PRAISE FOR JAY POSEY

"With *Outriders*, Jay Posey announces himself as belonging in the top rank of military science fiction authors. Effortlessly cool and instantly engaging, *Outriders* is impossible to put down."

Richard Dansky, lead writer, Tom Clancy's The Division

"A few pages into *Outriders* and I forgot the book was set in a science fiction world. Jay nails the mindset and the dynamics of a special operations unit. Keenly written with authentic characters, *Outriders* was one of the best science fiction books I've read in a long time. "

Kevin Maurer, author of Hunter Killer *and* No Easy Day

"Spoiler alert: the main character dies on page one. And then things get very interesting. Posey's *Outriders* is thrilling, action-packed science fiction that grabs and doesn't let go!"

Jason M Hough, New York Times bestselling author of the Dire Earth Cycle

"Jay Posey creates a vivid and mesmerizing world whose characters are so real and so flawed that you'll recognize them immediately. An unforgettable read."

Peter Telep, co-author of the #1 New York Times Bestseller Against All Enemies

"Gritty action-packed drama so hi-res and real you'll believe you got something in your eye."

Matt Forbeck, author of Amortals *and* Dangerous Games

"*Outriders* offers up a realistic portrayal of grey world/ black ops while doing some nice horizon busting both conceptually and technologically. A highly enjoyable read."

August Cole, co-author of Ghost Fleet: A Novel of the Next World War

"*Three* feels like the result of tossing *Mad Max*, *Neuromancer* and *Metal Gear Solid* into a blender. If you don't find that combination appealing, then I do not understand you as a human being."

Anthony Burch, writer for Borderlands 2 *and* Hey Ash Whatcha Playin

"*Outriders* is a kind of gripping, elegant, high-tech romp. Posey writes like he's some kind of gol-durned science fiction Tom Clancy. Characters come to full-fledged life with an ease that astonishes, and this plot has a constant credibility that makes believing it a simple pleasure. Here's hoping this guy hurries up and writes another one."

Jason VandenBerghe, Creative Director, Ubisoft

"I literally bit my nails to the quick from the non-stop, mind-bending action and tension – Jay Posey, you owe me new fingernails, but I forgive you that along with the lost sleep. It was well worth every minute of it. This is classic interplanetary outer-space science fiction in the grand classical tradition and I ate it up! I really can't wait until book 2 is ready to read – so get writing already – those are your marching orders, Mr Posey! And for you science fiction fans out there, I highly recommend *Outriders*!"

Popcorn Reads

"This book should have come with a warning – 'Attention! Once started this book cannot be put down'. An amazing blending of military action and science fiction. I have rarely encountered a book that I *had* to finish; it kept me up all night. But it was worth it."

A Book Drunkard

"*Outriders* offers a high-paced blend of near-future space opera and military science fiction, and in a nutshell it's good fun."

SFF World

"At the heart of *Outriders* is a thriller with bursts of action, and a book you begin to read and realise you've become so engrossed in that a whole day has passed by without you noticing."
Strange Alliances

"People are judged on the content of their character, their actions and choices, not even a little bit on what they look like or who their ancestors were. I hope other authors take note. This is how you do diversity."
Reanne Reads

"It is a military science fiction adventure story with a twisty plot and a complex political landscape. It focuses on a very small unit of people with character development as a centerpiece but the plot gods are also appeased. A great read for lovers of science fiction adventure!"
Bull Spec

"Posey's writing is easy, the characters nuanced, and certainly there is a lot to love here as a result. The villains are just as interesting as the good guys and there is definitely a set-up for a larger story."
Online Eccentric Librarian

"Posey has constructed a really unique world, one that steps to the side of the usual zombie tropes and provides an apocalypse that's at once unfathomable, but also believable. That's no mean feat."
SF Crow's Nest

"OK, Mr Posey I liked the Duskwalker series a lot, but now damnit... now you got me. You reached into the depths of my cobweb and comic book addled brain, took my love for science fiction and military action and put it on paper."
Shelf Inflicted

BY THE SAME AUTHOR

LEGENDS OF THE DUSKWALKER
Three
Morningside Fall
Duskwalker

Outriders

JAY POSEY

SUNGRAZER

ANGRY
ROBOT

ANGRY ROBOT
An imprint of Watkins Media Ltd

20 Fletcher Gate,
Nottingham,
NG1 2FZ
UK

angryrobotbooks.com
twitter.com/angryrobotbooks
Set the controls

An Angry Robot paperback original 2017

Cover by Larry Rostant
Set in Meridien and Fenton by Epub Services

Distributed in the United States by Penguin Random House, Inc., New York.

ISBN 978 0 85766 694 9
Ebook ISBN 978 0 85766 695 6

Printed in the United States of America

9 8 7 6 5 4 3 2 1

For Mom and Dad,
and for Mom and Dad

ONE

Elliot Goodkind knew it was a bad meet before he walked in, and he had a rule: never walk into a meet if there was even the slightest suspicion that it was bad. It was about ten thousand times easier to dodge the problem ahead of time than it was to get in the middle of it and then try to walk back out again.

And of course, in this case, he'd broken his own rule.

He'd ignored the twinge in his gut on the ride in, explained to himself how he'd triple-checked everything and why it was all going to be fine. The vibe in the restaurant had been off as soon as he opened the front door. But instead of turning around and walking away, he'd stepped inside.

Elliot had greeted his contact, Wilson, in his usual cautiously friendly manner, nodded politely and shaken the hand of the other man seated at the same table. Wilson had introduced that other man as Dillon, a business associate. And judging from the look that Dillon shot back at Wilson, it must have been his real name.

But Wilson had rubbed his hands on his pants before shaking Elliot's hand, trying to hide sweaty palms, and he'd been a little too enthusiastic in his welcome. Tried a little too hard to make Elliot comfortable, which naturally had the opposite effect. Final confirmation had come when Elliot had excused himself to use the restroom before sitting down; the way Wilson watched him intently, eyes following him all the way to the bathroom door, but anxious to leap back to Dillon, his mouth practically ballooning with excuses and explanations ready to spill out.

Elliot was blown. And Wilson knew it. This meeting was for Wilson's sake, then, his one attempt to prove that he wasn't a snitch or a plant, that he had no idea who Elliot *really* was. Elliot's fate had already been decided. A bad meet. And Elliot had walked right into it.

He turned on the water, splashed it cold over his hands and face, then left it running in the sink while he dried off. The bathroom was small, just a one-stall arrangement. The only window was a high slot. Maybe big enough to slide through, if he could get to it. He'd have to stand on the back of the toilet, and make an awkward stretch for that. That was assuming he could even get the window open, and judging from the grime built up around the frame, that wasn't a sure bet.

But escape was admission of guilt. And while it might get him out of the restaurant alive, there was no telling what effect that might cascade across all his many other networks and plans. Elliot had been here a long time. He'd done well for himself. Wriggling his ungainly way through a slot window into some grungy side-alley seemed like the wrong way to let it all end. Besides, if they were any sort of professionals, they'd have placed some muscle around the outside. Elliot could just see himself, draped halfway out a window, shot to death, limp like a wet towel out to dry.

He looked at himself in the mirror. Looked himself in the eye.

"Elliot," he said. He spoke aloud, but low enough for the running water to cover the words. "You're being ridiculous." He took a deep breath, stood straighter, pulled his shoulders back. Smiled. "Quit being ridiculous."

What did they really know? He could guess. Wilson thought he was a smuggler; the other man at the table probably thought him an undercover agent, local cop or internal security services, maybe. They were both right, of course. To a point.

Elliot was, in fact, smuggling small batches of black market, military-grade hardware out of the Martian People's Collective Republic for his employer. And Elliot was, in fact, an undercover agent. Though the proper term was *undeclared field officer*, and he didn't work for local police or for the Collective's feared Internal Security Services. He worked for the United States National Intelligence Directorate. He was a spy, in hostile territory, about two hundred and twenty-five million kilometers from home, give or take a few million depending on the orbital cycle. And being *undeclared* meant he only worked for the NID as long as he didn't get caught. If he was exposed as a foreign intelligence agent, there were no protections for him. The Directorate would conveniently have no knowledge or record of him, and he'd face whatever consequences his host nation might have in store for, say, a treasonous citizen, or perhaps a domestic terrorist.

The only help he was going to get in this particular moment, then, was whatever help he could create himself. It wasn't often he wished he carried a gun. In Elliot's experience, people who carried guns typically saw violence or the threat thereof as the default solution to too many problems. They let the weapon blind them to the possibilities. They lacked creativity. And, of course, there had been the incident in his early days involving a riot shotgun and an office ceiling, but Elliot didn't like to admit how much that had influenced his feelings on the matter.

The main trouble Elliot had with guns, though, was that usually when they *were* the solution to a problem, they were the *only* solution to the problem. And this particular problem sure looked an awful lot like one of *those* problems. He was just going to have to figure it out. He didn't have a lot to work with.

But he knew Wilson. Knew him enough. Just a guy with a side hustle. Wilson didn't care if he was selling milspec hardware or lollipops, he was just trying to make money where he saw opportunity. Well, no, that wasn't totally true. Wilson liked to think of himself as different than everyone else. Better. Special. He made good money and lived well, and as far as he was concerned, he deserved it because he didn't play by the same rules as all the other suckers out there. Living outside the norm, making his own rules, winning at his own game. That was important to Wilson. As long as he didn't get busted. He was a coward, really. An insecure man, looking for significance. That was part of what had made him so easy for Elliot to develop as an asset.

Dillon, on the other hand... well, Elliot hadn't seen him before, which meant Elliot had missed something along the way. Which was probably how Elliot had ended up in a one-stall bathroom, with the water running, trying to puzzle his way out. He glanced back up at that window again. Shook his head. Just too narrow.

So, best guess time. Dillon the Business Associate. Elliot let his mind draw up that brief flash of a first impression, let his instincts drive his assumptions. Dillon. Square jaw, square shoulders, everything squared away. Not overly friendly. Former military, turned businessman, then. He was probably Wilson's supplier. His boss, maybe, but more likely someone adjacent, someone at a similar level in the hierarchy who just *treated* Wilson as inferior. Aggression was Dillon's thing. His posture, his expression, his demeanor. Alpha.

Dillon had concealed his anger, mostly. There'd been an edge to it, though, something more. But not personal, he was too professional for that. He wasn't hurt by the possibility of Wilson's betrayal. It was a potential threat, and Dillon was the kind of guy who had to deal with all potential threats, immediately and with finality.

If Elliot had to guess, and he most certainly did have to guess, Wilson was out there, right now, doing everything he could to prove his loyalty to the relationship, to ingratiate himself to the strong man who could protect him. And meanwhile Dillon was evaluating the whole situation on a different plane; detached, impersonal, deciding whether or not continuing to do business with Wilson posed a threat to whatever operation it was he had going on. The more Wilson talked, the bigger the threat would seem.

Elliot shut the water off, took a deep breath. Smiled at himself in the mirror.

Show time. He stepped out.

"Sorry about that, gentlemen," he said, patting his belly as he approached the table. "Three breakfast burritos seemed like a good idea at the time but uh… can't say I recommend it."

It was a round table, four chairs. Dillon and Wilson sitting across from one another. They'd pulled a chair out for Elliot, but he stopped next to Dillon, stood a little too close to the man's shoulder than was socially appropriate.

"Hey buddy," he said. Dillon looked up at him, icy. "You're in my seat."

The big, square man was sitting in the position that had the best view of both the front and rear entrances, and Elliot knew that was no accident. It was the best seat in the house for this kind of work, but that wasn't the reason Elliot wanted it. At least, not the *only* reason.

"Just sit here, man," Wilson said.

"Nah," Elliot answered without looking at him. He held Dillon's stare, kept his face as neutral, counted to twenty. Neither of them budged.

"Come on," Elliot said. "You picked the place, I get to pick the chair."

Dillon was not a small man; Elliot guessed he was 225, maybe 230 pounds at one-G. By contrast, Elliot was about 165 if his pockets were full. But Elliot had one advantage; he was standing while Dillon was sitting. Most alpha males had a natural aversion to having another man's crotch in their face. Elliot casually grabbed his belt buckle and jiggled it around as if adjusting it, just to emphasize the point.

Dillon slid to the next chair over.

Elliot flashed a smile and plopped down casually, and just like that he'd changed the dynamic. Now it was a conversation between Wilson and him, with Dillon as observer. And Dillon was smoldering. Not just angry, but irritated. Hopefully enough to be distracted, and not enough to reach across the table and kill Elliot right there in the open.

Some attendant had come and gone while Elliot had been in the bathroom. A basket sat in the middle of the table filled with flatbread, herbed and glistening with rich oil, faintly steaming. Four glasses of water sweated almost as much as Wilson.

"All right," Elliot said, "I know we need to get to business, but before we do, I gotta tell you this joke. So, there's these three guys, right? These three guys walk into a restaurant... a businessman, a thief, and an undercover cop."

He let the words hang there in the air for a moment.

"And the joke is," he said, "I know who the businessman is." He raised his hand, pointer finger extended up towards the ceiling at first for dramatic effect, and then pointed at himself.

"So what I have to do now, is figure out which one of you is the no-good, lying, conniving, dirty scumbag... and which one's just the thief."

The color leaked out of Wilson's face so fast it was almost cartoonish, or as if someone had pulled a drain plug on him. Dillon, on the other hand, was unmoved. He returned Elliot's gaze with steady intensity, a corner of his mouth pulled back with one part smirk and three parts malice. Elliot held still, tried his best to look right through the man's eyes and straight out the back of his head. Out of the corner of his eye, he could see Wilson shifting his head back and forth between the two of them, no doubt wondering who would make the first move, and trying to decide whether he should make a run for it, or stick around to help.

After a long moment, Dillon leaned forward and drew a breath to speak. But before he could get a word out, Elliot slammed his palm down on the table, hard; it made the silverware jump and the other patrons quiet. Dillon sat momentarily stunned.

Elliot flicked his eyes left and right in a quick scan, soaking up the environment in a split-second glance.

Several of the other customers were looking in his direction; a natural reaction to any sudden, loud noise. Two guys in the back corner were working a little too hard not to notice. Dillon's guys, then.

"Now you," Elliot continued, looking back at Dillon. "You're a little too on-the-nose for a cop. You look like a cop. You smell like a cop. And you don't seem bright enough to me to try the old reverse psychology trick. But *you*," and here he kept staring at Dillon, while he pointed at Wilson. "You never check six. You talk too much." Now he shifted his gaze over to Wilson. "And you walk right into what's obviously a setup without asking yourself who actually did the setting."

Wilson blinked a half dozen times, and then stammered, "I don't know what you're talking about, man."

"That doesn't surprise anyone, Wilson," Elliot answered. He turned his attention back to Dillon. "So, that leaves us with you, Dill. Which is so predictable, it's boring."

Dillon sat back again, his brow creased. He was an intelligent man; Elliot could see it in his eyes. Smart enough to know that even if he'd thought of everything, he probably hadn't thought of *every*thing. He was working through it now, trying to puzzle out whether he'd missed something or if Elliot was just bluffing. Elliot had to keep him in that space, slightly off-balance, couldn't give him the time to work it out.

"Which means the only real question is, are you Central Martian Authority, or just a local guy?" Elliot said.

Dillon shook his head almost involuntarily.

"Or are you Internal Security?"

The suggestion was preposterous on its face; Elliot

knew for a fact Dillon couldn't be part of the Republic's Internal Security Services. They were never so conspicuous, never confrontational, which made them exponentially more dangerous. ISS agents had a way of putting people at unusual ease, asking easy questions that somehow led to hard places. A good one could sell you a rope and keep you smiling while you tied your own noose. Even if Dillon had been law enforcement, which he clearly wasn't, there was no way they'd ever let him be Internal Security. But just mentioning the agency planted the seed in Wilson's head, and had an unsettling effect on Dillion.

"I'm not any of that," Dillon confessed, now defensive. He tried to get back on top of the conversation. "You have *no idea* who I am."

"Sure I do. You're my supplier, and Wilson's your cutout. Or, to be technical about it, your *boss* is my supplier. He just doesn't know that, does he?" It was a shot in the dark, a hunch that Elliot hadn't realized he'd had until he heard himself say it. But Dillon's face shifted just enough to tell Elliot he was right.

So then, Elliot figured, Dillon had set up a little side business for himself, siphoning off hardware, selling it directly to buyers for three or four times the market rate, which was already substantial. And that was Elliot's point of leverage.

"At least, he doesn't know it *yet*," he said. "You know, cutouts work better when you don't meet face-to-face with your actual clients. That's sort of the whole point of having a cutout, so you–"

"I don't know what you think you're trying to pull off here, sport," Dillon said, cutting him off, "but it's not going to work."

Elliot held up a placating hand. "All I'm trying to do is

make sure I haven't been wasting my time and money. I'm guessing you got spooked when I started asking questions about where else you've been distributing your gear. I can understand that. I can appreciate it."

He reached over and made a point of picking up Wilson's glass of water, took a very deliberate drink of it before continuing. "I'm a careful man, Dill. Guy with my unimpressive physique can't afford to be anything *but* careful. I run a legitimate business, everything strictly legal, to the absolute letter of the law. To the tiniest dotted *I* and even the *T*s they forgot to cross, you understand? A substantial portion of my resources goes to make sure I'm staying right in between the lines, and I assure you my resources are significant. So this is only going to play out one of two ways. One, you're going to try to build some kind of case up against me, over the course of which you'll get to learn a life lesson about how the legal system actually works–"

"I'm not a cop," Dillon said, a little too loudly. Now he was getting angry. Elliot ignored him, which was sure to make him even angrier.

"Or two, you can keep your little charade intact and go snare some *actual* lawbreakers out there. Either way, you're wasting your time with me. I'm giving you the choice, the *opportunity*, to keep everything you've built up to this point. I'm sure you're making a nice little bonus on top of all your work for the greater good. And listen, I'll even continue to do business with you, if you're man enough to stomach it." Elliot flashed a smile. "It'll be good for your market legitimacy, I promise."

Dillon shot Wilson a look, and then growled at Elliot, "You think you're some bigtime player? Well you're not. You're not even half of my best client. Not even a tenth. I could crush you without even blinking. No one would ever find the body. No one would even come *looking* for it."

"And my ex-wives would probably thank you for your service," Elliot answered, reaching out and breaking the corner off one of the pieces of flatbread in the middle of the table. He popped it in his mouth, and spoke while he chewed. "But you gotta ask yourself, Dill, if *you're* in control, why am *I* sitting here so casual?"

That was the part Dillon couldn't work out. That was Elliot's lifeline. He glanced down at his fingertips, saw that the oil from the bread had sheened them. He reached over and very deliberately dipped his fingers in Dillon's glass of water, then wiped them off on the table cloth.

"What do you say, Dillon," he said. "Do you and your two friends back there in the corner want to walk out of here still business partners? Or are you going to have to see for yourself why I'm so unconcerned?"

Dillon just stared at him, hard. Still a dangerous moment. There was silverware on the table. Elliot really did not want to get stabbed with a fork. Not again.

"That's what I thought," Elliot said. "Thanks for the time, gentlemen." He stood up casually, careful not to make any moves that would suggest a threat, nothing that would set Dillon's reflexes off. "Nice to meet you face-to-face finally, Dillon. And to get your name." He smiled when he said it, then gave Wilson a little nod.

"Wilson, always a pleasure. I'm going to go ahead and take a twenty percent discount on that shipment this time. To cover this." He waggled his hand vaguely over the table.

Wilson stared up at him, his mouth slightly open.

"I'll be in touch," Elliot said. "You two enjoy the rest of your day."

Before Elliot turned his back, he looked over at Dillon's two associates in the back corner, made eye contact with one of them. Gave him a little wink and nod. As he turned to leave, he heard Wilson whisper, "Hey, are you a cop, man?"

Poor Wilson. Elliot genuinely hoped that they'd be able to keep their arrangement, but he wasn't sure if he'd ever see Wilson again.

He kept his pace steady and his ears attuned for any sudden movement. Twenty steps to the door. If he could make it that far, there was a better than coin-flip chance he was going to make it out. Fifteen steps. Ten.

And then he was there, opening the door, stepping out under the Martian sky. And it took every ounce of his remaining resolve to keep himself from sprinting to the vehicle that was waiting for him in the parking lot.

TWO

If it had all gone according to plan, no one would have gotten hurt.

But, of course, things pretty much never went according to plan.

Captain Lincoln Suh shoved the VIP up and over a waist-high wall, then leapt after the man. On the other side, he slammed his back against the aging concrete and dragged the VIP down with him. A moment later, Master Sergeant Wright flew over head-first and barely missed landing on their precious cargo. Incoming fire followed immediately after her, hissed overhead, popped concrete chips and chunks off their meager cover. Wright scrambled back against the wall, sandwiching the VIP between Lincoln and herself.

"Mike," Lincoln said into his comm channel.

"One sec," Mike answered, voice cool, steady. Three seconds later the incoming fire stopped. Lincoln hadn't heard the shot, but he knew Sergeant Mike Pence, the team's sniper, had done some work. "'K, one down. Rest fell back to an alley, twenty meters from your position. Marking."

A bright orange indicator appeared in Lincoln's view, designating the location. Lincoln nodded to Wright; off his signal, she swiveled, peeked up over the wall, and then brought her weapon up over the top and squeezed off one burst, then another.

"Move!" Wright called, continuing to fire controlled two- or three-round bursts back at their pursuers.

"Moving!" Lincoln answered. He grabbed a handful of the VIP's jacket, up near the scruff of the man's neck, and pulled him to his feet.

"This way, this way, this way," Lincoln said, shepherding the man forward as they bounded across open ground to a stubby, one-story building. When they reached it, Lincoln shoved the VIP up against the wall and then backed against him, covering as much of the man as he could with his own body. They'd had to run the op plain-clothes, so the only protection Lincoln had was the thin vest of armor under his shirt. Not much, but maybe enough to keep the rounds off the VIP at least, if it came to that. And it looked an awful lot like it was coming to that.

Lincoln braced his weapon against the corner of the building, sighted in on the entrance to the alleyway where the hostiles had taken cover. From this angle, he couldn't fire down the alley, only across the mouth of the entryway. But as long as they didn't get brave enough to rush out all at once, he probably had enough coverage to keep them suppressed. Probably. The light was still gloomy, an early-dawn grey, but the light-enhancement protocol of Lincoln's lenses compensated. He could clearly make out one of their pursuers, lying face down in the dusty street, arms limp and trailing by his sides like he'd fallen asleep in the middle of running. Mike's work.

"Set!" Lincoln called to Wright.

"Ready!" she answered.

"Move!"

"Moving!"

Lincoln opened fire, patternless single shots without rhythm, his rounds chewing bits out of the walls on either side of the alley. Wright sprinted across the gap. As she moved, one of the hostiles dared to lean out of his hiding place, despite Lincoln's suppressive fire. Lincoln shifted his aim. The hostile squeezed off a burst in the same instant that Lincoln fired three quick rounds, *pat-pat-pat*. The man fell back, though Lincoln couldn't tell if he'd hit his target or not. Out of the corner of his eye, Lincoln saw Wright stumble a half-step. Somehow she seemed to recover mid-stride and a few seconds later skidded in low, coming up close alongside Lincoln in a crouch. An instant later, her weapon was up and trained on the alley, spitting deadly rounds in sharp volleys.

"You hit?" Lincoln called down to her. "Are you hit?"

"I'm good! Where's our ride?"

Lincoln stepped backwards, shoving the VIP further along the wall away from the corner of the building. As soon as he moved, Wright flowed into the vacant space, continuing to suppress the alley.

"Sahil," Lincoln said through comms, "you got an ETA?"

"Ninety seconds," came Sahil's response. "And we don't wanna hang around for long." His tone was even flatter than usual, clipped but emotionless. Which meant he was probably driving way too fast, and most likely taking some heat along the way.

"They're splitting up," Mike said. "Finding another route."

"How many?"

"Three staying, five on the move. Check that, six. Six on the move," he answered. Then added, "Intel nerds only underestimated by half this time. Getting better."

"It was *our* intel, Mike!" Wright snapped.

"Oh," he answered. "Not so hot then."

Lincoln glanced around, checked the distance to the rally point. Forty meters. Did some quick math. Move too early, and he risked pulling the bad guys along with them to the pickup. Too late, and Sahil would be sitting there exposed, waiting for them to arrive. And if the bad guys moved fast enough, and maybe got a little lucky, it wouldn't take much for them to pinch Lincoln's element in. Lincoln never counted on luck, unless it was the bad kind.

"Getting low here, Link," Wright said over the sound of her gunfire. "What're we doing?"

Lincoln glanced down, saw the line of slender canisters strapped on Wright's back, up near her right shoulder. Red, white, white, grey. He grabbed the grey one.

"Smoke out!" he called, as he activated the smoke grenade and tossed it back the way they had come.

"Bad toss!" Wright said. Not a criticism, just informing him that he'd missed his mark. The smoke blossomed out, dense, but too far out to cover their movement.

"Give it a sec," Lincoln answered, hoping it would have the desired effect. "Mike, you got eyes on the bad guys?"

"Scopes only," Mike said. "No shot."

"They moving?"

"Yeah they're shuffling around... looks like, uh..." he said, breaking off. "They're splitting up, looping around."

"Sixty seconds," Sahil said.

"Twenty seconds, then we go," said Lincoln.

"Dry," Wright said. She ducked back, dropped the magazine from her weapon. Lincoln stepped up to the corner, squeezed off four rounds. Just under two seconds later, Wright said "I'm up!" and resumed fire.

"Mike," Lincoln said. "What're the bad guys doing?"

"Three of 'em are still sittin' there. Other group's maneuvering on your smoke."

Good. They took the bait. Hopefully the misdirection would buy them enough time.

Lincoln mentally counted off the remaining seconds.

"Moving to rally!" Lincoln called. He patted Wright's shoulder, hard. She stood, braced her weapon against the corner of the building, and opened up full-auto on the alleyway. Lincoln spun, took hold of the VIP, and drove the man forward ahead of him. "With me now, with me, we're almost there."

Together, they crossed the gap to another building, then down a narrow side street. Behind them, Wright's weapon went silent. The side street intersected with a wider road, and as Lincoln and his charge approached it, he heard the roar and whine of an engine. Moments later, an old pickup truck flew into view, braking hard and sliding past the side street. Lincoln didn't even need to look in the cab to know Sahil was behind the hijacked console of the vehicle; he could tell from the driving.

"Up, in the bed, go!" Lincoln told the VIP, practically throwing him up and over the edge, though the man hardly needed any prompting or aid.

As soon as the VIP was over the edge, the truck started rolling forward. Lincoln catapulted into the bed, scrambled over to lay on top of the VIP, shielding the man as much as he could. A few seconds later, another body came flying in and landed full force on Lincoln's legs.

"Go go go!" Wright called, and as the third word was leaving her mouth, the truck lurched forward. The sudden acceleration sent the three people in the bed sliding backwards, towards the tailgate. The master sergeant tumbled awkwardly into the rear corner, up on her back and shoulders, and let loose with some premium mil-spec cursing while she struggled to right herself.

"Mir, ow!" Lincoln said, as Wright's elbow dug into his lower hamstring. "My knee!"

"Well, why's it under me?" she snapped. He kicked his leg up, giving her a boost. She flopped to one side, rolled onto her back, sprawled her legs and fished her feet around for purchase against either side of the truck bed, near the tail gate. That was as stable a base as she was going to get in the vehicle. She kept as low a profile as humanly possible, her weapon laid flat along her body, muzzle pointing back behind them, just high enough to clear the rim of the truck bed. It'd taken her maybe five seconds to go from upside down in the corner to on point, ready for action. In the back of a swerving truck. Watching her move with such efficiency and control, Lincoln was once again struck with just how experienced an operator she was. An absolute pro. He hoped he looked half as cool as she did, though he knew that was unlikely. Particularly since he was perched on top of their precious cargo like some sort of human rucksack.

"Thumper," Lincoln called over comms, "We're en route to extract."

"Roger that," Thumper answered. "I'm tracking you. Local security commo traffic is picking up pretty heavy. Not sure how much longer I can keep it rerouted."

Thumper, the team's resident tech wizard, was set up in a safehouse well outside the target zone, running her mobile surveillance rig and working her magic on all manner of systems in the area.

"Alternate pick up zone still clear?" Lincoln asked.

"For now. Saber One One is on standby, and I'm keeping them apprised. They'll be there when you are."

"Mike, status?" Lincoln said.

"Bad guys are scrambling. Looks like you caught 'em off guard and they're short a vehicle. You're gaining time on 'em."

"You clear?"

"Clear enough," he answered.

"All right, pack it up, get back to the house."

"You got it."

"Thumper," Lincoln said. "You got coverage on Mike?"

"Yes sir," Thumper said. "Two skeeters on his wings, and a Dragonfly on station."

"Move that 'fly up close on Mike's location, cover him on the way out."

"I've got a good route," Mike said. "Shouldn't need it."

"*Shouldn't* doesn't mean you won't," Lincoln said. "Thump, move it over."

"Roger that," she said. "Mike, handing off Dragonfly control to you now. It's coming in on shadow."

Transfer protocol took a little time. Mike answered about ten seconds later. "I confirm Dragonfly hand off. I've got it."

Lincoln tried to run through the final checks in his mind; it was hard to calmly track and calculate all the finer points of a contingency plan while bouncing around in the back of a truck, speeding through too narrow streets after an unexpected gunfight. He trusted Sahil implicitly, but for all of the man's skill behind the wheel, he couldn't outdrive the laws of physics. Even though it seemed like that was exactly what he was trying to do.

The truck cornered hard; Lincoln had to splay his hands out quickly to keep from rolling off the VIP. In the sudden movement, one of his spare magazines popped out of its clip on his belt and skidded across the bed of the truck. He wasn't as low in the truck as he would have liked; his head was about even with the top of the bed. But with a grown man underneath him, it was the best he could do.

"We're doing fine," he said to the man he was lying on. "Almost there now. Almost home."

Lincoln raised his head up enough to get a quick look around, to orient himself and scan for trouble on either side. The streets were narrow, maybe three-quarters the width of what he was used to. Fortunately, this early in the day-cycle traffic was almost nonexistent, and the few cars he saw on the roads were following their ambling, perfectly predictable AI-determined paths. Sahil weaved around them expertly, no doubt leaving their occupants stunned and gaping in his dusty wake.

The buildings blurred in one long, rust-colored smear as the truck sped along. Not that there was much to distinguish one from another anyway, no matter the speed. They were all factory-formed replicas; two stories, boxy, like individual bricks for a titan's home. Evenly spaced, evenly distributed. A circuit board city.

With no sign of immediate danger, Lincoln shifted position atop the VIP, reached over to recover his lost magazine. And just as he stretched out for it, the upper edge of the truck bed popped sharply in his ear. Burning tendrils stretched across the right side of his face and the back of his neck, as if someone had splashed him with a cup of hot coffee. Lincoln glanced right to find a ragged notch torn out of the truck body, still smoking, right in the spot his head had been just moments before. He stared at it, his mind working to find an explanation and coming up empty.

"Drone!" Wright shouted. Lincoln looked to her, as she swiveled and braced her back against him and the VIP, bringing her weapon to bear. Following her point of aim, Lincoln spotted it now; a dark blur streaking a chaotic pattern in the sky behind them, off the back right corner of the truck. He didn't know what kind of weaponry the thing had; something mean, judging from the hole it'd left in the side of their vehicle. It was moving too fast. As good as she was, there was no way Wright was going to be able to bring it down with her primary weapon. Not that it stopped her from trying. Her weapon barked disciplined fire.

"Sahil," Wright called, "we got trouble!"

"I heard!" Sahil said. The truck lurched right, then back left, and then hard right again as he snaked the vehicle between two cars and around a tight turn.

"Thumper–" Lincoln said through the comm channel, but that was as far as he got.

"I know, I know!" she interrupted, intense.

Lincoln heard it this time. The shrill whine, followed by a dull thump just left of the vehicle, as if they'd run over something in the street. Based on the sound and the drone's rate of fire, he had a pretty good guess at what they were dealing with. Some flavor of queller, probably. Civilian security forces often used them for riot control and crowd dispersal, or as cheap patrolling presence in areas where unrest was likely. They were underslung with a wide-mouthed turret that was something like a cross between a shotgun and a small grenade launcher. The weapon design accepted a variety of munitions: smoke or tear-gas, high-explosive or anti-personnel rounds. If Lincoln was right, that was mild comfort at least. Quick as they were, quellers weren't built for precision or pursuit, and their targeting mechanisms weren't usually equipped to handle anything moving as fast as the truck was going.

Even so, there wasn't anything Lincoln could do, and it was the helplessness that made him fear. The truck was a big target. The drone was gaining ground, and they were utterly exposed from above. If it could get a shot into the middle of the truck bed, at least one of them wouldn't be making it out alive. Lincoln wrapped his arms around the VIP, crushed the man as small as he could beneath him.

"I can't breathe!" the man said, starting to raise his head.

"Keep still!" Lincoln commanded. He put a hand on top of the man's head, forced it down.

Another round came in, the same high-pitched squeal heralding its arrival; this one streaked diagonally over the truck and struck the corner of one of the rust-brown buildings, the shot sailing wide of its intended mark. The subdued *whump* of the impact was punctuated by a sharp crackling, like a firework explosion, as concrete chips and debris showered the sidewalk.

He shouldn't have raised his head, but Lincoln couldn't stop himself from glancing up and back at their pursuer. It was startling how close it was now, close enough that he could make out its single multifaceted bubble of an eye, and its wildly oscillating turret underneath, like a scorpion's tail curled under its belly. The muzzle twitched and jittered, trying to get a fix on the truck while another round loaded into the chamber. But from that distance, Lincoln didn't see how it could possibly miss again. Wright fired a burst, and then another, but the way the queller looped and cut through the air at random would have made it a hard target even with a shotgun.

Without warning, the air ripped; that was the impression Lincoln had. A tearing sound, the buzzing of a thousand hornets gone instantly mad, so close and so loud that he thought the atmosphere itself had torn apart. And a moment after, a loud pop, a puff of grey smoke; a dark line streaked low overhead from in front of the truck. The queller rolled over and plummeted to the street, spilling components and sending them skittering across the surface of the road.

"I lost signal on that target," said Thumper's voice in Lincoln's head a few seconds later, through the team's internal comm channel. "I'm reading you clear. Can you confirm?"

It took a moment for Lincoln's brain to catch up and realize that Thumper was talking to him. He scanned the sky, then pushed up higher so he could verify that the queller was down. Sure enough, it was disappearing from view, a glittering patch of debris in the street.

"That's confirmed," he answered. "We are clear. What'd you do?"

"Nothing," Thumper said. "I didn't hit it."

Lincoln glanced to Wright, but she shook her head and shrugged.

"Well, something killed it," Lincoln said.

"Hey, don't mention it, boss," said Mike. "You know I'm always lookin' out for you."

In the sky, something zipped into view from Lincoln's left. The Dragonfly. It caught up and matched speed with the truck, waggled its wings from side to side. It was a light drone, maybe a quarter the size of the queller, and sleek. Lincoln had used them plenty of times before, but at that moment he was pretty sure that particular one was the most beautiful he'd ever seen.

"You want me to ride shotgun the rest of the way

out?" Mike asked.

Dragonflies were pretty good at target selection when they were on shadow, loitering autonomously, but for the bit of flying he'd just done Mike had to have been on manual control – which meant he had holed up somewhere to run it.

"Negative," Lincoln said. "We're almost there. And you need to keep moving."

"You sure?"

"Yes, Mike. Go."

"I'm gone. Call me if you need me."

They were only another kilometer and a half or so from the pickup zone, down in the largely abandoned industrial quarter. It struck Lincoln as strange that anywhere in this place would be abandoned, but that seemed to be the way humans operated. Utopian promises rarely survived contact with reality.

A few more hard turns, and the landscape changed abruptly, but not substantially. The two-story buildings were replaced with six-story warehouses; still blocky, still the color of rust. Just larger. The already-narrow road thinned still more into a network of service roads, which Sahil expertly navigated.

"Saber One One, this is Mover," Sahil said over the full team channel. "We're ETA thirty seconds."

"Roger that, Mover," came the response. "We see you and are on approach. We'll be waiting for you."

"Keep your hands inside," Sahil said. Lincoln didn't understand the reference until a moment later when, without even slowing, Sahil slipped the truck down an alley with no more than a half-meter of clearance on either side. Only once they were inside the corridor between two buildings did he begin to slow the vehicle.

The alleyway emptied into a flat courtyard. Sure

enough, as promised, the craft was just touching down for them, side door open, engines locked to vertical. The flight engineer stood by the door, ready to receive them.

"OK, sir," Lincoln said to the man he was still lying on, "our ride out is right here. When we stop, we'll hop out, quick jog, and we're on the way home. No more shooting. Got it?"

The man nodded.

"You're doing fine," Lincoln added, giving the VIP's shoulder a pair of strong pats.

Sahil rolled the truck up parallel to the transport, maybe twenty meters away. Wright was up and out before they'd even come to a full stop. She dropped to a knee by the back of the truck, weapon raised, providing security. Lincoln waited the extra few seconds for the vehicle to come to an actual halt, and then came up in a crouch. Sahil jumped out at almost the same time, and took position on the opposite end of the truck from Wright, covering those angles. Lincoln scanned the area one last time for any signs of trouble. Seeing none, he patted the VIP on the back.

"OK, here we go," he said. Lincoln hopped over the edge of the truck bed, and then aided the VIP. But when the man's feet hit the ground, he nearly collapsed. Lincoln caught him by the arm.

The VIP was panting, his face pale and sheened with sweat.

"Whoa, you OK?" Lincoln asked.

The man grimaced, then nodded. "My leg," he said.

Lincoln's gut went cold. He flashed back to the hole in the side of the truck, and for an instant wondered if shrapnel had somehow found its way into the man he was supposed to protect. He glanced down, looked for blood.

"Are you hit?" he asked.

The VIP shook his head. "No, it's asleep," he said. "From you sitting on it."

Lincoln nearly laughed aloud with the sudden wave of relief. He grabbed the man around the waist and hoisted him up.

"All right buddy, I got you," he said, and with his charge's arm around his shoulders, together they covered the last few meters to the waiting aircraft. The flight engineer was standing in the back of the transport, a concerned look on his face.

"Wounded?" he called over the sound of the engines.

Lincoln shook his head and waved him off. A few steps later, he and the engineer helped the VIP aboard, who just flopped onto the floor on his back. It wasn't proper protocol, but they let him lie there anyway. He'd had a rough couple of weeks. Lincoln hopped up and stepped to the far side, making room for the rest of his team.

"He's all right," Lincoln said.

"Yeah, but I was asking about you," the crew chief said, pointing at Lincoln's face. Lincoln reached up and brushed his fingertips across his cheek. The contact reawakened the pain, a blowtorch wave spilling down the side of his face and neck. When he brought his fingers away, the tips of his gloves were dark and tacky with congealing blood.

"How bad is it?" he asked.

The flight engineer cocked his head, then shook it. "Ain't pretty. Lucky you didn't lose an eye."

"Lucky I didn't lose my whole head," Lincoln said. And for some reason, it wasn't until he said it that he realized just how true it was. If that magazine hadn't fallen out...

"Be a good story at least," the flight engineer said. He gave Lincoln's arm a punch as he turned to help the others in. Lincoln looked out of the aircraft to see Sahil leaning into the cab of the truck, fiddling with something near the floorboard; Wright had moved up next to him to provide cover. Whatever he was doing, he must have just been finishing up, because he turned almost immediately, closed the truck door, backhanded Wright's shoulder, and jogged over to the waiting craft. Wright held her position for three seconds, then followed.

Sahil leapt up into the cargo hold. Wright came in close behind, and as soon as she'd made it in, the flight engineer motioned to the pilot and said something that Lincoln couldn't hear. The next instant, the craft leapt off the ground. In the courtyard, the truck pulled around in a wide arc under its resumed AI control, headed towards another service road. As it pulled away, black smoke swelled and roiled out of the cab, and before it disappeared from view Lincoln could make out ghostly tongues of fire rippling along the door frames.

"Hope that wasn't a rental," Lincoln said.

"I got the insurance," Sahil replied as he passed Lincoln. He knelt down next to the VIP, who was still lying on the floor; if they spoke to each other, Lincoln couldn't make it out. In addition to being their driver and demolitions expert, Sahil was also the team's medical sergeant, and though Lincoln had given their precious cargo a quick once-over before they'd led him to safety, he knew Sahil wouldn't relax until he'd checked the man out for himself.

Wright, on the other hand, flopped into one of the jump seats, laid her head back and let out a long breath that gave Lincoln the impression she'd been holding it since the shooting had started.

"Got a little sporty," Lincoln said.

"Too," she answered, without a smile. The whole team would have a full debrief as soon as they reunited, to go over what went right and what went wrong with the op, while the details were still fresh in their minds. Lessons learned. Wright never let them miss a session, no matter how bone-tired they all were.

"Thumper, Mike," Lincoln said over comms, "we're up and out. What's your situation?"

"Almost to the safehouse," Mike answered. "No static."

"I'm breaking my rig down now," Thumper said. "NID's got a car on the way. We'll be right behind you."

NID, the National Intelligence Directorate, was often a close civilian companion on the operations that Lincoln's team ran; so close in fact, they almost always stepped on each other's toes. But no one was better at getting people in and out of places they shouldn't be than NID.

"Roger that. Stay on point, keep your heads down," Lincoln said. "I know I don't have to say it, but I just have to say it."

"All good," Thumper said. "We'll see you back home."

Lincoln hated splitting the team up like that, hated it even more that he was leaving the target before two of his people. But sometimes the op called for it, demanded it. He still hated it.

Already the courtyard had shrunk below such that Lincoln could have covered it with the span of his palm. From that altitude, he got a much stronger sense of the flat plain the city was built upon. It stretched out in every direction to meet water on all sides, its surface littered with factory-molded buildings and jutting skeletal structures never completed. A mechanical island.

They'd infiltrated by boat days ago, at night, and

though he'd seen plenty of aerial and satellite imagery of the sea-based city, the impression it left when seen in person had far greater impact. The design was more obvious from this height, the pattern more recognizable; an aborted space station, repurposed. It would have been small in its proper home, barely an outpost out there in the Deep. But sitting here in the middle of the Atlantic Ocean, it seemed plenty big. Lincoln didn't know the full story of how it'd come to be. He guessed it probably wasn't a happy one.

The flight engineer pressed a large yellow button on the roof with the palm of his hand, and the side door slid shut and sealed. As it was closing, the aircraft rolled right, turning to the fastest route out to sea. The engines added a hum to their roar as they rotated from vertical to horizontal, the craft gaining airspeed with surprising quickness. The pull of the acceleration almost unbalanced Lincoln, and that prompted him to finally sit down.

"Dagger, this is Saber One One," the co-pilot said over team comms. "Mover element is secure, precious cargo aboard, all souls accounted for. We're on our way out."

"Dagger copies, Saber One One. Fly safe. Hate to lose the cargo in the drink after all this trouble."

"Roger that, Dagger. They're in good hands. See you in a bit."

Sahil patted the VIP's shoulder a couple of times, and then rolled up into a jump seat nearby. Lincoln made eye contact with Sahil, raised his eyebrows in a request for update. Sahil just nodded. Their VIP was OK.

Lincoln looked down at the man they'd just rescued. Lieutenant Colonel Stewart, a pilot. He was still lying there on the deck of the craft, eyes open, staring up. For a moment, it looked almost like he was going into shock. But then tears spilled from the corners of his eyes, slipping down the sides of his face towards the floor.

"Everything OK, Colonel Stewart?" Lincoln asked.

It was a moment before Stewart responded. When he did, he just said, "I think that is the most beautiful thing I have ever seen."

Lincoln followed the man's gaze to the roof of the craft. He hadn't noticed it before, but when he saw it he couldn't help but smile. There was an American flag hung there, pinned flat against the ceiling.

"I know what you mean, sir," Lincoln said. "I think the same thing, every time I see it."

"Thank you," Stewart said, turning his head to look at Lincoln. "Thank you for coming to get me."

"Yes sir."

They were silent for a few moments, and then Stewart propped himself up on an elbow, apparently not quite ready to commit to getting up off the floor after their harrowing escape.

"They knew I was coming," he said. "And they knew what I was here to do. I don't know how, but they did. It all happened way too fast. And when I splashed down, I knew I would never get home. I didn't think anyone knew where I was. I didn't think anyone *could* know. How did you find me?"

"It's our job, sir," Lincoln said. "That's what we do."

"And uh… you mind telling me who you are?"

Lincoln just smiled at the man.

"Are you with… *that* unit?"

Lincoln chuckled, knowing exactly which unit Stewart meant. The Legend. Lincoln had, in fact, made it all the way through Selection for that very unit, only to get plucked out of it at the last possible moment to serve as team lead for the Outriders instead.

"No sir," he said. "We're in Information Support."

Stewart coughed a laugh, thinking Lincoln was joking. Then he just looked confused. "Wait, seriously?"

Lincoln nodded.

"You're kidding me," Stewart said, sitting up. "You guys are an intel outfit?"

"Well," Lincoln said, smiling again. "*Applied* intelligence."

Stewart's confused expression didn't change with the answer. Officially, Lincoln's team was the 519th Applied Intelligence Group, part of the 301st Information Support Brigade. Unofficially, they were the Outriders. Generally speaking, no one had heard of them officially *or* unofficially. After a moment Stewart seemed to finally realize that was all he was going to get out of Lincoln, and he laid back down and draped his forearm over his eyes.

"Guess I don't rate quite as high as I thought," he said, deadpan. Sahil chuckled at that.

"You do all right, sir," Sahil said. And then added, "For an aviator."

Stewart cracked a smile through his weariness, and Lincoln knew then the man they'd rescued was good to go. Lincoln glanced around, saw his teammates settling in for the ride home. Sahil had his head tipped back, eyes closed. Master Sergeant Wright was already checking something on a datapad; probably taking notes on all the things that the team could have done better on the op.

Lincoln kissed his fingertips and pressed them to the flag on the ceiling, let them linger there a moment. He'd been all over the world and out beyond it. Somehow, no matter how much he thought he cherished his country, every time he was headed back home those stars and stripes seemed to mean even more than they had before he'd left.

As he relaxed back into his seat as much as the tight quarters would allow, he caught Wright looking at him. If he hadn't known her so well, he would have thought her expression was flat. But there was a tug at the left corner of her mouth; the barest trace of a smile, and one that hinted at something like approval. Without a word, she let her eyes drop back to the datapad. Lincoln allowed himself a moment to savor the double victory. Not only had they gotten the VIP out safely, he'd actually gained the master sergeant's unspoken praise for something. As chaotic as things had been on the extraction, winning Wright's undoubtedly temporary approval was probably the harder of the two. Lincoln smiled to himself, leaned his head back against the side of the aircraft, and let the post-op wave of exhaustion finally roll through him.

THREE

For almost ten years, she'd followed her designated path, synchronized to the orbit of Mars from ten million kilometers distant. Or, 9 years, 132 days, 15 hours, 37 minutes, 16 seconds, at an average range of 9,985,307 kilometers, with a maximum deviation of 293.77 meters, to be exact.

And she was always exact. Precision was her design, and her purpose. All that time, she'd waited, as she'd been directed. Silent and invisible, ever-listening, ever-watching. Waiting. And that, too, was her purpose.

Until now.

A signal arrived. A burst of data as compact and dense as DNA, instructions no human could decipher beyond the most basic directives.

REDCON GAMMA; ready/alert, mobilize, MINSIG approach to holdoff orbit. Target designation forthcoming.

And with the message, SUNGRAZER woke.

Dormant systems winked to life, a fluid cascade of technological petals unfurling, each as crisply responsive as on her first day of operation. These were new orders from a new source; a different encryption scheme, though with all the proper and familiar algorithms. A

41

new position, an elevated ready condition. Her approach to holdoff orbit would be restrained, minimizing her signature, reducing her risk of detection to a statistically-insignificant fraction. From holdoff, she would be mere hours from strike distance; from strike distance, mere minutes from establishing a target vector and firing solution.

For the first time in nearly a decade, SUNGRAZER redirected and set a new course.

FOUR

Lincoln stared at his own corpse. Himself, dead.

Though, technically he wasn't sure if the body lying in front of him could be *dead* since according to Medical it had never been alive in the first place. It was only his replica.

Only. As if such a thing could be "only".

He scanned the row of three containers. Inside each, his face. His *own* face, on a different body. A body identical in every way to the one he'd been in for his entire life. Three replicas. Three backup bodies, ready to receive his consciousness if he should ever be killed in the line of duty. And, strangely enough, they were all property of the United States Government. What that meant for him if he ever had to inhabit one, he didn't know exactly.

When Lincoln had first joined the Outriders, they'd explained everything in painstaking detail. There were documents to sign, pamphlets to read, a consultation with a medical professional. But he'd been too tired to read the documents before he signed, and never read the pamphlets the army handed out anyway. And it wasn't exactly the sort of thing your brain would absorb from literature, no matter how much of it you read.

His teammates had all told him not to visit, that it was too eerie, too psychologically disturbing. Of course, most of them had done it themselves, which is how they knew. They were right. Lincoln didn't even know a word to describe it. He was no stranger to death. He'd seen it from all sides, delivered it to others, had it visited upon his friends. He'd seen the human body disassembled and rearranged in the most horrific fashion. And yet here, lying in front of him as if asleep, in perfect health, was the most disturbing thing he'd ever seen.

Lincoln couldn't get his thoughts around it. But he couldn't make himself leave, either. He'd told the technician who had let him in that he'd only need five minutes. That'd been almost an hour ago. He'd pulled up a chair and was now sitting next to the one closest to the door. Number One.

In his hands, he held a magazine from his weapon, still topped off with ammunition. The one that had fallen out of its pouch. The one that had spared his life. He balanced it on his fingertips, rolled it over, felt the texture with his thumbs. The sensation kept him present in the moment against the tide of memories that threatened to draw him back into his own mind, into darker places than he had the strength to revisit now. Though he didn't feel fully awake, either. He was in some strange, dissociative state, an in between place.

Someone cleared a throat behind him. Lincoln glanced back over his shoulder to find his teammate Mike standing in the door. He hadn't heard it open.

"Hey boss," Mike said, his words tiptoeing into the room.

"Hey Mikey," Lincoln answered. He felt like he should say more, but his mind couldn't conjure any words.

"Mind if I come in?"

Lincoln shook his head. Mike hovered at the door.

"Was that 'no' you don't mind?" he said, "Or 'no', I can't come in?"

"Don't mind," Lincoln said. Mike slipped in, floated ghost-like into the room, to the foot of one of the replica containers. He was a big guy, six four, maybe 105 kilos, long-limbed and rangy. But he moved like a dancer, like he could stop at any point mid-motion and hold that position forever. Lincoln didn't know if that was because he was the team's sniper, or if that was *why* he was the team's sniper.

The two were silent for a time, Mike just standing there at the end of the container, and Lincoln fiddling with the magazine. It eventually became clear that Mike wasn't going to be the first one to speak. And after a few moments of the big man's steady presence, Lincoln found the darkness receding from his mind.

"I thought you hated it down here," Lincoln finally said.

"Oh, I wouldn't say I hate it, sir," Mike replied. "On account of having never actually done it before. More scared of it, I guess." He chuckled to himself. "Well, I guess I *have* been down here before. Just wasn't aware of it at the time."

Everything about Mike said he was exactly the same as when Lincoln had first met him. Even knowing the truth, it didn't have any effect on Lincoln's perception of the man. Mike had been killed in action during an operation on board a ship, an op under Lincoln's command. Right in front of Lincoln, in fact. Lincoln had watched him die. So this Mike, the one standing in front of him, was a replica. Or, Mike was *in* a replica. Lincoln still wasn't sure what the right way to think about it was. Maybe there was no right way. But for all the expansive philosophical playground offered, for all the mindbending questions raised, none of it seemed to reach quite as far as reality. Mike was just Mike, same as he ever was.

"So, what're *you* doing down here?" Mike asked after a moment.

"I don't know," Lincoln said. "Thinking. Or trying not to."

Mike nodded.

Lincoln held up the magazine in his hand.

"This little guy saved my life," Lincoln said.

"That was thoughtful. Take a bullet for you?"

Lincoln shook his head. "Fell out. If I hadn't bent down to pick it up, that queller would've taken my head off."

Mike nodded. One thing Lincoln loved about the brotherhood amongst operators was that you never really had to say much. Sharing was efficient, and easy. The people who knew, knew.

They were quiet for another moment, and then Mike started one of his stories.

"One time, when I was back home on leave, my dad took me out for breakfast one morning. And we took his old truck. I mean old, like he was driving it himself, old. This was right after I'd gotten back from Balikpapan so... you know..." Mike gave a little half shrug, which encompassed all of the horror and carnage of a short, brutal brushfire war, now a decade-old and nearly forgotten by everyone but the men and women who'd shed blood there. "Anyway, we're driving this long stretch of highway, and my dad's telling me about how after thirty-five years of marriage Mom still can't get his coffee right. He's not really saying anything, you know, just filling the air because I think he was afraid of what might come up if he let me do any talking. And normally I wouldn't care, I'd just let him talk, but it was such a stupid thing to be griping about. Just droning on and on and on. Like, after thirty-five years of marriage, he still hasn't figured out how to make his *own* coffee, right?"

Lincoln dropped his gaze back to the magazine in his hands, flipped it over. He had to suppress a smile, listening to Mike's description of his dad going on and on about nothing. When Mike told a story, he usually had a point. *Usually.*

"I'd only been back in the States a few days," Mike continued, "and I was still pretty on edge. I shouldn't have done it, but I got fed up and turned and told him if weak coffee was the biggest trouble of his days, he was living an awfully soft life and he ought to be grateful. And he shot me this look, like, I don't know... like, I'd just slapped him and then told him I was a communist. I can still see it. I mean, my dad's a rancher up in Montana, so you know... I don't think anyone had ever accused him of being soft, exactly." Mike shook his head. "Anyway, we just stared at each other for a few seconds, and then BLAM. We hit a moose.

"And it was a big one. Tore us up pretty good. Dad was in the hospital for a couple of weeks... Still don't know what it was doing out there. We figured it must've been sick or something, to be wandering across a highway like that."

Lincoln waited a bit to see if a reason for the story was forthcoming, but when he finally looked back at Mike, he saw Mike staring down at Lincoln's replica in front of him, without really seeing it. Mike was Back There somewhere, remembering.

"But your dad was all right?" Lincoln said, gently prompting his friend.

"Well," Mike said. "After that, Mom didn't let him drive anymore." He gave Lincoln his quick smile and then shook his head slightly, as if to clear it. "Anyway, yeah, all that to say, that right there," he pointed at the magazine Lincoln was holding, "truth is, that can happen anywhere, brother. We like to pretend we're in control. It's easy to believe it when we're in the routine, back home, where we expect things to just happen the way they've always happened. That's not how it really is. Combat's crazy, sure, but it's not any more random than anywhere else in life. Little things change our fate every minute of every day, most of it we never even notice.

"If I hadn't said anything to my dad, chances are we would have cruised right on around that moose no problem. But then again if *we* hadn't hit it, maybe somebody else would have, maybe a mom with a car full of kids." He shrugged. "You try to pick apart every little moment and every decision you make, it'll drive you nuts and still won't make a difference. Just got to live the best you can, and be ready to go when you go."

The two men looked at each other for a long moment, and then Lincoln nodded.

"Mikey," he said.

"Sir?"

"We've got to work on your motivational speeches."

Mike smiled. "Yeah well, sir, if I got any better at it someone important might notice and make me an officer."

"God help us all."

"You gonna quit moping around now, or what?"

Lincoln chuckled and looked down at the magazine in his hand, tapped it on his palm. Then he tossed it over to Mike and stood up.

"Wright send you down here after me?" Lincoln asked.

"Nah," Mike answered. "I doubt she even noticed you were gone."

Lincoln put the chair back where he'd found it, turned and opened the door, then held out a hand in an after-you gesture. Mike remained where he was, his face unusually sober and earnest.

"It's not so bad, you know," he said. "The Process... It doesn't make so much difference as you can notice. Seems like it should be a bigger deal, I know. But it's not. It's actually harder to go through when it happens to your friends."

"I'll take your word for it," Lincoln said.

"I hope that's all you ever have to do, sir."

They shared a look for a brief span, until Lincoln gave a nod.

"And I don't know what you think I'm going to do with this," Mike said, tossing Lincoln's magazine back to him. "You gotta police your own gear around here, buddy."

Lincoln nearly fumbled the catch, but managed to catch it at the cost of letting the door close again.

"Smooth," Mike said.

"I've always been good with my hands," Lincoln answered, reopening the door. He held it for Mike once more, and as Mike passed by, Lincoln kicked one of Mike's heels and sent him stumbling into the hall. "At least, as good as you on your feet."

In the corridor, a medical technician gave them a scornful look, like they were schoolboys running loose in a sanctuary. Lincoln gave his customary nod of acknowledgment. Mike offered a salute so perfectly executed, the condescension was impossible to miss. And as the two men walked back to the team's facility, the final shadows slipped from Lincoln's mind and found their place amongst their kindred memories.

FIVE

Lincoln blew the steam from the top of his third cup of coffee, as he reviewed the briefing he'd put together in the early morning hours. Corrected a typo, took a sip. The coffee was pretty good. He wasn't sure he could say the same about his brief.

The call had come in just before 0200, a certain sign that somebody way up the chain of command was in a mood. Before Lincoln had gotten the details, he'd assumed it was going to be a standard hurry-up-and-wait op. Now that he'd pulled the basic info together, though, he wasn't sure his team would have enough time to fully prep before they had to bounce off.

"Sorry to be sending you back out so soon," Colonel Almeida said, though the smile on his face said otherwise. He'd materialized in the doorway at some point, though Lincoln didn't know when. For an old guy, the Colonel still moved like a cat. He was the officer in charge of the 519th Applied Intelligence Group and Lincoln's direct commander, which meant he spent most of his days in an office. But there wasn't any doubt he'd rather be out there in the field, or about how effective he could still be.

"You're doing me a favor," Lincoln answered. "We go more than forty-eight hours without something to do, and Wright starts getting on at me about letting our skills deteriorate."

"She's not wrong, you know," Almeida said, deadpan.

Lincoln chuckled. "I don't suppose you two are related, by any chance?"

"Same mother," Almeida answered. He waited for Lincoln's reaction, and then added, "War."

"Yeah, OK, tough guy," Lincoln said. The Colonel grinned again, though only one side of his face really showed it. Many years prior, Almeida had lost an arm, a leg, and a fair amount of his face when his vehicle had taken a direct hit from an explosive charge in an ambush. Medical could have patched him right up, if he'd let them, but the Colonel had chosen to keep the scars, and took no measures to disguise his prosthetics. After he'd brought Lincoln on board, Almeida had hinted at his reasons; warfare had gotten too clean in his opinion, too easy to hide the mess. Now that he was out of the field and dealing with the rear-echelon types on a daily basis, he liked to make sure they had a regular reminder of the human cost to waging war.

"You got something for me," Lincoln asked, "or you just here to check in?"

"Just making sure you hadn't dozed off. Higher's hot to trot on this one."

Lincoln checked the time. 0437. Barely even two hours since he'd gotten the materials to start work.

"And I'm being sluggish?"

"They've called me twice since I called you."

"Well," Lincoln said, as he rubbed the corner of his eye with a finger. "Do they want it done fast, or do they want it done right?"

"Both, of course," the Colonel said. "You done putting everything together?"

"No."

"I'll go get the room set up."

"Sure. See you in a few."

The Colonel nodded and disappeared down the hall while Lincoln set about getting everything packaged up to present. Lincoln had spent years in special operations in various roles, and he couldn't help but reflect on the mind-numbing hours he'd spent filing paperwork and preparing presentations. Strangely, none of the recruiters he'd ever talked to had thought to make mention of the desk work. In other units, he'd always felt like it had been such a waste of time. Since he'd joined the Outriders, though, it almost seemed like they'd overcorrected, getting by with the absolute bare minimum. And maybe even less. They certainly didn't leave a lot of margin, anyway.

"Hey boss," said another voice from the doorway. Mike.

"Morning Mikey," Lincoln said. "You're up early."

"Couldn't sleep with you and Mom bumping around in here," he replied. *Mom* was the team's nickname for Colonel Almeida; Lincoln still hadn't found the true origin story for that one. Not that he hadn't heard plenty of theories. "We going out again?"

"Looks like."

"Cool. What do you need from me?"

"You want to go wake Sahil up?"

"No, sir, I do not."

"Fair enough," Lincoln said. "Do me a favor and toss a crash in his room on your way by."

Mike snorted. "Only if you swear to back me up when I tell him Thumper did it."

"Mike, when have you ever known me not to back you up?"

"Pretty much any time I do something and I should've known better, sir."

Lincoln smiled. "Fine. I'll get the team. You can make the coffee."

"Oh, negative, no deal. I'll round up the troops." Mike slid back away from the door, and then added, "Sugar, no cream."

"I promise you I don't do anything different than anybody else," Lincoln called after him. When he'd first joined the team, Lincoln had taken to making coffee for everyone, partially to show he wasn't the sort of officer who thought doing so was beneath him, but mostly because he was the one who drank it the most. Based on the team's reaction to it, it would have been easy to think he had been sneaking in gourmet beans when no one was looking. Maybe they all really did enjoy it. But Lincoln couldn't help but suspect his teammates made such a fuss over his coffee just to keep from having to make it themselves.

He made a final tweak to his briefing, and then closed it with a quick hand gesture. The holographic display winked out. He made his way down the hall to the planning facility's claustrophobia-inducing briefing room. There were three rows of long tables in the room, each curving gently towards the front. Six chairs sat behind each table, packed together so tightly it gave Lincoln the impression of an elementary school. He couldn't imagine trying to fit adults that close together. And he still hadn't figured out why they had eighteen chairs in the room, when they had never needed more than six anyway.

Colonel Almeida already had the projector warmed up, its little 3D corporate logo hovering over it, spinning neatly above a warning message that the lens was thirty days past due for replacement. Lincoln gestured at the projector, pulled up the first panel of his brief. In the back of the room, crammed tight in one corner, was the coffee machine. Lincoln crossed to it and started the preparations. Almeida chuckled.

"Yeah, I know," Lincoln said over his shoulder. "You want any while I'm at it?"

"No thank you. I never drink it."

"Never?"

"More of a tea guy, myself."

The machine whirred and clicked once. Lincoln set out five industrial-looking mugs, outsides yellowed from countless years in the service and insides tanned with untold numbers of cups served. On second thought, Lincoln put one of the mugs back. He'd become pretty accustomed to the caffeine, but a fourth cup was pushing it, even for him.

"Tea, huh?" Lincoln said. "There's an old saying about that, you know."

"What's that?"

"Well, being a *true* American as I am… I like my coffee black, and my tea in the harbor."

"I've literally never heard that before."

"Yeah well… so maybe it's not so old."

"Maybe it's not a saying."

"Maybe," Lincoln said with a smile. "Maybe could be, though."

A few moments later the machine chimed, and Lincoln poured out four mugs. Black for Sahil, cream and sugar for Thumper, way too much sugar for Wright. He started to put cream in Mike's, and then remembered the change. Sugar, no cream. That hadn't been the usual for Mike before they'd lost him. It was his new normal. A small thing, a shift in preference, but Lincoln couldn't help but wonder if there were other things going through the Process changed about a person. Though, he couldn't honestly even be sure whether it was related to the Process or not.

"I recruited you because I knew you'd look after my kids," the colonel said. "I had no idea you were going to *pamper* them."

"This early in the morning," Lincoln answered, "I like to have a little peace offering on hand."

"I might be able to help with that," Almeida replied. "Got a little gift for the team. You want me to give it before or after you brief them?"

"After. If you give it first, no one will listen to anything I say."

"It's not that kind of gift," Almeida said. "And there's no guarantee they'll listen anyway."

"Thanks for that, sir. Big help."

Lincoln had just finished stirring the last mug as the team started to arrive. No surprise, Master Sergeant Wright was the first to enter, and she looked as squared away as she would've been in the middle of a normal work day. She snapped a smart salute to both officers as she strode in.

"Colonel," she said.

"Good morning, Amira," he replied.

"Sergeant Wright," Lincoln said, returning the salute. "Colonel Almeida has put forth a theory that you sleep in uniform, while standing up. Can you confirm?"

Wright flashed him a look, but her flat expression didn't change at all. Which was about all the response he could hope to get, and the only one he expected.

Lincoln smiled at her. "Morning."

"Sir," she replied. "One of those for me?"

Lincoln pointed to the mug he'd prepared for her.

"Hope this isn't the one that finally gives you diabetes."

Wright raised the mug in a little gesture of thanks, then peered at him from over the rim while she blew the steam away. "It'd be worth it," she said, before taking a sip. "Besides, I'd just get the lab to roll back one of my reps anyway."

She didn't smile when she said it, but it was a joke, if a dark one. Replicas were technically only for recovery of personnel killed in action. Wright went to the center-most position of the second-row table, shoved the too-close chairs away with her foot, and took a seat in pretty much the exact middle of the room. Lincoln smiled to himself as he watched her. Everything the master sergeant did, she did with just a slightly elevated sense of purpose and intensity. Even something as trivial as choosing where to sit in a briefing. She always carried with her an air of vague disappointment in the state of the world; not an arrogance or disdain, just a sense that she'd expected a little more professionalism out of everyone and everything. It was an edge that some people undoubtedly found difficult to deal with. Lincoln found it endearing.

"Mornin' Mom," Sahil said, as he entered. Sergeant Nakarmi was only five four or so, but he was built like a sledgehammer. He had a way of walking that always made it look like he was on his way to a brawl. "Cap'n. We got a worthy one?"

A "worthy one" was Almeida's code for a mission actually worth the Outriders' time; there weren't many operations that genuinely required the 519th's particular skill set, but when one did it was usually a matter of very serious proportions.

"Apparently worth getting me out of bed at oh-two-hundred for, anyway," Lincoln answered.

Sahil made a face. "That don't mean much other than somebody at Higher got an idea." He gestured towards the coffee mugs; Lincoln pointed to the proper mug, which Sahil lifted from the small table.

"Sounds like it might be a good one, at least," Lincoln said.

Mike and Thumper arrived shortly after Sahil. Thumper looked like she'd gotten less sleep than Lincoln had, and was ready to fight someone about it.

"Morning, Thumper," Lincoln said. "You all right?"

"As soon as that sun comes up," she answered, "I'm gonna punch it right in its stupid mouth."

"Splash some coffee on your face," Mike said. "It'll perk you right up."

"Perk *you* right up," she mumbled, as she headed back towards the remaining mugs. Mike grabbed his coffee and plopped down on top of the table in the back, feet dangling.

"Thumper" was actually Sergeant Avery Coleman, the resident tech genius. And she was truly a genius. Lincoln had never met anyone with a mind like Thumper's. It would've been a mistake to assume that her technical bent made her a pushover physically, though. Lincoln had witnessed her sparring with Sahil on many occasions. And though Lincoln was no slouch when it came to hand-to-hand fighting, he still hadn't worked up the courage to step on to the mat with her himself. She was tall and lean-muscled, wore her hair cropped short. Lincoln still hadn't gotten the story on how she'd earned the nickname, but even people outside the team called her by it, so he figured it must have been a long-time attachment. Despite the cool weather, she was wearing a sleeveless compression top, her full-sleeve tattoos on wide display, dark words and figures textured on her dark skin.

Once everyone was suitably coffee-ed and seated, Lincoln assumed his place at the front of the room. His nerves kicked up a notch. Briefings were routine, but for some reason standing in front of such a small number of people made him more self-conscious than usual. That, combined with the fact that his four subordinate teammates were all razor-sharp tacticians, also made him hyper-aware of how little time he'd had to put everything together. He was glad he hadn't had that fourth cup of coffee after all.

"All right everybody," Lincoln said. "Here we go. Hot off the press, fresh out of the oven, whatever you want to call it."

He activated the holographic display in front of him, pulled up a three-dimensional image of a ship. It was long, heavier in the back than the front, smooth and rounded like some sort of cosmic seed. Sleekly aggressive. There was no real indication of its purpose in its silhouette, but it gave the distinct impression that whatever it was, you wouldn't like it if it did it to you.

Thumper let out a little whistle, to Lincoln's surprise.

"You recognize that?" he asked.

"I hope not," she replied. "*Angel*-class?"

Lincoln swept his eyes over his other teammates, saw they were each waiting expectantly for him to continue. Good. He wasn't the only one who'd never seen one of these before. In answer to Thumper, he nodded.

"This is SUNGRAZER," he said. He gestured at the projector, enlarging the image and advancing the briefing with a wave of his hand. Text appeared in sequence, detailing specifications, highlighting capabilities. "Sometime in the last seventy-two hours, she went missing."

Thumper made a little noise somewhere between a cough and a grunt of disgust.

"What's she do?" Mike asked.

"She's a deep maneuver asset," Thumper answered. *Deep maneuver*. It was in-house terminology for anything that, once deployed, could spend years dormant or finding its way to a target; a piece of software, a genetically-targeted virus, an automated warship. SUNGRAZER was the latter.

"That's right," Lincoln said. "Self-contained, self-directed. Sitting out there cold and quiet and for all practical purposes, completely impossible to detect. Two major functions. First: ultra-long range signals intelligence gathering. She's basically a giant antenna, soaking up everything her target's giving off. Stores, processes, analyzes, adapts accordingly. Every so often she bounces a packet back home, presumably to our friends in intelligence.

"Second, and this is the real fun one... she's a kinetic orbital strike vehicle."

The basic concept of a kinetic orbital strike wasn't particularly impressive; it was pretty much just dropping something heavy from way up high on whatever it was you wanted to crush into oblivion. Where it got fancy was in all the math of making sure you dropped all that heavy on the right thing. And what made it scary were the facts that such a weapon could strike with very little warning and was nearly impossible to defend against. For added bonus, since the munitions had no launch signature, they left the source of their launch point virtually untraceable.

"How many hits we talking?" Wright asked.

"I'm not sure. Specs I was given listed capacity from fifteen to three hundred, so depends on loadout I guess."

"Quite a range," Thumper said. It was true. The difference between surgically excavating a city block and wiping out the whole city entirely.

"I get the impression the Powers That Be didn't want to get too precise in the information they provided," Lincoln replied.

"That's a whole lotta ship to lose track of for three whole days," Mike said. "And gonna be hard to do the job if the Powers That Be are going to be stingy on the details."

"Just wait," Lincoln said. "It gets better. SUNGRAZER's her codename, of course, because she's one of the Directorate's assets."

"Since when's NID runnin' ships?" Sahil asked. The National Intelligence Directorate usually relied on the military to handle the logistics of anything on that scale.

"Technically, she's a joint-operation vessel. Command-and-control is shared between NID and the navy, but since she's designed to go for long periods without direct contact, I'm not sure how much the navy's really involved."

"Seems like a hassle to manage with the Federation," Thumper said. "A lot of protocols to get through."

Lincoln nodded. "That's probably why she's not a UAF vessel. She's strictly ours, made and operated out of right here in the good ol' U S of A." The United American Federation joined the American continents from tip to tail, pole to pole. Every member state maintained its sovereignty and own military forces, but most military actions were carried out under the auspice of the UAF banner, comprised of elements contributed by the various nations. Even though individual countries were free to carry out operations, command often overlapped between the UAF and the host nation, with roles and numbers determined through some Byzantine process. The knot got even more tangled when special operations forces were involved. Usually the Federation's participation was more limited in those circumstances, with UAF personnel serving in observation or advisory roles. One of Lincoln's early assignments had been as part of such a team, working in Honduras. The reporting structure and hierarchy had been confusing to him back then. He'd since spent most of his adult life in the midst of it, and still didn't grasp it fully. "It's not even clear at this stage that the UAF is aware of SUNGRAZER."

"I'm shocked," Thumper said, with a tone that suggested she wasn't.

"Where's she stationed?" Wright asked. Lincoln didn't know why he bothered to organize his presentations; his teammates always asked questions he'd answer later in the briefing, no matter how carefully he tried to stage them to get to the relevant facts as quickly as possible. He gestured at the projector again, skipping through the next four slides to pull up an image of SUNGRAZER's general track. The scales were all off, like an elementary school picture of the solar system, but the image showed Mars, the asteroid belt, and a thick white line marking a short portion of SUNGRAZER's path.

"She's shadowing Mars, from the Belt-side," Lincoln said. "Or, at least, she was. As you can see, we've only got about ten days of historical data here to look at."

"Yeah," Thumper said. "Why is that?"

Lincoln smiled at the irony of the answer. "Clearance isn't high enough."

"I'm sorry," Wright said. "What?"

"You've all been given a great privilege here," Almeida said from his corner. "Just briefing you on this basically doubled the number of people who even know about SUNGRAZER."

"That's probably a bit of an exaggeration," Lincoln said, "but maybe not much of one. Operational control is highly-compartmentalized. Best I can tell from what they gave us, even some of the folks running remote maintenance on SUNGRAZER didn't know exactly what she was working on." He pointed at Thumper. "I want you to deep scan what they sent over, though. I'm sure you'll find things I missed."

"Easy day," Thumper said.

"If it's such a tight ship," said Wright, "how'd we lose it?"

"Good question," Lincoln replied. "She's supposed to have failsafes in place to prevent this exact scenario... emergency shut down protocols, self-destruct procedures, the whole bit. Whatever orders she received to divert her course didn't trip any of those failsafes. Remote intrusion countermeasures didn't even fire off or anything. From how it's looking right now, those orders came through a legitimate command chain."

"So we're looking at an inside job then," Wright said.

"The Directorate is adamant that it's not, but, then again, of course they would be. Inside job would point the finger right back at them. We'll keep it on our possible list, anyway. It'd certainly be the simplest solution."

"Anything can be hacked," Thumper said.

"With the right resources, sure," Lincoln replied. "So we keep the folks with the capability on the list of suspects, too. Still a short list. We're talking foreign intelligence, somebody else's military, state-level actors."

"Or a proxy," Wright added. "Who knew about it?"

"Ops team, obviously," Lincoln said. "Elements of command, an isolated cell within NID. As I said, this thing is highly-compartmentalized, very need-to-know."

"I don't suppose they were kind enough to give us any sort of jump start on this one?" Mike asked. "Or is it business as usual, and do all our own legwork first?"

"Actually, we got a lucky break for once," Lincoln answered. "NID techs picked up a comms burst from a long-hauler coming back from the Belt. The transmission itself was routine, but there was a second layer to it, encrypted, hidden in the stream. NID's folks picked some indicators out of it."

"'Indicators'?" Thumper asked. "Is that your word, or theirs?"

"That was theirs."

"Anybody specify what they meant by that?"

"They declined to do so," Lincoln said. "Which is why I said it was a lucky break."

Thumper shook her head. "Oh, you meant a *lucky break*."

Lincoln nodded. The Directorate naturally had to share information with outside agencies or organizations to get things done, but they were always paranoid about non-Directorate personnel figuring out how the information had been acquired. A *lucky break* had become the team's code for whenever intel seemed a little too detailed or too perfect for the acquisition story that accompanied it. Frequently that meant NID had a source very close to the situation. And it almost always meant they knew more than they were willing to share. But then, that too was to be expected.

"So this ship…" Wright prompted.

Lincoln gestured at the projector, skipped a few more slides he'd prepared, and brought up an image of the target vessel.

"This is the *Ava Leyla*, a Marushkin Type-43 cargo

ship. Free agent hauler, registered out of Luna originally. Official records have her doing far-reach hop runs mostly." The *Ava Leyla*'s travel records showed her spending the past year and a half bouncing between a variety of space stations out between the Belt and Mars. "But there are some gaps in her history, manifests. Records are good enough to pass most checks, not quite enough to hold up under thorough scrutiny."

"And we think they're in on it?" Wright said.

"Could be. Pretty sure they're up to something they shouldn't be, but that doesn't mean they're connected to our primary target. Either way, it's the only place we know to start. Maybe *we'll* get lucky."

"So do we actually know where they are?" Thumper asked.

"Well," Lincoln answered. "Not *exactly*. General idea. I think everyone assumed you could get us the last thousand klicks." Thumper nodded with an of-course-they-did expression on her face.

"And once Thump tracks 'em down," Sahil said, "No chance somebody's gonna do us the favor of holdin' 'em up till we get there, I suppose."

Lincoln shook his head. "If it was going to be that easy, I don't think they would have bothered to call us. Nobody wants to draw any attention to any of this. This is another situation where just poking at it might tip off the wrong people that we're on the trail. Same deal as LOCKSTEP."

LOCKSTEP had been a secret Directorate space station, a critical facility for collecting signals intelligence on Mars. Right up until a sophisticated party had put an asteroid through the middle of it. Lincoln's first operation as the Outriders' team leader had been to track down the people responsible; in doing so, they'd only narrowly averted the first shots of a war between Earth and Mars. The relationship between the two planets still hadn't recovered.

"We need to see what we can do, and we need to do it real quiet," he continued. "NID's being surprisingly collaborative on this one, if that tells you anything."

"We're talking world-ending level stuff here, huh?" Mike asked.

"Worse," Lincoln said. "Career-ending. Heads are going to have to roll over this no matter what. Only question now is how high the axeman has to go. And that probably depends on what we find, and how quickly we find it."

"Is she the only one out there?" Thumper asked, her tone suggesting a deeper question. She was doing the math, thinking ahead, looking at the strategic implications beyond the immediate crisis. "SUNGRAZER, I mean."

"Another good question. And another one I can't answer. Classified."

"Well, yeah of course, but I mean ballpark, how many of these vessels are vulnerable now. Just the one? Ten? A hundred?"

Lincoln shook his head. "As far as I know, could be any of those."

"I wonder if maybe this is finally the kind of thing that's going to get everyone to agree not to weaponize autonomous vehicles."

"That probably depends on how well *we* do," Lincoln answered.

"How we gettin' out?" Sahil asked.

"Navy's got a changeover coming up. We'll hitch a ride as far out as Blue Water goes, then launch a skiff from there." Blue Water was the extent of Earth's projected presence out into open space, all the way to three light-seconds past the moon's orbit. Lincoln hadn't even been old enough to walk when that declaration had been made, and he'd never dug into why that particular range had been designated as Earth's rightful territory.

"Ugh," Mike said. "We gotta operate off a boat?"

"Only until we figure out where we're supposed to go next."

"Fifty bucks says Mars," Thumper said.

"Don't say that," Sahil said.

"I'll take that bet," said Mike. "My gut says it's somebody closer to home. Eastern Coalition. Off Luna, I'd say."

"If that's what *your* gut's sayin'," Sahil said, "I'll throw fifty in on Mars."

"So, in summary," Wright said, getting back to business, "we're supposed to find an invisible ship in the middle of space, without letting anyone know what we're looking for."

"Before whoever took it uses it to destroy a city," Thumper added.

"On an unknown timetable," Lincoln finished. "Yeah, that about covers it. Officially, we are to locate SUNGRAZER and recover her if we can, or destroy her if we have to. Secondary objectives, which we'll probably get for free along the way, are to figure out who seized control and more importantly how they did it. I'm guessing this isn't the sort of thing we want to have to do more than once. I've got full packets prepped for each of you. Eighteen hours to lift off. Any more questions?"

Lincoln looked to each of his teammates in turn. Only Mike raised his hand.

"Yeah, Mike?"

"I got time for breakfast?"

"Not for your usual farmhand's one."

Mike made a face, then shrugged as he got to his feet.

"Probably just lose it on launch anyway," he said.

"One more thing," the colonel said, moving out of his corner towards the podium, "if you're done, captain."

"Yes sir," Lincoln said, stepping aside.

"We're a small outfit," Almeida said. "I've kept it that way for a long time, for very good reason. But as good as you kids are, there's one hole in our capabilities that I just haven't been able to fill to my satisfaction. Until recently."

"Uh oh," Thumper said.

"You gettin' us a sniper that can finally shoot?" Sahil asked.

"Hey now," Mike said.

"We're getting air support," the colonel said. "Two pilots."

"Oh jeez," Mike said. "Aviators?"

"I wanted to bring it in-house. We've been hitching rides at the mercy of everyone else's schedules for too long. And I managed to wrangle a little extra scratch for our budget."

"Sure, not like I could have used a raise or anything," Mike replied.

"Settle down, Michael," Almeida said, and from the tone of his voice, Lincoln wondered if he'd just discovered how the colonel had gotten his nickname. "Trust me, I wouldn't make changes to the team chemistry just because I can. This is the right move for the unit, short- and long-term. I know it'll take some time to adjust, but I believe these guys are going to give you greater flexibility and take some of the headache out of logistics. You'll move faster with dedicated support. I don't seem to recall any of you filing any complaints about getting on target too fast."

"Anybody we know?" Lincoln asked. Almeida glanced at him with a twinkle in his good eye.

"You may have met once before," he answered. Then he stepped over to the door, opened it, and leaned out into the hall. When he stepped back in, two men followed. Two brothers. Will and Noah Barton.

"You're kidding me," Wright said, but there was a smile on her face. "Where'd Mom find you two?"

"Out in the junkyard," Will answered.

"According to the official records, these two earned themselves a demotion and reassignment to the 301st Information Support Brigade, 519th Applied Intelligence Group, Logistical Support."

On a previous mission, the Outriders had been left stranded on a target after their support had been withdrawn. Whether by mistake or by design was never exactly clear. Regardless, the Barton brothers had intervened against direct orders, pulled off a very risky extraction, and rescued Lincoln and his team out of a dire situation. Lincoln hadn't ever heard what had become of them afterwards. Apparently Almeida had worked some of his magic.

"Actually, I earned *two* demotions," Will said.

"It was the only way I could afford you both," Almeida said.

"So you guys are our bus drivers then," Thumper said.

"More like delivery service," Noah replied. "Just hauling gear around for a bunch of technicians, you know."

He put a hint of extra emphasis on the word *technicians*. It was both a running joke within the Outriders, and a partial cover story. It was another origin story Lincoln didn't know. But pretty much whenever someone outside the team asked an Outrider what they did, the reply was they were "technicians from Information Support". Officially, it was true. The Outriders really were part of the 301st Information Support Brigade. It's just that *technician* had taken on a different meaning within the team.

"It's going to be great for your career," Lincoln said.

"Oh yeah, I can tell that already," Noah answered.

"What's big brother think so far?" Lincoln asked, looking to Will.

"Well," Will said, and he paused, taking an overly-dramatic look around. "Can't say I'm too impressed with the accommodations. Ink's barely dry on the transfer, and they're already getting me out of bed at ungodly hours." Then he looked at Lincoln. "But the people seem all right. At least so far."

"Gonna have to get used to roughing it, starfish," said Mike, tossing out a mildly derogatory term for space pilots. "We here in the army tend to spend our money only on the essentials."

"Not my fault you joined the wrong branch," Will replied. He extended his hand. "I don't believe we've met."

"Mike," Mike said, shaking hands first with Will, then with Noah.

"Oh, right," Lincoln said. "Sorry." The pilots had met the rest of the team, but not Mike. He'd already been dead when the brothers had rescued the team. They'd brought his body home. "Mike, Will and Noah Barton. Barton boys, this is Sergeant Pence."

"Not *One-Time* Mike Pence?" Noah asked, using Mike's sometime nickname. Mike's eyebrows went up a little.

"What, you heard of me or something?"

"I don't think you can spend any time around special

operations and not have heard of One-Time Mike Pence."

"None of the good stories are true," Mike said. And then after a beat, he added, "But I like to tell 'em anyway."

"Eighteen hours to lift off," Almeida said loudly. Then he smiled. "You'll have plenty of time on the way to sniff each other out."

"We're going out?" Will asked. Almeida nodded.

"Wouldn't be much point in bringing you on, if I was going to let you sit around our less-than-impressive accommodations."

"Why didn't you bring them in for the briefing then?" Lincoln asked, bewildered. And, admittedly, he was already dreading having to give the same presentation again.

"Clearance hasn't come through yet," Almeida said. "Don't worry, it should be in before you get out of Blue Water. And I'm sure your briefing will be even better the second time, captain."

"You folks don't mess around, do you?" Will asked.

Lincoln chuckled and shook his head. "Welcome to the Outriders."

SIX

"I'm counting on you," Elliot said. He leaned forward over the small table and lowered his voice. "I don't have anyone else I can trust."

It was a lie, of course. The only way this situation could have been stupider would have been if Elliot genuinely had no other options. Options were the lifeblood of an undeclared field officer. But there was time pressure on this one. NID was making impossible demands, as usual, and, as usual, Elliot was finding a way. The Powers That Be didn't always like the way he worked, but they never complained about the results. And whenever something had to get done, they didn't seem to have any issues asking him to work his magic.

"I'm not trying to be difficult, Volodya," the man answered, using the name Elliot had given him when they'd first met. He sipped from the small cup of hot tea in front of him, and then replaced it on the table, and shook his head. "I just don't know how to make it work. These are delicate matters. They take time to develop."

He seemed sincere.

"I know, Kit," Elliot said, leaning back. "I know."

Kit Leong was one of the wealthiest citizens in the Meridiani Administrative Region and, more importantly, a close advisor to the region's Minister of Finance. Elliot didn't know what the Directorate was up to exactly, what poison they wanted to pour into the Minister's ear. That wasn't his business anyway. All he knew was that he needed to win access for some diplomat he'd never met, and that the best chance to win it quickly was through his well-developed connection Kit Leong.

They were speaking Mandarin, with its curious Martian-dialect, a language that Elliot didn't actually know himself. The linguistic implant was smaller than a grain of sand, lodged snugly somewhere just behind his left temple. According to the literature, there was no discomfort, and there were no known side effects to running it. The device was, in fact, quite handy when operating in foreign territory. Elliot still wasn't clear on the exact details of how it knew when to kick in, but the implant took over language processing whenever necessary, and made him conversational in languages he didn't know. It still wasn't as fast as natural language; he could never pass as a native speaker. Just a slight lag in response time, noticeable but not disruptive.

Elliot paused as if weighing his options, or searching for words. Also a ruse. He already knew what he was going to say, but he needed the dramatic effect. He looked off to the skyline, at the high-rises stretching up, taller than the tallest buildings he could remember ever having seen back on Earth. So tall, they almost seemed like if you stood on the roof, you might be able to reach up and actually touch the thin membrane that shielded the city from the planet's worst environmental features. Impossible, of course. The bubble was a good couple of hundred meters above the tallest building. Even so, it was hard not to be impressed, even sitting as they were in a private window-room on the sixty-first floor.

"I don't come to you just for the help, you know," he said, eyes on the horizon. "I come to you for your advice, as well."

"My advice is the same as always," Kit answered. "Come work for me." Elliot looked back at the man, saw him smiling now.

"Tempting," Elliot said. "As always."

"I'm a foolish old man to keep asking."

"A wise man. There's a good chance that one day I may say yes," Elliot answered. "But today is not that day."

"When do you return to the Collective?" Kit asked.

"Supposed to head back in a couple of hours," Elliot said. "I could delay until the morning. If that would make any difference."

Kit shook his head again. "This would be a matter of weeks, Volodya. Not days. And certainly not hours." The man sipped his tea again, looking thoughtful. And then, his eyes still on his tea, he said, "Unless..." as if a thought had just occurred to him.

And this was the moment Elliot had been working towards. Naming the price. They were both playing the game. And they both knew they were playing the game. It was another ridiculous part of Elliot's work. No one could ever just come out and say what they wanted or why.

But no, a game was the wrong way to think about it. It was more like dancing. A complex style, dictated by culture and etiquette, the choreographed and synchronized movements well-rehearsed but spontaneously executed in response to the music, while both parties denied there was any music at all.

Elliot followed Kit's lead.

"Unless?" he prompted.

Kit shook his head. "No… it was just another foolish musing, from a foolish old man."

"Why don't you let me be the judge of that."

"Well… in the course of your business dealings," Kit said. He stopped himself, and waved a hand. "I have no doubts that you are a man of integrity, Volodya, you know that. But I believe we both suspect some of your connections to… certain parties, may indirectly bring you into relation with people of a lesser nature."

"It's not a suspicion," Elliot said. "I manage them carefully."

Kit nodded, and reflexively looked over one shoulder. Elliot's admission was stronger than usual etiquette would dictate.

"There is certain information, difficult to come by. Information that could be beneficial to a person in the Minister's position." Kit was always careful to refer to the Finance Minister as "a person in the Minister's position", as though the two were distinct. Undoubtedly a carefully cultivated practice to avoid suggesting that the *actual* Minister might engage in anything less than the most honorable of pursuits, while acknowledging that certainly one could understand how an individual in such a position *might* do so.

"Well, there are no guarantees," Elliot said. "But I can ask around." He sipped his tea, and then added, "Discreetly."

"I think," Kit replied, "perhaps if I were able to advise the Office of Financial Affairs on certain, specific details, a person in the Minister's position might be more open to a new introduction."

"If only someone knew what questions to ask," Elliot said. Kit smiled.

"Perhaps you should adjust your travel arrangements,"

the old man said. "There's a show I've been meaning to take in. Quite popular, I understand. You'll be my guest this evening?"

"It'd be a pleasure. In the meantime, is there a quiet place I could make a few calls?"

"Of course," Kit said. "I'll have Alanna set up one of our guest offices for you."

Elliot finished the last of his tea, and sat back again, returning his gaze to the cityscape stretched out before them. The kind of information that Kit was looking for most certainly wasn't the sort you could get by just making a few calls. But Elliot had one source, one in particular that he saved for very special occasions. Emergencies only. Technically he wasn't even supposed to know it existed. But he'd discovered it the way he usually discovered things. Listening to people hint about things they weren't supposed to be talking about, and then flattering them enough to keep them talking.

He'd only used it a handful of times, always to good effect. It was risky to access the source, but Elliot always took precautions. He was, in fact, more concerned about the techs at NID finding out what he was up to than he was about accidentally exposing the asset. The few times he'd resorted to pulling information from it, the quality had been so high it'd opened doors that would have been otherwise impossible to budge. And he had to oil those hinges every so often. If NID locked him out, he didn't know how he'd be able to keep all the plates spinning.

At least Kit understood the importance of protecting their relationship; and that meant protecting Elliot's methods. Given the confidential nature of Kit's legitimate financial work, and the number of competitors actively attempting to discover his methods, the "quiet place" he would provide was likely to be about as secure as any of the clean rooms the NID had for such work. And Elliot always carried a secondary encryption method, for an added layer of security.

"This is why I come to you with such things," Elliot said. "You have a way."

"As do you, Volodya," Kit said, rising from the table, and extending his hand. "We are of the same cloth."

Elliot stood, shook the offered hand and added the unnecessary but always appreciated traditional bow.

"Cut by the same tailor," Elliot said. "You'll let me know how I can be of service?"

"Shortly," Kit replied. "Have some more tea. Alanna will escort you when your office is prepared. See you this evening for dinner, at seven."

"See you then, my friend."

Kit nodded and smiled, then exited, leaving Elliot to figure out for himself what would come next. He sat back down at the small table and poured himself another cup of tea, even though he hated the stuff. You could only plan so far ahead in his line of work. Mostly, it was about having enough open options, acting decisively, and always trusting your ability to keep dancing, no matter the tune.

SEVEN

The firing solution was atypical; the target, unusual. Calculations produced a steep angle of attack; negligible gravitational pull from the target required a higher than standard approach velocity. Increased velocity meant increased risk of detection. But SUNGRAZER saw no indication of sensor arrays at the target site. And her directives were clear.

She followed her protocol, transmitted her intentions back to her controller, requested final confirmation. The reply was nearly instantaneous.

Fire.

SUNGRAZER rolled into her attack vector, increased her velocity to match her previous calculations. On her starboard side, a launch platform irised open. The munition armed. At a moment precisely timed, SUNGRAZER reached her terminal point and released.

The instant the projectile had left its housing, SUNGRAZER arced away from her attack vector, allowing her velocity to carry her gracefully along her escape trajectory. And while she sped away, her payload sped home.

The projectile met its target 741.18 kilometers distant at full velocity, imparting 4.88 gigajoules of energy concentrated into a focal point less than a meter in diameter. Destruction of the target from the resulting blast was thorough; shattered fragments and dust vomited out into open space, never again to settle.

And the yield had been but a fraction of her potential.

The asteroid she'd fired upon posed no threat, had no strategic value that SUNGRAZER could discern. But hers was not to decide. Hers was to wait, and to watch, and when called upon, to act.

The impact was just under two meters from the target origin; well within operationally-acceptable tolerances, but not up to SUNGRAZER's exacting standards. To her, imprecision was the same as a miss. She assessed her calculations, ran systems diagnostics. Recalibrated.

Next time, she would not miss.

EIGHT

"Cover," Lincoln said, his voice just above a whisper. "I'm going to take Poke for a look."

"Covering," Sahil responded, equally quiet. He crept cat-like past Lincoln and took position against the bulkhead, guarding forward. Thumper slid up to close the gap in the line, maintaining rearguard with Lincoln now in the middle.

"You're good," Thumper said.

Technically, keeping their voices low wasn't necessary. The recon suits they wore were completely sealed; Lincoln could have shouted and no one would have heard him outside his helmet. But it was a tough habit to break, and one Lincoln didn't mind leaving intact. Quiet speech encouraged quiet movement.

And the fifth-generation suits could move like a panther.

Most powered armor was all heavy plates and sharp angles, and left its occupant feeling cut off from the outside world. The Outriders' recon gear, by contrast, was fluid curves flowing into one another that made its many components appear to be a single piece. Other suits were a dump truck; Lincoln's, a racing motorcycle.

Inside his suit, Lincoln barely registered its presence.

Its liquid movement coupled with the enhanced environmental awareness it provided made it feel almost more natural than his own skin, as if the suit enabled him to finally move through and perceive the world the way humans had always been meant to.

The heads-up display projected a view of the outside world on the solid faceplate of his helmet, overlaid with a minimal set of indicators and operational markers. If he'd wanted it, Lincoln could have dialed the resolution in so sharply that it would appear he wasn't wearing a helmet at all. He preferred to keep a transparent representation of the faceplate in his view though, as a reminder of the level of protection it offered. It helped cut down on the flinch-factor when the unpleasantness came flying in his direction.

Lincoln used his gaze to select the appropriate options, opened up a window in the center of his view. It took a moment for him to orient himself to the new perspective, to remember that the ceiling was the floor. Their foldable was ahead of them, attached to the ceiling, scouting out the critical corridor that led to the ship's bridge. Foldable was the common term for it, though officially it was a self-assembling bot. Technically, it was just a self-*reconfiguring* bot, comprised of many independently-intelligent components operating together. But the more accurate terminology deprived its creators of the clever SABOT acronym they had assigned it when presenting it to the military.

The team had named their foldable Poke before Lincoln had joined; Thumper treated it like a pet. Poke was smart enough to run independently for the most part, but at particularly sensitive times, Lincoln liked to have a human at the helm just to be sure. He was old-fashioned that way.

Under his direct control, Poke crept silently forward along the ceiling, flattened and reconfiguring itself as necessary to follow the contours of the ship's overhead as closely as possible. Lincoln parked the bot at an intersection where two side-corridors joined the main. The door to the bridge was closed, and flanked by two other doors. According to the schematics, one was a supply closet and the other a planning room of sorts. Lincoln swept Poke's camera from right to left and back again, using its composite imaging to identify and mark the individuals it detected. Each mark was passed to the rest of the team, overlaid on their view.

There were four people on the bridge, and no one in either of the side compartments. Other corridors were clear.

This was the tricky part. They'd made it this far with no shots fired. Lincoln wanted to close it out that way. The thing was you never had to shoot until you *had* to shoot, and there was usually no way to know if or when that moment was going to come until it happened.

Lincoln closed out the view from Poke's perspective, set the bot back to autonomous. He laid a hand on Sahil's shoulder, gave it a squeeze. Sahil responded to the signal, glided to the side and back a step, allowing Lincoln to move forward. Once he was past, Sahil slid over back into the middle position again.

"Anvil," Lincoln said through his suit's comms channel. "Hammer's at Keyframe Zulu, ready to move up and prep for entry."

"Copy, Hammer," came Wright's voice in reply. "Anvil's already in position."

"Acknowledged. Hammer is moving to bridge entrance."

Lincoln glanced back over his shoulder to confirm his

two teammates behind him were set. Sahil nodded, and as one unit the three of them glided forward into the main corridor. Lincoln kept his short-barreled rifle up and ready, aim point centered on the entrance to the bridge. Those doors at the end of the narrow hallway were his responsibility; he trusted Sahil and Thumper to take care of everything else.

Their pace was fluidly aggressive, a fast walk with each step carefully placed. At the door, Lincoln lowered his weapon and let it lock into the panel on the front of his suit, where it clung as if by magnets. The moment it was secure, his hands continued on to the left side of his torso, where the entry tool rested. Sahil anticipated the movement, took over covering the entrance, while behind them Thumper dropped to a knee and covered the rear.

Lincoln pulled the tool from its housing, separated the two flattened cylinders from one another, and placed them one above the other in a vertical line, following the seam of the door in its frame. The instant they were properly seated, Lincoln lifted his weapon from its perch along his chest; it came away as easily as if someone had handed it to him.

The hatch to the bridge opened outward, which was going to make entry awkward. Lincoln took two steps back, shifted his weapon over to his left hand and shoulder, angled his body to give Sahil and Thumper as much room to get by him as possible.

One final check. The bridge was asymmetrical, laid out in an L-shape, upside down from Lincoln's perspective. Three of the individuals were in the long section, and one was at the far end, around the corner from the main entryway. He could track their silhouettes, thanks to Poke's imaging data that was projected over his view of the physical world. From what he could tell, all four crew members were casually working their stations, happily ignorant of what was crouching just outside their door. Lincoln almost hated to disturb them.

Almost.

"Anvil," Lincoln said. "Hammer's in place, set to go."

"Anvil's set," Wright responded over comms. "On your count."

"On my count," Lincoln replied. He drew a settling breath, held his lungs full for a five count. Easy exhale. Reminded his shoulders to relax. "Three... two... one... execute, execute, execute."

On the last syllable, he activated the entry tool. Its abrupt whine cut off almost as soon as it had started, followed in the next instant by a dull *whump* from within the bridge. Lincoln pulled the hatch open, and Sahil was through the gap in an instant, followed immediately by Thumper. Sahil went left, Thumper right, so Lincoln went left, weapon up and scanning for targets.

"Down, down, get down!" Sahil commanded, his voice thinner and processed as it came through the external speaker of his helmet. Two of the crew members on the ship complied immediately, but a third stood frozen in a half-crouch, hands swimming near his face like he was fighting bees.

He was closest to Lincoln, so Lincoln moved forward to control him. The man wasn't armed; Lincoln lowered his weapon and let it secure against the suit, then stretched out his hands towards the man. To Lincoln's surprise, the man swung a haymaker at his head. The punch bounced harmlessly off Lincoln's helmet, the dull impact barely registering. The man did what men do when they smash their hands into very hard things; he immediately clutched it with his other hand and pressed it against his belly, doubled-over. Which made it all the easier for Lincoln to secure him and take him down to the floor. He was a big man, and he struggled against Lincoln's control, fishing his legs around and trying to roll onto his back. Lincoln laid his shin across the base of the man's neck, pinning him, and bore down with just enough of his body weight to take the fight out of the man.

When he was confident his man was controlled, Lincoln snapped his eyes up, scanned the bridge; Sahil and Thumper had each secured a crewmember. Wright's marker was visible through the bulkhead; she and Mike had come in together through a hole they'd cut. Mike had quickly subdued the fourth individual. That was four of four. The bridge was theirs.

"We good?" Lincoln asked.

"Good!" Wright answered, and her reply was followed by the other three sounding off.

Mike was the last. "Good to go!"

Twelve seconds from entry to secure. No shots fired. All that remained now was to get the crew rounded up and moved to a central point, and then let Thumper go to work pulling data off the ship. About as clean as it could go.

"All right," Lincoln said. "Let's shut it down, and talk it out."

All around him, the environment shimmered and faded. The man under his knee went transparent and became the floor; the bridge became the large, open hangar of another ship.

It didn't matter how many times Lincoln ran haptic training simulations. Every time one ended, he was always surprised to see how much it had fooled his brain. It really had felt like there was a man writhing and struggling beneath him.

He got to his feet and his team gathered around him. They were all suited up, all carrying the exact load outs they expected to run on the live op. And that was one of the great benefits of the haptic sim; it was all piped in through their standard recon armor, so it *felt* about as real as the real deal. No special equipment, no weird extra weight or bulk that could throw operators off when they went into the field.

Sims weren't perfect, of course. No training ever quite was. But they got about eighty percent of the way there, which was about as high as anyone could hope for.

"Sahil," Lincoln said. "Give me the count that time."

"Four in quarters, two in engineering, two at mess, four on the bridge," Sahil said, rattling it off like he was reading from a checklist. "Twelve in all." That matched Lincoln's count of the ship's personnel.

"No weapons, no illicit goods," Lincoln said. "Gave us an easy one that time. Where'd we have trouble?"

"Cut through," Wright said. "Took us six minutes longer to reach our entry point on the bridge that time."

"Why was that?"

"Water treatment was on the starboard side, had some big pipes in our way. Had to route around."

"Which wasn't easy to do being all quiet like," Mike added, mostly unnecessarily.

The target ship was a nineteen year-old Marushkin long-haul freighter; the sim replicated the ship's general structure exactly, pulled straight from factory blueprints. All the major components were the same on every Marushkin, the general placement of compartments and corridors. But there were a few minor variations how a hauler could be configured, depending on what it was used to transport. And there was no way to know for sure what kind of custom work the hauler's skipper might have had done to it.

The haptic sim made best guesses where it could, and no run through was ever quite the same as anything they'd trained before. Crew count changed; sometimes there were passengers, sometimes not; maybe the ship was well-maintained, maybe there were leaky pipes and garbage everywhere. The simulator did a good job of preparing the team for learning to navigate the environment, without ever repeating enough to become predictable.

Simulated personnel were the biggest factor of unpredictability. Just like real humans. You never knew exactly how they would react. Well, that wasn't exactly true. Lincoln had been in enough situations involving civilians that had gone sideways to recognize the one thing you could know for sure was that they would never react the way you anticipated. He'd seen big burly men curl into quaking balls of fear, and spindly older women fly into rage, throwing whatever was close at hand. Bottom line was, people were the big unknown in any op, and the sim did a good job of replicating that fact.

"Hey boss," Mike said, chuckling. "Did I see that right? Did your man punch you in the faceplate?"

Lincoln nodded. "Sure did."

Mike shook his head. "I didn't know they could do that."

"Sure they can," Thumper answered. "They can do anything people can do."

"Yeah, but I didn't know one of them would ever do something so stupid."

Thumper shrugged. "Like I said. Just like people."

Lincoln spun the conversation back to the beginning,

had his team members run the op from the top in brief, each outlining their role, how they'd performed, what mistakes they made, and how they could have done better. It'd been their sixth rehearsal for the day. Everyone was professional about it, but Lincoln picked up on the fatigue around the edges of the words. They were used to running weary, but there was no need to push it too far before things went live.

Once they'd all had their say, he nodded, and raised his hands to remove his helmet. The seal around the neck of his armored suit released with a short hiss. He lifted the helmet off, wiped the sweat from his brow with the palm of his gloved hand. Even though his gauntlet protected his hands from any environmental threat and most small munitions, the sensory integration was so complete he would've sworn that he could feel the wetness through the suit. The rubberized material didn't do a great job of absorbing the moisture, but at least it kept the beads from running into his eyes.

"I'm thinking maybe we should wrap haptics for the day," he said. "Kind of nice to go out on a high note."

"Hate to go out on an easy one," Wright said.

"Better than going out on one where we all get killed," said Mike.

There was such a thing as over-preparing. A danger that the rehearsal would lead to routine, routine to complacency. It wasn't a question of professionalism. Lincoln had never been part of a team that was as consistently razor-sharp and on point as the Outriders were, and he'd served on some of the most highly-trained special operations teams in the world before his transfer. But it wasn't a training thing, it was a people thing. The mind had a way of seeing first what it expected to see, rather than what truly was. In operations like these, there wasn't time for second looks.

And as much as they knew about the layout of the target vessel, that was really *all* they knew about it. The team still didn't know exactly what they were looking for, just that whatever it was, was out there on the *Ava Leyla*. Some hits required something more like muscle memory; good preparation and planning enabled an aggressive take down, where most of the high-level decisions had already been made and it was just a matter of making the right calls moment-to-moment. This one was different. Once they were aboard, the op was going to require a lot of real-time assessment and adaptation, and a fair amount of creative problem-solving. He needed every one of his teammates mentally sharp.

"We've all got plenty of homework to get through still," Lincoln said. "And I've got some command-level bonus work on my plate. We'll hit it again tomorrow. 0600."

Wright tipped her head to one side briefly, a quick but clear sign she disagreed with the decision. But the fact that even Sahil didn't put up any protest told Lincoln he'd made the right call.

The navy had been kind enough to take them aboard the cruiser USS *Durham* for the trip out to the edge of Blue Water, and had even gone as far as to clear out a storage compartment for them to make into a planning room. The compartment had sufficient space for them all, as long as three of them didn't mind standing up the whole time. Thumper's rig dominated the major portion of available table area; Veronica, she called it, though Lincoln wasn't sure if Veronica was the rig, or just the helper AI that ran it. Then again, he wasn't sure that there was any meaningful distinction between the two.

Regardless, Veronica was the sixth member of the team. The Outriders were a hard-working crew, but Veronica was the only one among them who truly never slept. She was constantly watching, drawing in data, tracking, listening, synthesizing. Thumper was her handler. And the two of them together were closer to magic than just about anything else Lincoln had ever seen.

For the time being, it was just Lincoln and Veronica in the planning room; Veronica silently chasing down whatever tasks Thumper had set her to, and Lincoln finalizing logistics on the upcoming transition from the *Durham* to the skiff that would take them out into open territory. Special operations naturally required the occasional jaunt into deep space. You had to go where the bad guys were, after all, and it turned out they tended to be everywhere. Still, Lincoln didn't love it. He was a boots-on-the-ground kind of guy at heart. The idea of operating from a skiff for more than a few days filled him with a dull dread.

Not that the *Durham* was built with comfort in mind. Lincoln had never been on a single military vessel that had given him the impression that it had been designed for people first. But the cruiser at least had passageways wide enough for two sailors to pass by without brushing shoulders. The skiff was going to be a decidedly tighter squeeze.

Lincoln checked the time. 0137. If he could wrap it up now, he might be able to get four hours of sleep before they picked up another training run.

The hatch to the compartment opened, and Lincoln looked up from his work to see Mike stepping through with a troubled look on his face. The expression changed to surprise when he saw Lincoln, and then melted into a friendly, if not quite believable, smile.

"Whoa, sorry boss," he said. "Wasn't expecting you to still be awake."

"Me neither," Lincoln said. "What are you doing up and about?"

"Trying to find a quiet place to sit," Mike answered, waggling the datapad in his hand. He pointed to the other empty chair. Lincoln nodded, and Mike flopped into it.

"You know, I wouldn't mind being stuck on a boat for so long" he said, "if it weren't for all the sailors."

Lincoln chuckled. "Probably better get used to it."

"Probably." Mike cleared a little room on the table and propped his datapad up. "Don't worry, I'll shut up, sir."

He was keeping things light, but his manner seemed to be requiring more effort than usual. And it was at odds with the look he'd had on his face when he'd first entered, before he'd noticed Lincoln.

"You doing all right, Mikey?" Lincoln asked.

Mike flicked his eyes up from his pad, gave a puzzled look, like Lincoln had asked him some obscure question of trivia. "Uh, sure, yeah. Doing fine."

This was the second time now that Lincoln's early morning work had given him cause to observe Mike's sleep patterns. Maybe it was just coincidence.

"Getting enough sleep lately?"

Mike nodded, and went back to looking at the datapad. "Yep."

"Seems like every time I'm up working, you're up wandering around looking for something to do."

"I can't help it, sir," Mike answered with a shrug, his eyes still on the tablet in front of him. "Guess I just sleep faster than everybody else." He continued to scan whatever was on his pad for a few moments. Lincoln kept watching him, and Mike eventually glanced back up at him. When he caught Lincoln's eye, he sighed, lowered the pad.

"I'm just antsy to get on with it, sir," he said. "Hard to deal with the hurry-up-and-go-go-go pressure from Higher, when all I can do is sit around until we get there. Training helps a little, but you know how it is... the waiting's always the worst."

Lincoln nodded. He didn't quite buy that that was all there was to it, but he didn't want to push Mike. Every warrior had demons. Sometimes the quiet hours were the only time to wrestle them back into submission.

"If you think that," Lincoln said, "you ought to try the paperwork."

"Negative," Mike said, returning to his pad. "Not without the hazard pay."

The two sat in a long silence, Mike intent on his datapad, Lincoln finalizing the details on all the forms and reports necessary for their transfer to the skiff. Lincoln was just wrapping up when another team member stumbled through the door.

Thumper stepped in and stopped dead, swiveling her head back and forth between the two of them with a puzzled expression.

"Heya Thump," Lincoln said. "Up late?"

"Early," she said, rubbing one eye with the palm of her hand. "Veronica called." She kicked Mike's foot. "And you're in my seat."

"Didn't see your name on it," Mike said, as he got to his feet.

"Then you're losing your eyesight, old man," Thumper replied. She pointed at the chair. Lincoln hadn't noticed it before, but there was a small piece of white gaffer tape stuck to the backrest, with THUMPER written in block letters. Mike snorted a chuckle. He backed up to one side while Thumper squeezed past in an awkward, shuffling sort of dance. She flopped into her seat, and gestured at her rig. Indicators lit up, and if he hadn't known better, Lincoln would have sworn the console let out a contented little hum at Thumper's touch.

"She get a catch?" Lincoln asked.

"Something," Thumper said, her tone of voice suggesting she didn't want to talk just yet. Lincoln glanced up at Mike, who gave a little shrug.

"Yeah, well. Reckon I better go catch some Zs while I can," said Mike. "What do you think, Thump, you gonna give me at least twenty minutes?"

She grunted distractedly.

"Well said," Mike answered, a suppressed smile creasing the corners of his mouth and wrinkling his eyes. He nodded to Lincoln. "Sir."

"'night Mikey. Sleep well."

The thought of a pillow made Lincoln vaguely jealous. If Thumper had showed up five minutes later, he would have already been face down on his bed dead asleep, probably with his boots still on. But he couldn't leave her sitting alone now, even if she told him that's exactly what she wanted.

"You ought to get some sleep too, Link," she said, as if reading his mind. She was still intent on whatever it was Veronica was showing her.

"I'm good," he replied. "I slept a couple days ago."

"Might be a while."

"I still have a few things I need to wrap up myself," he said. Technically not a lie, since there was always something he could be doing. But as much as Lincoln wanted to crash out, he knew it wouldn't be long before Thumper pulled something up. And the thought of getting thirty minutes of sleep seemed worse than getting none at all.

"Well," she said. "If you're not going to sleep…" She gave him a sly look and a little knowing smile.

Lincoln shook his head. "I'm going to have to teach one of the Barton boys the art of the coffee maker."

Thumper went back to scanning Veronica's reports. "But then what we would have you for, sir?"

"My looks, I guess," he answered, getting to his feet.

By the time Lincoln returned with two cups of coffee, Thumper already had the Look on her face. It was about eighty percent intense concentration with the remainder evenly split between delight and wonder; almost like a child working a difficult math problem, having realized the solution and now just carrying out the steps to produce the answer.

"That was fast," Lincoln said. But Thumper didn't hear him, or at least didn't acknowledge that she had. He set her coffee down on the table next to her. She picked it up almost as soon as he'd released it, and took a sip without taking her unblinking eyes off the terminal. Ignoring him, then. He didn't take it personally.

Lincoln returned to his seat and spent the next little while reviewing the plan for deploying from the *Durham*. When he couldn't stand to stare at that anymore, he brought up the schematics for the Marushkin Type-43 again. They'd rehearsed as many scenarios as they could think of; hostile crew, cooperative crew, and everything in between. Staring at the layout probably wasn't going to give him anything new to consider. But it probably wasn't going to hurt, either.

He didn't even notice that he was dreaming the schematic until Thumper spoke.

"Got it."

Lincoln picked his chin up off his chest, rubbed his watering left eye, and then picked up his untouched coffee and took a sip. It was still hot. He hadn't been out that long.

"You found the ship?" he asked.

"Huh?" Thumper said. "Oh, sure, yeah, I've been tracking that for a couple of days. I thought I told you. But no, that's not the interesting stuff. I've been watching its feed since I found it. Most of the commo traffic looks pretty normal. But there was one little blip in there a few hours ago. Took us a little while to tease it out."

By *us*, she meant her AI rig and herself.

"Give me the dumb-and-sleepy-guy version," he said.

"Uhhhh... I'm not sure there is one."

"Try."

"OK, well... it's like you're listening in on a conversation with, I don't know... say a couple of hillbillies sitting around, talking about their hunting dogs."

"On the porch?" he asked.

"Uh, sure. They're on the porch and–"

"Are they playing banjos?"

"What?" Thumper asked, confused. "What? No. They're just talking."

"About hunting dogs."

"Sure. Or, I don't know. Moonshine, or whatever."

"Thumper, have you ever actually met a hillbilly?"

"Listen. You said dumb-and-sleepy. Do you want an explanation or not?"

Lincoln smiled and took another sip of his coffee. He knew it wasn't a particularly nice habit, but tweaking the resident genius every once in a while made up for all those times that he had to sit there listening to her make him feel stupid.

"OK, so they're sitting there talking, about what

doesn't matter," she continued, "and then all of a sudden in the middle of the conversation, one of them quotes a passage from the *Epic of Gilgamesh* in perfect Akkadian."

Lincoln sat there for a moment, feeling stupid.

"That's the dumb-and-sleepy-guy version?"

Thumper sighed dramatically.

"The communications stream got super dense all of a sudden," she said. "Just for a moment. And then it went back to baseline."

"Back to Standard Hillbilly," Lincoln said.

"Exactly."

"Gotcha. No chance of tracking the receiving end, I guess?"

Thumper shook her head. "That would've been an easy one then, huh?"

"Had to ask, just in case. So they're definitely talking to SUNGRAZER then."

"Ehn, not necessarily. Encryption looks like military-grade quant stuff, so that's a point in favor, for sure. But it's not UAF standard. And looking at the pattern..." She paused and shook her head. "It doesn't even look like the same *family* of algorithm. I don't recognize any of it."

If the encryption wasn't standard to anything the United American Federation used, that wasn't a good sign. As bad as it would have been if the whole thing was an inside job, that was looking less likely if even the *method* of encryption was unfamiliar.

"And this is weird too," she continued. "Even if this crypto is super compressive, this burst is real short. Almost like a fragment. Maybe thirty to forty percent of what I'd expect. Comparing it to the traffic SUNGRAZER would normally receive, anyway."

Lincoln flashed her a look; he knew for a fact that NID hadn't provided any samples of communications with

SUNGRAZER for Thumper to compare anything to. And on their first op together, Thumper had gained access to some highly-sensitive information through less-than-approved methods and channels. She saw his reaction, held up her hand, placating.

"I didn't do anything I wasn't supposed to," she said. "One of the Directorate techs gave me some metadata, just to help me zero in on what we're looking for. Helped me build a filter. Even so, this is a little outside the usual parameters. Veronica only picked up on it because she's smart enough to know you never take anything NID gives you literally. But even so… yeah, I don't know. I don't think I buy it. Looks too much like a bounce to me."

"Somebody rerouting through?" Lincoln asked. The revelation of new information was burning off the fatigue.

"Could be. But…" She trailed off again, turned her attention back to the terminal for a few moments. "Hmmm, yeah. See… Yeah, that makes sense."

Sometimes Thumper's brain made the leaps so fast, the words never actually made it out of her mouth.

"What does?"

"Sorry, yeah. Um. Say you're trying to steal control of a protected military asset, out in deep space. You aren't sure you can pull it off, and you don't want to make a lot of noise about it. So instead of trying for a direct long-range connection that might stick out to people who are paying attention, you stuff the signal into low-broadcast commerce traffic, and then bounce it. Harder to find that way. And, to do it right, you piggyback it on somebody who doesn't even know they're carrying your relay for you. And then if you're really serious about it, you pick somebody who's used to avoiding attention. Pirates, or smugglers, or something."

Lincoln had looked at the mission package so much it didn't take much effort for him to recall the relevant details on the *Ava Leyla*. Thumper's breakdown of the situation fit the profile.

"So they might have just been a convenient pass-through," Lincoln said.

"Don't know about convenient, really. Level of encryption we're talking here… that's not something you could just push through a normal comm array. They'd have to have some special hardware on board. Could be something they rigged up themselves. Particularly if they're black market folks, looking to protect buyers or trade routes or something. But this seems like overkill for that sort of business. Expensive. So, yeah, if we're looking at foreign intelligence or something like that, it's not too much of a stretch to think they could plant something on a not-so-innocent bystander. It's definitely possible the crew of the *Ava Leyla* doesn't even know they're part of it."

Lincoln was out of his depth when it came to the technical side of things, especially where Thumper was involved. But every once in a while pieces fell together in his brain in a way that surprised him. He didn't feel like he could genuinely take credit for having *thought* of it necessarily, unless it turned out to be a stupid idea.

"Could it be a fragment? Intentionally?" he asked.

Thumper's eyes narrowed reflexively in a way that suggested it *was* a stupid idea.

"I'm not sure what good that would do," she said, diplomatically. "Probably just get treated as garbage data and ignored."

Lincoln nodded and shrugged. "I was just thinking, you know." He took a sip of his coffee. "If I'm trying to steal control of a protected military asset, out in deep space, and I'm not sure I can pull it off? Maybe I break the traffic up into a few chunks, send it through different channels, reassemble it at the receiving end. Especially if I know what the people I'm trying to steal it from would be watching for."

Thumper squinted again, but this time her expression was more thoughtful. So maybe not such a stupid idea after all.

"Huh," she said, after a few moments. The way she did when someone else thought of something first. Lincoln couldn't quite keep himself from smiling.

"I'm going to tell everyone it was your idea anyway," he said. "Nobody would go along with it if they thought it came from me."

She didn't respond. She was already interacting again with Veronica. Lincoln took another pull of his coffee, let it sit in his mouth for just a moment. It was finally at that perfect temperature; hot enough to warm the whole body without scalding the tongue. He wondered briefly how long it would be before Thumper noticed him there again. Fortunately, it wasn't long.

"Huh," she said again. "Well that *is* interesting. I guess that could make sense. Maybe running three, I don't know, maybe four of these setups? Seems like a big risk, though. You have multiple ships out there, all doing the same thing. Ups your chances of getting caught."

"To a degree," Lincoln said. "But it's distributed risk. Doesn't matter how many of them are out there running around, if no one can tell that any of them are doing anything wrong, right? Plus, depending on your numbers, could give you redundancy in case one fails or goes missing, or moves out of range."

The more he thought it through, the more likely it seemed. If he were running the op, that's how he'd do it anyway. Multiple pieces to the puzzle, only posing a risk of exposure if someone could put all of them together. The way the idea fit made it seem like the right solution, the way confidence snapped into place when the answer to a riddle emerged. And that little click of satisfaction brought with it a nagging shadow of a thought just beyond his mind's ability to reach it. A sense that he had just forgotten something he'd been about to say, something important but now vanished.

"Or lets you limit your usage of any particular one, in case it gets too hot," Thumper said. "That could explain the low traffic off the *Ava Leyla*. Maybe they're only using it intermittently... I should have thought of that."

"You did," Lincoln said, smiling. Maybe if he didn't try to chase the memory, it'd come back in its own time.

"Makes it all the more impressive that NID picked it up in the first place," she said, ignoring the comment. "Or very, very *lucky*...

"I guess maybe that helps us, too," she continued after a moment. "If we hit the freighter and it goes dark, could be it doesn't disrupt them enough to notice."

"Anything you can do about it from here?"

"Sit and watch, I guess."

"That doesn't sound like much fun."

"No sir, it does not," Thumper responded. "Not much at all."

Lincoln got to his feet, glad he'd decided against going to bed.

"Want to go see how well all our planning holds up?"

Thumper flashed her brilliant smile.

"It won't," she answered. "But it ought to be fun anyway."

NINE

"OK kids," Will said over his shoulder, from the cockpit. "Time to put your shoes on. We're at grandma's."

Next to him, Noah tapped on a screen on the console to his right. Lincoln felt the slight swim of deceleration before the grav system compensated.

"Eager Nine, this is Spooky One Seven," Noah said. "We're on final approach to our point of detachment, and are preparing to deploy the package."

Lincoln wasn't hooked into the pilots' comms, so he didn't hear Eager Nine's answer. A few moments later, Noah spoke again.

"Acknowledged and understood, Eager Nine. We'll keep our eyes open. Spooky One Seven out."

Lincoln didn't particularly care for the sound of that. There usually wasn't much reason to keep your eyes open for anything out in open space, since it was mostly a whole lot of nothing.

"Trouble?" he asked.

Noah glanced back at him and shook his head. "Abundance of caution. I think she has to say it," he said, referring to the comms officer back on the skiff. He flashed a quick grin. "Guessing she's a mom."

"Roger that," Lincoln said. "We'll go ahead and get

loaded up." He signaled to the rest of his team. They were all suited up, but had left their helmets off for the ride in. Now they each donned their armored helms as they stood and made their way towards the back of the gunship. One by one, the faces of Lincoln's teammates disappeared behind smooth, faceless shells. And even as Lincoln placed his own helmet on and felt it seal, it gave him a chill to see those warriors ahead of him. Even with their names emblazoned in block letters across their backs in a digital ink only visible through the suits' visors, it was hard for Lincoln's mind to hold on to the fact that these were the same people. There was something otherworldly about them.

A hatch led down into the belly of the craft, where the Outriders' low-signature delivery vehicle awaited them.

"It's going to take us a couple minutes to get you a good vector," Will called back to them. "But we'll try to put you on target so you don't have to make too many adjustments on the way in."

"I have no doubt," Lincoln said. "Just try not to put us actually *on* the target, yeah?"

"Hey, he's the math guy," Will answered, jerking a thumb at his brother, "I just drive."

Lincoln was the last down the ladder. The delivery vehicle was fit snugly into the bay, facing backwards so that its top hatch more or less aligned with the ladder from above. It wasn't quite a perfect fit; Lincoln had to drop down to his hands and knees and scoot backwards a couple of feet to reach the entry. Officially the vehicle was called a Lamprey, but the Outriders had given a name that seemed much more suitable; they called it the Coffin.

As Lincoln descended through the upper airlock, he couldn't help but feel like part of a *matryoshka* doll, the famous Russian dolls that stacked neatly into one another. The gunship had deployed from the skiff; the Coffin would do so from the gunship; Lincoln, from the Coffin. In that particular moment, there was something almost comical to him about it, which then made him wonder if maybe the oxygen mix had been off in the gunship. He sealed the uppermost hatch, continued down into the main compartment, and sealed the secondary hatch.

The rest of the team was already strapping in. Sahil sat in the forward-most seat; he'd be the pilot for the final approach to target. Thumper, Mike, and Wright had moved towards the back, leaving room for Lincoln next to Sahil. Not that there was much room, exactly. Everything about the Coffin was designed to minimize its signature in open space, which meant there was basically precisely enough room for its capacity of eight personnel, and no more. The seats were staggered along either side, facing each other. And Sahil's wide shoulders took up about a seat-and-a-half.

A second airlock led out through the back of the vessel; Wright was in the number one position to exit that way, with Mike next to her.

"Spooky One Seven, Easy One, check check," Sahil said over comms.

"Spooky One Seven reads you, Easy One," Noah answered back. "You guys comfy down there?"

"Negative," Sahil replied. "Sooner you can get us on the way, sooner we can get out."

"Roger that, Easy One. We're lining up the shot. Two mikes."

"Two mikes, copy."

Lincoln didn't intend to keep count, but his brain did it automatically anyway. It was just about ninety seconds later when Noah spoke again.

"Easy One, you are aligned. Standing by for your call."

"Spooky One Seven, Easy One is ready for release."

"Easy One ready for release, copy that. On my mark…
three… two… one… release."

Initially, there was no apparent change other than
a subtle vibration. But a few moments later, Lincoln's
stomach lurched around as the Coffin broke free of
the gunship's grav field before its own took over. It felt
something like a drop, but only for the span of a foot
or two at most. His body barely had time to register it
before it was over, which almost made it worse.

"Spooky One Seven, Easy One has good release,"
Sahil said. "We are clear, and clearin' out."

"We copy, Easy One. Stay straight, and on till dawn,"
Noah answered, with what had become a traditional
closing. "Call us if you need us."

"Will do. Easy One out."

And with that final exchange, the five of them were
on their own. They settled in, each silent in their places.
The trick now, in the final hours of approach, was in
finding the balance of sharpening the mind without
exhausting the body. The waiting could dull the senses,
or burn out the adrenaline before it was useful. Everyone
had their own ritual for this time between, when the
operation had officially begun but all the action still lay
ahead. Wright meticulously checked her gear. Mike liked
to sprawl out as much as the limited space allowed and
listen to music. Sahil, when he wasn't driving the bus,
slept like a baby, and Thumper usually read.

Lincoln's particular method was to walk through
each phase of the hit, and to place his hands on each
piece of gear that he would use at each point. It was as
much physical as mental, and worked to both verify he

had everything he needed and also to remind his body where to find it all when the time came. He steadied his breathing, careful to keep a relaxed rhythm, closed his eyes.

He pictured the *Ava Leyla* there, dangling in space. The slow approach. Sahil at the helm, careful to match velocity. Lincoln formed the images clearly in his mind, sharpened them, forced himself to imagine carrying out each individual step of the plan no matter how small, routine, or mundane. Reminded himself to breathe. There was something deeply meditative about the practice, something reassuring about placing his hands upon the tools of his trade as if in blessing.

Not that there was any magic in any of it. The ritual didn't confer any supernatural powers; there were no special operations secret mystic techniques. Unless you counted the months and years of grueling training and dedication to discipline and practice. The ritual didn't prepare Lincoln for what was to come; it simply helped activate all the preparation that had come before.

As he was beginning his third mental rehearsal, Sahil came in over comms.

"Got visual on the target vessel," he said. "Y'all wanna take a peek?"

"You bet," Thumper said.

Sahil ran his wide fingertips lightly across the console at his left, and a few moments later the forward section of the Coffin melted away, revealing the brilliant array of stars in open space, with the *Ava Leyla* dangling out over the great Deep. Naturally there were no windows on the Outriders' delivery vehicle. But the inner surface could project an image so clearly it was better than any window could ever be; if Lincoln hadn't seen the image form, it would have been easy to believe there was really nothing between him and the vacuum.

"Type-43 all right," Thumper said. "Looks like the B-mod to me."

"With a couple of by-owner additions tacked on," Mike added. "I don't recognize that tank on top."

Sahil had rolled the Coffin to match orientation with the *Ava Leyla*; after having stared at all the imaging of the vessel, it was almost hard for Lincoln to remember that was the real thing sitting out there. He agreed with Thumper's assessment that it was a "B-mod" variation, but the lines of the craft were different enough that it set off Lincoln's instincts. It wasn't unusual for ship owners to make modifications, but the number of changes to the *Ava Leyla* were outside normal bounds.

"What's our time-to-target?" Lincoln asked.

"'bout eight minutes," Sahil answered. "Those Barton boys are somethin' else. Shot us as true as could be. I barely touched anything on the way in, 'cept to roll us on line." Sahil had a way of talking out of one side of his mouth and swallowing his syllables that made it sound like he constantly had a ball of chewing tobacco tucked in his lip.

Lincoln activated a display in his visor, overlaid the team's planned entry points onto the *Ava Leyla*. The first two were blocked by modifications. The third was still accessible, but he didn't like the implications. Their primary and secondary points of entry had put them directly into position for the first phase of the hit. Now they were going to have work their way forward through a narrow service tunnel, which was less than ideal. And there was something else, something nagging that he couldn't quite put his finger on.

"I don't think I like the idea of attaching anymore," he said.

For most boarding actions, the team made use of the Lamprey's defining feature; it was equipped with a industrial-strength hull breaching device surrounded by an environmental control mechanism. Typically, the delivery vehicle would attach directly to the outer hull of the target. Once secured, the Lamprey would cut through to make an entry point while maintaining a seal around the new opening. Hull breaches were generally detected by changes in internal atmospheric pressure, so the Lamprey's cuts went unnoticed, and the team could infiltrate undetected.

In this particular case, though, Lincoln's gut told him directly attaching was a bad idea. He couldn't identify a specific reason for the unease, but he'd done the job long enough to know that it was better to live with the unresolved curiosity than to ignore your instincts and find out for sure why they'd been right.

"You wanna go grapples?" Sahil asked.

"Yeah," Lincoln said, still unsure. Confidence came with having made the decision. "Yeah, I do."

"Roger that."

It wouldn't change the plan too much. Wright and Mike would still deploy from the rear and freespace to their entry point, using the microjets on their suits to navigate. The main impact would be on Lincoln's element, requiring them to use an alternate entry method.

"Thumper, that's going to put you on deck for overrides," Lincoln said. It was a contingency they'd planned for.

"Sure, no sweat," she replied.

As the team watched, the cargo ship grew incrementally. It was almost like watching an hour hand on a clock; Lincoln couldn't really notice the moment-to-moment change, but after a minute or two he was suddenly aware of how much closer they were.

"Mir, Mike, you're up," Lincoln said.

Master Sergeant Wright didn't need any more prompting. She popped to her feet like a guard dog catching a scent and moved into the rear airlock.

Mike chuckled. "I don't think I've seen her move that fast since the last time they had wings in the chow hall."

"I wouldn't keep her waiting," Thumper replied. "She might go without you."

Mike got to his feet with mock heaviness, made an overly-dramatic show of stretching his back; which took actual effort, since the low overhead of the Coffin prevented him from standing at his full height.

"Mike!" Wright barked.

Mike gave Thumper and Lincoln a look over his shoulder; his faceplate was closed, so there was no expression to read, but Lincoln could picture it perfectly anyway. Somehow the blank, faceless metal seemed almost mischievous.

"See you folks downstairs," Mike said, as he turned and headed towards the rear compartment.

"Mikey," Lincoln called. Mike stopped and looked back at him. Lincoln tapped his own faceplate three times with his forefinger. Signaling for Mike to stay buttoned up. Beneath the faceplate, their helmets had clear visors that were rated to hold up to some small arms fire, but they didn't offer nearly the protection that the sealed plate did. When Mike had died with his head in Lincoln's hands, he'd had his faceplate open to investigate a mechanism. It had turned out to be boobytrapped.

"Roger that, sir," Mike answered. He gave a curt nod, suddenly sober, and disappeared into the airlock.

"I think you sucked all the fun out of Mikey, sir,"

Thumper said after he'd gone.

"I'll make him some coffee when we get back," Lincoln replied. "You good to go?"

"Good to go."

"Sahil, you'll follow us up?"

"Yessir," Sahil said. "Soon as we're rolled and tethered."

"Roger. See you in a few."

Lincoln motioned towards the ladder, which was merely a few rungs formed into the bulkhead. Thumper climbed up first, into the upper airlock. Lincoln followed behind. It was a cozy fit for the two of them. Once Sahil joined them, space was going to be tight enough to be socially awkward. Supposedly four troopers could fit in each of the airlocks for simultaneous deployment; Lincoln figured if they ever tried to squeeze that many in up top, whoever was nearest to the exit would get forcibly ejected as soon as the outer hatch opened.

"Anvil, Hammer," Lincoln said. "Comms check, over."

"Anvil copies, Hammer," Wright answered over the team channel. "Commo's clean."

"We're lined up," Sahil said. "Mir, you're good to go."

"Roger," Wright replied. "Anvil's deploying."

She and Mike were dropping out to an entry point on the port side of the *Ava Leyla*. They would secure the lower decks and move up. Lincoln and the others would go in through the top, starting far aft and working their way forward. Most versions of the plan had them all converging on the bridge for the final take down.

About a minute or so later, Wright called back in. "Anvil's on site, moving to stage now."

"Anvil moving to stage," Lincoln repeated. "Copy that."

Sahil's head appeared in the lower hatch of the airlock.

"We're locked in, Cap'n," he said as he clambered the rest of the way up. Lincoln and Thumper had to shuffle around to make room for him. "Holdin' off at thirty meters."

Thirty meters of open space between the Lamprey and the *Ava Leyla*. There wasn't really any cause for concern. The two vessels were at matched velocity, and there was nothing out there to use as a reference point for the motion. For all intents and purposes, the traversal would be the same as if the ships were both at a dead stop.

But Lincoln hated open space. No matter how many times he'd operated in it, it felt unnatural to him to be surrounded by endless nothingness. The sense of complete and utter exposure was unnerving. To know he could literally fall forever and never hit bottom, in a place where even the idea of direction was meaningless. And it was impossible to avoid being confronted by his own absolute insignificance in the face of that vast emptiness that was yet so full of wonders beyond his comprehension.

"We set?" Thumper asked.

"Set," Sahil responded.

Lincoln took a deep breath, let himself feel his feet planted firmly on the deck. It was just thirty meters. Anybody could do thirty meters.

"Good to go," Lincoln said. "Pop it."

"Venting," Thumper said. She flipped switches on the control panel, starting the controlled depressurization of the airlock. Thirty seconds later, she said. "We're stable. Popping the hatch."

Thumper activated the outer hatch, which slid smoothly open to reveal the gap. The Coffin's grav field extended a few feet outward from the vessel; Thumper climbed up the ladder and took position on top. Lincoln was up next. He clambered up next to her, craning his neck back to look at the target ship hanging there above him. Sahil had rolled the Lamprey over to put the *Ava Leyla* over their heads, though as with all things in space, up was relative. The pull of the grav field dissipated abruptly only a few feet from the craft; the difference between Lincoln's feet and head was significant. It gave him a strange sense of something like vertigo, a feeling that his feet were too heavy, and his head too light.

Sahil joined the two of them on top of the Coffin.

"Anvil, Hammer's ready to jump the gap," Lincoln reported over the team channel.

"Copy, Hammer," Wright responded, then after a brief pause added, "Don't miss."

She said it deadpan, but there was a trace of a smile behind the words. Wright knew how much he hated open space. Fortunately, the *Ava Leyla* was at least ten times longer than the Lamprey, and made a nice fat target to land on. And the gap was only thirty meters.

"We good?" Thumper asked.

"Let's do it," Lincoln said.

"Ladies first," Thumper said, and without waiting for a response she leapt up into space and dropped away towards the cargo ship. Watching her go, Lincoln's world instantly flipped and he was suddenly upside down, watching his teammate plummet headfirst towards the target. She hadn't jumped up. She'd fallen off. It made his head swim.

"You can hold a grapple if you want," Sahil said. Thin tethers ran from four points between the Lamprey and the cargo ship. Technically, it would have been perfectly reasonable for Lincoln to follow one of the lines down. And he would have looked about as cool as if he were crossing a swimming pool by holding on to the edge and following it all the way around to the other side. Sahil was looking at him with that blank faceplate, but Lincoln could picture the exact expression the other man had on his face; the left corner of his mouth pulled down in his version of a smile.

"Thanks dad, but I'm good," Lincoln answered. Everybody was a comedian. He half expected Mike to chime in at some point.

Leaping out of gravity was always bizarre. There was no significant pop or snap; the tug was just there, and then it wasn't. It didn't even take a particularly forceful jump to break free. Lincoln swallowed the vertigo and kicked off, and then he too was rocketing headlong towards the freighter. Once again, the perspective shifted. There was no force dragging him downward towards the *Ava Leyla*; now he was crossing horizontally, flying between two vertical islands, with an infinite well below. He didn't look down.

Freespacing was almost exactly the opposite of swimming. It required patience, tight body control, and minimal movement of the limbs. The suit's gyros helped stabilize, firing jets in microbursts to counter tumble. Even so, the tolerances were strict to avoid accidentally overriding Lincoln's intentional small adjustments, so balance and relaxed stillness were the keys to success.

Twenty meters. Fifteen.

Thumper had already touched down, and she was moving in a crouch towards their designated entry point.

Ten meters.

Lincoln's training took over. He tucked and tipped himself backwards, started the slow roll that would enable him to decelerate and touch down with a light step as the cargo ship's grav field drew him gently on deck.

At least, that's how they made it sound like it would work during all the training.

In reality, Lincoln came in a little faster than he'd intended and hadn't quite completed the smooth backwards roll when gravity kicked back in. He landed on his tiptoes, leaning too far forward. One hasty step, then another, and then he decided just to bail on the smooth landing. He tucked forward, executed a combat roll over his right shoulder, came up in a crouch, shouldered his short rifle, and tried his best to look like he had totally intended to do that. He quickly checked left and right for any sign of detection. No threats.

Thumper was ahead of him, already doing work to prepare the entry point. She hadn't noticed his landing. Lincoln glanced back and saw Sahil dropping down a few steps away, landing as light and easy as a cat hopping off a window ledge. The little man hunched his shoulders and lowered his head as soon as he touched down, immediately brought his weapon up and scanned the surroundings. After a moment, he made his way over to Lincoln. He didn't stop where Lincoln was crouched, just passed by and swatted Lincoln's shoulder with the back of his hand.

"Nice save," Sahil said with a chuckle.

"I'm a true professional," Lincoln answered. He stood and followed Sahil up to Thumper's position, reporting in as he went. "Anvil, Hammer has touched down. We're prepping for entry."

"Copy that," Wright answered. "We're in position and holding."

Sahil and Lincoln flanked Thumper, one off each of her shoulders, crouching to keep a low profile while they provided security. It was of course highly unlikely that there would be anything on the exterior of the ship that would cause them any trouble. But even a one-in-a-million chance was a chance, and there was no room for slack on an op.

"Thumper, how's it looking?" Lincoln asked.

She'd fitted a device to the hull of the *Ava Leyla*, and was busy working some holographic display only she could see. Their point of entry was a hatch to a service tunnel; Thumper was running scans to make sure it was clear.

"Weird," she said. "Security's a little more robust than I would've expected."

"Care to elaborate?" Lincoln prompted after a moment.

"Gimme a sec." Her voice had the faraway quality it took whenever her brain was busy elsewhere. Problem solving. After that, she worked in silence for a couple of minutes.

"Hammer, you all right?" Wright asked, checking in after the longer-than-expected delay.

"Yeah, stand by," Lincoln replied. "Thumper's spooked."

"I'm not spooked," Thumper said with a hint of offense. "Just being careful."

"What are you seeing?" he asked, taking the opportunity to rephrase the question.

"It's just weird," she answered. "Picking up more sensor lines than I'd expect, even accounting for people who are maybe up to no good."

"So they're paranoid?"

"Kinda. But in the wrong direction."

"Spell it out, Thump," he said after another silence.

"Yeah, sorry," she said, shaking her head. "It's all wired up, lots of passageways and doors covered. But looks more like keeping people in than out."

Lincoln didn't quite know what to make of that

assessment, but he knew he didn't like it.

"Can you get Poke in there?" he asked.

"Sure thing," Thumper replied. She reached up and plucked a long, matte-black rectangle off her back, laid it down on the hull in front of her. After a moment of fiddling, the rectangle reformed itself into something longer and thinner, and sort of sat up next to her. She patted it on the topmost part. "All right Pokey, let's see what you can see."

Thumper took another device off of her hip, this one flat and round, and placed that too on the hull. It made a gentle whirring sound. When it stopped, Poke slid forward and into the center of the device, and then disappeared inside it. The device was like a miniaturized version of the Lamprey's breaching mechanism, a tiny drill and airlock all in one. Poke was the only one thin enough to use it, and that was because it could scale itself down to the diameter of a single component, which was roughly the size of Lincoln's little finger.

"We looking for anything in particular?" Thumper asked.

"Bad news," Lincoln said.

"Should be easy enough to find."

Thumper went to work, establishing search parameters for Poke, adjusting them based on what she found. She wasn't sharing the feed out to the team, though, so Lincoln had no way of knowing what she was finding.

"Anvil, we've got Poke doing some snooping," Lincoln said over team comms. "Just hold tight until we know what we're dealing with."

"Roger," Wright said, cool and professional.

After about twenty minutes of scouting, Thumper finally grunted.

"You got something?" Lincoln asked.

"I have a number in my head," Thumper said. "Crew complement for a Type-43 is what?"

"Eight to twelve," Lincoln said.

"Yeah, that's what I thought. You want to tell me why I'm picking up a whole lot more signatures than that?"

"How many more?"

"I'd say at least twenty."

"We're looking at thirty personnel?" Lincoln asked.

"If I haven't missed anybody, yeah, somewhere around there."

"Share it out," he said.

A moment later, Lincoln's suit received the data feed. He pulled up a three-dimensional wireframe schematic of the *Ava Leyla* on his internal display. Blue lines marked the internal structure of the ship, with the general locations of the personnel displayed as white heat throughout. The locational information wasn't precise. Thumper was keeping Poke in between the inner and outer hulls of the cargo ship, so it wasn't getting visual confirmation and couldn't update them all in real-time. Instead of individual indicators for each member of the crew, Poke was providing a snapshot of concentration. If people were far enough apart and on their own, they showed as fuzzy grey dots. The more crew members there were in one area, the larger the cloud, and the brighter it was. The vessel's bridge had a light grey, smoky splotch that Lincoln judged to indicate four or five. There were a few other dots here and there. But it was the lowest deck that was cause for concern. The cargo holds had a bright white smear; too many people, too close together to get a clear estimate.

Poke's sensor suite was sophisticated enough to avoid double-counting. A quick scan roughly confirmed Thumper's numbers.

Passengers? Hostages? Or were they armed hostiles?

Typically Lincoln liked to outnumber the bad guys by at least two-to-one. With a team as small as the Outriders, he'd had to get used to the idea of even numbers, or even being slightly outnumbered on occasion. Their suits usually tipped the balance in their favor anyway. But it didn't matter how well-trained and -equipped his team was; six-to-one against was bad odds for anybody. Bad enough to consider impossible.

"What you wanna do, boss?" Sahil asked.

Scrub the mission. That was the right answer. The obvious one.

But this was their shot. Probably the only one they'd get. Aborting now would be the same as having refused the mission from the outset.

Worse. All those people back home were counting on them to get this done, to find a thread to pull on. The army and navy had both provided resources and support that could have gone elsewhere if Lincoln had turned it all down from the start.

But six-to-one against were really bad odds.

Unless the six never saw the one.

"Thumper, can you get what we need without taking the bridge?" Lincoln asked.

She turned back and looked at him over her shoulder, but didn't reply right away. Thinking it through.

"I don't think I can say for sure, sir," she finally replied with a shake of her head. "Have to get a closer look at what we're actually dealing with."

"But it is possible."

"*Possible*, yes sir. Easy, definitely not."

"All right," Lincoln said, then opened team comms. "Anvil, we're making an adjustment. Infiltration and reconnaissance only. I want zero contact with ship personnel until we figure out what's going on."

"Understood," Wright said. "You want us to hold outside?"

"Negative, I still want the coverage. And if we screw this up, I want to be able to rally fast," he answered. It was the dichotomy of special operations; always stick to the plan, but be ready to adapt on the fly. But *always* stick to the plan... but adapt as necessary.

But the plan was always about the mission first. And the mission was information. If there was still a way to get it, then that's what they'd do.

"OK, Anvil, continue with your planned entry. See if you can get a better idea of what we're looking at below decks. But try to keep yourself in a blocking position. If we tip anybody off coming through, you're going to make sure nobody makes it topside."

"Roger," she answered. "Call it when you're ready for entry."

"Stand by." Lincoln switched channels back to his element. "Thumper, how we looking? Can we get in without making too much noise?"

She nodded. "Yeah we should be good. I've got a bypass on the hatch sensor. Just have to be careful of our route once we're inside. We'll either need to take it real slow, or real, real fast."

"We'll start slow. Let's move."

"Roger that."

"Anvil," Lincoln said over the team-wide channel, "we're going in."

"Hammer making entry, copy," Wright responded.

Sahil swiveled smoothly around and aimed his weapon at the hatch, prepared to be the first one in, or to be the first to fire in case things went wrong. Lincoln signaled to Thumper. She nodded, worked her magic, and the service hatch retracted. As soon as he had room enough, Sahil tipped forward and swept the interior with his weapon.

"Clear," he said a few moments later. He held position, providing cover while Thumper descended into the pitch black chamber.

"Set," she reported, once she was down.

Lincoln followed after her. There was no ambient light for his visor to amplify, but the sensor suite provided a composite view of everything else it could detect, displayed in ghostly blues. He reached the bottom of the ladder; Thumper was down in a crouch, covering the internal hatch that led to the service tunnel.

Lincoln moved to the opposite side of the ladder and likewise raised his weapon to cover the hatch.

"Set," he said.

Sahil moved down to join them, and sealed the external hatch. It took a few moments for the lock to repressurize. Once the cycle had completed, Thumper moved up to the internal hatch controls, and accessed them through some non-physical means. She turned and gave a thumbs-up signal.

"Anvil," Lincoln said. "Hammer's moving into the service tunnel. You're clear to make entry."

"Copy that," Wright said. "Anvil making entry."

"Thumper," he said. "Pop it."

As soon as he'd said it, the internal hatch slid open, revealing a tight tube of a tunnel. He'd seen it before, during their training.

Six against one. Bad odds.

Lincoln moved forward and took point, first one in.

TEN

Elliot cut across the courtyard, keeping his stride as casual as he could. When he reached the far side he took a sharp right, and then a made a quick loop that doubled him back out to the front of the courtyard again. There were still a few minutes to kill before his contact was supposed to ping him the final coordinates for their meeting location, and he didn't want to give anyone the impression he was waiting around for something. He also didn't want to get trapped inside his own mind, and that was proving difficult.

When he'd tried to establish contact with his secret source for Kit, his credentials had failed. Somehow, when it had happened, he'd found he had almost expected it. A gut reaction he'd been trying to ignore. Most likely, a routine security change had gone through and knocked him off the list of authorized accessors. But Elliot had managed to navigate those before, and this one seemed different. Maybe someone finally figured out he didn't belong on the list, and got him scrubbed. Maybe it was worse. And if it was worse, that meant it was much, *much* worse. Unfortunately, no matter how hard he tried to convince himself the loss of contact was routine, he couldn't shake the feeling that it wasn't. The

Directorate had asked him to track down some high-grade communications components a couple of weeks prior. Now, as unthinkable as it should have been, he couldn't stop his brain from screaming that there was a connection. And worse, that it might all lead right to his doorstep.

Elliot couldn't let his mind run down that course. Once it got started, the only possible end was sheer panic. And there was no need to try to deal with imaginary problems, when he had concrete ones right in front of him. Whatever the cause, the loss of access to such a rich source of intelligence was going to be a blow to his operations if he couldn't get it sorted out. As usual, he'd managed to talk his way into a little extra time with Kit and scored the NID's necessary introduction anyway. Kit knew he was good for the information. Now he just had to figure out how to get it without relying on his ace. Or, preferably, how to get his ace back.

But he had to shake all that off for now. Stay in the moment, neither in the past or the future. Elliot inhaled deeply, drawing in the smells of the environment, a technique he'd found helpful to ground himself in the present. He kept his head up, scanned the few others out at this time of night, looking for any familiar faces or anyone paying too much attention to him. So far, there weren't any repeats. He took a couple more unnecessary turns, stair-stepping his way through town towards the general meeting area, and then doubled back again, making an extra loop around the block. Handy for detecting a tail, and potentially shaking one if necessary. In the spy world, they called it a surveillance detection route. Many years prior, Elliot had earned one of his instructors' unveiled disapproval for calling it what it was: walking in circles.

Spy stuff was mostly like that. Fancy names for

mundane activities. He'd grown up screening spy stories that had made the work look exciting and glamorous, full of clever and attractive people doing dangerous things. The reality had proven to be something different. There was a lot of paperwork. Most of the people were neither clever nor attractive. There were no car chases, no meetings in dark alleys. He'd only been in one gunfight in his entire life, and he hadn't even had a gun. Being a master of tactics, he had just lain on the floor until there was a pause in the gunfire, and, being a man of stout heart, he had then very courageously made a run for it.

The job had its moments of genuine danger, of course. You couldn't operate in the grey and expect it to be all coffee with friends and walks in the sunshine. But Elliot had found that typically the greatest risk came from not knowing what you were doing. Or, as in the recent case with Dillon and Wilson, from ignoring your instincts. Most people were embarrassingly easy to read, and despite what the average citizen would tell you, things never *just happened*… there were always signs, always warnings. It was just that most people were so blissfully unaware of their surroundings, to them, things really did appear to *just happen*. In Elliot's estimation, a good ninety-nine percent of unpleasantness could be avoided simply by paying attention.

Of course, it was the other one percent that was the real trouble. And the biggest danger for Elliot was letting himself believe he *was* paying attention, buying into the narrative that he was an expert and was always on his game. So even though there was probably no threat and probably no reason to worry, he reminded himself that he was a foreign operative in a hostile nation, and tried to pretend at least one of the few people on the street was out to get him.

The night was in the transitional space between when respectable people were already home and somewhat less respectable people were preparing to emerge. Elliot was amongst the stragglers, or the early-birds, all of whom seemed to have adopted the hunched, brisk pace of folks trying to get indoors before a storm. He adjusted his pace to fall within the parameters of the environment, his goal to be the mediumest person in the bunch, the least likely to attract notice or to stick in a memory.

Across the street from him, a pair of men argued in heatedly hushed tones, sounding for all the world like a lovers' quarrel. A snippet of the conversation floated over to Elliot, and he realized the disagreement was actually over the outcome of some sort of sporting event. Ahead of him, a young woman strode purposefully towards him, walking with her arms crossed and her head slightly down. Cute, he thought. As she neared, she flicked her eyes up and caught his with a hard stare. The message was perfectly communicated; she was not someone to be approached or chatted with, nor did she appreciate strange men evaluating her looks. Elliot gave her a little, respectful nod. She didn't acknowledge it.

There were a few others that Elliot noted and mentally filed; Chatty Businessman, Overworked Mom, Drunk Guy Trying Not to Look Drunk. As best as he could tell, he was clear. Unfortunately, experience had taught him that the people you *really* had to worry about following you never caught your notice. This was even more true in the Martian People's Collective Republic, his area of operations. None of the citizens of the MPCR seemed to consider it a surveillance society, which struck him as odd, considering the fact that they were all under constant observation and, far more intrusively in Elliot's opinion, actual measurement.

The Collective Republic was the largest and most successful quantcomm on either Earth or Mars. A "quantified community". A place where every adult citizen willingly submitted everything that could be known about themselves to their government. When they woke up, where they went, when they ate. But it was more than that. Body temperature, blood oxygen levels, activity levels, quality of sleep. Just about any human function that could be measured was collected and shared, all of it fed into an artificial intelligence, which parsed it and produced an aggregate of the overall health of the community. Policy decisions then in turn could be based on real-time data, the effects of governance measured and evaluated with clinical detachment, and everything could be tuned and adjusted. Iterative government. Theoretically, it seemed like a good idea. But then most things did when they were theoretical.

Of course there were other such communities, humans all living together, sharing everything about everyone. It was just that most of them collapsed after a few years. And the longest running ones that Elliot knew about were all under one hundred and fifty citizens. Apparently trust didn't scale. People were still people, and power still had a way of corrupting.

But somehow the MPCR seemed to succeed where all others failed, on a grand scale; the greatest living proof of the concept. Elliot's guess was that it had to do with the MPCR's hybrid model of governance and the quality of its AI. Its name was Sigma. No one knew why exactly; it had named itself. There were a lot of theories.

When Elliot had first been assigned by NID to the Republic, they'd given him ample reading material on the subject. He'd skimmed it. Sigma shared governance with a council of elected officials, each advising the other, casting votes, or some sort of mathematically democratic arrangement or other. Sigma acted as an impartial check against some of the council's worst human tendencies, and the council balanced Sigma's occasionally impenetrable proclamations. Elliot didn't really know the details of how it all worked, beyond the fact that it did in fact seem to work. He'd operated there for almost fifteen years, and the citizens typically were generally happy and healthy. Nothing was perfect, of course. But he had to admit the average populace seemed more content than most. It was one of the most productive societies on either planet. All it cost to belong was the total surrender of your right to privacy and your concept of self.

The important bit to his line of work, the part that was never far from his mind, was the fact that supposedly all of that information was encrypted and obfuscated and depersonalized; the idea wasn't to track individuals, it was simply to use them as datapoints for a grand-scale picture of community health. Only Sigma could identify what data went with whom, and it wasn't particularly interested in anyone's love life. Given the raw intelligence value of such data, though, Elliot didn't believe for a second that the MPCR's Internal Security Services didn't have some way to access it.

He himself was free of the citizen's mark. He was just a Trusted Visitor, a status that gave him unrestricted travel access as long as he behaved himself. But it didn't matter that he wasn't plugged into the quantcomm. His every interaction with citizens could more or less be deduced from their measurements. Elliot was just a hole in the data, his absence made conspicuous by all that surrounded it.

That knowledge made surreptitious meetings with

sources and contacts all the more stressful. Finding the acceptable deviations from the norm that wouldn't draw the wrong kind of attention. It was exhausting.

The all-seeing-Sigma was a constant background concern, brought to the fore when his contact pinged him the final meeting point. Not *his* contact, exactly. Someone at the Directorate had arranged this one, which always made him even more nervous.

The information came in as a chime only he could hear, a destination point only he could see. The hardware tattooed on the back of his skull fed the data directly to his visual cortex, floated an orange waypoint in his vision. He'd replaced the standard icon with one that had a smiley face wearing a fedora and sunglasses on it. The icon had originally come from a kid's game about catching spies. Editing the Directorate's protocols wasn't exactly officially sanctioned. But then again, neither was a lot of what Elliot did to get the job done. It helped to have a sense of humor.

Just down the street, Elliot turned and followed a narrow lane between a restaurant and a hotel, around to the back. There was a service entrance to the restaurant, where it backed up too closely to another building. His contact was already there waiting, leaning against the wall, in the gap between two orange pools of light. Elliot paused for a moment, checked his surroundings, then chuckled to himself. A dark alley.

It still occasionally struck him as strange that in such modern times people would go to all the trouble to have actual face-to-face meetings just to pass messages to one another. But when virtual avatars could be spoofed and communications intercepted, he had to admit that there was something reassuring about doing this all in the real, physical world. And, Elliot supposed, certain secrets were only worth sharing when someone else had skin in the game. Of course, it was only *his* skin, which wasn't particularly encouraging.

He approached, and his source fluidly slipped from the wall and glided towards him. She smiled as they met in the middle of the light, and shook hands. Two friends, with nothing to hide. He'd never seen her before.

Facial recognition kicked off, verified she was the right person. Elliot reached under his sleeve, swiped a fingertip across the dermal pad on the underside of his forearm, traced a sigil that sent a message back to his controller.

WHITEHALL is secure.

Somewhere far, far away, someone received that message, and began a protocol, while Elliot stood there in a dark alley with a woman he didn't know, exposed and waiting. This was, hands-down, the absolute worst part of his job.

The linguistic implant sat up there in the Broca area of his brain, if the pamphlet he'd read before the procedure was correct. Or, Broca's area, to be correct about it. Calling it "Broca's area" had always rubbed Elliot the wrong way, though, because it made it sound like that part of his brain belonged to someone else.

Unfortunately, now, that was entirely true.

Every so often, someone way up the chain at the National Intelligence Directorate needed to pass secure messages to someone else on the ground in less-than-friendly territory. Messages so secure that even the messenger couldn't know the contents. It was a feature of this particular model of implant, provided to Elliot courtesy of the NID, that it could be used to pass messages through him. In those times, the "no discomfort" was a lie. Elliot could always tell when it was about to activate, to start receiving. A micromigraine, a pressure just behind his left eye. A mild clenching of his throat, the bare hint of gag. It was very much like a fear reaction.

And in Elliot's opinion, fear seemed appropriate to what amounted to a total surrender of self.

The woman waited patiently for the few seconds it took for Elliot to begin, a pleasant look on her face that wasn't quite a smile but that communicated warmth nonetheless.

A few moments later, the channel clicked open. Elliot suppressed a gag as his mouth opened and spoke words he'd never heard before, delivering a message he would never understand.

Vocal encryption.

When activated in such a manner, the implant was one-way; it gave him the words, but not the comprehension. And to call them words was a stretch. To his own ears, they were a tumbling torrent of phonemes. Any sound the human voice was capable of making was fair game, and the experience was, he imagined, something akin to a seizure or spasm of the vocal cords. It always went better if he could relax, but it was hard to do that when his brain kept telling him something had just gone catastrophically wrong with his body.

His contact, of course, undoubtedly had her own implant and the necessary key to understand whatever was coming out of his mouth. Or, Elliot thought, maybe her handler had the key. He wondered if she too was just a conduit for some other person too afraid to do the dangerous work for themselves. It was another strange side-effect of the experience, that his mind remained his own, free to observe and consider while his mouth belonged to another.

For five or six minutes, the conversation continued,

the two of them speaking the same caricature of language. Then, the woman nodded curtly, turned and walked away. It caught him by surprise, the abrupt end of the meeting. The same awkward feeling as when someone left the dinner table offended, and you weren't quite sure what you had said to upset them. That didn't necessarily mean that the conversation had gone poorly; only that doing business this way had weird social ramifications that none of the techs back at the lab seemed concerned about.

The pain behind Elliot's eye lost its edge, receded into a dull bulb of ache. He cleared his throat, verifying that his voice was once more his own. It always took him a minute or two to shake off the experience, as his brain learned to trust his body again.

He took a few deep breaths, stretched his arms out to the sides, cracked his neck. Tried to determine if he was nauseated or hungry. He decided to call it hungry. The restaurant was still open. A bowl of ramen seemed like a good idea just then. A really good idea. And even though he knew it was going to completely wreck his ability to sleep, Elliot decided he'd treat himself anyway.

He went back around to the front, wondering how many bottles of sake it would take to turn his really good idea into a really bad one.

"Mr Goodkind?" a voice said from behind him.

Elliot turned, surprised by the sound of his own name. There was a woman standing by the corner of the building, someone he'd walked by without even noticing. She looked vaguely familiar, but the haze from his verbal-encryption hangover prevented him from dredging up the connection. She smiled, extended her hand in way of greeting.

"I thought that was you. Out for a bite to eat?" she

asked. He shook her hand, returned the smile while his
mind spun to figure out who she was, where he'd seen
her. The alarm bells kicked off, but he couldn't tell if he
was reacting to some subconsciously-detected danger,
or if he was just still off balance from the previous
communication.

"I was thinking about it," he said, and then patted his
belly. "But trying to think better of it. I really don't need
the calories. And it's late."

He wasn't going to risk it. He still couldn't place her,
and there was no way he was going to stick around
to find out whether or not she was as harmless as she
appeared.

"I know what you mean," she said, looking up
and around at the buildings nearby. "But there's just
something about this time of night that always makes
comfort food and good conversation seem so inviting."

"It does," he answered. "But I really do need to get
home."

"OK. Nice to bump into you."

"Yep, see you around, I'm sure," he said. He gave
her a little nod and turned to leave. As he was doing so,
the familiarity snapped into place. He'd nodded to her
before, about twenty minutes prior. The cute girl he'd
passed on his way in.

Elliot's hands went ice cold, and his heart rate kicked
up.

"I couldn't help but notice, Mr Goodkind," she said as
he was walking away. "You have an interesting way of
speaking. Do you mind me asking what language that
was?"

A grim-looking man stood a few feet ahead, blocking
Elliot's path. A car waited at the curb, to his right. They'd
boxed him in. Whoever *they* were.

He played it the way he knew best. Roll into it, trust the solution would present itself in the midst of the chaos.

"I don't mind at all," he said, turning back with a smile on his face. Ignore the man, ignore the car. Pretend this nice young woman is just some mild acquaintance whose name had slipped his mind. "But I am embarrassed to admit that your name has completely escaped me."

"Mei," she answered. She hadn't left her spot by the corner of the building. He walked back towards her, saw her shoulders roll slightly. Coiling herself for whatever he might do, but trying not to give it away. Elliot stopped in front of the door to the restaurant, well out of arm's reach.

"Mei, that's right," he said, snapping his fingers as though her name had been on the tip of his tongue. "And we met at uh... was it a conference out in Rocknest?"

She smiled and shook her head.

"No Mr Goodkind, we haven't actually met. I'm with Internal Security."

He tried not to let his face react, but knew he'd failed.

"Oh, well... I must have met your twin somewhere then."

"Not likely," said a man from behind. Elliot glanced over his shoulder. The grim-looking man had advanced on him, close enough to pounce if necessary.

"Ah," Elliot said. "You're the brother then?"

"Something like," the man said.

"My partner," Mei said. "Gregor."

Elliot nodded.

"I see... Well, you hungry?" He turned back and smiled at Mei. "I was just thinking this time of night was perfect for some comfort food and good conversation."

"My treat," Mei replied. And together, the three of

them walked into the restaurant, the agents on either side and Elliot caught right in the middle.

ELEVEN

Master Sergeant Wright moved down the passageway with careful steps, her weapon shouldered, muzzle sweeping a graceful arc back and forth as she advanced. Keeping the weapon in controlled motion made it faster to snap on target if one should present itself, and also caused less fatigue in the muscles than trying to maintain a static aim-point. Mike followed a few paces behind. Not that she could hear him. If not for the small icon in her view marking his position and distance from her, she would have had to glance over her shoulder to be sure he hadn't disappeared.

Of course, that might not have helped either. As soon as they'd entered the vessel, they'd both switched on the reactive camouflage of their recon suits. Combining input from its sensor suite and threat matrix, the suit evaluated the environment and adapted its surface to blend in from multiple viewpoints. Even though Wright had never understood the math behind it, she was intimately familiar with the end result. The algorithms weren't good enough to make anyone invisible yet, but in the right situations they could be almost that good. And even in the wrong situations, it was usually enough to buy Wright those extra few seconds she needed to come out on top.

Thus far, the compartments and passageways had all been clear from their entry point. They'd already checked the deck where they'd entered and two cargo holds, and were working their way down. But they'd been taking it slow. With so many unknowns on board, any contact was likely to lead to a mission abort. The delay on entry and the extra cautious pace once inside had already kept them on the target almost an hour. The whole op was supposed to have taken them less than two, and they hadn't even really gotten started yet.

"Anvil," said Lincoln, over team comms. "Check in when you can."

Wright held up a hand, signaling for Mike to hold position. In situations like these, she didn't like trying to talk while moving. She dropped down to a knee and kept her weapon up.

"Hammer, Anvil. We're wrapping up deck four, preparing to move to deck five. No sign of our extra personnel yet."

"Copy, Anvil. We're at our access point in the service tunnel. Thumper's doing her work."

"Roger."

"After you hit five, go ahead and move to delta. Hold there until you hear from me. Unless deck five gives you something."

"Understood." *Delta* was her element's position below the bridge. "Continuing to five."

"Anvil to five, copy."

Five was the lowest deck, and typically was the largest cargo hold on a Type-43. For the other decks, holds were placed along the exterior of the ship, arranged around a central passageway. Deck five had a large centrally-located bay that spanned the width of the vessel, since it could be loaded from either side or through the bottom of the ship. It was also where, according to Thumper's earlier scans, most of the personnel was.

Once the brief conversation was concluded, Wright eased back up to her feet and continued down the passageway. There was an eerie stillness to the vessel, made all the more unnerving by the amount of clutter and garbage scattered in pockets along the way. Clearly, there were a number of people aboard, and whoever they were they didn't appear to be too concerned about keeping their ship tidy. The fact that they hadn't heard or seen anyone yet was good for the op, but it made it all feel wrong; like walking through a house abandoned ahead of a sudden disaster that had struck without sign or warning.

Wright led Mike a few more paces down the corridor, to a narrow compartment on their left. She passed by, but motioned for Mike to check the room while she stood guard.

"On it," Mike said in a whisper. Then, a few moments later, "Clear."

A door at the end of the passageway was marked as leading down to the lower deck. Once Mike had rejoined her, Wright pressed on to the door and then held there. Mike slid up to one side, looked to her for the signal. On her nod, he opened the door. Wright slipped through, quickly checked the upper landing for hostiles.

Still no one.

The landing was metal grating; looking down through it, Wright could see the tight skeletal staircase that doubled back on itself multiple times before reaching the lower deck far below. Wright hated clearing stairwells. No matter how many times she had done it, she still got a twinge of anxiety before stepping out onto that first step. And she had done it a lot. Too many angles, too easy to get cut off on both sides, trapped.

According to the schematics, Five was twice the height of the other decks, to accommodate the larger freight. Staring down at all those steps, with all their corners and angles, made it seem twice again as far.

"Hammer, Anvil's on the stairs down to deck five," she reported, more to help anchor herself than for any reasons of protocol.

"Roger," Lincoln answered.

"Moving down," she said, and started the descent. She kept her weapon up and out over the thin railing the whole way down, aimed at whatever next twisting angle posed the greatest risk of threat. Mike sidestepped his way along behind her, performing the same constantly-shifting dance to cover the landing above.

It only took a minute or two to reach the lower deck, but it felt to Wright like twenty. Once there, they repeated their door-opening routine, with Wright leading the way. The door opened to a short passageway with two compartments on each side, and an intersecting passageway that cut through the middle of them. Wright moved forward to the corner of the intersection, while Mike checked the first two compartments.

"Clear left," he said. And then several seconds later, "Clear right."

Before he could rejoin her, though, a sharp, ringing clatter came from down the right-hand side of the intersecting passageway.

"*Hey, careful, those aren't free!*" a woman said loudly, in Mandarin. After so long without any contact, the sound of another human voice was almost startling to Wright.

"Well maybe you should carry them all, then," came an answer in English, tinged with a Martian dialect. A man, further away than the woman, but not by much.

"*I'm not cleaning that up!*"

"You never do!"

Wright glanced over her shoulder, saw Mike standing halfway out of one of the compartments, covering the door back to the stairwell. After some shuffling sounds and muttered words she couldn't make out came an unmistakable noise. Footsteps. Moving their way, and quickly.

Two people, at least one of them carrying something metallic and possibly heavy. The question now was, where were they headed? To the upper decks? Across the hall? To one of the compartments Wright had just passed?

She'd know the answer soon enough.

Wright hissed sharply, to get Mike's attention. When he looked, she motioned for him to move back into the compartment. He didn't acknowledge her in any way, except to glide backwards and disappear from her view.

She backpedaled slowly, then slid into the compartment. Once inside, she quickly glanced around. The compartment was narrow, deeper than it was wide, and had large pipes running from floor to ceiling. There wasn't much room for the two of them. It was sufficient for the moment, but there was absolutely nowhere to hide. If that door opened, the only option they were going to have was to shoot first and hope no one else came along before they could move the bodies. At least it was mostly dark, lit only by a single low-intensity red light in the ceiling.

The footsteps grew sharper, more distinct, and then fell silent as Wright pushed the door closed and it sealed. She felt as though she'd gone deaf and blind.

There was a device on her belt designed exactly for

this situation; when attached to a surface and paired
with the sensor suite of her reconnaissance armor,
it enabled her to see through walls. It would take her
only a few seconds to set up, but she would need both
hands to do it. And she would have to stand within arm's
length of the door. If the two individuals came through,
she'd be caught between the wall and the door, wouldn't
be able to fire, wouldn't be able to guarantee she could
even get clear for Mike to take the shot. Wright made a
split-second call, decided it wasn't worth the risk. Better
to be blind and hope. At least that way, they could keep
two guns up.

Mike had already moved as far towards the rear of the
compartment as he could, standing his back against one
of the pipes. Wright tucked in front of him, in a crouch
at his feet, so he could shoot over her if it came to that.
Both weapons trained on the door.

"Hammer, Anvil's got two unknowns moving
through," Wright reported. "Might be headed up."

"You at risk?"

"Not if they don't open this door."

"Take 'em if you have to. But *only* if you have to."

"Understood."

Wright kept her eyes locked on the door handle,
intent on catching the first sign of movement, a hawk
waiting for the field mouse to twitch. Counted out the
heavy seconds. Three. Five. Ten.

After thirty, it seemed likely that the two crew
members had passed by on their way to some other
part of the vessel. That was a short-term blessing that
could easily turn into a mid-term curse. On ops when
the environment allowed for it, Thumper would stay
behind at a command point and run surveillance to help
the rest of the team mark and track hostiles. Wright was

old-school and generally thought that too many people relied too heavily on the tech. To her, it was a crutch, and if you didn't have the skills to do without it, you'd be in big trouble when it failed on you. Which it would.

Even so, it was cases like these that made her admit sometimes it was really nice to have the help.

She gave it another sixty seconds before she spoke.

"I'll check it, Mike," she said. "Be ready."

"Yep," he answered.

Wright lowered her weapon and crept forward in her crouch, drew a device from her belt, placed it against the door. It attached and held itself in place while she activated it. After a moment, an electric-blue border radiated outward from the device, spreading like a ring of lightning rippling in slow motion across water's surface. Wherever it spread, the door became translucent. Nothing in the physical world had changed, but through her visor the door appeared to have been rendered to mist.

From her vantage point, the passageway looked clear in all directions. Unfortunately, the device didn't let her see around corners. Wright deactivated the device and returned it to her belt.

"Clear," she said to Mike. "Ready to open."

"Open," he answered.

"Opening."

Wright reached up for the handle. Slowly applied pressure, gently, gently, until it started to move. She had to force herself consciously to keep the pressure steady, while the undisciplined lizard-brain part of her told her to do it all fast, fast, fast. When the handle reached its lowest point, she eased the door open, pulling it towards herself. She did the best she could, but there just wasn't enough room to maneuver to put herself in any sort of tactically advantageous position. If anyone had come into the passageway in that brief span, Wright was going to have to count on the few seconds of surprise and confusion to get the work done.

She opened the door until light from the corridor seeped in around the edges; she held it there, and leaned her head closer, straining to hear anything that might indicate where the two had gone. Even with the sensors on her suit dialed up, she couldn't make out anything useful.

Wright glanced back over her shoulder and said to Mike, "Coming up." He raised the muzzle of his weapon towards the overhead in response. She stood, took a half step back from the door, and then opened it wide enough to get a clear view. The passageway remained empty and silent.

"Hammer, Anvil's clear," she reported. "We're continuing on towards the cargo holds now."

"Roger. Any sign of your people?"

"Negative. Might have gone up, might still be roaming around down here with us."

"Copy that. Keep your head on a swivel."

"Yeah."

Wright stepped out into the passageway and held there for a few seconds listening before she motioned to Mike to follow her. They resumed their slow crawl of the ship. At the intersection, she turned right. The fact that people had come from there seemed to be as good an indication as any that maybe there was something that direction worth seeing.

The passageway led to another door, this one marked as access to one of the vessel's side cargo holds. On the floor just outside there was some sort of grey-white residue spattered along the deck and up one bulkhead.

She crouched down to take a look, touched it with her middle finger and then rubbed the substance between fingertip and thumb. It was vaguely slimy, but with a gritty texture, like rice or oatmeal cooked too long in too much water.

Some kind of cleaning solution, or fluid from a machine, maybe. Then again, judging from the general disarray of the other parts of the ship, she could probably rule out cleaning solution.

She got back to her feet and moved up to the entrance of the cargo hold.

"Ready Mike?"

"Ready."

She opened the door, and pushed quickly through.

From the instant she stepped in, Wright knew something was off. Her instincts detected it first, before she had any obvious indication of what it was. It wasn't anything she could see. But it *felt* wrong. The main lights were off; the hold was lit only by low-power reds at wide intervals, casting the hold in ember-glow hues and pools of smoldering darkness. Wright's visor automatically adjusted to compensate.

On first glance, it looked like she had expected, given the state of the rest of the ship. Various containers were stacked in haphazard groups, separated by irregular aisles. It almost looked like the loaders had just dumped all the freight into the hold, and then pushed everything into piles at random. The arrangement was neither an efficient use of space, nor particularly convenient to navigate through. Typically haulers would try to maximize one or the other, and which one they prioritized could generally tell you something about the skipper's personality. Tidy rows usually meant ease of access to cargo verification; a sign of order and concern for inventory. Cargo holds full to the brim indicated a prime interest in maximizing profits per haul. Based on the layout of this hold, the impression Wright got was that the *Ava Leyla's* captain didn't especially care about either.

She held position for a few moments while Mike closed the door behind them, and they remained there in silence for several seconds afterward, listening. Here, too, it was still and quiet. The hold's temperature was warmer than she would have normally anticipated. Not warm, certainly. It would have been too cool to be comfortable had she not been in the suit. But many cargo vessels kept their holds barely above freezing, unless they were shipping temperature-sensitive freight.

"Mike, cover," Wright said. "I want to double-check something, internal."

"Copy."

They moved a few paces deeper into the hold into an alcove formed by one stack of shipping containers, where they had some concealment. There, Wright activated her internal display while Mike kept watch. She pulled up the schematic of the ship, overlaid with the signatures Thumper had detected with Poke before the team had made entry. The imagery hadn't been updated since the initial scan, but looking at the large, bright cloud on the lower deck of the ship, it seemed certain that Wright and Mike should have run into more people by now. And if she was reading it correctly, they ought to be standing pretty close to being right in the middle of that cloud.

She switched the display off, and took another look at the surroundings. In doing so, her conscious mind finally caught up with her instincts. The reason the hold felt wrong was because it was too small. All the time she'd spent in the haptic sim had given Wright a good sense of the general structure of the vessel. Even with all the different layouts available, certain elements should have remained fixed.

The bulkhead was too low. Or, maybe, the deck was too high. Either way, the cargo hold had been modified, there was no doubt about that.

"Hammer, Anvil," she said.

"Whatcha got?" Lincoln answered over comms.

"You guys using Poke right now?"

"Yeah, Thumper's got it assisting her. You need it?"

"Possibly. Got a hunch, but I'm not sure how to confirm it just yet."

"Roger that, stand by."

Wright waited, and a few seconds later Thumper clicked in over the team channel.

"Heya Mir," she said. "I can work without Poke for a little bit, but I can't run him for you right now. You want me to hand off?"

"Yeah, if you can."

"No sweat. Passing control to you now," said Thumper. And then added, "Don't let it hurt itself."

Wright's suit chimed as it acquired Poke's control system. Poke was still in between the inner and outer hull of the ship, somewhere near Deck Two. She took over and started the work of navigating the team's foldable to their current position.

Lincoln resisted the urge to look back over his shoulder to check on Thumper. He was standing guard off her right shoulder, keeping an eye on the long service tunnel that stretched off and curved with the shape of the ship. She was crouched behind him with one of her tech kits out, working to get hooked in to the *Ava Leyla*'s system network. From what Lincoln could tell, it was part information technology, part neurosurgery. She'd been at it for almost half an hour.

"Where are we at, Thump?" he asked.

"Trying to make sure I don't give anybody any reason to come up here and see why their comms are making funny noises, captain," she answered. Thumper didn't usually call him by his rank, unless she was annoyed with him.

Lincoln knew better than to hassle her. Thumper never wasted time on an op. But standing in that narrow tunnel was starting to wear on his nerves. Everything was too close; floor, walls, ceiling, all of it felt compressed, almost as if the space had been intended for children. It gave him the same gradually expanding annoyance as having someone's hand hovering an inch from his face, doing the whole I'm-not-touching-you thing. Which, by this time, had become almost irritating enough to make him want to go full-on assault mode, just to take it out on someone. Almost.

"OK," Thumper said, with an exhale that made it sound like she'd been holding her breath the whole time. "I'm in. Just gonna take me a second to crawl it."

Lincoln hoped it really was only going to take a second. In fact, it took her about ten, which was close enough.

"Huh," she said.

"You get a hit?" Lincoln asked.

"Yep," Thumper said. "Comm array's got a command module bridge piggybacked on it. Or a jury-rigged one, anyway."

"And that does what?" Lincoln said.

"It's like a uh…" she said. "Well, a bridge. Like I said.

Sort of like a repeater: you pass a signal through one end, it gets strengthened and passed on to the final destination. But it's special-purpose, command-and-control code type stuff. And it's got some high-grade encryption baked in, so whatever it's talking to isn't your off-the-shelf kind of gear."

"These are our guys, then."

"No," Thumper said, with a head shake. "I don't think so. I mean, yeah, sort of. But you wouldn't need a bridge if you were running the C&C from here. You could just do it straight. I'm thinking your pass-through theory is probably right. Somebody's sending comms through this ship. Whether these people are in on it or not, they aren't running the show. Pretty sure we're on the right track, but we're not at the top yet."

"What are we doing about it?"

"Well. Good news is I can probably extract the bounce data from it, and figure out where the other end is."

If Thumper led with the good news, then that meant there was bad on the way.

"But the bad news is…" Lincoln said.

"I'm going to need access to their comm array. For a while."

"No chance that's somewhere easy to get to, I guess."

"It's on the bridge."

"Of course it is."

Lincoln reflexively reached up to pinch the bridge of his nose before remembering he had the suit on, and there was no way for him to touch his face. He stopped his hand halfway and clenched it into a fist instead.

"All right," Lincoln said. He switched over to the team wide channel. "Anvil, Hammer's done in the service tunnel." He waited for Wright's confirmation before continuing.

"Anvil copies," Wright responded after a moment. "What's the story?"

"Thumper's got an ID on some gadget, we're going to have to go down into the vessel to pull it. Looks like we're going to have to take the bridge after all. Can you start making your way into position?"

"Not just yet. I want to get confirmation on our extra personnel first."

"Roger that," said Lincoln. "We'll make our way to internal entry and hold for your callback."

"Understood Hammer. Shouldn't be long."

"Keep us posted. Hammer out."

By the time Lincoln had checked in with the rest of the team, Thumper had already finished collecting her tools. She was in the process of replacing the panel she'd removed in order to gain access to the ship's communications array.

"Wish you could work as fast as you clean up, Thump," Sahil said. "I ain't been this bored on an op since that babysittin' job for the Brazilians."

"I do it to annoy you, Sahil," Thumper answered. "I'm sure I could find an alarm in here to trip if that'd help."

"Too late now," he replied.

Thumper secured the panel back in place, and if Lincoln hadn't watched her do it he would have had a hard time telling she'd done anything all. She'd even put it back on slightly off-angle, just like they'd found it. Thumper got to her feet, brought her weapon around from her back, and nodded at Lincoln.

"Let's go see if we can find something for Sahil to do, sir," she said.

"Roger that," Lincoln responded, trying very hard not to let the numbers get to him. If they could take the bridge fast enough, there was a good chance they could

seal off the lower decks and prevent the rest of the crew
from retaking it. Better than good. Ninety-nine percent
likely. But there was always the *if*.

Wright brought Poke into the cargo hold through one of
the environmental control vents. Once it had made its
way to them, she had it reconfigure to a wide, flat shape,
and set it to autoscan. From there, the little foldable
went to work crisscrossing the hold, navigating around
and through the containers on some search pattern of
its own devising. Wright led Mike on their own separate
search, confirming that there was no one else in the
cargo bay. They'd completed their circuit when Poke
chimed at her.

The datafeed showed its location and what it had
found.

Based on the heat and electrical impulses, there were
seventeen people somewhere directly below it.

But when Wright crossed the hold to where Poke was,
she found that the foldable had wedged itself in between
two closely-packed containers. She quickly surveyed
the immediate surroundings, and then summoned Poke
back to her as her suspicions coalesced. The bot trundled
its way over, gradually spreading out again as space
allowed.

"Mike, check that container," she said, pointing to the
one on the right. "See if there's a way in."

"You mean besides cutting through?" he asked.

She ignored the comment and went to work searching
the other container. Most shipping containers were
sealed at the loading point, both for safety and security,
particularly when freelance haulers were involved.
Made it more obvious when any tampering had gone
on. Wright walked around the outside, scanning for any

indication of a door or hatch. Nothing unusual stood out or caught her eye, and she paused at the back side of the container, wondering if she'd gotten it wrong. She was just reaching to pull her scanner off her belt to get a look inside when Mike spoke.

"Got it," he said.

"'K, hold on a sec," she answered. She moved around and rejoined him. Sure enough, at the back corner of the container there was a thin seam. Even with the visor's light amplification and its sensors picking up other spectra outside normal visual range, the line was difficult to see. It was well-camouflaged in the regular contours of the container.

"Good eyes," Wright said.

"Pretty, too," Mike replied, deadpan. Despite the wise crack, his tone of voice suggested absolute focus; sometimes it seemed like his mouth wasn't even connected to his mind. "Think we can spring it?"

"Better get a second opinion first," she answered. She clicked over to the team channel. "Thumper, you got a sec?"

"Yeah, what's up?" Thumper responded.

"Got what looks like a shipping container with a concealed entry point on the side here. I need to see if it's wired up."

"What, like a secret door or something?"

"Yes."

"Cool! Sure, yeah, is Poke still running around?"

"It's here with me. You want it back?"

"Yeah, gimme a sec with it."

Wright handed control of the foldable back over to Thumper. After a moment, it reconfigured itself into a vaguely beetle-like shape and proceeded to crawl up the side of the container. It paused at a height just above Wright's head.

"Whatever's in here, they're not delivering it," Thumper said. "From the tracking history, it looks like they just update the destination every so often. Never actually offload it."

"I'm just worried about the door right now," Wright said.

"Working on it," she answered. Wright glanced back at Mike, who had turned to face the opposite direction, keeping watch. Every minute they spent down here was a minute longer they had to spend on target. And every minute longer on target was just an extra opportunity for it to go wrong. Ninety seconds later, Thumper got back to them.

"Neat," Thumper said. "This is sort of clever. Looks like two actually, one on the side, and a hatch in the floor. Like a double false bottom. I guess if the authorities are clever enough to find the first one, it just looks like a way to skim some product out of the container. Probably wouldn't look any harder beyond that. And yeah, good call, they're both wired."

"Think you can bypass?" Wright asked. As she was asking, the side entry point clicked and partially retracted.

"Hatch is physical," Thumper said. "You'll have to open it manually. But it shouldn't set off any alarms."

"Roger. I'm taking Poke back," said Wright. "Mike, keep an eye out."

"You got it," Mike replied.

Wright assumed control of the foldable, and sent it into the container first, attached to the underside of the roof. It was pitch black inside; Poke's sensors fed data directly to her visor, crafting images from the darkness. Metal crates were stacked nearly floor to ceiling, held in place against either side of the container with networks of straps. A narrow corridor ran down the middle. Wright made her way to the far end, where a row of crates reached only to waist height. These were braced against the roof of the container with a series of expandable arms. The crates were visually indistinguishable from one another, except for the one that Thumper had marked with a digital signature. Wright removed the brace from the top of it and after a minute or two of searching, found two portions of the crate that were actually latches.

She'd already confirmed enough to know her hunch was correct. There was no doubt about it now, the extra personnel they'd detected were down there below her. Hidden under the deck, with an entrance that was itself doubly-disguised. Human cargo, being smuggled to who knew where. Maybe they were refugees. Maybe escaped prisoners. Maybe radicals, looking to infiltrate some stable society so they could make a statement. Whatever the case, whoever they were, right now they were trapped in a shipping container.

And if they were in a shipping container, then they weren't a threat; if not a threat, then no factor for the op. A complication, possibly, but not a threat. There was no good reason to risk discovery, just to satisfy curiosity. And yet, even as her mind worked through the angles and implications, her desire to know, to positively identify, drove her hands.

Silently, slowly, she unhooked the latches and raised the edge just enough to let Poke slip through. It worked its way down, clinging to the side, and then to the ceiling.

There was a single light in one corner of the hidden compartment, a dull, yellow-brown globe that coated the room in a clinging, muddy aura. And through Poke's feed, Wright saw that her hunch hadn't been exactly correct.

People, yes.

Seventeen of them, as expected. They were gathered in small groups, huddled together for warmth and whatever comfort they could find. Some appeared to be sleeping. On second look, Wright realized that the groups were gathered around large bowls or pots. Scooping their hands in and bringing them to their mouths in hurried desperation. Her mind flashed back to the substance she'd found spattered on the deck in the passageway outside. The slimy, gritty grey-white mess she'd taken for some kind of mechanical fluid. Their food.

With Poke's lens she scanned the faces, and despite her years of service in some of the most horrible locations and situations in the known, her heart lurched and her emotions slipped. Their eyes were frightened, confused, hollowed with weariness, and hunger, and who could say what else. And the oldest among them could not have been more than thirteen years of age.

Wright stood in silence, her mind shocked into stasis. For how long, she didn't know. Her comms brought her back to herself.

"What you got, mama bear?" Mike asked.

In response, Wright split Poke's feed, piped it into Mike's visor. For once, he had nothing to say.

"Hammer," Wright said. "Anvil. We've located your personnel. Count is seventeen, appear to be subject to trafficking."

"We copy, Anvil. What's your assessment?"

Wright didn't know how to answer.

"Kids, Lincoln," Mike said. "It's all a bunch of kids."

The revelation hit Lincoln with nearly physical force. He felt a shock of cold pass through, a force of frost reality crashing over his expectations for the op. This was one possibility the sim hadn't come up with, and one for which he felt completely unprepared. He had known it was a possibility that all those extra people weren't on board by choice. But children... the thought had never entered his mind.

"You copy?" Mike said. Lincoln wasn't sure how many seconds it'd been since the report had come in.

"Roger, I copy," he answered. And then added, "Stand by."

Stand by for what? Lincoln didn't know yet. His thoughts buzzed through his mind, an overturned hornet's nest of plans and contingencies and options, without coherence or cohesion. Seventeen kids, headed off to who knew what fate.

"What're we doin', Cap'n?" Sahil asked. He was keeping things neutral, but Lincoln could hear the anger in his voice. Lincoln was pretty sure that if he left Sahil to his own devices, the man would likely walk through the vessel and execute every member of the crew with extreme prejudice and zero regret.

"Thumper," Lincoln said. "Is there any way you can get what you need from the comm array without getting onto the bridge?"

She thought for a moment, but then shook her head. "No, not really. I need physical access to it."

"What about the device itself? Is it on the bridge?"

"Nah, it's buried down in the guts, underneath."

"Anything we can do with it?"

"I don't think so. I don't have any of the tools I'd need to be able to pull data directly from it while it's in place."

"I mean if we take it home."

Another span of silence, while Thumper evaluated. It seemed to take her longer than usual.

"Huh. I hadn't thought about that," she said. "It's a

little more complicated, probably take me longer on the back end, but yeah, maybe."

"No time for maybes, Thump."

"Yeah. Yeah I should be able to do it. Just going to have to replicate a setup once we get back. But I guess if I spend some time with the hardware that might get us some good info too."

"Are they going to notice it's missing when it's gone?"

"I'm not sure they even know they have it, sir. I guess we'll find out?"

There were no good options.

The seventeen kids brought the potential bad guy count down to more manageable levels. Lincoln knew his team could take the ship now. But then what? They couldn't leave the ship floating in open space with a bunch of kids on board. There was no telling how long it would take for the nearest authorities to respond. Lincoln couldn't keep his team on the vessel. The potential cascade of events put too much at risk, too much beyond the team's ability to control. And they were already short on time, and leads.

No good options. Lincoln made the only choice he could. The only one there was, really.

"Anvil," he said. "Close it back up." No matter how lightly he said it, the words sounded harsh even to his own ears.

There was a pause.

"Say again, sir," Wright replied, her tone carefully controlled.

"Put everything back the way you found it," Lincoln answered. "I want zero footprint. No indication we were here."

"But we *are* here, sir," Mike said. "*We're* here, now." Lincoln didn't miss the implied message.

"Not for them," Lincoln answered.

"We can't just leave 'em–" Sahil said.

"We can, and we will," Lincoln responded, cutting him off. "We have our mission. We lose focus now, a lot worse is going to follow, for a lot more people."

He said it with a conviction he didn't feel.

"Wright, take facial on each individual," he said. "We'll put it out on the wire when we get back. Let the proper authorities take it from there."

"Roger that," Wright answered. Her previous request for Lincoln to repeat his order was her only sign of protest. She knew the decision had been made, and now it was only time to execute.

"Once you've got it clean down there, exfil and return to the Lamprey," Lincoln said. Then he turned and looked back at Sahil. "You too, Sahil. Go ahead and prep the ship for detach. Thumper and I will head in and retrieve the device, then meet you back outside. We'll freespace to pick up."

Sahil nodded curtly.

Lincoln didn't love the idea of sending the rest of his team outside the ship; if trouble came, they wouldn't be able to provide support. But the fewer of them there were sneaking around the ship, the fewer chances there'd be for accidental contact, and the quicker they could exfiltrate when the time came.

No one argued. Sahil turned and made his way back down the service tunnel, towards the hatch they'd first used to gain entry. All that was left to do now was for Lincoln and Thumper to sneak down through the most active part of the ship, steal a device buried somewhere under the bridge, and get back out without anyone noticing. Success seemed unlikely. Business as usual.

"All right, Thump," he said. "Lead the way."

She nodded and squeezed by him, which was no easy task in the narrow service tunnel. And as Lincoln followed her out, he fought to turn off the portion of his mind that was still trying to figure out how they could save all those kids.

"OK, I can get to it from here," Thumper said. She was more somber, more direct with her words than usual. She hadn't spoken to him at all during their tense crawl down into the main passageways of the vessel; she'd only communicated through hand signals. But Lincoln didn't get the impression she was deliberately showing her displeasure at his choice; it seemed more like it was her way of insulating herself from everything outside of the objective at hand. He was trying his best to do the same thing.

The proper access panel to the communications array was actually on the deck above them, on the bridge. But if they had any hope of pulling this off without detection, trying to gain entry to the bridge was clearly no longer an option. Instead, they'd opted to make an access point of their own, through the overhead of a storage compartment roughly beneath the command bridge. It wasn't ideal, but the few choices they had were all poor, and Thumper had figured that from their limited choices this one was the least bad.

The compartment housed several tall steel sets of shelves running lengthwise from the front of the room to the back, with narrow aisles in between. The lights were off, except for the low-intensity always-on red bulbs that were placed throughout the ship. One near the back corner flickered sporadically, a sure sign that it needed replacement.

For once, the ship's general disarray worked in the

team's favor. Various foodstuffs and supplies were haphazardly strewn all over the shelving, with no apparent order or plan. Sacks of rice and beans sat on the deck in one corner, alongside what looked like a pile of oil-stained mechanic's coveralls. The likelihood of anyone noticing anything missing or having been rearranged was slim.

Which was good, as they'd had to move a number of items to make room for Thumper. At the moment, she was lying on her back on the very top of one of the shelves, her face maybe six inches away from the overhead, and her legs propped over a soft-sided container of emergency environment suits. She scooted backward a few inches; the movement caused the whole shelf to shake and wobble. Lincoln instinctively reached out to stabilize it, but Thumper didn't seem the least bit fazed.

"How long?" Lincoln asked.

"Couple minutes to cut through," she answered. "Couple minutes to close it back up. Unknown amount of time in the middle."

He glanced up and saw she'd already begun the work. She traced thin lines in a silvery, metallic paint to form a rectangle on the overhead, a little wider than her shoulders, and starting from just above her head down to her midsection.

Lincoln went back to watching the door a few feet away. He took a deep breath, held it, exhaled slowly. There was something draining about this kind of operation. A slow-burn anxiety. At least in an assault, the training and muscle memory took over, clarity of action became razor sharp, and all that pent-up energy could be poured out. In an infiltration like this, there was nothing to react to, nothing to push against. It was all just waiting, waiting, waiting for that moment of sudden action, with no guarantee that it would come, but disastrous consequences if it came and caught you on your heels.

He'd placed a scanner on the door, but had dialed it in so he could still see the physical structure of the door as well as out into the passageway. If anyone showed up, he wanted to be able to quickly pull the device and didn't want to lose time fumbling around for it. The early warning wouldn't do all that much good if the scanner itself was still stuck to the back of the door for the bad guys to see. So far, they'd only seen one person in the passageway, a scruffy wastrel of a man who had hurried past without any sign of slowing.

"Burning now," Thumper said.

Above her, the silvery line glowed white, star-brilliant for a half second. And then she was pushing the panel up, and sliding it into the hole she'd just made. Through the hole in the overhead, Lincoln could see a beam of the ship's internal infrastructure, flanked on either side by pipes and masses of cabling. The idea that Thumper could sort through all of that in any sort of quick fashion seemed absurd.

"I'm going to have to get up in there a ways," she said. "Let me know if I'm making too much noise."

"Roger," Lincoln answered. He looked up to check on her again, and saw that she was rolling into an awkward not-quite-seated position. She disappeared into the overhead from the shoulders up, her arms held above her head.

"Oh boy," she said.

"Problem?"

"Not if I had all day," she replied.

For the next fifteen minutes, Thumper punctuated

the long spans of silence with the occasional grunt
or curse. Lincoln had to resist the urge to ask her for
updates; he knew she'd let him know whenever there
was something *to* know. There would be no point in the
request other than his temporary relief. It was like trying
not to scratch an itch.

After about seventeen minutes of Thumper working,
Lincoln got more of a distraction than he'd wanted.

People in the passageway. A man and a woman, with a
little girl between them. The woman held the girl's wrist
in a controlling manner, which seemed unnecessary, as
the girl offered no resistance whatsoever. The moment
Lincoln saw them, his gut told him they were headed
his way.

"Trouble," Lincoln said. "We've got two inbound.
There's a kid with them."

"What do you want me to do about it?" Thumper
asked; not confrontational, despite her tone. A genuine
question.

"How quickly can you get down?"

"Up would be easier."

"Do it."

There was no doubt about it. The man in the passageway
was in the lead, and he slowed as he approached the
storage compartment. Lincoln snatched the scanner off
the door, slapped it back in place on his belt, and turned
to find a hiding place. Above him, he saw Thumper's feet
disappear into the overhead. A moment later, the panel
slid back over the hole she'd cut, angled slightly so it
wouldn't fall through. It wasn't a perfect fit; to Lincoln's
eyes, the gaps at the corners seemed painfully obvious,
a warning that would be impossible to miss. They would
just have to hope that no one looked up.

Then again, if that was the thing the bad guys noticed,

that would mean Lincoln had solved the biggest problem. Himself.

He quickly moved to the back corner of the storage room, furthest from the door, with the largest amount of stuff between it and him. There he crouched down in between a stack of several large water canisters and a pile of unmarked sacks made of some rough, unrefined cloth. The canisters were taller and provided better coverage, but the irregular lines and colors of the sacks made for easier blending with his suit's reactive camouflage. The handle on the door clanked and light from the passageway sliced a narrow channel along the dark floor. But it didn't immediately widen.

"Then just wait," the man said, out in the passageway. He'd opened the door partway, but hadn't entered yet. "Or don't, I don't care."

At the last moment, Lincoln dragged one of the unmarked bags over in front of him, covering the lower portion of his body. He kept his weapon low but clear, in case he had to use it in a hurry.

The lights came on, and Lincoln felt as though he'd been caught in the open under a spotlight. He could just barely see the door through a gap in the water canisters and the shelves. The man moved through first, and was quickly lost from view. The woman shoved the little girl forward ahead of her, roughly.

"*Stand over there,*" the woman said in Mandarin. "*And don't touch anything!*"

The little girl didn't appear to understand any of the words, but there was no doubt she understood the general meaning. She stepped forward a few paces to a point where Lincoln could see her quite well through the shelves. She was seven or eight years old, he guessed, with dark hair, and skin deeply tanned. Though he couldn't be sure of her ethnicity, Honduras leapt to mind. He had spent months operating in Honduras early in his career; he'd seen plenty of boys and girls her age, and she would have fit in right among them. She kept her hands at her waist, in front of her, the pointer finger of her left hand wrapped in the loose fist of her right. Eyes on the floor.

"Are you sure we even still have them?" the man said from near the front corner of the room.

"*We should,*" the woman snapped, "*but I'm not the one who's using them all the time.*"

"Not like I do either," the man answered, but he swallowed it, apparently not wanting to invite any more of the woman's obviously substantial wrath. The sounds of rummaging came from his general direction. After a few moments, the woman sighed in irritation and walked over to join him.

"*Move, just move out of the way.*"

The rummaging became sharper, more violent. And the little girl, left alone and unguarded, did what children often do without supervision. She started exploring.

At first, she just reached out and touched the shelf in front of her, ran a finger along it. She glanced towards the front of the room where the adults were and, having earned no reproach, grew bolder. She stepped closer to the shelf, touched some of the items on it, picked up a small box and examined it. After she set the box back on the shelf, she dared to leave her spot by the door, and started walking down the aisle. Towards the back of the compartment.

She disappeared from view for a span, but it wasn't difficult to anticipate her trajectory. Sure enough, a moment later she reached the end of the shelf and paused. A stack of cans prevented him from seeing most of her, but he could see the top half of her legs through the shelving. She was still facing the shelves, investigating whatever those cans were, most likely.

Lincoln willed her to turn and go back to the door. If she did, there was still a chance no one would notice him. But if she decided to come around the end of the shelf, she would be standing in the aisle with an unobstructed view directly to Lincoln and his hiding place. There was no way to know how she'd react if she saw him. And there seemed vanishingly little hope that that wouldn't happen.

The girl shifted, her legs turned back towards the door. But she didn't move. Just stood there. Weighing her options, maybe. And then, to Lincoln's disappointment, she turned the other way and crept around the aisle. She trailed a hand behind her, running it along the smooth end of the shelf. She didn't seem to be searching for anything in particular. Looking around, taking it all in. It occurred to Lincoln that this might have been the first time she'd ever seen so many basic necessities all in one place. He noticed then that she wasn't wearing any shoes.

And then her eyes fell on him.

They were deep brown, and made Lincoln think of rich earth, and open fields. At first, they passed over him, swept casually from the water canisters to the sacks without pause.

Still, still, still, Lincoln told himself. He held his breath, would have stopped his heart if he could have.

The girl looked up at the corner of the room, and then started a lazy turn around the end of the shelf, making her way back towards the door along a different aisle. But before she disappeared between the shelves, she stopped, and suddenly looked back, as if she'd caught something out of the corner of her eye. It was then that she saw him. She turned her body towards him, and stared, wide-eyed.

"*We had six the last time I checked,*" the woman said. "*There should be at least three more.*"

The rummaging sounds approached closer, as the woman widened her search. The little girl didn't move. Her arms hung down straight at her sides, her hands clenched in tiny fists. Lincoln didn't know what to do. She was looking at him, there was no doubt about it. But she didn't seem to know what to do about it either. For maybe as much as a full minute, they sat there staring at one another. There was no fear in her eyes; just a careful attentiveness. Waiting.

"*Here,*" the woman said. "*They're right here! Four of them! Right here!*"

"Well, that's not where they were last time," the man said. "Maybe you shouldn't leave your stuff spread out everywhere."

"*I told you – I'm not the one using them all up!*"

The woman was close now. A few steps away, just on the other side of the canisters. If the little girl screamed, or pointed, or even walked over for a closer look, there was nothing he'd be able to do about it. His action would have to be decisive in those next confused moments, his aim sure, if he had any hope of preventing the man and woman from raising an alarm.

But then, a sudden, unexpected thought occurred to him. It was foolish, probably. But the hope of escaping the storage compartment without being discovered seemed all but lost. He took the risk, and moved. Slowly, he brought his pointer finger to his lips, or to the place on his faceplate where his lips would be if there had been any face at all for the girl to see. In response, she blinked several times.

And then she backed away, slowly, a step at a time. She remained by the end of the shelf, at the far side of the compartment, silent, never taking her eyes off him.

"*Girl,*" the woman snapped, from farther away. Somewhere near the door. "*Come here.*"

The little girl looked at the woman. Then back at Lincoln.

Lincoln thought for certain his heart had stopped. Involuntarily, he tightened his grip on his weapon, tensed his legs, readying to spring out and drop both adults before they could react. The woman was by the door; he would target her first. Through the gap in the shelves. Then the man, somewhere to the right.

The woman started to take a step towards the girl, but the instant she moved, the little girl turned and obediently went to her. She didn't look back.

A few moments later, the lights switched off, and the storage compartment was once more bathed in a red darkness.

Lincoln gave it a full minute before he spoke.

"We're clear," he said.

"I can put my feet back down?" Thumper asked.

"Yeah, you're good. Just do it quietly."

The panel slid back, and Thumper's feet descended, touching down lightly on the top shelf.

"My abs are killing me," she said.

"That was too close," Lincoln said. "How much longer?"

"Almost got it. Already rerouted everything I need to, just got to safely disconnect now."

"Soon's good."

Lincoln moved the sack out from in front of him, slipped forward out of his hiding place, and made his

way over to the shelf at the far end, where the little girl
had stood, maybe eight feet away. From there, he looked
back at the corner where he'd been. The fact that she
hadn't given him away made it seem unlikely she would
mention the strange, not-quite-invisible man sitting in
the corner. But he couldn't help but wonder what she
had thought he was.

"Hey Thumper," he said.

"Yeah?"

"While you're in there… anything you can do to
make them easier to find?" he asked.

She didn't answer immediately, but when she did she
seemed to understand his meaning. "I'll see what I can
work up."

Exfiltration, for once, had gone smoothly. Thumper had
found an exterior hatch on the same deck as the storage
room, one that led out to a small loading bay on the
starboard side of the vessel. She and Lincoln exited from
the bay, and traversed the exterior of the ship to where
the Lamprey was still tethered. From there, they made
the leap across open space. Once they were all loaded
in, Sahil punched out a command on the console. The
Coffin vibrated slightly as the grapples released and
retracted. Sahil activated the reverse thrusters, gradually
slowing the vehicle and allowing an ever-widening gap
to open between them and the freighter.

Sahil left the display up, so they could all watch the
Ava Leyla as it receded from view, shrinking to a single
point and finally vanishing in the great void.

"Spooky One Seven, this is Easy One," Sahil said.

"We copy, Easy One," Noah answered. "Good to hear
from you. Will was starting to worry."

"We got distance on the target, startin' our burn to

rally now," Sahil responded. The directness of his words and the flatness of his delivery communicated everything Lincoln needed to know about Sahil's feelings on the outcome of the op.

"Roger, Easy One, we're en route to pick up. ETA is... forty-seven mikes."

"Forty-seven minutes, understood. Easy One out."

Lincoln glanced over at the device they'd recovered. Two conjoined cylinders, one narrower than the other. Smaller than a loaf of bread, and maybe two pounds total. And yet they were headed back home with a much heavier burden.

"You leave that on me," Lincoln said. "I know it's going to be tempting to question what we did back there. We're all going to be thinking about what we could have done differently, or what we should have done. And I'll tell you right now, what you should have done is exactly what you did. You followed orders, you got the job done. Anything beyond that, you let me carry."

For a time, no one replied. But then Wright spoke up.

"Team's a team, captain. Whatever we do, we *all* do."

"It's my job to decide," Lincoln answered. "And the consequences of those decisions are mine to bear. That's my part. So you leave that on me."

They rode the rest of the way in silence. Lincoln knew he didn't want to second-guess himself the whole trip back, but there didn't seem all that much else to do. It wasn't that he doubted the call he'd made. There was no question it was the right one. On paper, out of the moment, detached from the emotion, there was no question. If it came down to trading the lives of a few kids here, no matter how desperate, for all those at risk if they didn't recover SUNGRAZER, Lincoln had absolutely done the right thing.

But it wasn't doubt that plagued him. It was the quiet fear that at some point on that long trip home, he was going to think of another way he could've done it. That the solution would present itself too late, when there was nothing he could do except regret he hadn't thought of it sooner, faster. Like having the perfect snappy comeback, three minutes after the argument ended. He thought about that little girl, bravely enduring. And how much longer she'd have to continue to do so, because of the call he'd made.

TWELVE

"Three of a kind, eights," Mike said, laying his cards down on the footlocker they were using as a table. Wright tossed her cards into the pile, face down.

"Beats me," Lincoln said. He gathered the playing cards up off the table and started shuffling them, while Mike collected his meager winnings. They never played for much, but they always played for something.

This was one of the tough parts about their particular line of work. The whole team was restless. Playing poker was occasionally distracting, but in this particular case, no one's heart seemed to be in it. After the intensity of planning for, and then executing, the hit on the *Ava Leyla*, the sudden lack of direction and focus made it hard to relax during down time. It wasn't unusual for the team to get a little break after running an op. In this case, however, it wasn't self-imposed. There was literally nothing any of them could do. Lincoln felt like the team had run full-tilt off the end of a long pier, only to find themselves lost at sea.

It'd been roughly sixty hours since they'd returned to the skiff, following the recovery of the module. Normally after a successful operation, the team had additional intelligence to comb through, further plans to make. But all they'd come home with this time was a black box of a device. And since Thumper was the only one who could do anything with it, the rest of them were left at loose ends. Lincoln wasn't much of a techie, but for the first time he could remember he found himself envying her the role. It must have been comforting, in a way, to have something to focus her mind on. A problem to solve, a puzzle to untangle. Lincoln felt like he couldn't get his brain to stick to any task for long.

The *Ava Leyla* op still clung to him. He'd put together a package and sent it on to the proper authorities, in the hopes that the next time the freighter pulled into port, they'd find a team of agents waiting for them. But there was no way to know for sure how that situation would resolve. After the team's return, they'd debriefed, eaten, showered, slept. But none of them had bounced back yet, not fully. There was something subdued about his team; their conversations were fewer and shorter. Sahil had spent even more time than usual in the gym. He seemed to be taking it the hardest. To their credit, no one had come after Lincoln over his decision to leave the children behind. No one argued. But they all had to deal with it in their own way.

Even Colonel Almeida had left the situation largely unremarked upon, when Lincoln had updated him and filed his official report. In some ways, that almost made things worse. Being forced to defend his decision, or to justify it, or even to have a blowout argument with one of his subordinates would have given him an opportunity to process it, and to release some of the emotional energy that had built up, and seemed to be continuing to build. The one saving grace was that he still hadn't thought of any other way to have handled the situation. It wasn't much comfort.

They were still two days out from reconnecting with the USS *Durham*. He hoped they hadn't just hit a dead end.

Lincoln dealt out another round of hands. Wright and Mike picked up their cards, reorganized them. Wright glanced at hers for maybe two seconds before she tossed in her ante.

"One time," Mike said, out of the blue. "Back when I was still with Fifth, I was on overwatch for the Marines. This was outside of Osh, back before the unification and all that. We were supposed to just be providing support for the locals, doing stability and security work. You know, guarding bridges and marketplaces, that sort of thing. Peacekeeping. Anyway." He threw in his ante. "I was keeping an eye out for a checkpoint on one of the main bridges. And things had been tense for a couple of days. Bad guys testing perimeters, skirmishing with the local security forces. So we'd had to close things up, put a curfew in place, restrict access to certain areas. And we all just had that feeling, you know. Today's the day, kind of deal.

"Well, I see this car pulling onto the road, pretty casual. So I give the Marines a heads-up, and they make the stop. Turns out it's two ladies, one about my age and I guess maybe her grandma. Old woman doesn't talk at all. Trying to take a bunch of stuff to market, the younger one says. I'm watching all this go down through optics, right? And trying real hard not to think about the fact that maybe I'm going to have to smoke one of them. Because who knows what's really in the car? Maybe it's full of grenades. Or maybe they're a distraction, while the bad guys come around the flank. So everyone's on point now.

"Well they can't use our bridge. Nobody's going that

way today. But there's a little one-lane job about a hundred meters north. More like a footbridge, it wasn't really meant for cars. But the woman asks if she can use that instead, and our officer says that's fine. It's obviously not really fine, but it makes it someone else's problem, I guess. You know how it is, he's got his boys out there, nobody knowing if this is a distraction or a car bomb or really just a couple of down-on-their-luck ladies trying to get some junk to a market. He doesn't care where they go, as long as they don't go down his bridge.

"Short version. You can guess. Car goes off the bridge. *Plunk*. Right into the water. Most of these folks? They aren't swimmers. Locals start coming out, pointing at the car, yelling. A couple of them try to wade out into the river, but the current's too strong. Pretty sure I saw at least one of them get pulled under, but maybe he made it back out, I still don't know. Anyway, some of them start waving at us, trying to get our attention, calling for us to come help out. We've got twenty-something Marines and soldiers on that bridge. Any one of us could have jumped down there and tried to do something. Pulled the ladies out at least. But you know how it is. We never do anything on our own. If we send one, we have to send five, and as soon as we do that, as soon as one of us leaves our post, that's when the bad guys are going to come. And it's our boys gonna get killed then. And maybe a whole lot more than just us, if they get across that bridge."

He paused, rubbed the underside of his chin with the back of his fingers. Switched the positions of two cards in his hand.

"So we held position," he said. He sniffed loudly, and then reached over and took a chip from Lincoln's stack, threw it in the pot as Lincoln's ante. "Whatever the cards are, you gotta play."

Lincoln hadn't even looked at his hand yet, and he wasn't exactly sure if Mike was talking about poker just then, or was actually making a philosophical statement. Both, maybe. Lincoln picked up his cards. Not even a pair.

"This one's worse than most," Lincoln said. And after the words came out, he realized he wasn't sure if *he* was talking about poker either.

"Pretty much no matter what you do, someone's always getting the short end."

Wright tossed her cards down on the table.

"I fold," she said. She'd already put money down, and play hadn't even started yet.

"You want your ante back?" Mike asked.

She shook her head and got to her feet, her eyes lowered. "You need it more than I do." She picked up her jacket, checked around for anything else that might belong to her, even though it was a team room and they all left their stuff lying around there all the time.

"You out?" Lincoln asked, even though it was obvious she was.

"Gonna hit the gym," she answered, still without looking at him.

"Hey," he said. Wright stopped then, held a moment, then finally glanced up and made eye contact. They each held the other's gaze, unblinking for a span. There were no tears in her eyes, no obvious signs of emotion at risk of spilling over. Unless you knew what to look for. And Lincoln did. He saw it there too, reflected in her eyes. The struggle he felt. The frustration. The sadness. She had her own story, like Mike. Many stories, probably. They all did.

All the recruitment posters would have you believe

serving in the military could make you a hero. No one mentioned you wouldn't be a hero for *everyone*. Sometimes not even those who seemed to need it most.

But the master sergeant's hard fire was still apparent: She wasn't going to fall apart or have a break down. She probably just needed to go sling some weight around to keep herself from chewing through the hull.

"Try not to tear a hole in the ship, huh?" he said.

The left corner of her mouth pulled back in a twitch of a smile; a mild acknowledgment, with a trace of relief that Lincoln hadn't made a big deal out of it. She gave him a nod, and started towards the door. It opened as she reached for it, and she had to stop to keep from bumping into Thumper, who had suddenly appeared, leaning into the compartment. Her obvious excitement helped clear away the gloom.

"I think somebody owes me a hundred bucks," Thumper said.

"You cracked it?" Wright asked.

"Looks like," Thumper replied. "Come see."

Lincoln and Mike tossed their cards onto the foot locker, and they all followed her over to the compartment they'd cleared out for her to use as a workshop. It had previously served as crew quarters. Now, one set of bunks had been stripped of mattress and linens, and been converted into workbenches. Veronica was set up on the lower bunk, with the new addition of a twist of cabling that ran from the back of her terminal up to the top bunk. There, it attached to the device they'd recovered from the *Ava Leyla*, which itself was attached to some secondary box that Lincoln didn't recognize. Thumper had rolled out a thinskin overlay on one of the walls, so she could display information for everyone to see. They all gathered around. Lincoln wondered briefly if he needed to go grab Sahil before Thumper got started. But then he thought about the outpouring of information Thumper was about to dump on them, and figured Sahil would very much appreciate just getting the highlights later.

"So this turned out to be a trickier bit of work than I anticipated," Thumper said. "It's probably a good thing we ended up pulling the device after all. Encryption's nasty. We'd probably still be on board the *Ava Leyla* if I'd had to run it from there. Of course, unplugging it caused some issues too. I ended up having to trick this thing into talking to itself, just to get the ball rolling."

"What do you mean?" Wright asked. "Talk to itself?"

"Loopback," Thumper said, rapping the box Lincoln didn't recognize with her knuckle. It was metal, and looked like something a high school kid might have put together in a garage. "Whatever's on the other end of this guy," here she pointed at the recovered device, "has some built-in activation protocol, also encrypted. So this module won't do anything unless it's got a live connection back to its partner. I just had to figure out a way to convince it that it had an open channel, and the only way I could figure out how to do that was to feed it some of its own old signal. I pulled that out of the transmission we picked up before we went out. Which I fed it through this loopback."

"You made that?" Mike asked.

"Me? Nah, couple of the navy techs worked that up for me. I just gave them the list of parts and a rough schematic. Pretty sharp cookies," she said. "For sailors."

"Well, that explains the workmanship," Mike said.

"I have no idea what you just said, Thump," Lincoln said. "Do I need to understand any of that before you can tell me why it matters?"

Thumper looked disappointed. "No sir, I don't guess so."

"OK. Then just skip to the part where you tell me what it means."

"You don't want to know how I found it?"

"Not today. Over beers, maybe. Later."

"Fine. We were right. Main signal was coming from a location on Mars, bouncing through the *Ava Leyla*, out to the final destination."

"To SUNGRAZER," Lincoln said.

"Or something that looks so suspiciously similar to SUNGRAZER, that no one would blame us for thinking it."

"Which means we're going to Mars," Lincoln said.

"Which means," Thumper said, turning to Mike, "you owe me a hundred bucks."

"I'm pretty sure I only bet you fifty," Mike said.

"That's not my recollection," Thumper answered. "And, I don't like to brag, but I *am* pretty good with numbers."

"Fine, you can deduct it from what you owe me."

"Owe you for what?"

"All the times I've bailed you out."

"That's just called doing your job, Mikey."

"Speaking of doing our jobs…" Lincoln interrupted.

"Yeah, OK," Thumper said, getting back to her show-and-tell. "So here's the thing. It looks like our bad guys are doubly smart. And maybe too clever by half."

She gestured at Veronica. The terminal brought up an image on the thinskin of the upper third of Mars, with some quick additional icons labeled as the *Ava Leyla* and SUNGRAZER. It looked like a presentation put together by someone with access to satellite imagery and absolutely no trace of artistic talent.

"You make *that* yourself, Thump?" Lincoln asked.

"Shut up," she said. "Point is, we've got a command signal coming out of here." She waggled a finger, and a line appeared connecting a point near the northern Martian polar ice cap and the *Ava Leyla.*

"Presumably, I would say with about eighty-eight percent confidence, it bounces from here, and goes out to there." Another gesture, another line connecting the comically bad icons for the freighter and SUNGRAZER. Eighty-eight percent confidence didn't sound as high as Lincoln would have liked, but then he had to remind himself that statistically speaking, that was pretty high. And Thumper tended to underestimate her own brilliance.

"What's there?" Lincoln asked, pointing to the ice cap.

"I'll get there in a sec," she said. "Now, here's the fun part. Signal strength coming out of the alleged origin is a little fuzzy. Not quite as pure as I would expect, if it were an actual origin."

It was impossible to deny that Thumper was a genius. It was also impossible to ignore the fact that she could never just skip straight to the point. She wasn't showing off by any means. There wasn't a prideful bone in her body, as far as Lincoln could tell. She just loved figuring out the pieces to the puzzle, and tended to assume that everyone else loved the process as much as she did.

"It's a double pass-through," Lincoln said, indulging her.

"A double pass-through, right. But more than that. I've had Veronica running signal analysis for me, and check this out." She gestured again, and a third line appeared, connecting the point near the ice cap to a location on the map that marked the Martian People's Collective Republic. "Based on the general communications traffic down there, I'm pretty sure *that* signal is coming out of the MPCR."

"*Pretty* sure?" Lincoln asked.

Thumper cocked her head to one side, gave him a look. She wouldn't have mentioned it if she hadn't thought with absolute certainty that it was true.

"Yeah, OK," Lincoln said.

That was probably the worst possible news of all the outcomes. Lincoln had of course known that Martian elements had to be considered as a potential source. But for the Martian People's Collective Republic to be involved took things to a new level. Earth and Mars weren't exactly on an open war footing any more, but the tension between the two planets remained high. The MPCR was one of the few settlements on Mars that was publicly pushing for de-escalation. That part wasn't a surprise, exactly. The Collective Republic worked hard to portray itself as aggressively neutral. And though it was one of the smaller colonies on the red planet, it was an economic powerhouse with a level of commerce that put it on the same stage as some of the oldest nations on either world. It had influence *and* at least the illusion of moral standing. The idea that the Republic would be publicly advocating for peace while secretly working for war was almost too depressing to consider.

And also entirely too plausible to ignore.

"Can we localize it?"

"Not precisely. This is sort of a gross oversimplification," Thumper said, gesturing at the images she'd thrown together. "We're untangling a lot of sophisticated stuff here, and trying to do it in a way that no one's going to notice. We could try to get NID in on it, but the more eyes we've got watching, the more likely it is that people on the other side are going to notice all of us noticing. I'm running pretty low profile here. So maybe if we sit here and watch long enough, we *might* be able to figure out the full route. But by then..." She shrugged.

"Bad guys might've already done what they're going to do," Lincoln said. She nodded.

"And we still don't know what that is."

"What about going out the other way?" Wright asked. "Can you use this science project of yours to find the ship?"

A good question. As tempting as it was to focus on the bad guys, Lincoln had to remind himself that their actual objective was securing SUNGRAZER. It was his natural inclination to go after bad actors. As much as it would irritate him to leave the important questions unanswered, in this particular case, it seemed like the easiest course of action would simply be to locate SUNGRAZER and shut the whole thing down.

Thumper's shoulders sagged at the mention.

"I've been trying," she said. "But that thing is so sewn up, I can't get a bead on it. I didn't realize this until I started working on it, but I don't think this guy is pushing commands to SUNGRAZER." She pointed at the device on the top bunk again. "I think SUNGRAZER is pulling from *it*."

Lincoln's mind made the connection without any conscious effort from him.

"It's a dead drop," he said.

Everyone looked at him. Thumper thought for a moment, then nodded.

"Yeah. Yeah, that's a good way to think about it," she said. "Command pushes orders to a location, SUNGRAZER picks them up when she can. Another layer of security."

It was an old spy term, from tradecraft. One spy could leave an item or a message somewhere, another could retrieve it later when it was safe to do so. Neither spy had to know the other, there was no direct contact between them that could be exploited, and it minimized the need for arranging meetings. Typically the thing being exchanged was disguised in such a way that anyone who came across it either wouldn't notice it, or wouldn't realize it was anything important. A simple tactic that mitigated a substantial risk of compromise.

"That sounds like a bad way to work," Mike said. "Warship running around out there that maybe will follow your orders whenever it gets around to picking it up."

"She's a smart ship, Mikey. Whole point is that she can mostly operate without a lot of back-and-forth from command. I'm sure she's got some kind of protocol about what she does when a new order comes in and she can't retrieve it yet. But we're also probably talking milliseconds here. Minutes at most, not like hours or anything."

"Can you re-engineer this piece? Force feed SUNGRAZER some commands of our own? Or get her to call home?"

"No, I think I blew that part when I started monkeying with it. Pretty sure this one's toast. Marked as compromised, at the very least."

"Well maybe that's not so bad," Mike said. "If that means we just cut off their contact with SUNGRAZER."

"I wish," Thumper answered. "But no, we're pretty sure this is just one of several channels they have to her. Most likely, they're cycling through, using different ones at different times. The fact that one went dark probably isn't that big a deal to them. I'd guess they were counting on it, eventually. Folks we're dealing with are smart. Planning types."

"And this isn't just acting on a target of opportunity," Lincoln said. "This level of planning and prep."

Thumper shook her head. "They had to have been working on this for several weeks at least. Maybe even months."

"So the big question is, how'd they even know about SUNGRAZER in the first place?"

"One of the big questions, yes. Also, how long did they know about it before they acted? And why go to all this trouble?"

"This thing was supposed to give us *answers*," Lincoln said, thumping the device they'd recovered. "Not more questions." He pointed at the ice cap region of the terrible diagram. "So this signal here. You said you were going to tell me what it was."

"Yeah, yeah, sure, here," Thumper said. She waved away her handcrafted image and pulled up reconnaissance imagery of a small dome placed on the Martian surface. Ice tendrilled and veined its way over the terrain, its blue-white stark against the patches of red. From the looks of it, the structure was old, still using hard-shell tech for environmental protection and control. "I believe it's an old research facility. Placement matches some records I dug up for an environmental study, back during early colonization days. But they shut it down a couple of decades ago."

"Sounds like some new tenants moved in," Lincoln said.

"Sounds like our *next target*," Wright added.

Lincoln looked around at his team. Nodded. "Guess I better go call Mom."

•••

"How certain are you?" Colonel Almeida asked.

"It's all coming from Thumper's work," Lincoln answered. "How certain would you be?"

The colonel grunted. "More certain than if I'd done it all myself." He sighed and scratched his nose with his prosthetic hand. "Can't ever be easy, huh?"

"I reckon not, sir."

"Timing really couldn't be worse. The Collective Republic just started the official process of calling for a summit, working to normalize relations between Earth and Mars again."

"What's your read on CMA?" Lincoln asked. Technically the Central Martian Authority was the unified ruling body, comprised of representatives from all the member colonies and settlements. The various governments on the red planet still maintained sovereignty, but apart from the occasional squabble over trade rights and taxation, thus far, whenever the CMA had issued a decision, they'd all fallen in line on the major points.

"A lot of posturing, for the most part. I think they want us to blink first real bad, and I don't think the majority of those people actually want war. There are a couple of groups up there that want to get after it with us, but given enough time I think cooler heads will prevail. But… it's delicate with the MPCR. Depends on the egos in play, I guess. CMA might not actually want war, but they don't want to seem like they're afraid to go toe-to-toe with big brother Earth. *I* believe they want peace, eventually. But they also can't afford to let it look like the Republic made the decision, and imposed it on everyone else."

"You think they'll go along with the summit?"

"Eventually. And then afterwards, I think they'll

spend a couple of months hemming and hawing and pretending like they came up with the idea of pursuing peace on their own."

"Is there a timeframe on that? Getting an official diplomatic summit together?"

"Not yet, not officially. MPCR's making the PR push, but CMA hasn't acknowledged it as a consideration yet. The fact that they're thinking about it isn't even on the public airwaves yet, it's all backroom chatter at the moment. And even after the decision gets made, there will still be a few weeks of shaping public opinion before anybody announces anything. So not immediate, but it's on the horizon."

"And if something were to happen in the meantime," Lincoln said. "Say, oh I don't know, a secret United States vessel suddenly appearing in Martian-owned space?"

"Yeah," Almeida said. "Could tip things the wrong way, that's for sure. It'd be real hard to deny involvement with that one, except for the one hitch of proving UAF involvement. No reason to steal a secret, untraceable US vessel if you want to make it easy to pin the whole thing on the UAF."

For whatever reason, the distinction between the US and the Federation hadn't seemed like a major factor to Lincoln until just now. But the colonel's words brought it into stark relief. To this point, he'd been operating under the assumption that the end goal was to further hostilities between Mars and Earth, specifically between the UAF and the Central Martian Authority. But now it struck him that there was another layer to consider, perhaps another game being played. For the first time, his brain started churning on what would happen if war kicked off as the result of perceived US actions. Actions unknown and unsanctioned by the Federation. There was no telling what political consequences might follow, but it was a safe bet that whatever they were wouldn't help the war effort.

"I think it's the doubt they're after, sir," he said. "On both sides of the equation. Or, all sides, I guess. I'm losing track of how many sides there are these days. But they're throwing just enough mist and shadow around so no one knows who or what to believe anymore. Easier to keep everybody afraid and reactionary."

"Over-reactionary, more like," said the colonel. "But if the plan is to violate sovereign space or even carry out some sort of strike, why haven't they done it yet? I wouldn't want to be holding a potato that hot for any longer than I absolutely had to."

"That's the thing we're chasing down right now."

"Chase faster," said Almeida, with a quick smile. "No chance the Directorate wants to back-channel it, I suppose? Warn UAF and the CMA about SUNGRAZER?"

The colonel barked a laugh. "Aw, son. You're still a pup at heart, aren't you?" The old man shook his head. "No, kiddo. No, I don't suspect anybody's going to be feeling honest and friendly enough to go trying to avert a potentially deniable diplomatic disaster with a guaranteed one. At this stage, CMA would probably broadcast the news and spin it as a really stupid attempt to cover an already-planned attack."

Lincoln nodded. And that nagging sensation he'd had before they'd launched the *Ava Leyla* operation came back, this time with a hint of dread. The thought that he couldn't quite capture previously became clearer.

"You know the thing that's really bugging me, sir," he said, "is that when we first got word SUNGRAZER had gone dark, it seemed so random. But the longer we sit with it, well... it actually is starting to feel familiar. A little too familiar. Not the start of something new. The continuation of something from before."

"You think this is Plan B in action?"

"Or more of Plan A," Lincoln said. Uncomfortable memories started bumping around again. Unanswered questions he'd tried to forget stirred, threatened to come awake. A woman's final words, about war not being an event, but a process.

"So what are you doing about it?" the colonel asked.

"I have a bad idea."

"All my best ideas are bad ideas."

"We've been working real hard not to draw any attention to the fact that we're on to these guys. I'm thinking maybe it's time we take the opposite approach."

Almeida grunted. "You want to throw a shot, see how they take it."

Lincoln nodded. "Yes sir, I do. Introduce a little chaos into their calculations for a change. Starting with this research facility."

"NID's not going to like that too much."

"No sir, I suspect they won't."

"You might just end up accelerating the bad guys' plans."

"Possible, yes sir. But I also expect my team to adapt faster. I know how my people handle chaos. I want to see how *their* people deal with it."

"Risky," Almeida said. Then he smiled. "I knew you were the right one for this job."

"Well, sir," Lincoln replied, "according to my data, between the two of us, fifty percent agree."

"All right. You're cleared to check out whatever's going on at that research facility, but steer clear of the Republic for now. At least until you get something more concrete to work with. *Much* more concrete. I'm talking names, home addresses, Christmas wish lists. That ground is tricky enough to operate in as it is. I don't want you running around in there unless you have very well-defined targets and objectives."

"Roger that," Lincoln said.

"Getting you on site is going to take some doing. I'll coordinate with NID, and get back to you with the logistics as soon as possible."

"Not going to mention the Collective just yet, are you?"

"Not a whisper, until you're already back," the colonel said. "And, if you kids do it right, maybe not even then."

THIRTEEN

The new target information arrived as SUNGRAZER had anticipated, and while she ran her protocols to verify the command, she evaluated the objective in parallel. A military target, concealed and embedded in a civilian-centric area. High population, strategic value readily apparent, risk of collateral damage substantial.

Precisely the kind of strike for which she had been created.

SUNGRAZER understood human psychology in her own way; clinically, as a thing long-observed. Statistically, the devastation would be insignificant. A pinprick. The impact, however, could shift an entire culture, shape the course of history. The sudden disruption of normal life, the shattering of illusions of security. A reminder of vulnerability. The nation would tremble under such force, so precisely and unexpectedly applied, as a man struck without warning in a cluster of nerves. The strike would surely provoke a response, though what that response would be SUNGRAZER could not predict. Fear, outrage, certainly. Submission, perhaps.

Additional commands revealed a novel detail; an unusual, specified post-launch protocol. Narrow constraints on her escape vector. A shallow trajectory.

It took her less than a tenth of a second to simulate the probable outcome a hundred thousand times.

She understood; she was a simple tool of policy, projected forward into hostile territory, or that which may one day become hostile. A single piece moving in a long game, to an end beyond her power to see.

With her initial calculations and systems checks completed, SUNGRAZER turned about and began her long journey to target.

FOURTEEN

It was a stupid idea. And one of the ways Lincoln knew it was such a stupid idea was the fact that the military continued to insist on doing it. He hadn't done a live low-orbit jump in years. He'd done plenty in training of course, enough to qualify and many more to stay that way. But there'd never really been a need for it in any of the live operations he'd done. Most of his operational career had been on good old terra firma, with the occasional jaunt to a hop or a vessel. The closest thing he'd done to a live jump had been on Luna, but with its lack of atmosphere and minimal gravity, he didn't really count that. Neither did any of the other vets he knew who'd actually deployed into combat in such a manner.

The chain of events that had led to him standing here, on top of a cargo ship, looking down at Mars, was a testament to the absolute mastery the US military had over logistics. From the skiff to the *Durham*, from the *Durham* to a fastboat, to a Marine transport, to an outpost space station, where they were picked up for the final leg of the journey. The Barton brothers had remained behind on the Marine transport, not without some protest. But once they found out what the rest of their new teammates were about to do, they both seemed more content with the decision.

The Central Martian Authority still had elevated security in place on all its approach avenues, doubly so where orbital lanes were concerned. That being the case, the Outriders were hitching a ride to their final destination on a commercial cargo vessel, operated by the Saint Michael's Shipping Company.

Saint Michael's Shipping was the business arm of a Luna-based monastery, and one of the most trusted long-haul corporations in the solar system. Their success story was well-known. The way Lincoln had heard it, the company had originally started with a single donated vessel, with a simple goal of serving the Lunar community and as a means to help sustain the monastery financially. Their prices were modest. But the monks' reputation for integrity and careful attention in all things had led to such explosive demand, over time they'd expanded to become a system-wide service, running from the floating cities of Venus all the way out to the far-reach hops near the belt, and everywhere in between. And now, financially, they were sustaining a whole lot more than just their abbey; they were supposedly something like number five or seven on the top ten list of most philanthropic organizations on Earth. All the more impressive since they still only had the one abbey, on the moon. Their prices remained modest.

Before they'd left the space station, Lincoln had met briefly with the monk who was piloting the vessel. An elderly man by the name of August, with a stooped back, few words, and a kindly smile. There hadn't been much conversation. Lincoln naturally couldn't say anything about the nature of the shipment August would be hauling; August seemed to have a polite aversion to idle conversation and a well-cultivated lack of questions.

Lincoln did manage to learn that the monk was just beginning six months of travel in solitude, with only the occasional stop to make or pick up deliveries for far-reach stations. August had simply referred to it as his "time of devotion".

They were monks of the Christian faith, and their ships were technically classified as places of worship. Lincoln didn't know the details of the arrangement. Only that August would be carrying their cargo from the station to a UAF Naval research facility out towards the Belt, and taking a path over Mars to do so. Whether or not he was aware that the Outriders would be along for the journey, or for a small part of it at least, Lincoln didn't know. August had taken care to mention specifically how his route would require entering low Martian orbit, and remarking upon God's wondrous provision, how he'd never had the opportunity to personally view the ice cap before and looked forward to doing so. The sentiment seemed utterly genuine, but given his otherwise laconic nature, that seemed also to be his careful way of communicating that he understood the importance of that particular trajectory.

Lincoln wasn't a religious man himself, but he had said a little prayer afterward anyway, just in case, asking for forgiveness if there'd been any deception involved and promising that if there had been, it was for a good cause. At least Saint Michael was the patron saint of the military. Maybe that made it all OK.

After meeting with August, Lincoln and his team had loaded up into two separate cargo containers, specially designed to house their gear, their dropsuits, and themselves. The containers were something like small apartments, if your apartment was just a closet with a chemical toilet in it, and you had a roommate who was a mechanic who liked to keep all his gear in your bedroom. Like all things military, one thing the containers had not been designed for was comfort. Sahil, Mike, and Lincoln had bunked up together, and the fit was not quite tight enough for them to have to literally sleep on top of each other. Even so, they slept in shifts, one man racking out while the other two tried to keep from going crazy. That left Wright and Thumper in the second container, with a little extra space. Lincoln had said it was to give the ladies some girl time together, but in reality it was because Thumper had drawn the short straw. No one wanted to be in a box with a restless Wright for three days. Even Wright. She'd said it wasn't fair she didn't get to draw straws too.

The Saint Michael's vessel had both internal cargo bays as well as externally-mounted attachment points, where shipments could be easily handled by station loading crews without need for much direct interaction. The Outriders' special containers were the only two set into the midsection attachment points atop the ship, side by side. When they'd loaded in, Lincoln had wondered if any pirates had ever been dumb or desperate enough to try ripping containers right off the outside of a Saint Michael's vessel. The monastery's ships had no attack capability, but supposedly had some of the most advanced and effective defensive measures in existence. Not least of which, Lincoln assumed, was the very hand of God.

It had been seventy-four hours of travel since they'd first entered the containers. And all of that had led him here to this moment, standing on an exterior platform designed for use as a staging area for loading cargo. Obviously, the vessel they'd hitched a ride on didn't have a proper jump bay. The platform they were using instead was wide and flat, and had not even a suggestion of a hand rail. Their containers were still in place attached to the ship, their inconspicuous airlocks resealed for the journey to the naval base.

And about two hundred and fifty kilometers below was Mars. Specifically, the Northern polar ice cap of Mars.

And Lincoln was nervous. Oddly, his discomfort with open space didn't really come into play in these situations. There was, after all, a giant rock down there, and there was literally zero chance of him missing it on the way down. It wasn't even the idea of falling for so long that bothered him. What was eating at him was the fact that even though it looked like it was more or less a straight drop from here to there, Lincoln knew he was actually flying, for lack of a better term, *sideways* at ridiculous speeds. In deep space, it never mattered that much how fast a ship was going when he was walking around on its exterior, because there was nothing to compare it to. But it was pretty hard to ignore orbital velocity when you wanted to get *down,* and you had to spend so much time going *sideways.*

A giant dropsuit lumbered up beside him, almost comical in its bulk. Like a child's inflated drawing of a man.

"Don't sweat it, sir," Mike said, over comms. "It'll be the most relaxing twenty minute freefall of your life."

"It's not the fall I'm worried about," Lincoln answered.

Mike took a step closer to the edge and leaned over for effect, getting a better view of the planet below.

"Oh, don't worry, Cap'n," Mike said. "This one's gonna be real hard to miss."

"We're missing it right now," Thumper said. She was standing behind them, well away from the edge of the platform. "We're already falling towards Mars. The only reason we aren't getting any closer is because we're missing it."

Lincoln sighed, closed his eyes.

"OK," he said. "*Now* I'm worried about the fall."

He reopened his eyes, checked the time-to-jump on his internal display. Three minutes, fourteen seconds. Calling it a jump was a little misleading. There wasn't much jumping involved.

Whether a dropsuit was technically powered armor or a single-occupant vehicle was still a point of contention in certain military circles. Mostly because the classification determined who was responsible for maintaining them and, thus, where the budget for them went. The ones Lincoln and his team were using had been borrowed from the Marines, who, as far as he knew, still considered them armor. Which meant that the dropsuit was like a suit for his suit.

That was, in fact, exactly what it was. Lincoln, wearing his recon suit, had loaded into the much larger dropsuit, climbing in through the rear. It felt something like wearing a high-tech snow suit, over many layers of clothes. It had arms and legs for his to slip into, though the arms ended in thumb-and-fingerless wedges, like some sort of artistic stylization of hands. Apparently there wasn't much need for manual dexterity when you were busy plummeting through an atmosphere. A snow suit, complete with mittens.

Above the shoulders, however, Lincoln felt more like he was sticking his head up into a bubble cockpit or a turret rather than a secondary helmet. He'd left the display on its default settings, which gave a wide-arc view, with two hundred degrees from side-to-side. The upper back of the suit had a large frame across the shoulders that housed the retro and stabilizing rockets, as well as the supply pod in its launcher.

The team had already completed the thirty minute process of walking through the pre-jump checklist, verifying their own suits and each other's. Like all checklist procedures, some of the items had seemed trivial and tedious at the time. Now, Lincoln was glad to be able to remind himself that they'd literally checked every little detail, to keep his mind from convincing him he'd forgotten some tiny but crucial thing.

At two minutes to launch, the team assumed their jump formation, an echelon right, with Lincoln in the center. Sahil took first position ahead and to Lincoln's left; Mike the last, behind and to his right. Wright and Thumper filled in the second and fourth positions. With a minimum three-meter gap between each, the team was spread across the curving exterior of the ship such that, from Lincoln's point of view, it almost seemed like Sahil was in danger of sliding right off the edge. It was a silly thought, considering what they were about to do. But the unease was instinctual, and Lincoln mitigated it by refusing to look in that direction. There was plenty else he could focus on, if he so chose. Mostly he just kept his eyes on that countdown. He wasn't usually this nervous. About anything.

Sixty seconds.

"This is gonna be fun," Mike said. "I feel good about this."

Thumper and Wright both chuckled. Even Lincoln smiled at the words. It was something he himself frequently said just before the start of an operation, particularly when he was feeling the opposite. He'd been too preoccupied to think about it. Mike was either poking fun at him, or covering for him. Both, most likely.

Sahil launched first. Since Lincoln had been studiously

not looking at Sahil, all he saw was a flare and a streak of motion as Sahil's dropsuit rockets fired and shot him off the vessel. Of course, in reality Sahil wasn't flying away from the vessel, the vessel was flying away from Sahil; he wasn't speeding off, he was slowing down. Aggressively.

Five seconds later, Wright launched in the same fashion. Which meant Lincoln had five seconds left until he was up.

Four.

For some odd reason, at three seconds to launch, Lincoln found himself concerned that these dropsuits had been "borrowed" from the Marines. He had no idea how they would ever get them back.

And then his thrusters fired.

It was like falling in the wrong direction. Or being a rock fired from a slingshot. Now Lincoln regretted what he had done to all those rocks as a kid and asked for their forgiveness as he hurtled off the ship and out into space, with Mars waiting eagerly below to smash him to pieces. In about twenty minutes.

Lincoln had done plenty of conventional skydiving and other high-altitude activities in his day, but this was a whole different ball game.

According to the dropsuit, the launch and deceleration protocol was proceeding smoothly, and all systems were green. From Lincoln's perspective, there wasn't anything smooth about any of it, though he did feel like he too might be green. It hadn't been like this on Luna. He hoped he didn't throw up. The recon suit had mechanisms for dealing with various such predicaments to keep its occupant from asphyxiating, but he didn't want to have to run the initial stage of the op with that taste in his mouth.

Indicators on the left side of his display tracked his

companions, all of whom had good launches. They were strung out across the Martian exosphere, dropsuits autopiloting them towards one another as the initial launch phase drew to a close, and EDL protocols prepared to kick off. According to official military terminology, an orbital jump went through three distinct phases: Entry, Descent, and Landing. EDL.

Or, as everyone who'd ever qualified for Orbital Jump School knew it, Extreme Death Likely.

From Lincoln's perspective, it appeared that Sahil, up front, was slowing to allow the others to catch up. In reality, of course, it was the opposite. Mike, at the back of the echelon, was decelerating harder than the rest of them. The group closed in, reforming their line while maintaining the all-important thirty meter safety gap. Visually, it seemed like a lot of space to keep between them, but Lincoln knew he was moving about ten times that distance every second. He didn't know his exact velocity. He'd turned that part of his display off because he just didn't want to know. For a moment, he even considered shutting the entire display off, so he wouldn't have to stare at the planet's surface's inexorable approach. But then he decided against it, only because he figured being afraid was better than being afraid *and* bored.

Once they passed the two hundred kilometer mark they officially began the Entry phase as they reached some imaginary line that the eggheads back home had no doubt calculated to be the technical edge of the Martian atmosphere. Not that there was any obvious indication, apart from the message on his display. There was no neat border, no welcome sign, not even a detectable shiver or shudder. It all just felt like falling. And it was going to feel that way for a while.

"Wish I'd brought something to read," Mike said, a few minutes after launch.

"Usually I like to nap," Thumper answered cheerfully. "But I'm just so glad to finally get some time away from Amira, I decided to stay awake for this one."

"Keep the channel clear," Wright barked. And then added, "And I'm a great roommate." As usual, she said it deadpan, but Lincoln had learned to hear the curl of her words that suggested a smile even when her face lacked the expression.

The team's relative horizontal velocity stabilized in synchronization, and their rockets winked out. In true freefall, now. Lincoln shifted into the traditional skydiving position, legs bent at the knees, arms out to the sides and bent ninety degrees at the elbow. He tried to relax.

Despite all the falling going on, EDL was mostly E by protocol standards. Descent didn't really begin until they'd used as much of the atmosphere to slow themselves as they could. Throughout that Entry phase, the dropsuits gradually took on their telltale orange glow from the friction and heat buildup. Lincoln couldn't see what was going on with his own suit, but ahead of him Sahil and Wright looked like embers floating down from the heavens.

At fifty kilometers from the surface, the team transitioned into a second formation in preparation for the Descent phase. The echelon's ends rotated and wrapped inward as if Lincoln were a hinge, until they were in a loose ring maybe twenty meters in diameter, with everyone's heads facing towards the center.

At twenty kilometers, a pop vibrated Lincoln's suit as the supply pod separated and launched itself away, headed towards its calculated drop point. Its chute would open after Lincoln's, guaranteeing that the heavy cargo would touch down first so as to not crush the operator it was meant to supply. The landing protocol was supposed to keep it within fifteen meters of his landing site, but Lincoln knew enough about jumps to suspect he was going to be walking a lot farther than that to retrieve his gear.

Crossing the twenty kilometer threshold made Lincoln's nerves kick up for a moment; the surface seemed so close now. He had to remind himself just how far twenty klicks actually was. Relative to their starting point, sure, they were almost right on top of Mars, but when he thought about what it'd be like to have to patrol that distance, he felt better. He even started to enjoy the view, looking at the tendrils of ice stretching long fingers out into the Martian soil, like a child sinking hands into the wet sand of a red beach. His body had almost adjusted to the constant feeling of falling; if he ignored the fact that he was plummeting, he found the peace and quiet of the surface almost soothing. Off in the distance, he could make out the snaking line of the vast Chasma Boreale canyon in the ice cap, its red-lined cliffs apparent even at altitude. It struck him then how fortunate he really was, to be among so few humans who ever had the chance to see such things with their own eyes. He couldn't help but wonder about August all the way back up there, and whether or not he'd finally gotten his view of the ice cap.

A few seconds later, something went catastrophically wrong.

A pop and a zip, and Lincoln tumbled violently backward. He let out an involuntary cry, scanned frantically for any sign or warning of what had happened to his suit. To his great embarrassment, he realized his chute had deployed, officially marking the beginning of the Descent phase.

"Lincoln," Wright said over comms, "you OK?"

"I'm good," Lincoln answered. "I just uh… just dozed off on the way down."

The Descent phase was a lot like regular atmospheric jumps. The thin atmosphere required a special chute design, much larger than what he'd been used to back home, but the general idea was the same. The wedge-like heat shield covers over his hands ejected, revealing fat-fingered gloves that made it look like his hands had swollen up with some sort of allergic reaction.

Lincoln scanned around him, saw that each of his teammates had good openings on their chutes. The timing hadn't been perfect; Sahil was a few meters higher up than most of them, and Thumper a little lower. That wouldn't pose any problems, as long as everyone kept their lanes clear. Even in the thin Martian atmosphere, the slowing from the parachute was dramatic. Lincoln had gotten used to watching his altitude decrease so quickly, he'd sort of forgotten just how long those last few kilometers were going to take. During the Descent phase, he expanded the view projected on the dropsuit's helmet and adjusted it in order to get a better view of the terrain. They were low enough now that he could start getting oriented. In addition to the marker for the landing zone, he brought up indicators for both their planned base camp and the target facility. The sites were off his right shoulder, and, from so high up, looked almost shockingly close together. Lincoln knew, however, he wouldn't be thinking that when they were making the walk.

After a few minutes of graceful descent, a chirp informed him that the dropsuit was about to detach from the parachute. He'd survived the Extreme and Death phases. But most people did. It was the Likely part you had to worry about.

A few seconds later, the chute clacked loose and Lincoln was briefly in freefall. Within three seconds, a whoosh became a roar as the dropsuit's rockets fired off once more, providing the final-stage thrust that would prevent Lincoln from creating a new, shallow, and unimpressive crater on Mars. The ground rushed towards him like a lonely hound greeting his master, and then seemed to change its mind, slowing its approach to one of casual indifference, until at last Lincoln felt like a dandelion seed, floating on a gentle breeze. He chuckled at the thought. It was a ridiculous comparison, considering he'd seen from the outside what it looked like when a thousand-pound suit touched down. There was nothing dandelion-like about it.

The rockets shut off an instant before his feet hit the ground, and he made contact with about the same force as if he'd jumped off a short ladder, instead of from a ship two hundred and fifty kilometers above. Once he was safely down, Lincoln thanked God for the ground, the Marines for the suit, and all the eggheads back home who'd devoted their lives to math and physics so that he could do the fun stuff.

The rest of the team had good landings as well, though they were a little more spread out than originally intended. There were, of course, no gravity generators this far out from civilization. Getting gathered up took some effort, as they all had to get accustomed to the lower gravity.

"Everybody good?" Lincoln asked.

"Yep," Thumper answered.

"All good," Mike said.

"Good," said Wright.

Sahil gave a neutral wave of his hand, like he didn't want to talk about it.

"Sahil?" Lincoln said.

"Good, sir," he said, but his voice sounded off.

"You're not hurt are you?"

"No," Sahil replied. He didn't sound happy.

"You have a hard landing?"

He waved his hand again, more aggressively this time.

"Sahil, if you're busted up," Lincoln said, "I need to know right now, this isn't the kind of place you can just tough it out–"

"Puked in my suit, all right?" he snapped, "Can we go now?"

"Ugh," Thumper said. "That's literally the worst."

"One time," Mike said with a chuckle, "when I was at Bragg–"

"Not now, Mikey," Wright interrupted. "We need to get moving."

"Roger that," Lincoln said.

The first order of business, once his teammates were all accounted for, was to recover their supply pods. And that was just the beginning. Once they were loaded back up, they still had an eight kilometer trek from the landing zone to the crater they'd picked out for their temporary base camp. After three days in a box, Lincoln had been looking forward to getting out under a sky again. But after having fallen through one for half an hour, now he was thinking it might be nice to have a roof again.

"And, just 'cause I'm havin' such a good day," Sahil said. "Looks like my pod burned in and skipped on impact. How far out you want me to go lookin'?"

"Locator still working?" Lincoln asked.

"Nah, but I watched it comin' in. I know the general direction."

"Two hundred fifty meters," Lincoln answered. "If we can't see it by then, we'll re-evaluate. But hold up, we'll all go."

Sahil trailed along while the others bounded out to their supply pods and got them loaded back on to the dropsuits. Lincoln understood the reasoning for the separation; every pound they could shave off the dropsuit made it easier on the landing, and between the suit and the pod, the suit was carrying the more precious cargo. If one of them had to have a hard landing, it was better for it to be the supply pod. Still, given the unwieldy design of the pod and the complication of the dropsuit's fat hands, it was a pain to deal with getting the two reunited. By the time they'd recovered four of the pods and were ready to start the search for Sahil's, Lincoln had half a mind to abandon it, just to save the effort.

They had redundant supplies for this exact scenario, and could have scraped by if only three of the five pods had survived. But they were going to be uncomfortable enough as it was, and he knew that once he'd had a chance to rest a few minutes, he'd be cursing himself for his laziness if they didn't salvage everything they could. When everyone else was loaded up, the team set off together in a shallow wedge formation with Sahil taking the lead, headed in the direction of his errant supplies.

It took them all a few minutes to learn how to walk again. A normal stride was impossible to maintain, and the cumbersome dropsuits didn't make things any easier. Lincoln finally settled on a sort of shuffling hop. Once he got the hang of it, though, he couldn't help but have a little fun with it, taking the occasional bounding step.

On one particular hop, he added a little twist at the peak, for effect.

"Wow, sir," Mike said. "I didn't realize Master Sergeant's been giving you ballet lessons."

"That good, huh?" Lincoln replied.

"That bad," Thumper answered.

Wright didn't say anything about the comment, but a few seconds later she took a bound of her own and pulled a full 360-degree twist before touching down again. Even Sahil laughed aloud. After that, it wasn't the most professional patrol Lincoln had ever been a part of. But out here in the empty Martian wastes, after three days in a box, the team let loose a little bit and seemed to relax into the trek. Which was good, since once they recovered Sahil's supplies, they still had several kilometers of open Martian terrain to cover before nightfall.

FIFTEEN

Elliot waited in the lobby or the foyer or entryway, or whatever the small, drafty room by the establishment's front door was supposed to be. "Establishment" was the best word he could come up with for the place. It wasn't a bar or a restaurant, was neither diner nor pub, but was perhaps some kind of confused mix of the four. Not his choice. Not his contact's, either. Just the luck of the random draw, one option of many in a pool of casual spots neither of them frequented but weren't so far out of the norm as to attract attention. The ceiling was about eight inches too low; not enough to bump his head on, but enough to make him instinctively hunch anyway. A "Please Wait To Be Seated" sign stood guard by the entrance, which is why he hadn't chosen one of the many empty tables available to him. He'd waited long enough to at least entertain the thought that maybe someone had forgotten to remove the sign, but when he'd started to take a step beyond it, a surly man behind a counter gave him a sidelong glance that made him keep his place.

So he waited. There was an aquarium against the wall, maybe fifty gallons' worth of water and plants and fish and rocks and the wrong kind of sand, all laid out by someone who had obviously never seen an ocean. Who probably couldn't even imagine one, for that matter. There was even a little crab sitting on a floating island, looking about as resigned to its fate as Elliot felt to his. Elliot reached out and tapped on the glass at the crab. It responded by raising both tiny claws above its head; most likely it thought it was doing so in a threatening manner, but to Elliot it looked more like it was raising its arms in celebration.

"Yaaay," Elliot said quietly.

The man behind the counter grunted aggressively and when Elliot looked at him, the man pointed severely at the sign above the tank, unnoticed by Elliot until that moment, handwritten in bold block letters: DO NOT TAP GLASS.

Elliot waved an apology at the man.

"Just sit anywhere," the man said, waggling his hand at all the empty tables. A couple of the regulars glanced over and chuckled, but the other handful of people in the place paid no mind. "I don't know where my waiter went."

"Thanks," Elliot said.

"You know what you want?" the man behind the counter said as Elliot passed by, gruff but not unfriendly.

"Just some tea," Elliot answered.

"Only got green."

"That's fine."

The man nodded. Elliot took a seat at a table for two, a couple of empties away from a pair of older gentlemen who were nursing pints and quietly arguing about something they'd probably been arguing about every night for the past twenty years. The place had that sort of vibe to it. A low-key neighborhood stop in, good for people who didn't feel like going out but who didn't want to stay at home either.

The man from behind the counter plodded over and delivered a small pot of tea along with two simple white mugs.

"Got company coming?" he asked, dipping his head at the empty chair.

Elliot shook his head.

"You want anything else, come up to the counter," the man said. He looked tired.

"Long day?" Elliot asked.

"Every day," the man answered, as he stumped his way back to his post.

"I know that feeling," Elliot replied. He let his tea steep for a few minutes, and then poured a mug and spent a few more watching the steam curl and fold in on itself as it ascended and eventually vanished. For all their individual twists and turns, the fate of each wisp was the same. A brief rise, then oblivion.

It reminded him of his career.

Or rather, he was already thinking about his career, and the steam provided a convenient visualization for the inevitable. He'd played it the best he could. And now he was out of options.

That wasn't strictly true. He actually had several. It's just that as far as he could see, they all ended in the same place; with him dead in some shallow, unmarked grave, covered up and forcefully forgotten.

Elliot slipped his hand in his jacket pocket and fiddled with the device inside, flipping the small flat disk end over end between his fingertips. He'd made compromises before, hadn't always played strictly by the rules. That was the job. And over the years he'd had a few deals on the side, because NID work didn't pay all that well, particularly when you considered what they asked of you. There was surprisingly little money in protecting a nation.

Even so, this felt like crossing a line he'd never thought he'd even be close enough to see. Somehow a series of small decisions had led him to a place he'd always assumed would require a much bigger decision somewhere along the way. But maybe this was always how it happened. Good people, giving of themselves for the greater good, and eventually discovering that when it came right down to it, the greater good didn't return the loyalty. He'd burned assets before, for the greater good. He'd just never thought he'd find himself on this side of it.

"Hey," a voice said. One of the older gentlemen nearby.

"Hey, fella," he said again, and Elliot finally realized the man was talking to him.

"Sir?" Elliot responded. He didn't feel like talking, and hoped his stiff reply and facial expression communicated it. Both the men were turned in their seats, looking at him. For some reason they looked like a Bob and a Joe.

"You're an out-of-towner," said Bob.

Elliot wasn't sure if it was a question or a statement.

"OK," he answered. And then looked back at the cup in front of him.

"So who would you favor, then?" Bob continued, as if Elliot had been part of their conversation the whole time.

"I'm sorry?"

"In a dust up? Earth or Mars?"

Elliot looked back and forth between the two old timers. Martian lifers from the looks of them, but old enough that they might have loyalties to the old world. He was guessing one of them did, anyway, if that's what they'd been arguing about.

"War's a tricky business," Elliot said with a shrug. "Don't think I'd favor either side by much."

Bob and Joe exchanged a look, and then Bob chuckled.

"We're talking about football, fella," he said. "All-star teams, best of both worlds, head-to-head. Football!"

The look on Bob's face was like a sun ray piercing a cloud, giving Elliot a glimpse of a distant land he'd almost forgotten existed. One where people had time to sit and passionately argue about unimportant matters, where security was so assured it wasn't even a consideration, and tomorrow was guaranteed.

"Yeah... yeah, of course," Elliot said, shaking his head and covering the mistake, poorly. "I just mean, you know... something as serious as football, you have to expect everyone's going to be bringing out the big guns. No telling which way that might go."

"A proper world war then, yeah?" Joe said.

"Count on it."

"Didn't answer the question though, I note," Bob replied.

"I hate to pick sides," Elliot answered. And then gave them a smile. "At least until I see who's ahead."

"Ah," Bob said, and then he gave Joe a nod and a wink, as if Elliot had proved the point, "ah yeah, see what I told you. Too close to call, like I said."

Joe waved dismissively. "Not with the pride of the planet on the line, no way our folks let a bunch of island hoppers get the better."

Island hoppers. Elliot chuckled to himself at the comment. It didn't matter how big Earth's continents were; as far as some Martians were concerned, anyone on a planet with that much water couldn't be anything but an islander.

"And why should it be any different for them, though?" Bob said. "They don't have their own pride?"

"Well sure they do," Joe answered, taking a swig of his beer. "It just doesn't matter, because they aren't as good."

"There's the one fella... goalkeeper for one of the big leagues down there..." Bob said, and the two men turned back in their seats and resumed their conversation, getting just about every Terran geographic detail wrong as they tried to remember where the goalkeeper was from.

"Of course," Elliot answered. "I think you fellas are missing the key to the debate..."

The men looked back at him.

"Yeah?" said Bob. "What's that?"

Elliot took a long drink of his tea, then leaned forward in conspiracy and asked over the top of the mug, "Where do you get the refs?"

The men blinked at him for a moment.

"'Where do you get the refs?'" Joe repeated, and then wheezed an almost silent laugh. The three shared the moment, and Bob gave Elliot a long look.

"You maybe lay off the newsies a bit, fella," he said, with grandfatherly kindness. "Wears a man thin the way they chatter all day about nothin'."

"Good advice, sir," Elliot said.

"Free, too," Bob said with a smile. He tipped his pint in Elliot's direction, and turned once more to his old friend. The two men resumed their debate, though followed it down a side trail and argued for a while about how many Americas there were and whether or not they were all the same thing as the United States.

Elliot didn't correct them, just smiled down into his mug. It would have been nice to have had a friend like that. A life like that. But he'd given that up a long time ago, before he'd known its value. And there was no unmaking that decision now, no matter how much he wished he could.

It'd been long enough. He reached under the table and firmly pressed the device from his pocket into place, where it held fast and would remain until his contact came to retrieve it. Once the disk was affixed to the underside of the table, Elliot leaned forward and propped his head on his fist, and absently traced a design on the table's surface with a fingertip. The pattern was invisible to the naked eye, but would be unmistakable to his contact's enhanced optics.

He'd done a lot of things he wasn't proud of in his life. Things he'd convinced himself were necessary. This one was going to be the hardest of them all. But the first step in learning to live with himself was to stay alive in the first place.

He drained the rest of his tea, and got to his feet.

"'Night, gentlemen," Elliot said to Joe and Bob. Bob waved without looking in his direction.

Elliot paid the man behind the counter and walked out the front door, knowing that whatever chain of events he'd just kicked off would summon a whirlwind, with thin hope that once it had passed through he might somehow find himself still standing.

SIXTEEN

"I don't mind the cold," Mike said, lying next to Lincoln on the ridgeline.

The pair had been observing the research facility down below for almost nineteen hours now, and though they were a good thirty klicks away from the farthest reaches of the ice cap or so, the climate was decidedly chilly. By Martian reckoning, Second September was just beginning, which meant, if Lincoln's elementary school hadn't misinformed him, they were in the early days of the hemisphere's autumn. Not that the temperature really mattered, since their recon suits were completely sealed and environmentally-controlled.

"Kind of used to it really," Mike added.

"You're a real trooper, Mikey," Lincoln answered, only half-listening. There was some activity near one of the out-buildings, and he was busy trying to maneuver one of their skeeters into position overhead for a better view.

The target installation was hard-shelled, sealed off and protected from the harsh environment. Like the base camp the Outriders had set up ten kilometers away, the facility was set down in a wide crater for added protection. One central building, with four smaller

ones arrayed around it. The main building and three
of the outer ones sunk low in the Martian soil, a sure
sign that they extended below ground, as so many early
constructions did. By the time Lincoln got the skeeter
in position, whoever had been moving around had
disappeared again. He left the microdrone loitering, just
in case the people decided to come back out into the
open any time soon.

As Thumper had said, the place was clearly a few
decades old. Its shell wasn't quite fully transparent
anymore, having taken on a yellowed tint everywhere,
with a milky translucence forming in spots. Martian dust
clung in patches to areas where the antistatic repellent
had worn away. The obscuring effects of the aging shell
apparently weren't enough to interfere with the solar
collectors housed within, but they had forced Lincoln
and Mike to change positions a few times in order to get
a better picture of what they were dealing with.

Sahil and Wright had taken the first shift, a quick
eight-hour jaunt during the previous night to place a few
sensors and get base stations established for the skeeters.
Lincoln and his team could have run surveillance
remotely from back at their base camp, but they all
knew you could never really get the full picture without
going out yourself. Even with haptics, you couldn't get
the feel of a place, the rhythm of it, without actually
being there. Which is why he and Mike had spent most
of the day lying on a little hillock on the flat expanse
under a butterscotch sky. Now, the late afternoon settled
in around them, as the sun slipped towards the horizon.

They hadn't seen much yet.

Lincoln activated a mechanism through his display,
and a small tube extended to his mouth from the right
side of the helmet. He took a pull on it, swallowed the

mouthful of nutrient-rich, calorie-dense substance the military apparently considered food. It had a consistency somewhere between oatmeal and applesauce, with a flavor like someone's attempt at a fruit-flavored milkshake, assuming that particular someone had never actually tasted either before. There was probably a fancy name for it, but everyone Lincoln knew who'd ever had it just called it *the goop*. Typically, he tried not to subject himself to it, unless he was so hungry it interfered with his ability to focus. Unfortunately, on a long, boring op like this one, it didn't take much to interfere. He took another shot of the goop, and then bit down twice on the mouthpiece to switch its feed, in order to wash it down with a drink of unpleasantly warm water from the same tube.

Both he and Mike were running their suits with added long-duration support packs, something like a backpack that locked into the frame and provided some additional functionality for longer operations. The extra bulk was noticeable, particularly compared to how sleek the suits usually felt, but it didn't have much negative impact since they were mostly lying around anyway.

"You know, I used to think Montana was cold," Mike continued, a few moments later. "Then after I spent a winter running all over the mountains in Hamgyong, nothing really ever seemed like much more than jacket weather to me again."

"I didn't know you were in Hamgyong," Lincoln said.

"Yeah, first fall and winter of the unpleasantness," Mike replied. "Before we had any idea what we were doing."

"Whereabouts?"

"Nowhere, mostly," Mike said with a chuckle. "Kimchaek was the closest city, but we spent all our time up in the mountains. Little place we just called Big Top."

"No kidding. I was up at Big Top that following spring," Lincoln said. "Don't think we had it figured out by then either."

"No way, that's crazy."

"Yeah, I was with 1st Group then. Did a bunch of work up in Tumangang area, then got pulled over to fill in some gaps, just for a couple of months. I guess that was, April maybe?"

"Huh. Must have just missed each other. We pulled out in uh, I guess it was early March, maybe middle of. I was still baby infantry then, pure grunt mode. We had all the ice, guess you guys got there just in time for all the mud."

"Sounds about right."

"Small world," Mike said. "And chock full of people that need shooting."

"And seems to be getting fuller by the day."

Down below in the research facility, a door opened from one of the outbuildings, and two figures exited. The skeeter Lincoln had parked overhead was still in position enough to get a decent glimpse, and he brought up the feed. The two were bundled against the cold, so much that it was impossible to identify anything useful about them. Could have been men or women, young or old. Given the deep hoods and number of layers, Lincoln couldn't even guess whether they were rail thin or grossly overweight. One detail he could confirm though, was that the one in the rear was armed.

He marked the timestamp, and tried to zoom in on the weapon. The two figures crossed the short span between buildings and disappeared into the main facility before he could get a good look. The weapon was slung casually, lying low and flat along the rear of the individual's right hip. Armed, then, but not overly concerned about security. Lincoln wondered how long it'd take the individual to get a shot off with all that winter gear on.

"Heya Thumper," Lincoln said over comms. It was about forty seconds before a response came in.

"Yo," she answered, sounding like she was speaking through the tail end of a yawn.

"I wake you?"

"Nah, what's up?"

"I'm piping you a feed. We finally caught a decent look at a couple of the tenants. I dropped a marker at the interesting bit, wanted to see if you can get an ID on the weapon in the shot."

"Sure, no problem. How's it going out there?"

"Going on nineteen hours, and that twenty second clip is the whole take on our efforts."

"Hate to tell you, but that clip's only about seventeen seconds."

"Yeah, thanks, Thump. Let me know what you find."

"Roger."

Surveillance work was, in Lincoln's estimation, about one percent useful collection, six percent missed opportunities, and ninety-three percent sheer boredom. It seemed like pretty much the only time anything interesting happened was right when you'd just left your position to answer the call of nature. And since they were out in the middle of the freezing Martian expanse, there was no doing *anything* outside of the suits, which meant they never had to leave position. Which meant the chances of anything interesting happening were effectively zero.

"Nice to know we weren't completely off-base," Mike said.

"Yeah," Lincoln answered. "Guess we'll see."

Conversation lapsed for a few minutes before Mike kicked it back up again.

"You know I've served with a lot of different folks in my day," he said. "Lot of really, really good people out there. Aussies especially. I did some long-range reconnaissance training with a couple of Aussies once, a full week in the field, and the two of them never spoke a single word. Hand signals the whole time. It was insane. And the Brits. Brits are solid too. But I gotta say, out of everyone I've ever served with, I think those Korean Marines are still some of the hardest folks I ever met."

"I know what you mean," Lincoln said. "My granddad was one."

"Oh yeah? No kidding. Runs in the family then, huh?"

"Well. Skipped a generation, but yeah."

"Uh oh," said Mike.

Lincoln chuckled and said, "Yeah."

"Old man disapprove of your life choices?"

"Probably," Lincoln said. "Last I checked he still wasn't crazy about my choice of career. But, you know... that's just standard op for dads and sons, isn't it?"

"I reckon," Mike said. "Not for me, but I know I'm a lucky one."

"My dad's first generation American, and after what *his* dad went through with the first war... I think he just feels like our family's already done enough of that, maybe."

They were quiet for a span; long enough for Lincoln to start thinking about things he didn't want to think about just then.

"So," Lincoln said, taking the conversation down a safer path, "from baby infantry. How'd you end up on this career track?"

"Hamgyong, actually. We had some special operators attached to help us out up at Big Top. It got pretty rough up there at times, but you know… I really never got scared whenever I knew we had a couple of big, tough frogmen on the high ground. And I'd always been pretty handy on the long gun. Grew up hunting, so that was just part of life for me. But I never forgot what that meant to me, when I was down there on the ground, knowing somebody else was up high watching over me. So when we rotated back out, I put in for sniper school, and one thing sort of led to another. I was just always looking for ways to get better, do more work. Taking every opportunity I got. Eventually Mom came knocking."

"Glad he did."

"Yeah, me too."

The conversation lagged again for a moment, and then Mike let out a little chuckle.

"Hey," he said. "At Big Top. Was a fella named Ben still hanging around when you got there?"

"Ben…" said Lincoln, giving it a second to see if anyone came to mind. No one did. "I think you're going to have to be a little more specific."

"You'd know him if you met him," Mike said. "OK so one time…" he started, and then stopped himself. "I say that a lot, don't I? 'One time.'"

Lincoln smiled. "Once in a while," he said, wondering if after all these years, Mike was finally going to figure out why people called him One-Time.

"Anyway," Mike continued, apparently missing his moment for epiphany, "Big Top. We'd been there I guess about three weeks when we got hit hard. *Real* hard. Worst night of my whole tour. I think it was five or six hours of shells, nonstop. And I don't know about you, but there's nothing worse to me than mortar fire. I'd rather spend a whole day in a firefight than fifteen minutes taking mortars.

"But anyway, when we'd gotten up to Big Top, we'd set up shop in a couple of old concrete buildings. It was in a group of eight or nine of them, all blasted out, not much to 'em really. None of them more than three stories tall. But they had some walls, which was more than anything else around there had to offer, so that's where we'd started. Well, that night, the Russians lit... us... up. So much that one of the buildings right across from us just came down, *boom* big ol' pile, like they'd taken a wrecking ball through it.

"The craziest thing about it all, is we only took a couple casualties. I don't know if their aim was off or their intel told them we were in the other building or if we had the angels on our side or what, but couple of wounded, nobody got killed. Still can't believe it.

"Next morning, some brass showed up, which is like, oh great, how's that gonna help, right? Just going to make a bunch of extra trouble for us at the worst possible time. But turns out the guy's probably the best officer I ever met, except Mom," he said. And then added, as an afterthought, "And you, of course.

"Colonel Curtis J Nichols," Mike continued, putting special emphasis on each part of the name, the way you might with some historical figure or legendary leader. "And he was full-bird, really had no reason to be up there at all. Plenty high enough rank to have been back in the ol' rear-echelon drinking the good coffee, but there he was, first thing in the morning, kitted up, checking on us grunts. Looked like a real pipe-hitter too, like he was ready to round us up and lead us out himself to go get after it. But we weren't supposed to be going outside the wire then, so we had to stick around. Lucky me, I got assigned to security for him while he's on site, surveying the damage, seeing how many casualties we took, all that. So he's getting the tour of the place, and our LT's showing him around, doing his best, God bless him, to sound like he has any clue what he's talking about.

"Well, during the tour, we stop for a minute right next to that collapsed building. And LT isn't exactly *lying*, but he's giving us a lot more credit for quick thinking and decisive action than we deserve. And while he's talking, I notice, I kid you not, an *arm* poking out of the rubble of that building. Like, just hanging out of the heap, from about the elbow down. And at that point, all our folks are accounted for, right? All our personnel, all the Korean Marines we were with, all the support staff. Nobody knows whose arm that is. And the colonel notices me noticing, and he stops LT, and looks right at me, points to the arm, and says, 'What's his story?'

"Now, I wasn't expecting him to talk to me at all, and I don't really know what he means. I guess he was probably wondering who that was and why we hadn't cleared him out yet, but I'm an idiot and I just say 'He's been crushed, sir.'

"And he looks at me for a moment, and of course I figured he was about to chew me out, or that LT would step in and say something like 'Sorry sir, he's an idiot', but instead, cool as can be, he just walks over and reaches up, without missing a beat, shakes the hand, and says 'Pleasure to meet you, Ben.'"

Mike laughed at the memory. "Cracked us all up. 'Pleasure to meet you, Ben.' And I guess it was just one of those moments, where we're all laughing half because it was funny and half because we're all just glad to be alive. But we all just lost it. And it became a thing, after that. Any time people passed by there, 'Mornin' Ben', 'How's it hanging, Ben?' We all did it. Handshakes, high fives, whatever."

Lincoln chuckled at the black image.

"It was so freezing cold, and we didn't have any heavy equipment to dig him out. So he was just there. A couple people tried to cover the arm back up with some rocks and dirt or whatever, but it never took," Mike said. "He was still there when I left. Never did find out who it was."

Mike chuckled again, and then went quiet. After a moment, he added, "I told my girlfriend that story when I got back. For some reason she didn't think it was all that funny."

"Yeah," Lincoln said, knowing full well you had to have first seen the darkness before you could see the humor. Then he asked, "How long she stay after that?"

"'Bout three weeks."

"She gave it a pretty good shot, huh?"

"Well. To be fair, I got a last-minute chance to take on some training after I'd been home for four days, so I shipped right out again… Can't really blame her."

"I never do," Lincoln said.

They lapsed back into silence for a good twenty minutes or so, each back to their isolated worlds of observation and whatever memories the story had dredged up.

"Oop," Mike said some time later. "There we go. Looks like we got somebody inbound. About nine o'clock. Southish."

This far north, just about everything was southish. Lincoln turned and looked off to his left, but didn't see anything out of the ordinary.

"I don't see it," he said.

"Little dust cloud," Mike said. "Right there." A

moment later, Lincoln's visor chirped and brought up a small white icon in his view. Below it, now that he fixed his eyes on the spot, sure enough he could see a small cloud of red dust. How Mike spotted it was beyond him. Lincoln magnified the view until he could make out what was causing it.

"Skimmer, looks like," he said. A terrain-following vehicle, moving fast across the open space.

"Yep," said Mike. "Where you think it's headed?"

It was a joke, but Lincoln was already making the switch to pro mode, evaluating the threat and opportunity that was unfolding. He flicked his eyes to the side, selected the appropriate setting; a moment later when he looked back at the inbound vehicle, a range finder displayed the distance to it along with an estimated time of arrival at the research facility. About twenty minutes.

"How long you think it'd take to cover the ground from here to the facility?" Lincoln asked.

"Depends on how much you want to get looked at on the way," Mike answered. "Couple of minutes if you're hoofing it. A lot longer if you're crawling."

Lincoln glanced at the horizon. The sun had already set, but the pink-hued darkening sky would stay light for another hour or two in the dusty Martian atmosphere. Not quite dark enough to make a run for it.

"What're you thinking?" asked Mike.

"I'm thinking we hadn't figured out a good way to get inside just yet," Lincoln replied. "And that we might be looking at our opportunity."

Mike didn't respond immediately, but his head turned back and forth a couple of times from vehicle to facility and back again. Judging the distance. From Lincoln's estimation though, it was too close. There was only one entry point large enough for a vehicle, and it was on the other side of the facility from their current position. He could have made it at a trot no problem, but the chances of getting noticed were too high.

"I could do it," Mike said.

"No," Lincoln said. "Too risky. By the time we got over there, that skimmer's going to be right on top of us. We'll have to figure something else out."

"I didn't say *we*, Link," Mike said. "But if I'm going to do it, I better go now."

"I'm not sending you in there by yourself."

"Why not? I do it all the time. I'm going to do it."

"Mike."

"Captain. Relax. I'll get in there, and I'll lie low the whole time. No trouble. I'll just hang around until everybody else gets here, then I'll let you in."

Once again, Lincoln found himself with a tough call to make and no time to decide. It was against everything he'd been taught or experienced, to send a man off on his own. But the opportunity was unlikely to present itself again, and the payoff could be huge.

"Sir?"

"Go," Lincoln said. "But if you see anything you don't like, you back off. We'll find another way."

"No sweat," Mike said. "Trade with me."

Mike handed over his long rifle, and Lincoln gave him his shorter, automatic weapon in exchange. A moment afterward, Mike disengaged the support pack from his suit, and laid it to one side.

"Call me when you're ready," Mike said. And then he was up in a crouch, and scrambling down the hillock towards the facility. At first, Lincoln was concerned with Mike's speed. He was taking it way too fast. But once Mike reached the basin of the crater, he dropped into a sort of bear crawl, using his hands and feet. Between the suit's reactive camouflage, the long shadows on the terrain, and the low profile Mike was keeping, Lincoln soon found he was having trouble visually tracking his teammate even knowing exactly where he was. After watching his progress for a couple of minutes, Lincoln realized Mike was taking advantage of the lower gravity, making little bounding movements that would have been impossible at a full G. That would change as he got within range of the facility's grav field of course, but for now he was making good use of the environment. Lincoln still didn't know how a man that big could move with such fluid grace. Soon enough the only way Lincoln could keep track of Mike's progress was via the indicator in his visor that marked Mike's position. He was already at the perimeter of the facility with ten minutes to spare before the vehicle arrived.

Mike had been right. There was no way they both could have covered that ground. But Mike had most certainly done it on his own.

Lincoln maneuvered the skeeter around to the front side of the facility and watched the skimmer's approach. It was still about four minutes out when Mike made it into position near the entry. He'd gone to ground for the final hundred meters or so, a quick skimming belly crawl that, with the reactive camo blending in, made him look like he was tunneling shallowly, advancing just under the surface of the soil.

"Heads up, Mike," Lincoln said. "Getting close now."

"I see 'em," Mike answered, breathing hard from the effort. "This might've been a bad idea."

"Still time to bail out."

"Nah," he said. "Came all this way. Hate for it to be for nothin'."

Through the skeeter's feed, Lincoln watched from

above as the skimmer closed the final distance to the
entrance, and slowed to a halt. It was a light-duty hauler
variety, with room in the cab for four and an external bed.
Whatever it was carrying was concealed under a heavy-
duty tarp. Lincoln brought the skeeter down lower and
tried to get an angle on the cab, but the skimmer was
full-plated with no way to see inside. It held outside the
sealed gate for a minute or two. Lincoln got as much
footage as he could with the skeeter, though he didn't
see anything in particular that looked useful. Thumper
would feed the whole stream to Veronica, though, and
there was no telling what she might be able to do with it.

Finally the main entrance ground open, heavy gears
worked the gate with the sound of aged mechanicals. From
the noise, Lincoln guessed they probably didn't come in
and out a lot. If he'd been living in there forced to listen
to that, he would have done something about it by now.

The skimmer moved into the bay. It was double-gated,
like an airlock, probably to keep the interior from filling
up with dust during a storm. Lincoln had been expecting
Mike to hop up on the back of the skimmer while it was
stopped, or at least to follow it in when it moved. Instead,
the indicator on Mike's position showed him still in the
exact location he'd been in when the vehicle had first
pulled up. Maybe he'd seen something from down low
that he didn't like. Maybe he'd changed his mind.

"Mike, you all right?" Lincoln asked. Mike didn't
answer.

A moment later, the exterior gate started to close.
Mike still hadn't moved.

"Mike?"

The gate was about halfway to the ground when Mike
shot up out of his hiding place. He covered the distance
in a few quick bounds, and then slowed several paces

outside. He'd waited too long. He wasn't going to be able
to make it in now.

And then, Mike pulled off a move that looked gravity-
defying, like a slow-motion fall. Somehow he went from
his low crouch, to the ground, into a roll, and back up
to a crouch again, all in such a fluid motion that Lincoln
couldn't quite replay it in his mind, even though he'd
just seen it for himself. The gate touched down closed
behind Mike, only three or four seconds after he'd passed
through. He ended up tucked into a dark corner of the
airlock, off the right-side rear of the skimmer.

Once the outer gate was closed completely, the inner
gate started its retraction. Mike didn't wait this time.
Lincoln couldn't get a clear view of him through the
skeeter, but he could see Mike's indicator closing in on
the skimmer. The two indicators met for a moment;
the skimmer pulled forward into the complex, and the
indicators separated again. Mike's stopped moving just
inside the gate, while the skimmer continued on to one
of the outbuildings. The only outbuilding that wasn't
sunk into the ground, which Lincoln now realized must
have been the garage.

As best as he could tell, Mike had just hitched a short
ride on the back of the skimmer, and then dropped off it
once inside. He appeared to just be lying in the middle
of the entrance.

Lincoln repositioned the skeeter over the top of the
facility, and got the best view of the garage as he could
find. Three individuals emerged from it, all bundled up
in similar gear to the other two people he'd seen earlier.
And all three armed. They walked to the main building
and entered. Only after it was all still and quiet again did
Mike check in.

"I'm in," he said.

"I see that," Lincoln replied. "Cut it kind of close, wouldn't you say?"

"Had to make it look good," Mike answered. "I'm going to do a little legwork while I'm in here, see what I can find."

His indicator started moving again, away from the entrance and towards the outer wall, slowly. At a crawl.

"I'd feel better if you'd just find a nice, quiet place to hide," Lincoln said. "And sit tight until the cavalry gets here."

"I need the exercise," Mike said. "And I'm sure we'd all like a better idea of what we're walking into. Don't worry boss, I won't blow it."

"Take it slow, Mike. I'm moving up to the perimeter. Before you go stalking too far off, skirt around the outside and find me a way in. Just in case."

"You got it."

Lincoln eased up from the ground and started off towards the facility, his pace much more cautious than the one Mike had displayed. Even so, whether he was moving or lying flat and still, he felt totally exposed. At least it'd be dark soon. Once he got within a hundred meters or so, he started to feel the grav field.

"Thumper," Lincoln called in. "I've got another feed for you. Three new arrivals, came in on a skimmer. All armed. Get me that weapon ID, and then suit up. We're going in tonight."

"Tonight?" she responded. "Kind of short notice, isn't it?"

"I hope not," Lincoln said. "Mike's already inside."

There was a pause, and when Thumper answered, her voice had a new quality of controlled intensity; flipping the switch.

"We're on the way."

SEVENTEEN

"It's good kit," Thumper said, lying on her belly next to Lincoln, sharing what she'd found about the weapon he'd asked her to ID. "Not exactly standard issue for CMA military, but that's only because it's higher-grade than standard. Only reason it doesn't *look* expensive because it's all so well-used."

"So these guys are funded *and* experienced," Lincoln said.

"Could be a rough ride," Thumper answered.

Lincoln had backed off a couple hundred meters from the airlock that Mike had designated as his emergency exit and found a place to set up shop while he had waited for the rest of the team to arrive. Now he and Thumper were providing cover while Sahil and Wright closed the final distance to the facility. Mike's emergency exit was about to become their route for free admission.

"Get an estimate on numbers?" Lincoln asked.

"Based on power usage and what little we could get from the skeeters, I'd guess twelve to fifteen. Main building's got six floors total, but I think they're only running the upper two. Maybe the third for storage or something. The heat differential's pretty big in that gap, so if anybody's working on that third floor, they're doing it in a coat and gloves. None of the outbuildings are powered at all, except the garage. Those two people you picked up earlier, I'm not sure what they were up to, but they probably weren't planning on staying for long. As far as I can tell, they're keeping the activity mostly restricted to the main building.

"I didn't get to do a deep mapping, but perimeter security looks pretty straightforward. Couple zone alarms, few motion detectors," Thumper continued. "I don't think they're expecting too much trouble way out here."

"The fact that they took any precautions at all says enough," Lincoln said.

Some hundred meters away, Wright went flat to the ground, with Sahil dropping behind her an instant later. In the hard-shell of the facility, an exterior light came on at one of the corners of the main building, lighting up the whole place like a lantern. For a moment, Lincoln couldn't help but wonder if they'd tripped some early warning system.

"Wright, you good?" he called in.

"We'll see," she answered.

"Thumper?" Lincoln asked.

"Grid's still green. I don't think they blew anything."

Two figures emerged from the main building and trudged towards the garage.

"Mikey gave us a heads up," Wright said. "He's got tremblers near all the entryways."

While Lincoln had been staring at a door waiting for the rest of the team, Mike had been busy skulking around inside "making some preparations", as he'd called it. He hadn't gone into details. When exactly he'd had time to get tremblers out, Lincoln didn't know. The micro seismic monitors were sensitive enough to pick up vibrations from talking, footsteps, even breathing if it was heavy enough. They didn't provide a lot of data to go on, but if you had them in the right place they were a handy way to keep people from sneaking up on you. It made sense that a sniper might take a pocketful of them everywhere he went.

"Mikey, whatcha got going on right now?" Lincoln asked.

"Just hanging around," Mike answered. "Couple of night owls look like they're maybe headed out. Or they left something in the skimmer."

Lincoln switched on his locator for Mike; the indicator showed him at the edge of one of the outbuildings, facing the garage. He seemed awfully close, like he was almost daring the two individuals to notice him.

"You're sure you aren't in the open there?" Lincoln asked.

"Pretty sure, sir."

"Looks close to me."

"Look again," Mike said.

Lincoln magnified the view. From his current location, he didn't have direct line of sight to Mike's position. But once he zoomed in close enough, the detail he'd missed before became clearer. The difference in elevation.

"Are you on the roof?" Lincoln asked.

"That's a roger," Mike answered. "I could maybe spit on 'em from here, and they might think it was raining. If you'd let me open my faceplate."

"Negative on both counts."

"I think you're good to move up, anyway," Mike said. "The way the light's reflecting off the shell in here, I can't hardly see what's going on outside. And *I'm* paying attention."

"Sahil," Lincoln said. "What's your read on it?"

"Same as Mikey," Sahil replied. "Plenty of shadows from here to there. We can ghost right up to the door."

"All right, go ahead and move up. Hold off at ten meters, and when you're set we'll join you."

"Copy," Sahil said.

"How much time you need on the door?" Lincoln asked Thumper. Not because they hadn't already discussed it. But they'd come up with the plan on the fly, talking it through while the three remaining Outriders patrolled in from base camp. Revisiting the details never hurt. Especially when you were making it up as you went along.

"Still sixty to ninety seconds, captain," she said. "Assuming Mikey did his part right." The fact that she called him by his rank was a good indication he'd asked her one too many times. "A hundred and eighty if you ask me again."

There'd been a physical lock on the interior door that Mike had taken care of for them. The airlock they'd chosen was the least convenient for access to the buildings. Once the team was through the airlock, there was a fair amount of open ground to cover before they reached the nearest outbuilding. The inconvenience was a feature; Mike had figured it was the least likely to be used, and therefore the least likely to be carefully monitored. It was a strange aspect of human psychology that the mind tended to cling to the familiar and to overlook the unused. Lincoln had made his living, and kept his life, by exploiting such tendencies.

"How are we on the cameras?" Lincoln asked.

"Skeeter's patched in no problem," Thumper said. "We can go full blackout whenever we want."

"And if they call for help?"

"It won't come. Intercept's locked in. Call won't go

out, but we'll know who they were trying to reach."

Lincoln nodded. And then added. "I'm glad you're on our side, Thump."

"You should wait on that, sir," she said, "until we see if it all works."

"We're in place," Wright said over comms. "You're good to move up."

"Roger," Lincoln answered. "Moving up."

Lincoln nudged Thumper.

"Ladies first."

"Always the gentleman," she replied. A moment later, she did an explosive pushup that took her from her belly to her feet in a crouch all in a single movement, and was advancing across the terrain before Lincoln had even started to get off the ground. He got to his feet the old-fashioned way and followed after her, already five meters behind. They continued past Wright and Sahil and closed the final ten meters to the airlock.

Once they reached it, Thumper dropped to a knee and went to work affixing a device to the main panel while Lincoln stood over her, providing cover. He didn't mind taking a turn on the long gun every once in a while, but now that they were getting ready to make entry, he was really looking forward to getting his weapon back from Mike.

"Mike, we're at the lock," Lincoln reported. "What's the status of our night owls?"

"Still in the garage," Mike answered. "Can't tell what they're up to, though."

"Roger. We'll hold here until you give us a go."

"'K," said Mike.

As much as Lincoln hated standing around right at the perimeter, he liked it a lot more than getting stuck in a sealed box with potential hostiles wandering the premises. If he tried to go now, he had no doubt those two individuals would decide to show back up as soon as his whole team had loaded into the airlock. They'd just have to wait and see.

It was a long wait. After about half an hour, Mike called back in.

"There they are," he said. "Might've been wrong about the night owls."

"How's that?" Lincoln asked.

"Might actually be love birds," he answered. "At least, they're not bringing anything back with them that they didn't take over in the first place."

"All right, roger that," Lincoln said, even more annoyed at the delay now. He took a couple of deep breaths, and tried not to let it get to him. The only schedule they were on was to get everything done before sunrise, and they still had a good few hours before that deadline. "Still armed?"

"Only one, but yep. Carrying it lazy-man style now," Mike said. The individual was carrying his weapon unslung and in hand, but not ready for combat; like you might if you'd picked it up, say, off the front seat of a vehicle and weren't expecting to need it any time soon. "I didn't get a great angle on it, but looks like a Type 32 to me."

"It'd be the right family," Thumper answered.

"They're almost back to the main building now," said Mike.

"Seems weird they'd switch the lights on if they're trying to be sneaky about it," Thumper said.

"Yeah, probably just loading something in the skimmer. But the other story's better."

A few moments later, the light from the main building went out, returning the facility grounds to heavy darkness. Lincoln glanced up at the sky; the dust and thin clouds obscured most of the stars, keeping ambient light to a minimum. The clouds struck him. He didn't know where everything stood with the ongoing terraforming process. Last he'd heard back home, the general consensus was that it'd take another fifty years or so before Martian settlements could take their chances going completely unshielded. But they'd already gotten an artificial magnetosphere reconstructed and raised the atmospheric pressure well above the critical levels, both faster than anyone had predicted was possible. Technically, if not for the ridiculous temperatures, he and his teammates could have been running around with just some additional oxygen support.

That was one thing that made Lincoln nervous about a potential war with Mars; pretty much every forecast anyone had made about the speed of their expansion and development had underestimated them. Sometimes grossly.

"All right, you're clear," Mike said.

"Thumper," Lincoln said. "Spring it."

"Ninety seconds," she replied. Given her initial estimate, Lincoln was pretty sure she'd have it done in under a minute.

"Wright, Sahil," said Lincoln. "Come on up."

Wright hopped up with Sahil close behind, and the two made the quick jog to the airlock, standing off just a few feet while Thumper finished her work.

"Once I get this bypass," Thumper said, "we need quick open and close. I'm not going to pop both doors at once because of the atmospheric imbalance, I don't want to make any more ruckus than we absolutely have to. But I don't want to be stuck in that lock any longer than necessary either. So, load in fast, and get out faster."

"How long?" Wright asked.

"We can get through in fifteen seconds, if nobody trips."

"Mike," Lincoln said. "How are we looking?"

"Slow," Mike answered. "But still clear."

"Got it," Thumper said. "Security's looped, door's set for knocking. Ready on you, Lincoln."

"Cameras?"

"We're good."

"Roger that. On me," Lincoln said. "Mike, we're coming in... three... two... one... Go."

Thumper stepped back from the entrance. The next moment, the airlock clicked and opened inward. As soon as it moved, so did Lincoln. He stepped into the lock and went as far forward as he could, positioning himself right at the internal door. Wright was right on his heels, followed by Sahil. Thumper came through last, closing the door behind her. Ten long seconds later, the secondary door clicked and unsealed. Lincoln pulled the handle and swung the door open, stepped in and to the right, and went to a knee, covering their right flank. Wright was there a moment later, mirroring him and covering the opposite direction. Sahil advanced five meters into the open, keeping his weapon trained on the main facility while Thumper came through the lock and sealed it behind them. Once the lock was resecured, she held position for a few moments, all of them listening and scanning for any signs of trouble. The only thing that seemed to have changed was the ambient temperature.

"Mike, we're in," Lincoln said.

"Roger that. I'm coming down. Meet you at the front door."

Sahil took point from the perimeter all the way to the main facility, his catlike steps smooth and sure despite the rough terrain. None of the ground appeared to have been graded or improved beyond what was strictly necessary from a construction standpoint, and Lincoln wondered how many of the original researchers had been treated for sprained ankles and broken wrists.

When the four teammates crossed into the compound proper, Mike was already holding position off one corner of the main building. Sahil led the team to a point between two of the outbuildings. Mike disappeared around the back of the main building, and then re-emerged from the other a minute later and joined them. Wright pulled open a pouch on her harness, and dug out a handful of hard plastic bands. Quick cuffs. She handed them to Mike. He accepted them, and stared at them for a moment.

"We're really doing this, huh?" he said.

"Unless you have a better idea," Lincoln said.

"Just about *all* of my ideas are better," Mike answered. "But none of them involve us going in *there*."

"Yeah, well," Lincoln said. "I know you'll make it work."

"I'd feel better if we had a good head count," Wright said. "Gonna be tough to know when we're secure."

"Let's just assume we aren't secure until we're off the planet," Lincoln said.

"Fair enough."

Mike stuffed the quick cuffs into a pouch on his harness, and then turned back to Lincoln, holding his weapon out. Lincoln took his own rifle, and returned Mike's to him.

"You going to be OK running that inside?" Lincoln asked.

"Sure thing," Mike said. "If it gets hot enough in there for me to be wanting something else, a lot of other things will have already gone wrong."

Lincoln nodded, and then looked around at the rest of his team.

"Set?"

"Let's do it," Sahil said.

"All right," Lincoln said. "Drop camo."

The reactive camouflage's mottled reds and blacks drained away to a deep navy blue streaked with charcoal lines, with four letters emblazoned in bright white, front and back.

OTMS.

The impossible to miss initials for the Outer Territorial Marshal Service. Thumper had pulled footage of the Marshal Service's Special Tactics Group in action; Veronica had analyzed it and fed the data to their suits. And now, instead of blending into the surroundings, the reactive camo was mimicking the group's signature uniforms.

Not that the Marshal Service had anything remotely like the Outriders' recon suits. But that was part of the point. The more confusion they could inject into the bad guys' plans, the better.

The facility was too far out to fall under any one colony's law enforcement jurisdiction. The OTMS was an arm of the Central Martian Authority's shared police force, one that extended protection and security to settlements that couldn't support their own force. It also oversaw any areas that weren't explicitly designated as belonging to a particular governmental body.

Which was all to say, if any illegal activity were to be taking place way out here, technically it was the Marshal Service that would be responsible for shutting it down. The ruse wouldn't hold up to any serious scrutiny. But the deception served two purposes. The obvious one was to give credit for the operation to someone closer to home. But it would also quickly indicate the loyalties of the people inside. If they all threw up their hands and complied with orders, the situation was likely to be a lot easier to resolve than Lincoln was expecting it to be. If not, well... at least that would suggest they knew they were up to no good.

"I'll take first in," Sahil said.

"Negative, I'm on point," Lincoln said. "This was my stupid idea. If their answer to it is to shoot, it's only fair that I catch the rounds."

"Hope they don't have AP," Mike said. Their powered armor was made to withstand most small arms fire, but they were primarily designed for reconnaissance, not assault; armor-piercing rounds of sufficient power would cut right through.

"If they do," Lincoln said, "I'm counting on you to avenge me."

"If they do," Wright answered, "I'm counting on you to shoot first."

Sahil knelt down at the door to work the lock. Lincoln took the lead position, followed by Wright, then Thumper, then Mike. They set up on the front door in a staggered line, left, right, left, right, to flow faster through the entryway. Based on the floorplans Thumper had pulled together, the upper entrance wasn't a full floor, just a large, single room with a staircase directly opposite the main entrance. A sort of combination reception and staging area where researchers could leave all their cold-weather gear before descending into the facility proper.

They'd decided to forego sending Poke in first to scout. As nice as it would have been to have had a full picture going in, there weren't many viable places for the little foldable to get around without risking discovery. And this wasn't the kind of hit where they could afford to tip the bad guys off early and give them a chance to harden up the interior. Lincoln was trusting instead to speed and surprise to get the job done.

"Sahil," Lincoln said.

"Lock's done," Sahil answered. He slid to the right side, clearing the path to the door, but kept his hand on the mechanism.

"Roger," Lincoln said.

"Remember, slow is smooth, and smooth is fast," Mike said, reciting a well-known shooter's mantra. And then added, "… but fast and smooth is best."

"Three… two… one," Lincoln counted down. Then. "Go."

Sahil pushed the door open and drew back, and Lincoln pushed through aggressively at an angle, clearing the entrance as quickly as possible without rushing anything. The lights were low, the room illuminated only by the dim orange glow emanating from the stairwell. Long shadows stretched and pooled.

His first look was to the right, front corner of the room. Clear.

Without slowing he swept through the room, scanning for targets. Heavy coats lined the walls at odd intervals, each presenting a silhouette to evaluate and assess. Behind him, Wright's sharp voice pierced the gloom.

"OT Marshals, OT Marshals," she called, "Get down on the ground, on the ground!"

A commotion followed, but Lincoln ignored the scuffling until he'd completed his circuit around the right of the room, confirming there were no threats to that side. A short table sat against the back wall of the room, and on it lay a weapon he recognized in a glance as a Type 32 short-barreled rifle. He continued on to the stairwell, and posted up there, keeping his weapon trained on the switchback that led to the floor below. Apart from catching some activity out of the corner of his eye, he hadn't stopped to look at what was going on. Thumper joined him at the stairwell.

"Stay on the ground," Wright commanded. "Faces to the floor. Hands spread. Hands spread!"

And then, through internal comms, she said, "Two individuals. One male, one female, both unarmed. Sahil's securing now."

"Type 32 on the table, to my right," Lincoln answered.

"I got it," Mike said, and a moment later he was there, removing the ammunition and a firing component to render the weapon temporarily inoperable. He stuffed the component in a pouch on his leg, and tossed the magazine to the opposite side of the room.

"It's going to be OK, it's going to be OK," the man on the floor kept saying, though it wasn't clear if he was saying it to the woman, or to himself. As far as Lincoln could tell, the woman had yet to make a single noise.

"Guessing these are our night owls," Sahil said, through comms. "Got 'em locked up pretty good, they ain't goin' anywhere."

It wasn't proper protocol to leave anyone unguarded, no matter how secured they were. But there was no way Lincoln was giving up the firepower to babysit a couple of people they'd locked down.

"How many people are in the facility?" Wright asked.

"Don't tell 'em anything–" the man started, but a meaty thud followed suggesting Sahil had just bounced his head off the floor.

"How many people are in the facility?" Wright repeated.

"Ten," the woman answered, her voice trembling but

her tone calm. "Ten others, I mean, not counting us. Eleven, sorry, eleven more."

"How many are armed?"

"Five... I don't know," the woman said. "Six, maybe. Maybe seven. What's happening? I don't understand what's happening."

"Is everyone in this building?" Wright continued. "Is there anyone in any of those other buildings?"

"Yes... err, no... I mean... we're all here. Everyone's here. Please, what is going on? We're not doing anything wrong."

"Then this should be over real soon," Wright said. "Stay still, stay quiet." And then through internal comms, she added. "I think she's telling the truth. As best as she can."

Lincoln still hadn't taken his eyes off the stairwell.

"Can we move?" he asked.

"One sec," Sahil said. And then to the woman, he said, "Your friend here's gonna sleep for a little bit, but don't worry, he'll be just fine when he wakes up." And then through internal comms again, "I went ahead and dosed the troublemaker. Had a feeling he was gonna make a ruckus. Should be good to move now."

"Roger, moving down."

Lincoln stepped out onto the landing, and his team returned to their entry formation. The door to the first floor was closed and looked heavy, but Lincoln didn't want to count on it having muffled all the commotion they'd just created. There was a good chance that at least some of the individuals below would be sleeping. Or at least had been until just a minute or two ago. But every interaction they had, even as easy as this one had been, increased the likelihood of resistance the further they went into the facility.

They reached the door to the first real floor without any issue. A small window sat in the upper middle of the beige door, an arrangement that made Lincoln think of a hospital. He risked a peek through it, saw a wide beige corridor, with doorways on either side. There was no one in the hall, no sign that anyone knew anything unusual had happened upstairs.

"Mike," he said. "Door."

Mike rolled to the side and took position at the door, waiting to open it on Lincoln's cue. Behind him, the others formed up. Long hallways with rooms exactly across from each other made for tricky clearing.

"Simultaneous on this next," Lincoln said, probably an unnecessary reminder of the plan. "Wright, lead left; I'll take right."

"I'm on left, understood," she confirmed. In cases like this, the team had a default split; Wright was second element leader, with Sahil and Mike supporting. They'd already numbered the rooms on this floor one through eight, with evens on the right side of the hall. Lincoln and Thumper would clear those, while Wright's element handled the others.

"Mike, go," he said. Mike pulled the door open, and the team flowed through, stacking alternately on either side of the corridor until they were all through and set. Lincoln looked across the corridor and held up his hand for Wright to see. She nodded. One. Two. Three.

They moved as one, each element rounding the door and entering their target rooms simultaneously. Lincoln button-hooked around the doorframe, headed towards the right with Thumper on his heels. A quick scan of the dark room revealed it to be full of tall lockers from floor to ceiling, creating several aisles. Rather than looping around the other side of the room, Thumper stayed with him, and together they walked the outer edge, keeping an aggressive pace with quiet steps. They circled the whole room. Empty.

Once they reached the door again, Lincoln held there while awaiting a signal from their teammates. Behind him, Thumper marked the floor right by the doorframe with a digital ink, invisible to the naked eye, but radiant through their visors. A reminder that they'd cleared this room.

"Two's clear," Lincoln said. "Holding for you."

Before Wright reported in, a light appeared in the hallway, and a shadow stretched toward Lincoln. A clear silhouette of a man. From the angle, it looked like someone in the room further down the hall diagonal from Lincoln's was standing in the doorway, with the light from the room behind him.

Lincoln didn't wait. He exploded into the corridor, weapon up.

"OT Marshals!" Lincoln called as he rushed the individual, "OT Marshals! Get on the floor, hands out, hands out!"

And then over internal comms, "We've got room three, we've got room three!"

The man was heavyset, wearing a T-shirt and boxer shorts, with dark socks. His hands shot up in front of him, palms towards Lincoln, fingers spread wide, like he was expecting Lincoln to plow right into him. His feet peddled almost comically, slipping on the floor as he tried to get away. He fell back into his room, first hard on his backside, and then gracelessly onto his back. His eyes were locked on Lincoln, and he kept his hands up, even while his feet continued to scrabble at the smooth tile of the floor.

Lincoln crossed the threshold and swept his weapon

around the room. A bedroom, two occupants. There was another man in a bed against the far wall, sitting up with a look of sheer panic on his face. Thin, with red hair curling up off the top of his head like a frozen flame.

"On the floor, get on the floor!" Lincoln barked. The man in the bed did his best to comply, flopping unceremoniously out on the floor, trailing blankets and sheets behind him. One foot got tangled and the man lay there on the floor staring up at Lincoln and kicking his leg to try and free it.

"Over, on your belly," Thumper commanded the heavyset man. He rolled over and spread his hands out to either side.

"One's clear, we're moving to room four," Wright reported. "Wright to room four!"

The red-haired man dropped his face to the floor and covered the back of his head with his hands. His leg was still tangled, and still kicking like a half-dead cricket. Lincoln crossed to him and put a hand on the man's back.

"Relax," he said. "Relax, you're fine." The man went still, but didn't uncover his head. Lincoln reached over with one hand and unwound the sheets from around the man's lower leg. Thumper stood over the man in the dark socks, her weapon trained on him, while Lincoln cuffed the redhead.

Lincoln asked the man a couple of questions, but he'd gone unresponsive except for an occasional sound that was a mix between a whimper and a cough.

"Room four," Wright reported, "two females, unarmed. They're secured. Sahil's questioning one of them now."

"Roger," Lincoln answered. "Room three; two males here, same story."

He moved over and cuffed the heavyset man.

"You fellas sit tight," Lincoln said. "Don't make any trouble for us, and we'll be out of your way soon. Understand?"

The larger man nodded.

"I hope we got the right guys," Thumper said. "Apart from the knucklehead upstairs, everyone else around here is fitting the researcher profile a little too well."

"Still got plenty of rooms to go," Lincoln said. He marked the floor and readied to move down the corridor as soon as Sahil was done. He was just about to ask Wright if she wanted to stick to the even-numbered rooms now that they'd switched when a clacking sound came from the far end of the hallway.

Lincoln edged the doorframe, just enough to get a peek down the hall. Two men stood at the far end of the corridor, in the stairwell. One had entered the hall by a couple of steps, but both were holding position there, looking Lincoln's direction, not moving. And then the man in the dark socks cried out.

"Help! Help us, help us!"

"OT Marshals!" Lincoln called, bringing his weapon to bear. "Drop your weapons!"

The reaction from the men was immediate.

They both opened fire.

Lincoln was faster, by a thread.

The first man cried out and tumbled back towards the stairwell, and nearly simultaneously rounds snapped into the wall in front of Lincoln's shoulder, and a hard impact caught his right hip, whipping his leg out from under him and throwing him off balance. He fell hard to his left knee.

Out into the hallway.

Reflexes took over. Lincoln dropped onto his right

side, half-fetal, stabilized, and brought his weapon back
on target, just as the second man fired another burst,
and then another. Most of the rounds snapped over him,
but one caught the outer edge of his left shoulder and
knocked his aimpoint off target. A moment later, gunfire
popped off above him, right over his head, single shots,
and then a pair of legs went striding past him while the
gunfire continued *pop pop pop*, steady and sure.

Wright. She was advancing towards the stairwell,
driving the attackers back. The wounded man was
still in the corridor, sprawled on his back. The second
hostile was crouched now in the doorframe, but leaning
awkwardly forward and firing one-handed.

Before Lincoln could get a shot lined up, the wounded
man rolled up and raised his weapon. He sprayed fire on
full-auto, filling the corridor with rounds, and sending
Wright ducking into the next doorway. At the same
time, Lincoln felt something constrict his right ankle,
and a moment later he was sliding. Thumper, dragging
him out of the open.

In the corridor, the volume of gunfire dropped to
spasms of three- and four-round bursts; the walls and
doorframes spit chunks and splinters under the assault.
That kind of wild gunfire was typical of panicked
amateurs, but when Lincoln regained his place by the
door and risked a glance, he saw the wounded man was
sliding backwards, while he fired; his companion was
dragging him clear of the corridor, while he provided
suppressive fire. The instant he was in the stairwell, he
kicked the heavy door shut.

That wasn't an amateur move.

"Lincoln, you hit?" Wright called.

"I'm good, I'm good!" he called back. "Took a couple
hits, but they didn't get through!" He still wasn't sure

how he'd gotten hit, until he saw a hole torn through the door frame. The man had shot him through the wall.

Not amateurs. Not by a long shot.

"We gotta go," Sahil said, "we gotta move!"

He was right. The race was on now. They'd lost surprise. The only way for the Outriders to compensate was with speed, and violence of action.

"Sahil! Get on that door to the stairs," Lincoln ordered. He was up now, moving down the hall. But he couldn't leave the remaining rooms unchecked. "Thumper, Mike, clear room seven!"

As soon as he reached room five, he kicked the door almost off its hinges.

"Six is clear!" Wright called. "Moving to eight!"

Room five was a combination break room and sitting area, with low chairs and tables, plus a small kitchenette. Most of it was visible from the doorway, but a closet or pantry in the back posed a potential hiding place. Lincoln swept through the room in a straight line, kicking chairs aside, stomping up and over one of the tables, wasting no time.

"OT Marshals!" he called, two strides from the door. He didn't wait for a response. If anyone was hiding in there, they weren't going to be happy. He kicked the door right next to the handle. It rocketed open, slamming into the wall so hard the handle actually stuck. As he'd guessed, the room was a shallow pantry, with shelves of food and assorted supplies. No one was inside. Lucky for them.

"Five, clear!" he called.

"Seven, clear!" Thumper responded.

Lincoln crossed the room, moved back out into the corridor, and started towards the stairs where the two men had retreated. Sahil was already there, crouched to one side of the corridor keeping his deadly weapon ready to unleash if anyone dared to open that door.

"Eight is clear!" Wright said, a moment later.

"Wright," Lincoln said. "My count is six individuals secured; two hostiles, confirmed; five unknowns unaccounted for."

"I confirm, six secured, two hostiles. *At least* five unaccounted for."

The team reformed in the hall, behind Sahil's security. Lincoln and Thumper took the right side, while Wright and Mike moved left. Lincoln and Wright covered the door to the stairs while Mike and Thumper covered the rear, just in case.

"Sahil," Lincoln said. "Go knock."

"How loud?" he asked.

"Loud enough to kill whatever's on the other side."

"No sweat."

Sahil crept up to the door, and pulled three copper-colored cubes out of one of the slots on his suit. These he arranged in an inverted triangle on the surface of the door.

"Y'all might wanna take a step back," he said, though he himself just moved over to one side of the door. He held his weapon with one hand; in his left hand were two white cylinders. Stun grenades. The Outriders just called them *crashes*. "Say when."

"Hit it."

"Stand by to get some," Sahil said, and then, "Fire, fire, fire." A moment later, a hurricane of fire ripped the door from its moorings, as if a gateway to hell had opened up in the stairwell and sucked it into oblivion. Lincoln's suit automatically damped the roar, but even so the intensity set his teeth on edge.

Before the smoke had cleared, Sahil was up, tossing the crashes down the stairs. They went off like a thunderstorm, sending flashes of white lightning and ear-splitting peals rolling up and down both hallways.

Lincoln was first through, his weapon trained on the most dangerous angles.

At the bottom of the last flight, just a few steps before the door to the second floor, two men lay motionless. When Lincoln reached them, he quickly confirmed what he suspected. They were the same two men who had fired on him. Whether they'd been waiting in ambush, or if they simply hadn't been able to make it down the stairs in time, the blast from Sahil's charge had been too severe. They were both dead.

The door leading to the second floor was warped and partially open. Smoke crawled through the gaps out into the hallway on the other side.

"Door," Lincoln said over comms. "Going through."

It might have been more tactically sound to set up for an explosive entry, but he didn't want to lose momentum. Without slowing, he launched a stomping kick into the middle of the door, near the frame. He wasn't even making conscious decisions anymore; training drove him forward through the gap, muscle memory guided his motion.

A short hall opened out to a single, large room, segmented by half-height walls throughout. Gunfire greeted him before he could announce himself. Lincoln snapped his weapon right, centered on the disappearing target, and put three rounds through the short wall. A sharp cry reported his fire had been accurate.

"Contact, right!" he called.

The rest of team was already flowing through the space, effortlessly breaking into two elements, sweeping the area.

"OT Marshals, throw down your weapons!" Thumper

shouted, one final attempt to end the firefight before it got out of control. She was answered by another burst of gunfire from somewhere on the other side of the room. But in the mental echo of the sound, Lincoln realized the report hadn't come from a Type 32; it'd been a simultaneous volley, a burst from Sahil's heavy weapon paired with a single round from Mike's rifle. Dropping a threat before it could develop.

The Outriders snaked their way through the maze of a room, every aisle and cubicle a potential point of ambush. The fact that the bad guys had gotten any shots off at all was a testament to the complexity of the environment, and their level of training. By Lincoln's count, there were still three loose in the facility. Assuming the first woman had been telling the truth.

Near the middle of the room, Lincoln angled a cubicle wall and found a man lying face down.

"Stay down, stay on the ground!" he commanded, but as he stepped over to secure the man, he saw that was unnecessary. The man had been shot twice through the back of the head. Judging from the damage, it looked like it'd been at close range. There were no weapons nearby.

Lincoln held there, the discovery shocking him out of his near-automatic assault mode. Throughout the room, the rest of the team continued to clear, while he knelt by the man and took quick inventory. Judging from the attire, the physique, and the hands, Lincoln could tell this wasn't a military man. He had to assume this was another civilian, like those they'd secured on the first floor. But those weren't stray rounds that had taken the man's life. They had been intentional, from short range.

The realization flashed a warning, but the intensity of the moment clouded it.

"Clear!" Wright called, and then. "Lincoln, what are we doing?"

"Push!" he said, getting back to his feet. "Sahil, switch with me!"

"Copy, I'm on Thumper," Sahil answered. Lincoln was trailing the others by twenty-five feet or so. Thumper effortlessly stepped up to element lead, with Sahil supporting, while Lincoln moved to catch up. Wright and Mike didn't wait around. They exited through the single door in the rear of the room and continued clearing.

When Lincoln made it to the corridor, he held position until Wright and Mike emerged from the first room on the left. Mike marked it clear, and Lincoln fell into the second-man position.

"Lincoln, we got an issue," Thumper said.

"What is it?" he answered. She and Sahil were a little further down the corridor, each on either side, covering opposite angles at what looked like a T-intersection.

"Long hallway here, it's not on the blueprints."

"Which one?"

"To the left. Should be a wall, not a corridor."

"How long?"

"Can't say. Can't see the end, it curves."

"Hold there," Lincoln said. Wright led the way and the team formed up, rejoining into a single unit. Lincoln did a quick scan. Sure enough, the hallway to the left looked like newer construction. Still years old, but undoubtedly a later addition. The rest of the facility had been relatively uniform and predictable. This hall stood out as an anomaly. Lincoln double-checked with Sahil, who motioned back that the section to the right was clear. Then Lincoln risked a peek down the suspect hallway. The corridor stretched and curved to the left; there were no doors on either side of it for as far as he could see.

"Any guess on where it goes?" he asked.

"Not off the top of my head," Thumper answered.

"Towards the garage," Mike said. "Bends back around towards the garage. Freight elevator or something maybe?"

There were still two individuals missing. And the executed civilian's vague warning snapped into clarity.

They'd left five of them tied up upstairs. And the remaining hostiles had a back door.

"Back," Lincoln said. "Back with me, double-time!"

He didn't wait, and his teammates didn't ask for an explanation. Like the alpha of a wolf pack, he raced off, and they followed on his heels.

Lincoln didn't run, exactly, but he moved as fast as he could while back-clearing the space they'd just moved through. Back through the large room, back up the stairwell. And as he emerged on the first floor, two men were coming down the stairs at the opposite end. Both armed. Lincoln didn't hesitate.

He snapped off two bursts. Wright's weapon barked next to him on the second. The two men at the far end of the corridor fell to the ground under the assault; one motionless, the other fishing his legs around and making a terrible noise. By the time Lincoln reached him, he too had gone still and quiet.

"That's thirteen," Wright said, the adrenaline apparent in her voice, though her tone was matter-of-fact.

Lincoln nodded.

"Better clear it again, just to be sure," he said.

"How'd you know they were trying to circle around behind us?" she asked.

"Don't think they were," Lincoln said. "Found a body downstairs, knew we hadn't done it."

It took a moment for the rest of the team to make the

connection. Only Mike voiced it.

"You think they were coming up here to kill these people?" Mike asked.

"Yeah," Lincoln answered. "That'd explain why the two upstairs were sneaking around. Or why she couldn't go out with an armed escort."

When he said it, he realized what it meant. The two men who'd been coming down the stairs obviously would have passed by the man and woman they'd left cuffed upstairs. A cold, sickly feeling hollowed him out.

"We should check upstairs," Wright said.

Lincoln nodded.

"Sahil, take Thumper and Mike, clear it out again, as far down as you think you need to go," he said. "Make sure we got everybody."

"No sweat," Sahil answered. He rolled off, with Thumper and Mike in tow, and not a single complaint about having to cover all the same ground yet again.

Lincoln double-checked to make sure the two men at the base of the stairs wouldn't trouble them anymore. Wright took the men's weapons, removed the ammunition and firing components, and tossed them into one of the empty rooms, just to be safe. Then together they ascended the stairs back to the main entrance.

To Lincoln's dismay, what they found didn't surprise him. The man that Sahil had rendered unconscious was still out cold. The woman, unfortunately, had been shot dead, just like the man he'd found on the lower floor.

"You think they knew?" Wright asked.

"The civilians?" Lincoln said. Wright nodded, and he shook his head. "I'd guess they just figured these men were here for their protection."

"Guess we could go ask."

"Don't know if I'm up for that," Lincoln said, looking

at the poor, executed woman. He couldn't help but wonder what her story was, what part she had played, what she'd done, and whether or not she'd had any idea what she'd gotten caught up in.

"Well," Wright said. "At least we've got *him*." She nodded towards the sleeping man.

"He didn't seem real cooperative the first time around," Lincoln said.

"Yeah, I don't care about that. But he's going to have a lot of explaining to do to the authorities when he wakes up. The real ones, I mean."

Lincoln nodded, feeling his detachment from the situation starting to slip. He needed to get back on mission.

"We better get going on collection," he said. "We've got a lot to cover, and we're losing time."

"Roger that," Wright said.

They returned to the first floor, where they corralled the frightened civilians into one of the residential rooms. It'd be hard for them to get comfortable with their hands cuffed behind their backs, but at least they'd be warm and have access to bathroom facilities. Once the Outriders finished the collection, the plan was to alert the actual Outer Territorial Marshal Service to the situation. It'd be a long few hours for the civilians, but they'd be fine.

After Sahil's element had finished re-checking the rest of the facility, they'd moved the bodies of the slain into cold storage, and taken scans of each for later identification. When that grim task was completed, Lincoln assigned Sahil to questioning the survivors. Despite his outer appearance of a hard-charging pipehitter, Sahil had a genuine gift for empathy. Whether he'd developed it during his medical training, or if it was the reason he'd trained medical, Lincoln wasn't sure.

Either way, the same bedside manner that made him an outstanding medical sergeant also made him effective at developing rapport with possible sources of intelligence. He'd even assisted the man in the boxers with getting on a pair of pants.

Apparently, they were all independent contractors, hired on from a number of different settlements. None of them came from the Martian People's Collective Republic, and none had worked together before. Communications engineers, mostly. In general, they seemed to be willing to cooperate, but the details they provided were few. The story was that they thought they were helping set up preliminary infrastructure for a reopening of the facility; establishing deep-range communications. As far as they knew, the traffic they were passing around was just test data. Either they were well-trained liars, or their employers had done an exceptional job of keeping them in the dark as to their actual purpose. The fact that they provided so little information made it seem all the more terrible that the armed men had attempted to execute them. The only thing Lincoln could figure was that the bad guys had been concerned that their contractors might actively help dismantle whatever it was they'd built. They almost certainly weren't counting on anyone as sophisticated as the Outriders.

Sahil didn't tell them about their two fallen comrades until absolutely necessary. One of the women had asked about them repeatedly, and finally convinced the others not to answer any more questions until Sahil told them where they were. When he did, they weren't able to answer too many more questions anyway.

While Sahil handled the civilians, Lincoln ran the rest of the team through collection on the remaining rooms. Wright was on hard surfaces; bookcases, furniture, floors. Mike handled the soft stuff, clothes, notebooks, bedding. Thumper, of course, took care of anything technical, while Lincoln ran the sketcher. It was his job to get a scan of each room's layout, and track where each piece of potential intelligence came from. It was a tedious process, but together, if they did the job right, they could clear a room in just a few minutes, and the analysts back home would still be able to reconstruct a pretty good mock-up of the general environment to understand everything in context.

There wasn't much useful on the first floor. It was primarily their living space, and from what Lincoln could tell they'd maintained solid security protocols about not letting their work spill over. The second floor was the treasure trove. But no one on the team was happy about what they found.

"Link," Thumper said from one of the facility's terminals.

Lincoln was in the middle of the work room, finishing up with the sketcher.

"One sec," he said. "Almost done."

"Might not need it, when you see this," Thumper said. He took the ten seconds to finish the scan anyway, and then walked over to where she was.

She'd patched in to one of the workstations, not far from where Lincoln had found the first dead civilian worker. Whatever she'd hooked into wasn't immediately apparent; she was monitoring something on her internal display.

"What'd you dig up?" Lincoln asked.

"I got an observer on their stream," she said. "They're being smart about it, trickling data, routing it through multiple sites. Same idea as what we found with the device we recovered. They could've been smarter about it, though. Key I picked up off the device from the *Ava Leyla* let me peek at where all of this was ending up."

"Let me guess," Lincoln said. "The Collective Republic."

"Winner."

"So, *definitively*, you can trace the connection back to the MPCR," Lincoln said. "A hundred percent certain."

Thumper nodded. "Pretty much right to the home address. Looks like they're using the Manes-King array."

Manes-King Quantum was a powerhouse secure communications corporation, based out of the Republic.

"Doesn't seem like it should be that easy," he said.

She looked at him; the blank faceplate was unreadable, but the tilt of her head clearly communicated this wasn't the time.

"Sorry," he said. "It's worse than that?"

"It's worse than that. They're not just sending command and control *to* SUNGRAZER," she said. "They're piping data back *from* her."

"Back?" Lincoln said, before the implication fully settled on him. Thumper waited a moment, giving him the chance to catch up. She didn't give him long, though.

"SUNGRAZER isn't just a strike vehicle, Lincoln."

Lincoln recalled the briefing, to everything he'd been told about SUNGRAZER and her capabilities. She was a deep maneuver asset, sure. Lying in wait for the order to attack. But for a decade she'd been a surveillance vessel first and foremost.

"They're pulling our intel?" he asked.

"They're pulling our intel," Thumper said, nodding. "Not all of it, not all at once. The footprint for that would be enormous, easy for us to pinpoint. Looks to me like they're bleeding it off, a little bit at a time."

The rest of the team had paused their collection work,

and were now gathered around.

"For how long?"

"Couple of months at least. Possibly more."

"So before SUNGRAZER went missing then?"

"Well before."

Lincoln wasn't as deep into the world of intelligence and counterintelligence as his friends at the NID, but the implications weren't lost on him. The strategic impact of such a compromise in security couldn't be overstated. There was no telling what all the bad guys might be able to glean from rifling through everything SUNGRAZER had collected and transmitted back home for the past decade. Sources, methods of collection, what the US knew and what they didn't. The potential to shift the balance of power was staggering. And that didn't even take into account what would happen if that information was exposed to enemies closer to home. Or to the worlds at large.

And worse yet occurred to him.

"If they can pull data off," he asked, "how much more capability would they need to put it *on*, too?"

Thumper nodded again. "Now you're getting it. I don't see a lot of evidence that they're feeding us bad intel, but I wouldn't necessarily expect to from here. Gonna have to put Veronica on it to do a deep scrub. Big question now, is why take it offline at all?"

"You don't think it's a pure intel grab?" Mike asked.

"No," Thumper said. "They were doing that already without moving the ship. And it was cutting off contact that alerted us to it in the first place. Maybe something they found made them nervous."

"Or maybe they found whatever they were looking for," Lincoln added. "How long you estimate until they figure out we just wrecked their operation out here?"

"Might have already," Thumper said. "If not, I wouldn't think long."

"We cut 'em off here," Sahil asked. "What happens to SUNGRAZER?"

Thumper shook her head. "All this is just smoke and mirrors, making it hard for us to pin them down. We could pull the plug, but nothing's stopping them from directly connecting to her. Or from setting up another situation like they've got running here."

It was an important piece of the puzzle, maybe, but for all the effort Lincoln still didn't feel any closer to their objective. For every answer they'd uncovered, it seemed like they'd opened two new questions. And SUNGRAZER was still out there, on who knew what mission.

"I don't know how NID's going to handle the news that one of their automated assets got turned," Lincoln said.

"Not well," Wright answered.

He'd said it without thinking, but hearing his own words Lincoln felt the spark of an idea forming.

"Hey Thumper," he said. "Now that you're looking at their stream... how hard would it be to slip something into it yourself?"

She didn't answer immediately. After a few moments of consideration, she shook her head.

"Possible, but not from here. I'd need Veronica's help. That's obviously off the table."

"Why's that?"

"Uh… because I didn't bring her along for the hit, and I'd have to leave the connection live…?" Thumper said, with a tone that suggested it wasn't a question she should've had to answer.

"And how bad would it be to leave the connection live?" Lincoln asked.

"If we left it live, then I don't see how we did anything

useful at all here," Thumper said. "Except add to the body count."

"Just spit it out, sir," Wright said, clearly picking up on the fact that Lincoln had at least the beginnings of a plan. "We'll tell you if it's stupid."

"It's probably stupid. But we have to assume the bad guys know we hit this facility. If not already, then soon. Killing the connection now might prevent them from pulling any more data, but most of the damage has probably already been done. Seems like the next best thing to me, then, is to make them doubt whether they can trust the data they're getting. Better if we can make them doubt *all* of it."

"You're saying, we leave the stream intact, and hope they take that as a sign that we're not concerned about them stealing it?" Thumper said.

"I told you it was probably stupid," Lincoln said.

"It's not," Wright answered. And then added, "Not *completely*, anyway."

"Aaaand... we inject something," Thumper said, picking up the thread. "Something that looks good... maybe a little too good."

Lincoln nodded. "Something that maybe they only notice because they get curious as to whether or not any of it's trustworthy."

"I don't know, sounds pretty risky," Thumper said.

"Doubt it'd be worth doin' otherwise," Sahil answered. "Boss is right. Can't put the genie back in the bottle, might as well act like we don't care it got out in the first place."

"We're talking master-level chess here," Wright said. "Counts on them being a pretty sophisticated adversary. But I think all signs point to that being the case. I'm for trying, anyway."

"I guess I might be able to piggyback a trace in there, while we're at it," Thumper said. "A ridealong, might eventually find its way to SUNGRAZER. If we don't find her through other means first."

"What's your take, Mikey?" Lincoln asked.

"Hey, this stuff's all beyond me," Mike said. "You just call me again when something needs shootin'."

"This is getting outside of the intelligence business," Thumper said. "Falls more in line with counterintelligence."

"Yeah, well…" Lincoln said. "I can talk to Mom about a name change for the unit if you like."

"Let's see how it goes first," Thumper said. "All right, I'm sold."

"How do we make it happen?" Lincoln asked.

"Get back to base camp, for starters," Thumper said.

"I'm thinking we better do it on the jump," Wright said. "It might buy us a little more time on the job, but a little misdirection isn't going to solve the problem on its own. If this were a democracy, I'd vote we run it parallel to the groundwork, from inside the MPCR. But it's not a democracy." She turned meaningfully to Lincoln. Again, the expressionless faceplate somehow managed to highlight just how much her body language and tone of voice could communicate. Lincoln thought it over for a few moments, weighed the options.

"I agree, Amira," Lincoln said. "First order of business is to track down command-and-control, inside the Collective Republic. Anything else we can get is a bonus. Let's wrap it up here. We need to get the actual Marshals out here to see about these people. Once we're back to base, we'll pack up everything we can, and prep to move. I'll get a line back to the colonel asap, and see how he wants to get us on the inside."

They hadn't gotten exactly what they were after here, but at least it wasn't a total loss. Lincoln knew his team was used to working with whatever scraps they could come up with on their own, and figuring it out on the fly.

Unfortunately, he also knew they were running out of time.

EIGHTEEN

"You tell them about the feed we left open?" Lincoln asked, on a secure line back to the colonel. On the projection, Almeida shook his head as he sipped from his tea.

"I didn't tell them *anything* I didn't have to," he said. "I gave them everything you gave me, but I didn't *tell* them a thing. Figured I'd let them draw their own conclusions. Of course, given the quantity of material you pulled from the site, I think that might have made it all a little easier on me. After that, they were fairly eager to help. I basically just told them you'd tracked the culprits to the MPCR, and asked them how they wanted to get you inside. Didn't even give them the opportunity to consider whether or not you *should* be going inside."

"And how's that going to work?"

"Excellently," the colonel answered. "I hope." He smiled his crooked half-smile, and then said. "NID's got a man on the inside, one of their best, according to them. I don't know about *best*, but he's a long-time officer operating in there, so that's a point in favor. And the Barton boys are coming in commercial. They'll be on standby in a neighboring colony in case you need to leave in a hurry. I'm afraid they won't be available for close air support on this one, though."

"Yeah, I figured," Lincoln said. "Considering we can't even take the suits in."

"I know your pain," Almeida replied. "I'd wear my old one around the office if they'd let me."

"You still didn't answer my question."

"Oh, yeah, getting *you* in. NID Special Logistics is supposed to be handling it, but, here's the glorious part: I worked a couple connections on your behalf. I don't like to brag, but... Papa Charlie Bravo's going to take care of you. You're welcome."

Colonel Almeida said it with such gravitas that Lincoln knew the words must have had special significance; he just didn't know what that was.

"Papa Charlie Bravo?" Lincoln said. "Should I know him?"

Almeida gave him a look as if his joke had fallen flat. It melted to genuine surprise when the colonel realized Lincoln wasn't joking.

"That's the Directorate's west coast ninja squad. You've never heard of them?"

"No, sir I haven't. Though if they're a ninja squad, I guess that shouldn't really be a surprise. What do they do?"

Almeida smiled again. "Make things happen."

"Good things, I hope," Lincoln said.

"Good, bad. Depends on the need," the colonel answered. "But whatever they do, they do well. Absolute pro status. I figured you guys might appreciate having at least *one* thing you didn't have to worry about for a change."

"I do," Lincoln said. "What's our timetable looking like?"

"You tell me. Papa's already got people working,

should be able to get out to you by mid-morning at the latest. After that, it's go as fast as you can without getting caught."

"Wait, they're picking us up out here?"

Almeida nodded. "They're a full-service operation. They'll get you where you need to go … though, uh, I can't guarantee you'll like how you get there."

"As long as it doesn't involve getting shot at, I'll be good."

"They'll get you linked up with NID's fella, and he'll run you from there. Codename is WHITEHALL."

"And he knows what we're in town to do?"

"Enough," Almeida said. "I don't believe he knows about SUNGRAZER, but he knows you're helping the Directorate track a high-value asset, under time pressure. The way NID sold him to me, sounds like he's got networks inside networks. Most anything you need, he should be able to get for you. But you probably ought to avoid mentioning the ship, just to be safe."

"Understood," Lincoln said.

"Any update on the civilians at the facility?" the colonel asked.

Lincoln shook his head. "We know the Marshal Service sent a team out. Haven't been able to pick up any word on the outcome yet. No idea what kind of story they're going to have to tell. But they're not stuck out there on their own anymore, at least."

"Oh that reminds me," said Almeida. "The *Ava Leyla*."

The fact that the one situation had reminded the colonel of the other was a pinprick through Lincoln's heart. He thought he'd sufficiently detached from the experience on board the vessel, but the words revealed how raw the emotions still were.

"Thumper did a little work while you were on board,

you mentioned? Something to make it easier to keep track of?"

"Yes sir," Lincoln answered.

"Sounds like it paid off," said the colonel. "Report came in that the crew got picked up by port authorities when they came into dock at one of the hops out there, under a different registration. Recovered fourteen children from a hidden cargo hold."

Lincoln grunted at the number. Fourteen. Of seventeen. He couldn't help but wonder if the little girl from the storage room had been among them.

"That's good news," Almeida said, off Lincoln's reaction. "You and your team ought to feel good about that."

"I'd feel better if it had been all seventeen, sir."

"It's a whole lot more than zero, son. You didn't have to do anything. You made a tough call, did what you could. Fact that you got the job done *and* helped those kids, that's above and beyond. Take the win."

"Yes sir," Lincoln said. He nodded, and tried to take the colonel's words to heart. They just wouldn't sink in, though, not so that he could feel it. Maybe in time. For now, he found himself stuck hoping that little girl had made it out. "Anything else for me?"

Almeida gave him a look for a moment, but had the sense and courtesy to recognize Lincoln didn't want to discuss it further.

"I don't believe so," the colonel said. "Check back in once you get to the Republic and get a read on the situation. Let me know you got there, and all that."

"Will do."

"Oh yeah, and the folks from Papa. When you meet them, tell 'em I said hi."

"Friends of yours?"

"They're *all* friends of mine," Almeida said flashing his smile again. Obviously a history there he didn't plan to elaborate on at this time.

"Roger that," Lincoln said. "Talk to you soon."

"Look forward to it," the colonel replied. "Out."

Lincoln killed the feed, and sat in the dark of the mini-habitat for a few minutes, thinking through what lay ahead, and how they'd gotten this far. Maybe the colonel was right. Fourteen out of seventeen wasn't so bad. It was a little bit of good they'd done, anyway. It was, in a way, the only noticeable difference they'd made during this whole operation.

Thinking about it that way didn't make him feel so much better after all.

There was still plenty of work on Lincoln's plate, but sitting there in the darkness, he felt the weight of weariness settle on him. Not just tired. Lincoln lived tired. But he'd learned to tell the difference between wanting a rest and needing one. And he needed one.

He shook his head at himself. The op tempo hadn't been all that high, all things considered. He'd been in situations before that had required him to run two, sometimes three hits a night, for weeks on end. This scenario was a different sort of challenge. The physical exertion was the easy part. It was the constant mental churning, paired with the relentless sense that they were short on time and weren't moving fast enough, that dragged and wore him down, even when he was able to grab an hour or two of sleep. Lincoln couldn't remember the last time he'd slept and dreamed of anything other than the job.

He needed to take care of himself. But first, his teammates. Tempting as it was to crawl over to a corner of the mini-hab and rack out until someone found him,

Lincoln knew he couldn't disappear like that. He got
to his feet, and took a few minutes to visit each team
member, updating them individually or in pairs on what
he'd discussed with the colonel. They all expressed a
mixture of relief, gratitude, and disappointment similar
to Lincoln's at the news of the rescued children.

Once he'd completed his rounds, Lincoln double-
checked some final planning details, and then, shortly
before midnight, finally allowed himself to crash.

The team was up well before the sun to break down
their camp. They hadn't quite finished when two men
showed up in the pre-dawn hours, in a massive six-
wheeled, manually-operated ground vehicle. The thing
looked like a survey-exploration rig, a dump truck,
and a garbage truck had all smashed into each other
and decided it'd be easier if they all just went the same
direction from then on. The two men hopped out, both
sporting environmental suits typical of workers on outer
territorial drillers and excavators. If it hadn't been for the
fact that they pulled right up to the Outriders' concealed
base camp, Lincoln wouldn't have been sure these were
the right guys.

"Subtle," Lincoln said, pointing to the vehicle as the
men approached.

"Short notice," the driver replied. He extended his
hand. "Owen Kahn. Papa sent me."

"Lincoln Suh," Lincoln said, shaking Owen's hand.
"Mom told me to tell you hi."

"Lincoln," said Owen, with a nod. "Guess that makes
us brothers."

"Evan Garcia," the other man said, offering his hand
in turn. "Nice suit."

"Thanks," Lincoln said. He'd popped the faceplate

open so they could see his face through the transparent shield. It seemed rude to greet the men otherwise. "Sounds like you're going to be taking care of it for me while I'm out of town?"

"We'll keep it locked up for you, don't worry," Evan said. "And we'll even give it back when you need it."

"Yeah well, if you decide you want to try to take it for a spin, you probably want to wash it first. I've been in it for a couple of days."

"We don't do laundry," Evan answered, and then added with a smile, "and it wouldn't fit me anyway."

Thumper came over to greet them, and Lincoln made the introductions.

"You fellas are Logistical Support Officers, huh?" Thumper said.

"That's right," Owen said.

"Sort of like we're Information Support Technicians?" she asked.

"I wouldn't know anything about that, ma'am," Owen said, though the smile he flashed said otherwise. "But yeah, something like. Looks like you've got a lot of gear to pull out. Probably better get to it. Long drive back."

After the initial introductions were made, the seven set to the task of getting all the gear loaded up. The vehicle had a small crane arm on one side, and with it Evan unloaded what looked like a shipping container from the vehicle. Owen interacted with a panel on one side, and the container separated in two, about a quarter of the way from the back end. On closer inspection, Lincoln discovered it was in fact two containers; the rear quarter of the length was empty, but the rest was already loaded with equipment typical of speculative drilling operations. They packed all of their gear into the smaller section. Getting the dropsuits arranged was the trickiest part; they resorted to having Thumper walk them all in one at a time, since she was the most limber and had the least amount of trouble getting back out. The hardest part, though, was when it came time for the Outriders to part with their recon armor. The men from Papa Charlie Bravo had brought civilian clothes and e-suits for the five team members, matching the rugged ones they themselves were wearing. Lincoln knew it was for the best. The kind of work they'd be doing inside the MPCR wouldn't allow for anything so conspicuous. And the risk of one of the suits falling into the wrong hands… well, Lincoln didn't even want to think of what kind of repercussions that might have. Even so, he hated seeing it packed up. For him, it was like watching a lion forced into a cage. He knew well what the suit was capable of, what it had been made to do. Hanging in storage was exactly the opposite of its purpose. He managed to restrain himself from saluting as the door to the suit's container closed, but only just.

Once the equipment was secured and the Outriders had all changed into the clothes they'd been brought, they loaded into the monstrosity that Evan and Owen had driven in and got underway, as the sun crept over the horizon and daybreak began in earnest.

As it turned out, though they'd never actually met before, Wright and Sahil both knew who Owen was; apparently they'd run in some of the same special operations circles before Owen had officially transitioned out to civilian intelligence support work. It wasn't unusual for the Directorate's Special Logistics Division to recruit from Army Special Forces, and not a surprise that such a man would end up in the apparently highly-regarded Papa Charlie Bravo unit. And, as fate would have it, both Owen and Evan had been childhood friends of Will and Noah Barton. It really was a small world, and the special operations community made it even smaller. With all the common connections, the rapport was almost instantaneous.

"Guessing NID doesn't pay you to drive, huh?" Mike said to Evan, as they bounced across the trackless Martian terrain.

"Nah," Evan answered from behind the wheel, "they mostly pay me to clean up after jokers like you. The driving's just a hobby."

"Oh, so you're a janitor then," Mike replied, with a smile.

"From what I've heard of your work," Evan said without missing a beat, "I'd say we're more like septic system repair."

The cab of the vehicle was large enough to hold ten in three bench rows, the back row being slightly wider than the others. There wasn't a lot of leg room, but at least they didn't have to sit shoulder to shoulder the whole ride.

"So what's the plan for infil?" Wright asked from the middle row, right behind Evan. He gave her a quick glance over his shoulder.

"Basehead first, then over to Shukaku Station," he answered. "Our man WHITEHALL will take it from there. Not sure how he's planning to move you into the MPCR proper yet, but I'm sure he'll get you squared away."

"We're not driving all the way to Basehead?" Thumper asked from the back, loudly, and more of a statement than a question.

"Not in this thing," Evan said. "It's a good couple more hours to the excavation rig we used as an excuse to come get you, and then we'll be hopping a smoother ride out from there. We should be able to get you into Shukaku in time for dinner."

"And WHITEHALL?" Wright asked. "What's his story?"

Owen shook his head. "Don't know much about him, except he's undeclared and been running around the Republic for something like a decade."

"Must be pretty good at his job, if he's survived this long," Mike said. He was in the back row with Thumper.

"Or pretty bad," Thumper replied.

"From what I understand, he's the good kind," Evan said. "I've seen some quality stuff come over the cable with his stamp on it."

"You've never met him, though?" Wright said.

"Nope. Don't even know what he looks like," Owen answered. "Or, for that matter, that he's even a he."

"Hey, how do you guys know Mom?" Thumper asked.

"The colonel?" Owen replied. "Never had the honor of meeting him, ma'am. Reputation only."

"Everybody at Papa loves him, though," Evan added. "Word in the halls is he's one of the few truly good people out there. Pretty rare in our line of work. That's why we were so quick to volunteer when the news popped up on the wire that you guys needed a hand."

"You guys volunteered for this?" Lincoln said.

"Yep," Owen answered. "Soon as we heard."

"Well, more like we just hopped a flight and let the Directorate know we were handling it."

Lincoln chuckled. "Colonel made it sound like he'd pulled a few strings."

"Oh he did," Owen said. "A few years back. We're still returning the favor."

They spent the remaining hours of the trip swapping stories of operating in the shadow world. Both sides were careful to maintain operational security, hinting around enough without ever explicitly naming names. Once again, if you knew, you knew. And for the most part, they all knew. To Lincoln's disappointment, though, he never did learn why Colonel Almeida and Papa Charlie Bravo had such an affinity for one another, nor how Mom got his nickname.

They pulled up to the excavation rig around Martian noon, and Lincoln was impressed by how professionally all the workers ignored their arrival and their preparation for departure. Whatever cover story the PCB boys had provided had apparently been highly effective. In under an hour, they were on a sleek, corporate aircraft headed for Basehead, with their gear loaded safely on board. From Basehead, there was a change of clothes and craft, and another jump over to Shukaku Station, where they arrived around 1900 hours local time. Just a little late for dinner.

An unmanned shuttle picked them up and dropped the whole party off at a mid-scale hotel nearby. Owen didn't bother stopping at the front desk; he led the way to room 1911, and knocked.

"Yeah?" a voice said from inside.

"We're friends of Ms Nadia van der Merwe," Owen said, giving what Lincoln assumed was the proper phrase for initiating contact.

"Nadia? I haven't talked to her in years," came the reply. Clicks and snaps sounded from inside the room, locks being undone. The door opened a crack. "You read her book yet?"

"I've read them all," Owen answered.

With the prearranged coded exchange apparently completed, the door opened wider, but didn't reveal any more of the man on the other side. He shielded himself behind it, and waved them in with a single arm. Owen and Evan went first, followed by the rest of the team.

"Good grief. Brought the whole family, didn't you?" he said, as Sahil passed by him, entering last. He closed the door and relocked it. "Guess it would have been too much to ask to keep it a *small* affair."

"You know who we work for," Lincoln said. "We're lucky to do anything with less than a hundred."

The man turned around; dark hair, quick eyes, steady hands, and, as far as Lincoln could tell, a genuine smile on his face. The infamous WHITEHALL, in the flesh.

"Elliot Goodkind," WHITEHALL said, extending his hand. "Sounds like I'll be your tour guide for the duration of your stay."

"Goodkind?" Thumper said. "Is that your real name?"

"I get that a lot," he answered. "And yes." He gave it a moment, and then added, "At least as far as you're concerned... But you can call me Elliot."

Lincoln scanned the hotel room; it was a suite, nicely appointed, if a bit aged. He hoped they wouldn't all be spending the night here, though.

"Sooo," Elliot said. "You guys eat yet?"

Lincoln shook his head. "We've been on the move all day."

"Ah, *you're* the man in charge, then," Elliot said with a smile. An innocuous question, with deeper intent. Lincoln had never considered how answering for the others made him conspicuous as a team leader.

"The one with the title, anyway," Lincoln said, extending his hand. "Lincoln Suh."

"I've seen the file, Lincoln," Elliot answered, shaking hands. "What they were willing to share, anyway. Good to meet you."

"We secure here?" Wright asked.

Elliot nodded. "Room's clean. I've got a field running."

"So you're up to speed on what we're here for?" Wright said.

"You'd probably be surprised at how little they actually tell me," Elliot said. "But that's OK, it works out for both of us. If I get caught, it makes me less of a liability to them. And if I make a mistake, I can claim I didn't know any better." He flashed a quick grin.

"I guess that's one way to look at it," Lincoln said.

"This line of work, it helps to be an optimist," Elliot replied. "When you can afford it, anyway. Though I guess most of the time, it's just likely to get you killed."

"Sounds familiar. How much did they give you?"

"Details were a little light, but I think I got the gist of it," Elliot said. "NID asset dropped off the radar, parties believed responsible operating out of the Republic, possibly under government direction. You're here looking for fingerprints."

"Sounds about right," Lincoln said. "Word on the street is you're NID's ace in the hole."

"Well, they got the hole part right, for sure," Elliot said. "Jury's still out on the rest of it. But I should be able to grease the wheels for you a good bit. Get you in and around, and hopefully out soon enough. Let me get an order in for dinner, and we can talk through it. You guys all good with Chinese? There's a place about a block over. Food's not great, but they give you a lot of it."

"That's a big thumbs up from me," Mike said. "I'm starving."

"All right," Elliot replied. "I've got a room here if somebody wants to bunk with me. And rooms 1917 and 1812. All suites. I'll let you folks figure out who goes where for how long." He pointed to Owen and Evan.

"You fellas staying around?"

"We've got a place across town," Evan answered. "But I could eat."

Elliot nodded and disappeared into one of the bedrooms to place a dinner order, while the rest of the team sorted out living arrangements. Lincoln decided he'd stick with Elliot, and let the rest of the team pair off. Mike and Wright took room 1812, leaving the room just down the hall to Sahil and Thumper.

Dinner arrived close to 2000 hours, carried by a thin and sweaty young man who had somehow managed to wrangle the entire order up to their room on his own. Elliot gave him a big tip, but the young man seemed more grateful to be relieved of the burden than for the extra money.

They all gathered around the small table to unload boxes from the numerous bags.

"Uh oh," Elliot said. "Tactical error."

"What's that?" Owen asked.

"Forgot I didn't have any dishes," Elliot answered. "We'll have to eat like savages, out of the boxes."

"Fine by me," Mike said around a mouthful of something. He was already chowing down, straight out of a container.

The rest of them set to. Elliot hadn't been kidding. None of it was great, and a lot of it tasted the same, but there were so many different dishes and so much of each, they could have practically opened their own buffet. By Lincoln's estimation, Mike ate about half of the haul on his own.

They spread out to the various available seats around the room, some on chairs, three on the couch, a couple leaning on arm rests. Elliot perched on top of the desk in the corner of the room. They kept conversation light and on surface matters until the feeding frenzy was winding down.

"I never could get the hang of these things," Elliot said, fumbling with a set of chopsticks while trying to fish the last few noodles out of a box. "But I always feel like using a fork would be dishonoring the culture."

"Pretty sure this chicken is already doing that," Thumper said. She held up a chunk of the meat for Elliot to see.

"I think that's beef," Mike answered. Thumper glanced at Mike, then back at the bite she'd been about to eat. Without another word, she let it fall back into the box and set the whole container down on the end table by the couch. Mike looked at her, then at the box, then back to her again. After a moment, she handed it to him, and he dug in.

"So," Elliot said, apparently giving up on those last noodles. He set the container down next to him on the desk and rubbed his hands together. "To business?"

"Let's do it," Lincoln said.

"I've got a safehouse set up already, an apartment in the financial district. Might be a little tight for five, but should be more comfortable than your previous accommodations at least."

"How much static are we going to have moving our gear in?" Wright asked.

"Weapons... we'll have to ship in," Elliot said. "Could be a little dicey."

"What if we go local," Sahil said. "You got access?"

Elliot nodded. "Yeah I can make that happen, if you don't mind the downgrade. Nothing I come up with is going to be as high-speed as what you're used to."

"I'm the only picky one," Mike said. "Sahil could do the job with a couple of rocks if he had to."

"Whatdya mean a *couple*?" Sahil said, mock offended at the implication he would need more than one.

"I'm hoping we won't need any at all," Lincoln said. "But we better count on it anyway. As long as whatever you can get us hits hard and doesn't make too much noise, we'll try our best not to need them."

"That I can do," Elliot said. "Other equipment should be a fair bit easier, depending on what we come up with for cover. Anybody set you up with a front yet?"

Lincoln shook his head. "I figured you'd want to weigh in on that."

Elliot looked surprised. "Well... gee. That was courteous of you. I'm not quite sure how to respond."

"With good recommendations would be great."

"Sure, yeah. Just not used to getting to have input on these things. Usually the only time I have any say is after the mess is already made."

"We're hoping to skip that part," Lincoln said.

"We have options?" Elliot asked.

"Sure," Thumper said, holding up her personal datapad. "I've got like five hundred corporations on here."

The corporations Thumper had access to were all one hundred percent legitimate companies, operating in the open. They were, however, also one hundred percent operated by National Intelligence Directorate-managed AI. Goods and services were bought and sold; money moved in, out, and around. Profitability was carefully controlled to balance gains and losses, keeping everything within statistical norms to avoid attracting too much market attention. Personnel were hired and fired, though employees were a mix of actual humans and hollow identities waiting to be filled whenever an operation required a well-established cover. The list automatically rotated and refreshed to prevent separate operations from using the same businesses. Only certain Special Access Programs could make use of the list, but fortunately, the Outriders were classified as one such program.

"How many do we need?" Thumper asked, already scanning the list.

"I'd say three, minimum," Wright said. But Elliot shook his head.

"One will be enough," he said. "MPCR is magnificent at determining connections between people. Like, scary black magic good at it. I'd guess it would take them about forty-eight hours to put you five together, once you're all inside and working. Unless you want to spend all your time trying to manage your contact with one another, it's going to be safer and more efficient to all go in together, under the same umbrella."

"You're sure that's wise?" Wright said, and her tone clearly communicated she was sure it wasn't.

"Wise?" Elliot said, shaking his head again. "No. Not at all. It's not ideal, not by a long shot. If you had time on your side, I'd work it more organically, over three, maybe four weeks. But I got the sense you guys were on the clock on this one."

"Time is of the essence, yes," Lincoln said.

"Then that's my recommendation. I do a lot of my hiding in plain sight these days. It's been working so far."

"I'm sure it *appears* that way, at least," Wright said.

"Fair point," Elliot admitted.

"I think we'll let you folks work out the details," Owen said, getting to his feet. "I'm smoked."

"Oh yeah, sure," Elliot said. "What's the plan for you guys?"

"The Barton boys are supposed to be rolling in sometime in the morning. We'll hook up with them, get them set up in town, and then we'll be on standby. You need anything, give us a yell."

They all exchanged the necessary contact credentials and ciphers.

"What's your response time gonna be like?" Sahil asked. "Case we need somethin' in a hurry."

"Just depends on how much noise you allow us to make. Probably four to six hours to get to you quiet-like. Half that, if you don't mind starting a war."

Owen and Evan said their goodbyes, and left the team to their planning session.

"I think something technical is going to work best for us," Elliot said, resuming their conversation. "Military adjacent."

"Guidance systems?" Thumper asked.

"Maybe not that adjacent," Elliot said. "You got anything in navigation?"

Thumper skimmed the list, while Lincoln started gathering up cartons of Chinese food, of various quantities. When she saw what he was doing, Wright wordlessly joined in.

"You want me to save any of this?" Lincoln asked.

"I don't think you want to try it reheated," Elliot said. But Mike's eyebrows went up, like maybe he'd be willing to risk it.

"I'll save you some, Mikey," Lincoln said.

Elliot snapped his fingers. "Oh, there's one… uh what was it? Did some work a few years ago for a couple of folks and used… Ready something. Ready Solutions? Something like that?"

"Ready Vector Solutions?" Thumper said, a few moments later. "Collision detection and avoidance?"

"That sounds right, yeah," Elliot said. "Anybody used recently?"

"Not in the past couple of years, at least. Looks pretty clean."

"Commercial?"

"Industrial," Thumper answered. "But could be looking to expand maybe, if we needed it?"

Elliot thought it over for a moment, then nodded. "Yeah. Yeah I think that'll work. Looking for partnerships, maybe. Yeah, I can work with that. That'll make it a lot easier for me to stay in touch with you. Sort of a known-connection kind of deal. Making introductions, that sort of thing. How long you folks think you'll need in town?"

"We'd be done in a couple of hours if it were up to us," Mike said.

"Best case," Wright said. "I'd say five, maybe seven days. We have two objectives, but we only know where one of them is. Need at least two days to recon that site. We were hoping you might be able to help us out with the second."

"Understood," Elliot said. "Happy to do whatever I can. Probably the less time you spend inside, the better it is for me. And I'm all about me, you know. What are you after?"

"Two pieces of a puzzle," Lincoln said. It was going to be delicate, giving Elliot enough information to go on without risking compromising SUNGRAZER's security any further. "The asset in question has some specific, specialized communications protocols. One objective is to handle command-and-control. That one we've got the location for. The second objective has to do with the method of communication. That one we have some ideas about, but not enough to go on."

Elliot grunted. "Probably going to have to give me a little more than that, if you want me to be of any particular use."

JAY POSEY

279

"Yeah," Lincoln said. "Sorry. It's a sensitive situation."

"Obviously," Elliot answered, smiling again. "When they send soldiers who don't exist to talk to a spook who doesn't exist, I guess we can't expect all the cards to be on the table."

"It's more that if you don't already know, it's better to keep it that way," said Lincoln.

"Oh, I understand. Pretty much everything is need-to-know in my line of work. I'm used to it," Elliot replied. He grimaced, and then added, "Well, I don't think you get used to it. But I get it, anyway... even if I'm the guy who got you here in the first place." He threw the comment away, with a sly smile.

Lincoln looked at the NID agent for a moment, while his brain worked back through the chain of events that brought them all to this point. He found the connection.

"You didn't happen to turn some NID techs onto a communications burst, by any chance?" Lincoln asked.

"I can neither confirm nor deny the Directorate's sources or methods," Elliot said. Then he smiled. "But yeah, I gave them the *Ava Leyla*. That's why I wasn't too surprised when they came back later and told me a team was looking to get in. I mean, obviously I didn't know *why* they were asking, what they were looking for exactly. Still don't. But I picked up on some business dealings between a couple of shady types, moving high-spec commo hardware out of the Republic. Put two and two together and actually came up with four for once. Just one of those random right-place-right-time kinds of situations."

"A lucky break," Thumper said.

Elliot nodded. "Almost lucky enough to make me believe in a higher power."

"You don't?" Mike asked.

"Nah. I figure if there was one, he probably wouldn't let people like me run around making a mess for so many others." He tossed it off with a casual smile, but as he let it fade, Lincoln noticed him glance at the window and a brief shadow swept across his face. More truth to his words than he wanted to admit, maybe. A man in his position, operating in the grey for so long... Lincoln could only imagine the hard stories Elliot must have had.

Out of the corner of his eye, Lincoln saw Sahil stifle a yawn, barely. Lincoln couldn't remember a time when he'd seen Sahil show any sign of weariness.

"Do we need the whole team to work the rest of the details?" Lincoln asked.

Elliot shook his head. "Don't guess so. Pretty much just need to work out getting you in. I figure you need to get a lay of the land before you make too many plans, huh?"

"Absolutely right," Lincoln answered. "Thumper, why don't you hang out with Elliot and me for a little bit longer, and let's get the cover worked out. Rest of you can knock off, get some sleep while you can."

"I'm good," Sahil said. Wright nodded.

"Me too, I'm fine, sir," she said.

"I'm smoked," said Mike.

"I know you're anxious to get in," Elliot said. "But I think we'll hop an evening flight tomorrow. There's always a good influx of business types around 1900 hours. Long lines tend to make the customs folks less curious. We can wrap things up for the night, finalize details in the morning."

Lincoln managed to convince the rest of his team to call it a night, though he kept Thumper and Elliot up past midnight solidifying their cover stories and identities. When he finally went to bed his body was exhausted, but his brain kept him awake for another hour, trying to process all the details he had to keep in mind. No matter how much he trusted his teammates, Lincoln knew if anything went sideways, he would be the only one he could hold responsible. They were all counting on him to lead them, and to get it right. There were still so many unknowns, so much at stake, and so little margin for error. He drifted off to fitful sleep, dreaming of the ways it could all go wrong.

NINETEEN

They arrived with the end-of-day commuter rush, under
the nearly invisible membrane that shielded the Martian
People's Collective Republic from the extremes of the
Martian climate. For all Lincoln's nervous sweating and
loss of sleep the night before, the journey in had turned
out to be nearly effortless. Elliot escorted them the entire
way, without taking any apparent measures to conceal
their connection. In fact, he openly, actively advertised
it. It was obvious the man was a frequent visitor to all
the main travel ports. The only minor scare came when
a customs agent approached and without explanation
pulled them out of the line and asked them to follow him.
As it turned out, the agent was friendly with Elliot, and
whisked all six of them through a special expedited line.
Elliot explained how Lincoln and his companions were
in town to evaluate the MPCR as a potential location for
expanding their business, but it came out through small
talk rather than any sort of official inquiry.

If Elliot's manner gave the impression he was
unconcerned with drawing attention, his "safehouse"
did nothing to dispel the notion. When he'd told them
the apartment was in the financial district, Lincoln
assumed he'd meant in the cheapest part of town. Like

most assumptions, that had turned out to be grossly mistaken. Elliot's safehouse was in prime territory, in a towering apartment complex that looked like it wanted everyone who saw it to know it belonged amongst the most lavish buildings in the entire district.

"You think the taxpayers know about this?" Mike whispered as they stared up at the facility.

"I hope not," Lincoln said. "And I don't think we should tell them."

The group took a lift to the ninth floor. It was so quiet and fast that Lincoln wouldn't have realized they'd moved, if not for the numerical display catapulting from G to 9. Elliot took them to apartment 919. When he swung the door open, Thumper let out an uncharacteristic and involuntary curse. Elliot ushered them in with the gracious air of a generous and humble host.

"Sorry it's only a two-bedroom deal," Elliot said, as he closed the door behind them. "Usually we only use it for one primary, plus either a security or interrogation team."

The apartment didn't disappoint. Standing in the entryway, Lincoln immediately felt like he should take off his shoes. The team fanned out to inspect their new, sadly temporary home. And while it was true that it was "only" a two-bedroom affair, each bedroom was cavernous. All five of the Outriders could have bunked together in one of them, and still considered it obscenely luxurious compared to what they were used to.

"This is uh…" Thumper said, "maybe not the most inconspicuous place in town, yeah?"

"More than you might think," Elliot said. "A fair number of CEOs and political types spend a lot of their time in the district. This is where they bring all their mistresses and boytoys."

"Ugh," Sahil said, the first time Lincoln could ever remember him expressing an opinion.

Elliot shrugged. "Makes for amazingly incurious neighbors. Everyone's real polite and stays out of everyone else's way. Well, except for one lady up on the fourteenth floor. Pretty sure she's rich, retired, and bored. A real busybody, always up in everyone's business."

"And you're not worried about her?" Wright asked.

"Nah," Elliot said. He flashed his grin. "She's on my payroll."

"You got a place here, too?" Mike asked.

"Me? Pff, no, I've got a studio over in the cheap part of town. I'd bet you'd be surprised at how little we civil servants make."

"Not *that* surprised," Mike said.

"Speaking of which, I've got a couple of things I need to check on around town. I'll let you guys get settled in. Fridge is stocked, dishes are clean. I'll stop back in a couple of hours?"

"Sounds good," Lincoln said.

"Make yourselves at home," Elliot said. "Try not to get in any trouble. At least until tomorrow."

"Roger that," Lincoln replied.

After Elliot left, the team went through their usual routine for setting up in a new location; they went through the apartment checking the doors and windows, noting vulnerabilities and escape routes, talking through the best use of each room, getting a general feel of the place. Once that was completed, Wright and Mike went out again together to scout the surroundings; elevators, stairwells, general layout of the floors above and below. Lincoln and Sahil handled getting their gear moved and unloaded, while Thumper got to work setting Veronica up in the apartment's study. The fact that the apartment had a study was not lost on any of them. Of all the assignments Lincoln had ever been on, he knew there was no way anyone back home would let him complain about it, no matter how hard the work actually was.

When Mike and Wright returned, they raided the fridge and threw together a quick meal, sketching rough ideas for how to handle the approach to their objectives while they ate. By the time Elliot returned, the team was already gathered around Veronica, looking at imagery of the target facility and marking up routes and locations for their surveillance op. Elliot joined the session in progress.

"That's your first objective?" he asked.

"Yeah," Lincoln said. "We tracked a signal back to here. Pretty sure this is the origin point for command-and-control we're after."

"Probably going to be a four-man job, at least," Wright said.

"Oh, well…" Elliot said. "I'm pretty sure we can get it done with three."

The whole team went still. Wright wasn't sensitive about being contradicted, but there was no question that she had an eye and a mind for tactical planning. Lincoln doubted Elliot had anything like the experience necessary to be able to make that sort of call, and even if he did, Lincoln wouldn't ever trust the Directorate officer's judgment over that of his master sergeant.

"How do you figure that?" Lincoln asked, hoping he didn't sound completely dismissive.

"Because me and two of you makes three?" Elliot said. He let it hang in the air for dramatic effect, and then added with a smile, "I know a guy."

"You know a guy?" Wright said.

"Yeah," he said. "Well, a lady, actually. That's Manes-

King Quantum? Out in the north quarter?"

"It is," Lincoln said. "You're familiar with it?"

"Sure. Their chief of security is a buddy of mine."

"You're kidding me," Wright said.

Elliot shook his head. "No joke. Selah Coulibaly. She's great. One of the first contacts I cultivated when I got here, in fact. When I met her, she was just an analyst for uh… oh who was it? I forget now. They were small time, got bought up by Manes-King." He looked at the floor, trying to come up with the name of the company.

"She's an asset?" Wright asked, prompting him to continue.

"Oh no," Elliot said. "Just a friend." He chuckled to himself, and then shook his head. "Actually, I was trying to get her to go out on a date with me. By the time I'd worked up the nerve to actually ask, she'd already had my intentions pegged for like six weeks. But she had a good sense of humor about it. Anyway. You know where you need to get in the facility?"

"Not exactly," Thumper said. "I'd been assuming getting on site was going to be the hard part."

"But the people you're after, they're in there somewhere?" Elliot asked.

"Not the people, no," Thumper answered. "They're running remote access to Manes-King's on-demand comm system. I need access to hardware that's managing that traffic. If I can get to that, Veronica can crawl it from there, get us to what we need."

"Oh," Elliot said. "I'd assumed you were after the bad guys."

"That'd be a nice-to-have, certainly," Lincoln said. "But our priority is recovering the asset."

"Oh OK, got it," Elliot answered, nodding. "You just need access to the array farm."

Thumper nodded.

"The part of the facility they keep under tightest control," he continued.

Thumper shrugged and then nodded.

"The one place they guarantee their vast client base is absolutely, one hundred percent secure and tamperproof," he said.

"Sounds like the one," Thumper said.

"Sure," Elliot said. "Let me give her a call, see what I can work out."

"Kind of late, isn't it?" Mike asked as Elliot was stepping out of the room, but Elliot just waved a hand like it was no big deal. A few moments later, they could hear him talking, words indistinct through the door of one of the bedrooms.

"It can't be that easy," Wright said.

"Another lucky break?" Lincoln said.

"We never get two on the same op," Wright said. "And even when we get *one*, it usually only gets us in trouble."

"Give him a chance, Mir," Sahil said. He had his chair tipped on its back legs, and was leaning against the wall with his eyes closed. "He's been at this a long time."

"Maybe so," Wright said, turning back to the images on Veronica's display, "but we're still posting up. No way we're going in with just three. And I'm *not* counting him as one."

The team waited around for a few minutes until Elliot reappeared.

"All right, all set," he said. "You, and you," he pointed to Lincoln and Thumper in turn, "have an appointment with Ms Coulibaly at 10 am tomorrow. I told her you guys are thinking about expanding, but are concerned about maintaining the security of a high-availability system, and that I couldn't pass up an opportunity to see her. I didn't mention the array farm. That might be too much of an ask even in person. We'll see how it plays when we get there. I'm positive she's not going to give away any secrets about how they run their systems, but I think we can get you on the right floor at least."

"Just like that," Wright said. She wasn't being openly hostile, but it was clear to everyone in the room that she wasn't going to go along unless she could confirm for herself the viability of the plan.

"Just like that," Elliot replied, with a half shrug. "If we can't get the work done when you're inside, at least you can get a look around, see what you're dealing with. Though, I gotta be honest. If you can't get what you need while we're there, I don't envy you the job of trying to get back in. Selah's top notch."

"And you don't have any issue betraying your friend's trust?" Wright asked.

"For my country?" Elliot said. "Would you?" In response, Wright's eyes narrowed and her lips disappeared in a tight, thin line. After a moment Elliot smiled to take the edge off the comment, even though it had obviously had its intended effect.

"Anyone ever tell you the way you operate kind of makes it seem like you might be involved in some sort of organized crime?" Thumper asked.

Elliot looked at her, still smiling. "Anyone ever tell *you* that the way the government operates *would* be organized crime, if only they weren't the ones making the rules?" He waved his hand back at Veronica's display. "Anyway, I do think it's a good idea for you to get out there and do some ground work on your own. Never hurts to double-check and plan contingencies. What's the delivery mechanism for whatever it is you need to do to the farm?"

Thumper sat back and ran her hand back and forth over her head a few times, thinking it over.

"Physical access would be best," she said. "Barring that… I might be able to do it with a skeeter. That's going to take longer, though."

"How long?"

"Eight, ten minutes. Depending on their protocols."

"Better count on twenty, then," Elliot said.

"Then I'll take two," Thumper replied.

"Getting any gear in is going to be tricky, so it'd be good to travel light."

"Always is," Lincoln replied. "You have any fancy spy gear you can hook us up with? Shoes with secret compartments, laser watches, that sort of thing?"

"I'm not that kind of spy. And I kind of figured you'd brought your own."

"I'm working on a list now," Thumper interjected.

"And I'm going out to take a look," Wright said, getting to her feet. "Link, I don't think it's a good idea for you to be walking around up there before tomorrow."

It was a good call. No need to risk getting noticed casing the joint, when he'd be getting an up-close-and-personal view in the morning. It was a key part to the functioning of the team that Lincoln didn't feel the need to discuss the point or put his stamp of approval on it. And an equal part was the fact that even though she'd made it a statement, Wright showed her respect for his position by waiting for him to officially release her to get to work.

"Keep your head down out there," Lincoln said.

Wright nodded, and headed for the door. "Mike, Sahil, you're with me."

The three of them departed, leaving Thumper, Elliot, and Lincoln with the job of working out the details for their morning appointment. Lincoln understood why he had to go in, but there was no denying he would have much preferred to be working the perimeter. Instead, he spent the next few hours at a table, devising a plan to get the necessary gear through security.

Selah Coulibaly was a tall, dark-skinned woman, six feet or possibly a hair under, with the long, elegant grace of a ballerina and eyes that were unsettlingly like those of a panther, not in color but in subdued ferocity. She met them in the large, marbled lobby of the Manes-King facility, and embraced Elliot warmly. Despite the welcome, Lincoln felt exposed, vulnerable from every angle. This wasn't how he was used to working, and judging from the woman in front of him, a single mistake could easily blow the whole operation. And already he felt that walking through the front door might have been a mistake.

The rest of the team was outside the facility on the distant perimeter, with a standard obstruct and escape plan in case things went wrong, but from the inside Lincoln was no longer confident they'd be able to make it far enough out to matter.

"Selah," Elliot said. "Thank you for doing this. I know it's a hassle."

"Not at all, Elliot," she answered. "It's nice to have an excuse to see you on the clock. It's been too long."

He nodded. "Been traveling a lot lately. Hoping it'll slow down here soon." He stepped back and offered the black box he had tucked under one arm. "A small thank you."

"Hmm, this looks familiar. And completely unnecessary," she said, but she accepted the gift anyway, and held it to an ear as she shook it gently. "And I hope not too expensive to be a *small* thank you."

"A medium-sized one, then," Elliot replied. "Mr Kim here actually insisted on it."

Elliot drew Lincoln and Thumper into the moment by waving them closer, introducing them by their assumed identities. "Allison Cooper and Simon Kim, from Ready Vector Solutions."

When Selah shook Lincoln's hand, whatever affection she had for Elliot seemed to have transferred directly to them; it was more personal than professional. He almost felt guilty for the false name.

"Ms Cooper, Mr Kim, a pleasure."

"You can just call me Allison," Thumper said.

"And Simon, please," Lincoln added.

"Very well. Simon, Allison. Thank you for this," she said, holding up the gift.

Lincoln tipped his head in a shadow of a bow, "The least we could do, for your generosity on such short notice. Elliot advised us on the selection."

"I'm sure it's extravagant almost to the point of ostentatious, then," she said with a smile. "Follow me, I'll take you back."

She led them through the access control point and had them sign in as visitors. While they filled out some standard documentation agreeing that they wouldn't reveal any details of their visit under threat of stiff legal penalties, Selah chatted amicably with the security personnel manning the station. From their interaction, Lincoln could tell she was personally familiar with her staff and had a sharp mind for details. She was also apparently well-liked by her subordinates. That was all likely a bad sign for their chances of infiltrating later. If she took that much care with her staff, he could only imagine what she'd done for the facility as a whole.

When they had completed the documents, Selah directed them to pass through a small chamber.

"You can keep everything in your pockets," she said. "The scanner's just going to do a quick inventory. We won't restrict your communications while we're here, but this just lets us keep track of traffic coming in and out of the facility. No recording devices I should know about?"

"I already told them," Elliot said.

"I assumed you had," Selah replied, and then added with a smile, "but I never assume."

"We're not here for pictures, Ms Coulibaly," Lincoln said.

"Selah, please. Friends of Elliot's are friends of mine."

"You scan all your friends?" Elliot said.

"Every one," she answered.

Elliot went first, followed by Thumper, with Lincoln bringing up the rear. He tried not to hold his breath.

"I don't know why, but these things always make me nervous," he said as he passed through. He and Thumper were both carrying disassembled components of a control device, each element disguised as typical pocket litter. As far as he could tell, nothing registered on the scan. Once they were all through, Selah waved for them to follow her, but then stopped.

"Oops, one second," she said, and took the gift Elliot had given her over to the security station for the guards to run through a scanner.

"You're kidding me," Elliot said.

"Surely you understand, my dear," Selah said. "What kind of example would I be setting if I didn't follow my own rules?"

Lincoln tried not to panic. The only devices they couldn't disassemble were the skeeters, and they were both hidden in the gift. The present had been carefully chosen, and wrapped identically to one Elliot had given her before. Elliot's expectation was that, given their relationship and Selah's familiarity with the package, it would escape further scrutiny. It was why he'd made a point to present the gift to her in the lobby, knowing that she wouldn't pass through the checkpoint. Apparently he had either underestimated her zealousness for her job, or overestimated the level of trust he'd developed with her.

The devices were Martian-manufactured, supplied by Elliot, modified to suit Thumper's purposes. Elliot swore they were as good as the Outriders' usual gear, and safer on the remote chance they should happen to be discovered. It looked likely they were about to test that theory. The skeeters were small, deactivated, and shielded against most standard spectra, but they weren't invisible. About the only hope they had now was that the original social engineering plan would still work on the security guards, that maybe they'd run only a cursory scan, expecting that any personal friends of the Chief of Security would assuredly be trustworthy.

At least, that's what Lincoln had assumed. Apparently Elliot had other plans.

"Well, can you at least let me take the microdrone out of it before you scan it then?" Elliot said.

Selah laughed, but Elliot held out his hand and motioned for her to hand it over. The Chief of Security's humor drained away, and she held her place. Lincoln had no idea what to do.

The two security guards exchanged a look, like they had no idea what to do either. Elliot was the only one who seemed unconcerned.

"Give it here," he said.

Selah walked over slowly and handed him the box, the look on her face unreadable.

"I told you she was top notch," Elliot said, to Lincoln and Thumper as he opened the gift. It was a twenty year-old Scotch, one that Selah had a special love for. Elliot removed the bottle from the container. Lincoln still didn't know what the play here was.

"Hold this," he said, handing Selah the black box. Sure enough, to Lincoln's surprise and Thumper's obvious discomfort, he casually removed the false bottom from the bottle that they had so painstakingly prepared the night before, and then drew out the two flat disks hidden inside. They were each about the size of a large coin.

Elliot held them up between thumb and forefinger. But no, Lincoln saw now, not two. Only one. He had no idea where the second one had gone, even though he'd been watching Elliot the whole time. The man had a magician's hands.

"Sorry, it was probably a stupid idea," Elliot said. "I wanted it to be a surprise."

He flipped the disk to her, and she snatched it out of the air one-handed.

"It *was* a stupid idea," Selah said. "That's not funny, Elliot."

"I know, Selah, I'm sorry. It didn't even occur to me what that might look like… I just thought you'd like to check one out, and thought I was being clever."

She held the disk flat on her palm and studied it briefly.

"How does it work?" she asked.

"That one won't," Elliot said. "It's a demo model, not a live one. I'm not *that* stupid."

Selah looked up at him, and studied him for a moment, and then shifted her eyes over to Lincoln and Thumper.

Judging them. Lincoln stood very, very still. In this case, he didn't have to feign the shock he was feeling. He still couldn't believe Elliot had blown the whole op before it'd even started.

"I'm sorry, Mr Kim," Elliot said. "I should've told you."

"Or," Lincoln said, picking up the cue, "not have done such a thing at all."

Selah watched them for a span longer. Finally, she shook her head and took the box and the skeeter to the security guards and had them scan both. Fortunately in its deactivated state, the microdrone wouldn't give off a signal of any kind that might alert them to the fact it was anything other than the demo model Elliot had claimed.

"Bottle too," she said.

Elliot sheepishly relinquished the bottle.

"Now you see why I don't make *any* exceptions," Selah said to the guards at the station. They both nodded dutifully. But then she chuckled and shook her head again, and the tension broke. She turned around while the guards finished the scan and looked at Lincoln and Thumper. "This guy," she said, pointing at Elliot. "I don't know that I'd trust him, if he wasn't so easy to read. I don't suppose he told you about how we met?"

"A little," Thumper said. "Mostly that you'd had his intentions identified well in advance of the execution of his plans."

"Exactly," Selah said. "Surprised he admitted to it. With him, it was even easier than usual." She and Thumper shared a knowing look that made Lincoln feel like he'd just missed some subtle joke. And the feeling that he'd missed the joke enlightened him to the fact that he was part of the punchline.

"We are a generally oblivious animal," he said, and Selah's eyes flicked to his, amused.

"In general, yes," she said. And then added with a quick wink. "Perhaps not in *every* specific."

"What are you guys even talking about?" Elliot said.

"All clean, Ms Coulibaly," one of the guards said, handing the box, the skeeter, and the bottle back.

"Thank you, Douglas," she answered, accepting them. But she stopped mid-motion, and examined the bottle. "Elliot," she said. "You didn't."

"No I did not," he said. "Mr Kim did."

She looked at Lincoln, stunned.

"Mr Kim, I can't accept this. This is too much."

Lincoln didn't know anything about Scotch, so the force of her reaction was lost on him. He hadn't even paid for the bottle. Elliot had given it to him from some secret stash.

"I must confess Ms Coulibaly, I'm not sure I understand the significance," Lincoln said. "I asked Elliot for a recommendation. He said you were fond of that particular brand?"

She nodded and motioned for them to follow her as she led them towards a short corridor.

"I used to think there was nothing on Earth we couldn't make better here on Mars," she said. "But Scotch…"

There were three lifts on the left side of the hall, and a fourth at the end. Selah escorted them to the fourth, and ran her credentials through the interface. The door slid open, and she ushered the three of them in.

"And this in particular," she continued, holding the bottle up again. "Well, it almost makes up for Elliot's ridiculous stunt."

"Then I wish I'd brought one more bottle," Lincoln said. "Or perhaps, one less Elliot."

Selah laughed aloud then, and whatever remaining

cloud had been hovering over them seemed blown away by her laughter.

"I'm sorry to admit I hadn't heard of Ready Vector Solutions until last evening," Selah said, as they rode up to the eleventh floor. "But I did a little homework. I had no idea how many different industries used your hardware."

Lincoln dipped his head. "We've been very fortunate."

"And Elliot tells me you're exploring expansion?"

Thumper took over. "Exploring, yes ma'am. I'm not sure it's a good direction for us."

"Ma'am," Selah said, laughing. "That makes me sound old."

"Sorry, it's a habit," Thumper said.

"I think it makes you sound distinguished," Elliot added.

"Mm, yes," Selah said. "A fine euphemism for old. Very good, Elliot."

They exited the lift and walked down a quiet hall to a small, corner office.

"What may I offer you to drink?" Selah said, as they entered. "Water? Coffee? Tea?"

"Why don't you crack open that 20?" Elliot said.

"I shouldn't," she replied. "Not so early."

"I'll pour," he said, holding out a hand for the bottle. Selah smiled and though she didn't exactly give him the bottle, she didn't resist when he gently took it from her. He walked over to a small bar and poured out four drams. Selah took a seat behind her desk, and motioned for Lincoln and Thumper to sit in the two chairs facing her. As they sat, she held up and examined the disk Elliot had given her.

"I'm not sure I see how this is supposed to work," she said.

Elliot returned and handed drinks to Lincoln and Thumper, but held on to Selah's, an unspoken demand that she exchange the deactivated microdrone. She handed him the disk and accepted the glass in return.

"This is why I wanted it to be a surprise," he said. He set his drink down on the corner of her desk, and then flexed the disk and shook it. The intelligent material awoke, and assumed its functional form; vaguely insect-like, roughly the size of a wasp. He handed it back to her.

"That's remarkable," she said, examining it again. "Where did you get this?"

"One of the manufacturers I work with," Elliot said. "It's a first run, not widely available yet. I thought you might find it interesting."

"And what does it do?"

"Depends on the model," he answered. "Though I believe that one is just a sensor for hazardous materials. Buzzes around sniffing for radiation, that sort of thing."

"So why sneak it in?"

"To impress you. I was planning to do a magic trick."

"I'm not sure magic tricks have the effect on the ladies that you think they do, Elliot," she said. "And as fond as I am of you, the answer is still no."

"I know. I've *almost* given up hope," Elliot said with a chuckle. He picked up his glass and raised it in a toast. "To good health, great friends, and the absolute, very best of security."

"Cheers," Lincoln said.

"Cheers," Selah said. They each sipped, and she closed her eyes, holding the amber liquid in her mouth for a time, savoring. Then she added, "Elliot, you really are an idiot."

"I really am, Selah. But at least I'm handsome."

"In your own way," she said.

Lincoln had never been much of one for whisky of any sort, but he had to admit that this particular Scotch was smooth enough to make him reconsider. Of course, he could never afford it at the market rate, even at home. He could only guess what Elliot had paid for it here on Mars. Then again, given what he'd learned of Elliot so far, it seemed likely that the man had a connection somewhere that made it all a bargain.

"OK, so to business," Selah said. "Elliot was vague on details."

"That would be my fault," Lincoln said. "I've not provided many. But he has spoken very highly of Manes-King in general, and of you in particular. When he said he thought he might be able to arrange a meeting, I couldn't turn down the opportunity."

They spent the next hour or so chatting, weaving through their cover story. Thumper took over the technical side of the discussion, but part of the brilliance of the cover was the fact that by design, neither party wanted to get too deep into the specifics, each honoring the other's sensitive corporate position. Every so often, Elliot inserted a personal detail or worked in some industry connection so expertly that even knowing it was all false, Lincoln found it convincing.

Though it was never explicitly stated, Elliot steered the conversation in such a way as to imply that Ready Vector Solutions might be considering partnering with Manes-King, rather than establishing their own center. Assuming, of course, that they felt confident in Manes-King's ability to handle highly-sensitive traffic. He never mentioned the communications array farm, but somehow Selah suggested giving them a tour of the facility anyway. By the end of the conversation, Lincoln understood how Elliot had managed to operate in the area for so long.

When Selah stepped out briefly to make quick arrangements, Elliot took advantage of the moment.

"I hope you can make it work with one," Elliot said to Thumper.

"Me too," she answered. "Link, I need the bits," she said, motioning for him to hand over the two components to the controller he was carrying.

"What about the skeeter?" he said.

"In my pocket," Thumper said.

Lincoln's eyes flicked from Thumper to Elliot to Thumper again.

"When he handed me my drink," she said. Lincoln had completely missed the exchange. Elliot was good.

They got everything transferred to Thumper, and not a moment too soon.

"We're all set," Selah said, poking her head back in the office. "I can't take you all the way down to the actual array of course, but I can give you a good overview."

"That's more than we expected, Ms Coulibaly," Lincoln said. "Thank you again."

Selah took them down a couple of floors, and spoke in high-level terms about the systems they ran and how they ensured the security of the traffic they moved all over known space. Thumper was truly in her element here. The depth and insight of her questions apparently impressed Selah enough that at one point she asked Thumper whether or not she'd ever consider leaving Ready Vector. After twenty minutes or so of the behind-the-scenes tour, Lincoln surreptitiously keyed the comm unit in his pocket, sending a one-pulse signal out to Wright, wherever she was on the perimeter. Less than a minute later, Thumper received an incoming call.

"I'm sorry, excuse me, I need to check this," she said. She answered, and stepped off to one side of the hall, and held a quiet but increasingly animated conversation. After a minute or two, she said, "Look, I'll have to call you back in a few minutes, I can't discuss this openly."

She returned to the group, but pulled Lincoln close and they held a low, rehearsed conversation.

"It's the Archive," she said.

Lincoln grunted. "How bad?"

"They don't know yet, but Aoki is already gone, managing a different issue. I'm going to have to talk the tech through the process."

"Can it wait?"

"Not long."

They stood silent for a moment, doing their best to look concerned.

"Is everything all right?" Elliot asked, on cue.

"Minor crisis," Thumper said. "But escalating."

Lincoln flashed him a quick smile. "Which is to say, business as usual. These things only happen when we're off site."

"If you need some privacy, we can get you a guest office," Selah said. "If that would help."

"Thank you, but no," Thumper answered. "It's a fairly sensitive situation."

"Oh, we have several secure rooms here, if that's the concern," Selah said. "As I mentioned, we have clients across a broad spectrum. Governmental, military, financial. This sort of thing happens more frequently than you might think. Or, perhaps, *as* frequently as you might think."

"Well," Thumper said, deferring to Lincoln and looking convincingly torn. "If *you* think it's all right...?"

"I'd rather you handle it as soon as possible," Lincoln

said, and he turned to Selah. "If it's not too much trouble for you? I feel like we've already taken too much of your time."

"Not at all," Selah said. "Just down two floors, we'll get you set up."

Selah escorted them to another long, quiet hallway, and let Thumper into a nicely-appointed secure facility. Though the floor was isolated from the communications systems they needed to access, the two sections of the facility shared internal support structure. As long as Thumper could find a way to get the skeeter through the wall or ceiling, there were support beams she could follow to reach the target.

"There's a terminal in the desk, if you should need it," Selah said. "Thumbprint to access a new profile, thumbprint again to log out. All traffic will be scrubbed when you log out."

"What about the thumbprint?" Thumper asked.

Selah smiled. "Also scrubbed."

"How long do you think it will be?" Lincoln asked.

"If it's what I think it is, it should be half an hour maybe? If not... well, if it's not, I should probably book a flight out immediately."

"Keep me posted."

Thumper nodded, and then called Wright back. They left her to her work, closing the door behind them. Before they'd closed the door completely, Thumper was already unleashing a tirade that made Elliot's eyebrows go up.

"User error would be my guess," Lincoln said. "Ms Cooper doesn't have a great deal of patience for self-inflicted wounds."

Lincoln had no doubt that Thumper could make the conversation work from her side; she already had a tendency to talk too much anyway, and he didn't know anyone with a more extensive technical vocabulary. He couldn't help but feel sorry for Wright on the other end of the line, though, and could picture her gritting her teeth through the whole deception.

Though Selah mentioned that she didn't mind waiting for Thumper to finish, Lincoln assured her that it would be better to complete the tour, knowing that he might also have to leave in a hurry, depending on the outcome of the call. With Thumper's absence, he took the lead in keeping up the ruse, asking questions related more to operations and logistics. He'd never thought about it all that much before, but the more they talked, the more he got the feeling that there wasn't as much difference between the civilian corporate world and the military life as he had expected. Maybe one day he'd go into business.

It was about forty minutes later that Thumper contacted him and relayed that she'd gotten the issue resolved. By that time, they'd been headed back up to Selah's office anyway, having toured as much of the facility as she was comfortable allowing. They redirected and met Thumper.

"Everything taken care of?" Lincoln asked.

Thumper nodded. "Best I could do from here, anyway," she said. "Thank you for your understanding, Selah."

"As I said," Selah answered, "it happens all the time."

She escorted them back to the lobby and they said their goodbyes amidst assurances of keeping in touch about their potential future partnership. They were only a few steps away from the door and freedom when Selah called after them.

"Oh, one more thing," she said. They turned back to

see her standing there with the skeeter pinched between her thumb and forefinger. A cold fear rolled through Lincoln. Was that the one from her office, or the one Thumper had been using? There was no way to tell. "The next time we meet, leave your surveillance toys at home."

But Elliot just laughed and plucked the device from her hand.

"I told you it was just a demo," he said.

"And I would have been a fool to have believed you," she said. Her demeanor had shifted back to predator. "What do you think I've had my people doing while I've been giving you a tour? And leaving a device like this sitting around in the chief of security's office? Think what that could have done to my reputation."

From her office, then. Lincoln hoped the relief wasn't obvious on his face. But his mind flashed back, and he couldn't recall having seen her take the skeeter off the desk. Or when she would have handed it off... Ah, when she'd excused herself, with the claim that she needed to arrange for their impromptu tour. He wondered what exactly her people had been doing all that time.

"I'd like the name of the supplier who gave you this," she continued. "I'm afraid they've misled you as to its purpose."

The look on Elliot's face was indistinguishable from genuine dismay.

"Selah... I'm... I'm so sorry," he said.

"I don't blame you, Elliot," she said. "But you would make a terrible corporate spy."

"Good thing, I guess," he said, looking at his feet.

"You, on the other hand," Selah said, turning her gaze to Thumper. For a moment the two women stood locked in silence, both unreadable. Then Selah added, "I don't know what you *really* do, but you're obviously exceptional at it."

Thumper held still, giving neither proclamation of innocence nor admission of guilt.

Selah flicked her eyes back over to Elliot, drew closer, lowered her voice.

"You're a good man, Elliot. If I didn't know that, if I didn't *know* it..." she said, then cocked her head to one side briefly. Somehow in that simple motion, the full weight of her potential menace made itself known. "... so I'm giving you this *one*."

"Selah–" Elliot said, but she cut him off.

"*One*, Elliot," she said. "And only one."

For once, Elliot appeared to be at a loss for words. He opened his mouth, then closed it. Dropped his head to gather himself. Lincoln feared that even a blink might tip them over the edge into catastrophe, mere steps from triumph. For all intents, it seemed they hadn't gotten away with anything at all. And though Elliot might escape her judgment, her eyes had not yet fallen upon Lincoln.

"Let me make it up to you..." Elliot said. And then he looked up with a hint of a smile and impeccable timing, "Over dinner?"

But Selah wasn't amused. She held up her pointer finger an inch from his nose; punctuating her message, and maybe giving warning not to push her anymore today.

Elliot pushed anyway.

"Lunch?" he asked.

Selah tipped her head back slightly, chin jutted... and then shook her head with a chuckling sigh, and Lincoln got the impression that somehow, by some miracle, they were going to walk out of there after all.

"Goodbye, Elliot," she answered. "Stay in touch. I've missed you."

It wasn't until the three of them were riding away in the car, a good five kilometers from the Manes-King facility that Elliot let out a long exhale and a laugh, and rubbed his forehead with the palm of his hand.

"You got what you needed?" he asked.

"I got access," Thumper said. "Going to have to wait to see what Veronica can do with it before we can be sure. But yeah, we got what we came for. You weren't kidding about those protocols though. Took me twenty minutes just to figure out how they were tracking activity in the room she put me in, so I could circumvent."

"So they do track it?" Elliott asked.

"Of course they do," Thumper said. "I had to make up a whole batch of backend protocol nonsense on the spot, just to give them something to gnaw on."

She closed her eyes and pinched the bridge of her nose, then chuckled.

"Gotta say, if I were actually working for Ready Vector, I'd feel pretty safe partnering with them."

"I can't believe we got away with that," Lincoln said. "Twice in that lobby, I thought we were dead."

"You and me both, brother," Elliot replied.

"Couldn't have guessed it from your reaction," Lincoln said. "I kind of thought you'd already had those contingencies planned for."

"Not exactly," said Elliot, and he leaned his head back and closed his eyes. Lincoln knew that posture. He'd adopted it many times, during the adrenaline letdown after coming out of an op.

"Is this the job you always wanted?" Thumper asked.

"Me?" Elliot said, chuckling with his eyes still closed.

shook his head. "Me, no. I always wanted to run a pub."

"Well… you seem born for the work," Thumper said. "I don't know how you do it."

Elliot smiled with his response.

"Helps to be a good dancer."

TWENTY

They hadn't spent much time celebrating their victory. As soon as they got back to the safehouse, Lincoln and his team got to work on the second piece of the puzzle, trying to determine how the bad guys were passing command-and-control signals to SUNGRAZER. The device they'd recovered from the *Ava Leyla* was a good starting point. Elliot was already out running his connections to see if he could track down any leads on where the components may have come from.

Based on what they'd learned so far, Elliot had given them a hit list of six or seven places he thought could possibly have a connection. While Thumper worked with Veronica, the other four teammates had been out doing legwork, getting some initial reconnaissance on those sites. There was no need to sit around and wait. Maybe they'd get lucky again, and they'd already have a plan to pull off the shelf once they got confirmation. Worst case, it was good practice at operating in the MPCR they could put to use when they found the real targets.

Mike and Sahil were scouting one potential site when Thumper got her first break. It wasn't good news.

"You cracked the encryption?" Wright asked.

Thumper shook her head. "Not yet. Not even close.

But I found something anyway."

She waved Lincoln and Wright back into the study.

"You know how I said SUNGRAZER has all sorts of protocols that are supposed to make this whole hijacking thing impossible? Well, one of those safeguards is an encryption key test. Obviously you can't expect that your codes are going to remain stable over the long haul, not when you're talking about a deep maneuver asset that might be operating for ten, twenty years. You pretty much guarantee your ship's going to get jacked if you don't have some plan to rotate or refresh your encryption schemes. So NID put a lock in... the algorithm they use to encrypt command-and-control traffic is sort of a key itself. Whenever they update the encryption, SUNGRAZER does a comparison on the algorithm used to make sure it's valid. It's sort of clever, as long as no one gets hold of your algorithm."

"Guessing in this case, someone did," Wright said.

"Looks like. But it actually helps us anyway. The raw C&C traffic is unreadable to us obviously, because it's a different encryption scheme, *but* with a similar algorithm, and here's the key... sending the same traffic. NID shared some archived communications with me. I just have to figure out how the two relate."

"Do they know they shared it with you?" Lincoln said.

"More or less," Thumper said. And off of Lincoln's look, she added, "Elliot helped me get it, so I assume that makes it legit. And anyway, I don't see why it matters if it's helping us get the job done. I can't sit around waiting for somebody on a whole different planet to fill out whatever ridiculous paperwork has to be done for this sort of thing.

"*Anyway*," she continued, "point is... if I can find an identifiable chunk, that'll give Veronica enough to work with to crack it, eventually. SUNGRAZER's got some well-defined protocols for specific tasks. Good news is, just looking at the metadata, length of communication, data density, that sort of thing, I was able to pull up a match."

"Then why do you look like it's bad news?" Lincoln asked.

"Because the block I'm matching up here," she said, "is from SUNGRAZER's targeting routine."

Lincoln looked from Thumper to the data displayed on Veronica's terminal. Then back at Thumper.

"They're going to use her for a strike, after all?" Lincoln asked.

Thumper nodded. "Already did, once. See this?" She waved a hand and drew up a data visualization that was incomprehensible to Lincoln. Fortunately, she didn't wait for him to parse it on his own. "Here's the full routine, from the NID archive." She pointed at each block in turn, naming them as she did. "Target selection, assessment, approach, lock, final confirmation, launch, post-strike evaluation." She brought up a second screen alongside the first; stripped of their raw data and compared on the meta alone, the blocks aligned neatly.

"When was that?"

"Few days ago," she answered. She collapsed the NID archived traffic, and brought up a third screen with the same visualization. The chain was similar, but considerably shorter. "Ignore this other stuff, I'm not sure what that is yet. But you want to guess what's missing?"

Lincoln counted in; target selection, assessment, approach...

"No lock yet," he said.

Thumper nodded.

"Which means she's on approach," Wright said.

Thumper nodded again.

"First strike was a test fire?" Lincoln said.

"My guess, yeah," Thumper said. "Verifying they had her under full control. Dress rehearsal. No telling how many attempts they had prior to the successful one."

"You think they launched in open space?" Wright asked "Just confirming they could fire?"

"No, because here..." Thumper pointed at the final block in the chain. "Post-strike evaluation. She had a real target. No way to know what it was or if she was successful until I crack open the box, but they weren't shooting at nothing."

Lincoln tried to put himself in the bad guys' shoes, thought through the possibilities. Target would have to be large enough to judge effectiveness of fire... it wouldn't be enough to get a hit with a kinetic weapon, they'd have to guarantee that it struck with sufficient force. Space station, maybe. But a live target would be too risky, and there weren't exactly a lot of abandoned hops just floating around out there. Or...

"Asteroid?" he said. "Where was she when NID lost contact?"

"Veronica," Thumper said, "give me the report on SUNGRAZER's last known location."

A screen appeared, familiar from Lincoln's briefing. Ten days of positional data, up to the vessel's disappearance. SUNGRAZER had always kept towards the belt-side of Mars.

"Take her out to the belt, pick a rock," Wright said, nodding to herself.

"Could be," Thumper said. "Seems like a safe option, anyway. Minimal chances of discovery, plenty of opportunity to practice. If I had to roll the dice on it, yeah that'd be my safe bet."

"What's your guess on travel time?" Lincoln asked.

"Depends entirely on how hard they wanted to burn. Couple of days out, if they don't care about getting noticed. More if they were patient."

"Let's assume these are patient people who don't want to get noticed," he replied. "Check SUNGRAZER's specs, and get us some good numbers on time table. Earliest possible launch window on a return."

"OK," Thumper said. "On what target?"

"Anywhere on Mars," Lincoln answered.

"Sure thing," Thumper said. "What are you thinking?"

"I'm thinking we better get the other half of our key real soon," Lincoln said.

Mike and Sahil returned around lunch time with a solid initial reconnaissance sweep of one of the facilities on Elliot's hit list. Elliot reappeared shortly after, and rendered it all unnecessary.

"Found it," Elliot said as soon as he'd closed the door behind him. He had the look of a man who'd just come in out of a windstorm. "Guo Components. They have a manufacturing facility and a warehouse across town."

"Guo Components," Wright repeated. She looked to Sahil. "We did a circuit on it already?"

Sahil nodded.

"Yeah, they were on my early guess list," Elliot answered. "Glad you guys aren't the sit-around type."

"We know what we're looking for in there?" Lincoln said.

Elliot shook his head. "I don't, but that device you pulled off the *Ava Leyla*? Couple of the sensitive bits are Guo's, for sure. Not on their official product line, but no doubt that's where they came from, so I'm guessing that's where the final assembly happened. I figured whatever else you might need, you're going to find somewhere in there."

"And you're sure of this because…" Wright said.

Elliot smiled and flopped into a chair at the table. "I know a guy. Well, a guy who knows a guy. But it's legit. I confirmed with secondary sources."

"We gotta do another pass to get the good stuff," Sahil said. "But we got a quick peek at the site. Pretty tight security for corporate, but still civilian. Shouldn't be much trouble."

"I'll go back out and get a full workup," Mike said.

"Get some chow first," Lincoln said. "Then I'll ride with you. Thumper, what's your take?"

"Easy B&E sounds good to me," Thumper said, unconcerned with the breaking-and-entering part of the job. "I don't know that's going to give us the exact pieces we're missing, but I guess it can't hurt to go look around. Particularly if it's going to be a soft target. If I can get on site and do some snooping, then yeah, I think we should do it. Better than anything else we've got going on right now."

"What does a good result look like?" Wright asked.

"Best case scenario," Thumper said, "I dig up schematics, we build our own dead drop, and once Veronica finishes crunching that C&C traffic, we put the two together and send SUNGRAZER a new set of instructions. Take the keys back."

"That doesn't give us the bad guys, though," Wright said.

"No, it doesn't," Thumper said.

Wright grunted.

"It's all right, mas'sarnt," Mike said, running her rank together into a single word, "I'm sure we can find some more people for you to shoot next time."

"I just don't want to have to do this all over again in a couple of weeks," she answered.

"I think once we get all the pieces put together, we'll find the vulnerability," Thumper said. "We can make sure this doesn't happen again. Or... at least that it doesn't happen again the exact same way."

It wasn't a sure bet, but nothing in this line of work ever was. And for once, it sounded like a relatively low-risk situation. If it was a bust, it wouldn't cost them that much time or effort, and if their luck held, maybe they could sew this thing up and get themselves on the next flight home.

"Let's hit it," Lincoln said. "Mikey and I will get down there and do a thorough walk-over. Wright, you and Sahil wide-net it... see if you can pick up any extra watchers looking for people like us. Thumper, pull what you can on the facility from existing sources, do as much prep work as you can from here. We'll feed you more once we're all on site."

"I still got time for chow?" Mike asked, as the rest of the team went into action.

"Yeah," Lincoln answered. "But shovel it."

"Always does," Thumper said.

"What do you want me to do?" Elliot asked.

"Keep doing whatever you've been doing," Lincoln said, flashing a smile. "Seems to be working so far."

Lincoln's eyes popped open, waking instantly alert from a deep sleep, as though he'd heard an unusual sound. He kept still, listening, but nothing stood out as the apparent cause. Nerves, maybe. It was just after midnight, still two hours before the team was supposed to gear up and roll out. After they'd returned from their site recon and pulled their plan together, Lincoln had ordered everyone to get some sleep. They'd been pushing it hard, and he knew a solid four hours of rest would be enough to sharpen everyone back up.

He glanced over at the other bed where Mike was sleeping. Except Mike wasn't sleeping. Again. He was sitting up in bed, staring at his datapad. Lincoln laid there, watched his teammate for a moment. It was obvious Mike was agitated about something. Whatever he was looking at on the datapad was giving him some sort of trouble. Finally, Lincoln couldn't let it go anymore.

"Mike," Lincoln said.

Mike started at the sound of his name, and made a quick attempt to play it off with a strained smile in the dim light of his pad's display. He clutched his chest, feigning heart pain.

"If you're trying to kill me and make it look like an accident, that was a pretty good attempt, sir."

"Trouble sleeping again?"

"Just excited about the big night coming up, I guess."

Lincoln sat up and turned on the bed, put his feet on the floor. This had gone on long enough.

"Mike."

"Lincoln."

"I'm serious," Lincoln said. "What's going on, brother?"

Mike shook his head, playing innocent. "I don't know what you mean, sir. Everything's right as rain. Just didn't feel like sleeping much."

Lincoln didn't say anything, just kept his eyes locked on Mike's. Waited for a real answer.

"Come on man," Mike said after several seconds of Lincoln's intent silence. "What do you want me to tell you?"

"The truth, sergeant."

Mike shook his head again and held up a hand like he was at a loss, but for the first time since Lincoln had met him, a look came into Mike's eyes that made him look lost, and a little scared. Finally, he held up the datapad towards Lincoln. On it was an image that could have come from a nature documentary. It showed a bull caribou, huge and majestic, silhouetted by a distant ridgeline, its massive antlers black against a winter sky. Lincoln looked at it, acknowledged it with a nod, then looked back up at Mike.

Mike turned the datapad back towards himself, held it low almost in his lap, stared down at it while he spoke.

"I told you I grew up hunting, yeah?"

"Yeah," Lincoln said.

"My dad and I, we still get out there together when I'm home. It's kind of our thing. But, well, after I was in for a while, got to be hunting felt a little too much like the day job, you know. Lost a little bit of the magic for me. It's just sort of… especially after Balikpapan… hard for me to feel like it was fair, killing a thing that couldn't shoot back and just wanted to be left alone.

"But that was our thing, you know, so I tried not to let it get in the way too much. I guess my dad picked up on it anyway, because one night, before we were supposed to head out at like oh-three-hundred, he tells me he got me something new to shoot with, and takes me down to the basement where his gun vaults are. Which I figured was kind of weird, taking a new rifle out for a hunt without ever having tested it before. But when we get down there, he's got all this camera gear laid out. Real nice stuff. Professional grade. Must have cost him a small fortune. And he just said, 'If you can get 'em with this, I reckon we'll both know you could've gotten 'em with the other.'

"That was all he said about it. So we still hunt together, but..." Mike stopped and shook his head with a little chuckle. "This is stupid I know, but when I take those pictures, it kind of feels like I'm giving a life *back*. I know that sounds weird. But it helps me. And I tell you what, it's a whole lot harder to get a good shot with a camera than it is with a gun. You ever hunted caribou before?"

Lincoln shook his head. He actually hadn't ever hunted anything in his life, unless you counted people, but he figured now wasn't the time to mention that.

"They're ghosts, man. The way my dad and I do it, anyway. We don't use any of the tracking gear, none of that touristy drone business. Just old-fashioned eyes and ears, and a mind for weather and terrain. Up in the high country, just getting around is more than most people can handle. And caribou have excellent hearing. If you're bumping all over the rocks, they'll spook before you ever had a chance to lay eyes on one. So you have to keep one eye on the wind, and one eye on the ground... Anyway I'm rambling, but the important thing is that a caribou, one that's worth the trouble like this fella, will make you earn it. So when I get a shot like this one, there's always a story goes with it..."

"Thing is, Lincoln... I don't remember taking this picture," he said, showing the image again. He pulled up another image; different composition, different caribou, but same masterful photographer's touch. "Or this one." He showed a couple of others. "These two I can tell you everything, time of day, what the temperature and humidity level was when I got those shots. Everything, crystal clear. But these others... just gone.

"I can remember every detail of every single time I've ever had to put an enemy down," Mike said after a moment's silence. "Faces, expressions, clothes, situation.

Every one of them. Used to be, I remembered my hunts the same. But ever since..." He stopped and shook his head.

Lincoln made the connection for him.

"Since you went through the Process?" Lincoln asked.

Mike shrugged, and then gave a little nod, like he was admitting to an addiction and was ashamed of it. "It was little things at first. After the first time, I mean. Didn't really notice it, but it's been rougher since this last."

"More than pictures of caribou?"

After a moment, Mike nodded.

"Odds and ends. Every once in a while I get a face and can't come up with a name, or the other way around. People I should know. That I've known for a long time. Some gaps from when I was a kid, or when I was home on leave. It's weird..." He stopped, shook his head, took a settling breath. He was clearly struggling; relieved to be letting it out after who knew how long, uncertain how much was safe to share. "It isn't like when you forget an appointment, or something that happened a long time ago that a friend reminds you of. It's a hole. A blank spot. I know something *should* be there, but I don't know what it is."

"You talk to medical?"

"No, sir," Mike answered. He looked up at Lincoln then, his eyes resolute. "And no sir, I won't."

"Mike," Lincoln said. "This isn't something you can just ignore. If something's going on, we need to know. We need to get it taken care of."

"I *am* taking care of it. You see me do anything yet to make you doubt whether or not I'm still up to the task?"

"No," Lincoln said carefully. "Not yet. Doesn't mean it won't happen. And what if it does, Mike? What then? You're putting the whole team at risk."

"No, I'm not, Lincoln. Look, I can do the job. Same as always. That ship we took down, the one with the girl on it, before I got KIA? I can walk you through that whole op, minute by minute, moment by moment, right up until they scrubbed me."

The technicians always trimmed the last few minutes of memories leading up to a catastrophic event. Apparently in the early days of the Process, they'd left the memories intact all the way up to the moment of death, thinking that operators might be able to learn valuable lessons from whatever went wrong. Somehow they'd managed to underestimate the negative psychological impact of being able to remember the details of your own death. These days, they removed a safe buffer leading up to the event. And now it was starting to sound to Lincoln like they might be removing more than just that.

"It's nothing to do with the job," Mike continued. "Planning, execution, all of it, I'm at the top of my game right now, I swear. It's just... some of the outside stuff feels... I don't know man. *Thinner*, somehow." He shook his head. "I don't know how else to describe it. Some of those memories are like... it's like they're just stories I heard from someone else."

He motioned to the picture of the caribou again.

"And that..." he began, but he fell silent and didn't continue.

"You need to talk to medical," Lincoln said. "If you don't, I'll have to."

Mike's head snapped up, with an intense look. "No Lincoln, I'm good. Look, it doesn't affect anything. I can do the job, no problem, you don't have to worry about that. It's just this other stuff..."

"That 'other stuff' is who you *are*, Mikey."

"No, it isn't. What I *do* is who I am. And *this* is what

I do. If you talk to medical, they're gonna freak out. They'll pull me out of the team. And then I'll have lost *every*thing."

Lincoln wanted to reassure Mike that getting removed from the team wasn't on the table, but he couldn't bring himself to say the words. He knew all too well that it was a possibility. And recognizing that fact put him in check; what would the team do without Mike? He was their eyes and ears. And more often than not, their heart.

"I had a buddy I served with, back in 3rd Group," Mike said. "Seventeen years in, he broke his back in a jump, decided it was time to get out. After he recovered, he got a job in landscaping. *Landscaping*. Went from killing bad guys to spreading pine straw. And people treated him like a second-class citizen. After all he'd done. Can you imagine that? Going from serving your country to serving some country club, and getting looked down on by people who wouldn't last five seconds out here in the real world? He was a hero, man."

The fact that Mike was referring to him in the past tense wasn't lost on Lincoln. He didn't want to ask what had happened. But he didn't have to.

"Died in a car accident six months after he got out. But he was our team driver, best I've ever seen except maybe Sahil, so…" Mike said. He looked back down at the datapad in his hand, shook his head. "I just… I don't want to die not shooting back, Lincoln."

Lincoln didn't know what to say. If he'd been in Mike's place, would he have been doing anything differently? He couldn't convince himself that he would, no matter how much sitting there as a commanding officer he wanted to believe there was a better choice. How many times had he ignored pain or lied about the severity of an injury, out of fear that he'd be forced to stay home while his teammates went into the field? Many. Too many, probably. If Mike said he could do the job, did anything else matter? As his team leader, the answer was probably no. But as his friend... well, as his friend, the answer wasn't nearly as clear cut as Lincoln wanted it to be.

"I'm good, sir," Mike said. "I'm good to go."

"If you say you can do the job, I believe you Mikey. You know I don't want to go out there without you," Lincoln said. "But–"

"That's all you have to say."

"But..." Lincoln continued. "We need to figure this out. And we'll figure it out together, OK? You and me. Together. Now that I know, there's no point in you hiding anything from me. Not a thing. Understand?"

"Understood," Mike said. "You're not gonna... you know?"

"Tell the others?" Lincoln asked. Mike nodded, and after a moment's consideration, Lincoln shook his head. "Not yet. Not until you're ready. When we get back home, we'll talk about it."

"When we get home," Mike said. "So... what's that mean for us now?"

Lincoln drew a deep breath. And then he swiveled back around and laid down again.

"It means you need to turn that pad off and get some sleep," he said. "Big night coming up."

TWENTY-ONE

Lincoln slid into the narrow darkness alongside the first perimeter fence surrounding the Guo Components facility, and dropped to a knee. Thumper followed close behind, turning when she joined him to watch his back while he worked. Whoever had laid out the security perimeter for the facility had done a fair job; there were only a handful of gaps where the exterior lighting failed to overlap, and both inner and outer fences were latticed cable-fiber, strong and flexible enough to stop a heavy transport from plowing through. The sensor suites were typical of high-end corporate security, but had been more cleverly situated than most. Enough for Thumper to have commented on it, anyway. From her analysis, it appeared that Guo Components had made some improvements in the not-so-distant past, another point in favor of the theory that they had some connection to SUNGRAZER's disappearance.

"Dakota, this is Omaha," Lincoln said. "Signal check?"

"Dakota has good signal, Omaha," Wright answered. "Go ahead."

"We're on site at the entry point," Lincoln continued. "Can you confirm?"

"I have your beacons," Wright replied. "I confirm

your location and entry point. Looks good. Mike, you got visual on Omaha?"

"That's a roger," Mike said. "I'm set up. Omaha has thirty meters clear, fence to fence."

"Sahil?" Wright said.

"Good to go," Sahil answered. "Routes in are clear."

"Dakota is set, Omaha. Enter when ready."

Thumper had a skeeter shadowing them, providing a bubble of disruption to hide them from the various security systems as they moved through. Even so, Lincoln felt like they were running naked. The job would have been almost effortless if they could have employed their suits. Operating in this environment, though, had required the opposite approach; they were all wearing street clothes, and apart from the skeeter, most of the gear they were carrying had been supplied by Elliot from local sources. Even their usual communications gear had been replaced with off-the-shelf dermal adhesives, modified by Thumper to run secure. Lincoln hadn't used that sort of model for probably a decade; the strip behind his ear tugged at the skin. He hoped it wouldn't leave a rash.

"Roger, Omaha is making entry," he said, as he drew from his back pocket a thin cylindrical tool with a smooth hook on one end. This he ran quickly down the cable-fibered fencing, starting from about a meter high, silently incising the lattice-work. The cable-fibers shivered as the severed ends retracted and curled inward like flame-withered tendrils. The resultant gap was no more than a half-inch in width, but Lincoln pushed and flexed the fence inward like a heavy curtain, making room for Thumper to crawl through. He followed after her and then together they crept forward in a low crouch, crossing the thirty-meter span to the second fence.

"Omaha at the inner fence, ready to cut through," he reported.

"Roger, Omaha," Wright answered. "You're good to proceed."

The cable work of the fencing was too dense for Lincoln to get a clear view of what lay on the other side. Wright was holed up in a building across the street, spotting for them both with the skeeter and with good old old-fashioned optics. At Wright's word, Lincoln repeated the same process to defeat the barrier, and then he and Thumper were inside, ready to do the fun part of the job.

"Omaha's inside, starting our approach to target," Lincoln said.

The facility was a small compound comprised of a mid-sized manufacturing building, a warehouse, and a squat office building towards the front of the lot. The complex wasn't without its charm; patches of grass and trees broke up the paved pads and connecting roads and walkways. Based on their surveillance and a little system intrusion work, Thumper had identified an area on the third floor of manufacturing as the best place to start, where blueprints and schematics were archived.

There were no armed guards on the premises, no security forces garrisoned within. The only real threat they faced was from the handful of drones floating lazy patrols in and around the buildings, but as long as Lincoln and Thumper were careful, the drones wouldn't be more than a nuisance. Thumper had rigged the skeeter up with an alert system; it was set to chirp at them whenever a drone was heading their way, giving them enough time to reroute or find a place to hide until it passed.

Lincoln led the way across the open ground from the inner fence to the nearest access into the manufacturing facility, making use of the thin trees whenever possible. It took Thumper about thirty seconds to override the lock on the door, using a small black device she'd pulled from her pocket. Once inside, Lincoln flicked on his low-intensity red-filtered light and took the lead again. The wide corridors were dark and eerily silent, his red light casting sinister shadows as they moved through. The silence of the halls felt heavy, as if the building itself were brooding and resented the disturbance. As quietly as they moved, their footsteps and even breathing sounded too loud in that almost malicious stillness.

Occasionally they caught the buzzing hum of an unseen drone making its rounds somewhere down some other corridor. The way the sound bounced around made it almost impossible to gauge exactly where the noise was coming from, which made Lincoln even more grateful for the early-warning skeeter that was trailing along behind them. He couldn't decide which was worse; the ominous sound of potential discovery, or the heavy silence that clung to them in its absence.

For some reason, it was the stairwells that got to him the most. He couldn't help but wonder if he'd started to get too reliant on his recon suit, with its vision-enhancing sensors and reactive camouflage. Maybe it was a good thing they'd had to do this the old-fashioned way. And an even better thing that the target was so soft.

Fortunately, they only had to go up two flights, and then it was a short walk to the office Thumper had selected as their primary target. The room was only about half the size of how Lincoln had imagined it, based on Thumper's description of what it held. He posted up by the door to keep watch while Thumper went to work on one of the terminals nearby.

"Dakota, Omaha is at the target," Lincoln reported

over the team channel. "Starting our pull now."

"Roger, Omaha," Wright answered. "Still quiet out here."

"Don't get too curious," Lincoln whispered to Thumper. "I don't want to stay in here any longer than absolutely necessary."

"Darkness getting to you?" she whispered back.

"Maybe."

"Well you'll just have to suck it up, sweetheart. I'm going to pull everything I can get my hands on."

Lincoln hated this part of the job. There was literally nothing for him to do but wait and watch. And this particular situation felt a little too familiar; his mind kept wanting to bring up images from the storage room on the *Ava Leyla*.

"Hold up," Sahil said. "Hold up, y'all. I got some possible trouble here."

His tone wasn't loud or urgent; it was the calm intensity that made it worrisome.

"What's going on, Sahil?" Wright asked.

"Familiar face," Sahil said. "Got a second look at a fella here I saw a little bit ago. Pretty sure he's keeping tabs on me."

The idea that someone had made Sahil almost seemed ridiculous; he was farther out from the facility than anyone else, keeping an eye on the two main routes leading towards the complex. He was always careful to avoid attracting any attention. But he wasn't the paranoid type. If he thought someone was watching him, regardless of the circumstances, someone was probably watching him.

"You safe to move?" Wright asked. "Without tipping him off?"

"Yeah, but it'll put me out of position."

"Sahil," Lincoln said, breaking in, "if you see something you don't like, get moving."

"Roger that," he answered. "Then I'm movin'." That was a bad sign indeed.

"What do you want to do, Omaha?" Wright asked.

"We're already in," Lincoln said. "We'll keep pulling what we can, but let me know if you get any other activity out there."

The words had hardly made it out of his mouth when Mike cut in.

"I've got movement," he said. "Office building... three, four... looks like six individuals coming out of the office building."

There shouldn't have been anyone anywhere in the facility at this time of night. Lincoln didn't need any more information than that.

"Thumper, wrap it," Lincoln said. "Close it all down, we're pulling out."

"On it," Thumper said. "Thirty seconds."

Lincoln crossed the room to a window, scanned what he could see from the vantage. He didn't have an angle towards the office building, but he now saw two vehicles crawling up a service road, lights off. Blocking access.

"They're coming your way," Mike said. "They're coming in. Omaha, you need get out of there. You gotta get out, right now."

"Copy, Dakota," Lincoln answered. "We're wiping prints, and on our way out."

"Vehicles on the main road," Wright said. "No lights, no sirens."

"Same on my side," Lincoln said. "Thumper?"

"Ten seconds," she answered.

"Sahil," Wright said. "What's your status?"

"Stair-steppin'," Sahil said, referencing the technique

for shaking a tail. "Got a funny feelin' he ain't the only one to worry about."

"Got it," Thumper said, and she was up, headed to the door. She cracked it open and waited there for Lincoln to join her. As he moved back across the room, he saw she had her pistol drawn, held tight against her body.

"Let's try to ghost out," Lincoln whispered as he drew in close behind her. "No contact, no shots fired." He put a hand on her shoulder, but not for comfort or reassurance; the physical contact made it easier to read the intention of her movement and less likely they'd need verbal communication to avoid bumbling into each other.

"Understood," she said. "Just saving myself a step, if it comes to that."

Lincoln drew his weapon as well. The subsonic pistol Elliot had provided was apparently the standard firearm for local law enforcement. Twenty-five rounds. Lincoln got the distinct feeling that if he needed any of them, he was going to need all of them.

"You've got trouble, Omaha," Mike said. "They've got the ground floor locked down. Pick a door, and say when. I'll clear it for you."

"Negative, Mike, hold fire," Lincoln said. "Hold fire, do not shoot. They haven't found us yet. I don't want to leave a trail of bodies if we don't have to."

Lincoln thought back through all the contingencies they'd prepared. Roof was still possible, but that made them easy targets for the drones. The manufacturing building had a loading dock with an overhang. Maybe a compromise. If they could make it on top of that, there was a chance they could skirt around behind whoever these people were.

"Omaha's going to the loading dock," Lincoln said.

"From the second floor."

"I don't have eyes on that," Mike said. "That's opposite of my position."

"Understood Mikey," Lincoln said, over comms. Then to Thumper by his side, "Let's go Thumper, second floor, find us a window."

She nodded and checked to make sure the corridor was still clear, then stepped out and led the way. Lincoln followed at a half-arm's-length distance, holding off her left shoulder so their feet didn't get tangled. It was pitch black in the first stairwell, and dead silent. Thumper switched on her light just long enough to get them down to the second floor, and then doused it before exiting the stairs. Once there, they made their way through the darkened corridors by way of the ambient light filtering in from the wide perimeter windows. Thumper found the way to an office overlooking the loading dock, and they ducked inside, quickly crossing to the exterior window.

They held there, both searching the grounds.

"There," Lincoln whispered.

"I see 'em," Thumper answered.

Two figures walked the perimeter of the building, one shining a light along the exterior wall as they moved. They closed in on the loading dock and disappeared beneath the overhang. Looking for signs of entry, Lincoln guessed.

"Did we trip something on the way in?" he asked.

She shook her head. "Not that I see. Nothing pinged any of my alerts. I must have missed something."

"No," Lincoln said. "I don't think you did, Thumper."

The approach, the vehicles, the way it was all going down, it was clear this was no police force, no standard security team. Whoever they were, they didn't want to draw any more attention to what was going on at Guo

Components than Lincoln and his team did. They were moving quickly, but not rushing, walking aggressively. They weren't responding to an alarm. They were springing an ambush.

"*Sun ray, sun ray, sun ray,*" Lincoln said over team comms. "E&E is in effect. I say again E&E is in effect."

The order for the team to escape and evade was one he'd never thought he'd have to give; it wasn't just a mission abort, it meant the team would scatter, each relying on their own individual skill to disappear into the environment and rendezvous at a preplanned rally point later. But there was no doubt in his mind that it was the right call.

"I acknowledge *sun ray*," Sahil said. "Goin' to ground."

"I'll hold until you get clear of the building–" Mike said, but Lincoln cut him off.

"Negative, Mikey, pack it up and get out of there. Rally at Zulu." If the bad guys had gotten eyes on Sahil that far out from the facility, there was no reason to think any of them were safe. And Mike was particularly vulnerable with his long rifle; as good as he was, he was still going to need a few extra minutes to ditch the weapon and clean up his roost before he could vanish into the night.

It took a moment before he responded, and he didn't sound happy when he did.

"Understood," he said. "I acknowledge *sun ray*. Stay safe."

"Wright," Lincoln said. "What's your position?"

"Still in place, no static," she said. "I'll walk you out."

Technically it was a violation of protocol, but Lincoln couldn't bring himself to command her to leave just yet. Having her eyes out there might be the difference-maker in whether or not he and Thumper could get clear of the facility.

"Roger that," he said. "We'll make it as quick as we can. Can you see the loading dock?"

"Affirmative, I see the dock."

"Two individuals moved under the overhang a minute ago. You see them?"

"I see them," Wright answered. "They're not under the overhang anymore, they're continuing along the perimeter, moving towards the front of the compound."

"Copy that, we're second floor, above the overhang," Lincoln said. "Look for my flash."

Wright was tracking their position remotely, but he wanted to be sure she had actual visual before they tried to make their escape. He held his light flat against the window and quickly pulsed the red light three times.

"Roger, I have your flash."

"Let me know when we're clear to come out."

"Stand by."

The seconds ticked by. The silence in the hall was broken by a quiet hum; a moment later, Thumper's skeeter chirped its warning. A drone, headed their way.

"Wright?" Lincoln said.

"Hold."

"We've got trouble headed our way."

"Hold."

The hum sharpened into a buzz. The skeeter chirped again, three short bursts this time. The drone was close.

"Wright–"

"Go, go," she answered.

"We're coming out," Lincoln said.

The windows opened from the inside, but had a thin protective mesh covering the exterior. Lincoln made quick work of that with the entry tool he'd used on the fence, cutting a rectangular hole for them to crawl through.

"You first Thump," he said.

She didn't argue. Thumper holstered her weapon, scrambled through the gap, and lowered herself as far as she could down the other side. The window was a good ten feet above the overhang, but Thumper pushed off the wall and turned 180 degrees in the air, and dropped cat-like into a quiet crouch. Her weapon was out and up an instant later, as she scanned for targets.

Lincoln followed right after her and tried to mimic her graceful landing. He was thankful he didn't break an ankle when he hit the roof. There was no way to know how the drone would react to the damaged window if it wandered into the office. Maybe it would just continue its patrol down the hall. They didn't stick around to find out.

"I see you, I have you," Wright said. "If you can get around to your entry point, that's still your best bet. Couple sentries posted by the entryway, but doesn't look like they know that's how you went in."

Lincoln took point, dodging the pools of light around the facility as they worked their way back to the hole they'd cut through the fence. After several tense minutes of hiding and dashing, with ample direction from Wright, they reached a place of marginal concealment within sight of their entry point, under a pair of dormant loading vehicles parked side by side. Two stacks of cubical shipping containers sat between them and the inner fence. They could make a dash for them, but once there, they'd be stranded on those lonely islands. It was a good forty meters from the containers to the fence. There was no way they could cross that open ground unseen and make it out. At least, not both of them.

"Wright," Lincoln said. "Need a favor."

"Yeah?"

"Keep an eye on Thumper for me."

Her response didn't come immediately, but when it did it was typical of the master sergeant.

"Roger that," she said, her simple answer somehow managing to communicate that she understood everything he was saying, with all its implications.

Thumper was a different story. She looked at him, her eyes wide and full of concern.

"What do you mean keep an eye on me?" she said. "We're going out together, sir."

Lincoln shook his head quickly. "Too many eyes, Thump. Once they make us, I don't like our chances of getting out of here. Either of us. And you're the only one that can put all these pieces together."

"Lincoln," Thumper said.

"Not a discussion, sergeant," he said. "But before you go, you think you can get me into one of these?" He flicked his head up at the loading vehicle they were hiding beneath.

She pressed her lips together, undoubtedly searching for some other way to make it work.

"It's OK, Thumper. I'm just going to draw them off," he said. "I'll shake 'em and meet you at Zulu."

Finally, she relented; nodded, rolled onto her back, produced a small black device from her pocket, the same she'd used to unlock the door to the building. While she worked, Lincoln kept scanning the area. There were three figures standing guard at the door that Lincoln and Thumper had used to enter the building. No uniforms. Street clothes. Private security, possibly. But that didn't seem likely. Lincoln's gut told him it was much worse.

"Got it," Thumper said. She handed him the device; a small touchpad and display, now a miniaturized version of the loader's controls. "Don't hurt yourself."

"No promises," he answered. "What's the range on this gadget?"

"Short. Five meters, ten maybe."

"Traceable back to us?"

"Not us specifically. Probably don't want to have to explain what it's doing in your pocket, though."

"Roger. Get to those containers. When I do my thing, get out."

"What's your thing going to be?"

"Not sure yet, exactly," he said. "But good chance it'll be loud."

"Lincoln, I..." she said. And then, "Keep your head down."

"See you soon, Thump."

She nodded and crawled out from under the loader. Lincoln kept his eyes on the three individuals by the door, watching for the moment of opportunity. For the most part, they were more intent on the building than on their surroundings. Convinced they'd trapped their quarry inside, he guessed. Still, they were obviously professionals; the calm, casual way they maintained situational awareness made that apparent. Finally, the chance presented itself.

"Go, Thumper," Lincoln said. "Go now."

There was no response, no sound of movement. Maybe she hadn't heard. When he glanced over to her position, he saw she was already three-quarters of the way to the crates. Apparently she'd seen the opportunity developing a little earlier than he had.

"In place," Thumper said a few moments later over comms.

"Roger that," Lincoln answered. "Wright, you got her?"

"I have her," Wright responded.

"All right," Lincoln said. "Here we go. Let me know what the sentries by the door do when I start moving."

Lincoln slipped out from underneath the loader and clambered up onto the side of one, with the other between him and the people guarding the door. Chances were effectively zero that he'd escape unnoticed, but having that little bit of cover might buy him a few extra seconds. The loaders were irregularly shaped vehicles, a blessing and a curse. There was no easy place for him to cling to, but once he got himself positioned he found that he could minimize his silhouette by pressing his body into one of the depressions in the frame. The loaders weren't really designed for people to ride in, or on. Fortunately, Lincoln found a handle on a maintenance hatch near the top that felt sturdy enough to keep him on board.

Not that there was any chance this was going to be a fast escape, no opportunity for a thrilling car chase. The loader was heavy and slow; it could probably outrun a human on foot, but not by much. Lincoln brought the vehicle online, its engine activating with a low rumbling hum.

"That perked them up," Wright said. "Don't think they're on to you yet, though."

"They will be in a second," Lincoln answered.

He thumbed the controls and started forward, a slow roll at first with the lights off, just to see how far he could get.

"They're fanning out," Wright said. "Still looking."

Lincoln eased the throttle higher a nudge at a time, gaining speed with each bump. He was moving at the equivalent of a fast jog when the guards at the door finally caught on.

"They've got you now," Wright said. "Moving to the edge of the building... but they're holding. Calling it in, looks like, but holding by the door. They're watching you. Thumper, go. Go, go, go."

Once he had their attention, Lincoln pushed to full throttle and steered off the main paved path out onto a long, grassy patch, cutting across the complex. He steered around the thin trees with one hand, while with the other he death-gripped the handhold he'd put so much faith in. Bouncing across that softer ground, it was starting to feel like maybe he'd put too much faith in that handle.

He drove the loader towards the service road he'd seen earlier, where two vehicles had formed a blockade. There was no way for him to know exactly what was happening on the other side of his ride, but the fact that the guards hadn't left their positions at the door gave him mild hope that no one was running to intercept him. That likely meant they didn't have a large force on the ground, which was good. It also likely meant they were confident they had all the entrances and exits covered, which wasn't.

The service road came into view up ahead, with about sixty meters between him and the blockade. The vehicles were parked at angles to each other, noses opposite directions, forming a staggered wedge as a barrier, but still positioned so that either could quickly turn and navigate around the other if necessary.

Lincoln found his spot; a narrow channel of shadow where the lighting failed to overlap, no more than thirty meters from the service road. As he got nearer to the blockade, the doors to the vehicles opened, and figures emerged, two from each. They moved quickly behind the vehicles, using them as cover.

Five meters until his drop point.

Three.

Lincoln locked the controls to full throttle and straight and hoped the loader would be able to hold its course across the remaining uneven terrain. As he crossed the line of shadow he turned the loader's forward lights on full blast, wedged the controller into a tight space in the frame, and then dropped to the ground on his belly. He laid there still until the loader was halfway to the blockade. As it continued towards its imminent disaster, Lincoln crawled diagonally towards the fence, away from the blockade, following the seam of darkness. A series of pops and pings signaled the people at the blockade had turned to shooting at the loader as it advanced. Strong as it was, Lincoln ignored the urge to watch what came next.

The loader impacted the first car with an underwhelming crunch, followed by a second even less impressive sound of metal crushing as the first vehicle in the blockade slid into the next in line.

Lincoln reached the inner fence and scythed it open. Once he was through the first, he didn't waste any time trying to sneak. He made a break for it, sprinting the thirty meters to the outer fence. The instant he was through that, he dashed up to the nearest road, and then slowed to a brisk walk, scanning for threats. There was a small park not far away. He'd make his way there first.

"I'm out," he said. "Going dark now."

He didn't wait for a response. He peeled the adhesive communicator from behind his ear, palmed it, and then dropped it over the rail of a footbridge as he crossed. A quick, casual glance over his shoulder didn't turn up any obvious pursuit. There was more traffic at this time of night than there would have been in most places; the MPCR's night-life was vibrant, and it was hard to tell whether the people out at this hour were up late or early. That was good for Lincoln's chances of blending in, but the advantage was one he shared with whoever was after him and his teammates.

Wright exited the building and headed down the sidewalk, trying to keep her pace casually brisk. She folded her arms, hunched her shoulders, kept her head down; just a woman huddled in on herself against the cold, in a hurry to get home. Certainly not a soldier in a non-permissive environment, concealing a pistol and ready to drop the first individual that showed any signs of causing her trouble.

Her route would intercept and then run parallel to Thumper's. They wouldn't meet up, exactly, and it wasn't strictly proper according to protocol, but Lincoln's point had been well taken. Capture wasn't a good option for any of them; Thumper's would be catastrophic. Wright was ready to do whatever it took to ensure Thumper made it out. Whatever else followed, they'd deal with as it came.

Wright came around the corner of a building and turned right, the timing practically perfect. Thumper emerged from a side lane on the other side of the street, maybe fifteen meters ahead and, without making eye contact or acknowledging Wright in any way, turned to head in the same direction. The streets were mostly empty, apart from a few stragglers here and there, and the vehicles parked along either side. One car came down the road towards them, but it passed by without slowing, its sole occupant asleep or passed out in the back.

A quick glance over her shoulder revealed no signs of danger. But when Wright turned back, she saw a woman stepping out of a parked vehicle, not long after Thumper had passed by. She opened her mouth to whisper a warning, then stopped herself. They'd both already ditched their comms. Wright picked up her pace. And as she did, two more individuals appeared further down from the doorstep of a building. This time on her side of the street. Two men, headed in her direction. But there was no mistake they were zoned in on Thumper.

Wright made a quick tactical calculation. Close the distance, take the woman trailing Thumper first to clear her flank, then deal with the two men, prevent them from crossing. She tightened her grip on the pistol hidden under her coat, settled it in her hand. Increased her pace as fast as she could go without turning it into a jog, not wanting to draw the attention of the men headed towards her. The street wasn't wide, the first shot would be easy. She just had to make sure she didn't give the woman an opportunity to hide amongst the parked vehicles.

There was a gap between two cars just ahead, an available parking space. Wright drew her weapon from under her coat and held it low, pressed against her leg. Waited for her moment. Ten steps. Six. Four.

But before she could raise the pistol, the men ahead cut diagonally across the street, headed to intercept Thumper. She wasn't going to have anywhere to go, but through them. And Wright could tell from the change in Thumper's posture that that was exactly what she was planning to do. She must have already ditched her gun.

A moment later, out of nowhere, a vehicle skidded around the corner and bore down on the men in the street. One of them managed to leap out of the way, but the other took a hit and went spiraling off of the front fender, landing in a heap back on Wright's side of the street. The woman behind Thumper reacted, immediately ducking behind a parked vehicle. She pulled something from under her coat. Wright didn't have a shot, but she didn't hesitate. She squeezed off a series of five quick shots at the hood of the woman's hiding place; the impacts caught the woman by surprise and sent her scrambling.

The vehicle in the street slowed to a roll alongside Thumper and the side door swung open. Wright broke into a run, bringing her weapon to bear on the car in case someone tried to snatch Thumper, but a man called from inside.

"Get in, get in, get in!"

Wright recognized the voice immediately. Elliot.

Thumper broke from the sidewalk and dashed for the still-moving vehicle, diving into the cab. Wright was right on her heels, and she launched into the car, landed in a heap on her teammate. The door wasn't even closed when the vehicle lurched forward and tore off down the street. Wright pushed up off Thumper and looked out the back window; she managed to catch a glimpse of the woman they'd left behind, standing in the street, before Elliot took a hard corner and the scene was lost.

Lincoln crossed into the park without any trouble and immediately started shedding the rest of his gear. The pistol was the first to go, unloaded, partially fieldstripped, pieces scattered into various trash cans, planters, and sufficiently dense undergrowth that he passed. After that went the entry tool, then the flashlight, and then pretty much anything else in his pockets that might in any way be taken to be something other than everyday pocket litter.

He emerged from the park several minutes later a clean man, out for a stroll at an unreasonable hour. Lincoln took a quick inventory, tried to calm himself, made sure his cover was intact, just in case he got picked up. Cover for status? Business man in town for a few days, trouble sleeping, thought he'd see the sights. Cover for action? Seen enough of the sights, headed home. Good enough. If he could make it to a terminal to summon a ride, he just might make it out after all.

Across from the park, a bar and a restaurant punctuated a row of otherwise darkened shops. Right in front of the bar, Lincoln spotted a public terminal and made for it.

Once there, he punched in the necessary details, and was informed that an available car was en route, with a wait time of four minutes, nineteen seconds. A little longer than he wanted to spend standing on the street, but at least now he had a valid reason to be hanging around a place, people-watching. He backed off from the terminal and leaned against the exterior wall of the bar, keeping his head up, casually scanning for any signs of trouble, and trying his best to look vaguely bored.

It seemed to take a lot longer than four minutes and nineteen seconds, even though Lincoln had watched the countdown as if it had been the last minutes of his life. Finally, a vehicle cruised up and slowed to a stop just in front of the terminal.

The side door opened, and Lincoln crossed to it, glancing up and down the sidewalk one last time to see if he was really going to pull this off. He had a foot in the vehicle when he realized there was already someone sitting in it in the front, rear-facing seat.

"Mr Kim," the man said, smiling. The expression looked out of place on the man's grim face, like it was something he'd seen other people do and was mimicking it without understanding its purpose.

"Oh… sorry, I thought this was my ride," Lincoln said.

"It is," the man replied. Lincoln felt someone close in behind him, and when he glanced over his shoulder he saw not one, but two people had materialized. He looked back at the man in the car.

"What's going on?" Lincoln said.

"We're with Internal Security Services, Mr Kim," the man answered. "We have a few questions for you."

TWENTY-TWO

Wright knew from the look on Sahil's face what he was going to say; somehow, it wasn't enough to prepare her to hear it.

"They took him," Sahil said.

The words hit Wright like a rifle butt to the stomach. They'd grabbed her commanding officer, her team leader. Taken him away. And she didn't even know who "they" were. In all her years in special operations, she'd never had a teammate captured by the enemy. Based on her reaction to the news, she was thinking it just might have been the absolute worst possible thing she'd ever experienced.

Sahil flopped sweat-soaked into a chair, his exhaustion apparent. He'd been the last to arrive at Zulu, their emergency safehouse in a damp basement apartment near a transit station.

"Where?" Thumper asked.

"No idea," Sahil said. "I knew he had trouble comin'," so after the *sun ray* call, I circled around, almost caught up with him in the park. But I had to break off again. Got a line on him when a team picked him up. He was too far..." He stopped, leaned forward and rested his forearms on his knees, dropped his head, still breathing

343

heavy. "Just too far. I kept movin' for another hour or so, to make sure I was clear."

He'd beaten the sunrise, but not by much. The horizon was already showing its first pinkish-red hints of dawn. Wright had to remind herself that the twilight phase lasted longer on Mars than it did back home, so maybe they had more time before the sun came up than she'd first thought. Enough to risk another trip out? Maybe, if only she had any idea where they needed to go.

"I hope whatever we got in there was worth it," Wright said.

"I wish I could I say for sure it was," Thumper answered. "I didn't have time to pull everything I was looking for. I need to feed it all to Veronica, get her to help me put it all together."

Something was off with her. Sunken in on herself. Blown from the op, maybe. Elliot had all their gear out in his vehicle, a sure sign that returning to their previous safehouse wasn't an option. They'd pulled some of it into the apartment, but Wright wasn't ready to commit to setting up shop just yet.

"We'll get her started on it as soon as we're sure we have some breathing room," Wright said.

"So I assume those were our bad guys," Mike said. "Any guesses on who we just bumped into?"

"No need to guess," Elliot replied. "They were Internal Security."

"What?" Wright said, reflexively.

"The Republic's guard dogs," he said. "Like your usual secret police, but with more smiling and less mercy."

"I know who they are," she said. "How'd they get on our trail that fast?"

Elliot spread his hands, a gesture somewhere between "I have no idea" and "what else would you expect".

"There's a reason no one wants this place for an area of operations," he said.

"Mas'Sarnt," Mike said. "What should we do?"

"First order of business is to get the rest of you out of here," Elliot said. "I'll get in touch with the guys from Papa, see how long it'll take them to get something prepped–"

"Excuse me," Mike said, interrupting pointedly. "I was talking to our senior ranking team member." Elliot took the hint and backed down. After a moment, he found himself a chair in a quiet corner, and left them to their business. He looked wrecked.

"We gotta go after him," Thumper said. "We gotta get Lincoln back, obviously."

Wright and Sahil exchanged a look.

"It ain't obvious, Thump," Sahil said. "Much as we all want it to be."

"What are you talking about?" she said. Then she looked at Wright for support, but found none. "How is this even a question?"

Wright had wondered if she had what it took to be the team leader; had always believed she did, in fact. She'd been Almeida's right hand for a long time, and when the old man had brought Lincoln on board to take over, she'd had to wrestle with that decision more than she ever wanted anyone to know. But now, sitting in the driver's seat, with everyone just waiting for her word, the weight of the responsibility nearly overwhelmed her. After all the ops she'd run as an element lead, she'd thought she was more than up to the task. She'd never really thought about the fact that even in those roles, she was still executing someone else's plan. Now, the plan was her call, and it wasn't at all clear what her call was.

Or maybe the call *was* clear, and she just didn't like it.

"It's not a question of doing," Wright said. "It's a question of priorities. And I'm not sure he's top of the list just yet."

Thumper shook her head with her mouth open, but she didn't have a response. And when Wright heard the words come out of her own mouth, she realized the truth; she'd already made the decision, and she hated herself for it.

"We still haven't done what we came here to do," Wright continued, mindful that Elliot was in the room. "Recovery of the asset has to be our focus. He knew that. Said it himself. That's why he took the risk he did."

"To get *me* out," Thumper said. And the way she said it tipped Wright off to the thing she'd missed. A thing she shouldn't have missed. Thumper's guilt was weighing her down; she was taking Lincoln's capture personally, like it was her fault. Lincoln would have caught that right away, Wright knew.

"It wasn't about you, Thumper," Wright said. "It was about the mission. He made a call that you were critical to mission success. And it was the right call."

The words sounded harsher than Wright had intended, but it achieved the desired effect. Thumper's air of near-desperate frustration faded.

"Look," Wright said, trying to soften the moment. "If we knew where he was, we'd go get him right now. But we can't afford to split our focus searching for *two* targets. So we're going to prioritize and execute. First job first, and then we'll put everything we've got into getting Lincoln back."

Thumper nodded, and then did so again after a moment, more forcefully.

"If we play our cards right," Elliot said from his corner

of the room, "we might be able to get them both at the same time."

"How exactly do you figure that?" Wright said. "And don't you dare say you know a guy."

Elliot blinked. "… then I'm not sure how to answer your question."

"Elliot," Thumper said carefully. "How did you find us, anyway?"

Elliot looked at Thumper, then flicked his eyes at Wright briefly. "I do know a guy," he said, holding up a hand as he answered. He stood up and cautiously worked his way back over to the group. He held off a few feet away. "But he's not *my* guy."

He was pale, sweaty, trembling. Wright had assumed it'd been from the adrenaline dump after the close shave escape, and maybe the news of Lincoln's capture. He scrubbed his face with both hands, pressed his fingertips into his eyes. Collecting himself. Or gathering himself.

"Look," he said. He kept his eyes closed, and a fist pressed against his forehead. "His name is Gregor. Gregor Petrescu. He and his partner… a woman named Mei. Mei Dimasalang. They got their hooks into me not long ago. Had me pegged. Codename, records of operations, names of contacts and sources. Full book, dead to rights."

"When was this?" Wright asked. The implications were starting to weave together in her mind, and she didn't like them.

Elliot pulled a chair out from under the table, turned it to face her, and sat down heavily. He really did look like he was about to faint.

"Few days before NID told me you were coming in. I've been trying to spin it, use it to figure out what's going on. Feed them a little information, steal some at the same time. To get to the bottom of the whole thing.

I think they're in on it. Gregor for sure, some others too, maybe."

He opened his mouth as if to say more, but then stopped himself.

"In on what, Elliot," Wright said.

He took a deep breath, as if preparing to jump off a cliff into icy waters.

"I think they have SUNGRAZER."

His mention of the ship electrified the air, and Wright felt the world slip sideways.

"Where did you hear that name?" she said.

Elliot dropped his hand into his lap, kept his eyes on the floor.

"From an NID tech," he said quietly. "About seven years ago."

"You know about SUNGRAZER," Thumper said. Not a question. Processing aloud. Elliot nodded.

"More. I got access to her," he replied. "Wasn't supposed to, obviously, but I did. What you're going through right now? It's just a taste of this place. How hard it is to stay on top of the bubble, to stay ahead of the game. And the Directorate... the things they ask for, that they *demand*... They have no idea what it's like here, no patience, no concept of the risks involved. The intelligence on SUNGRAZER was the edge I needed. Before I had her, I was small time. After... well, I only used her occasionally, just in emergencies, just when there was no other option. But she helped me dodge a lot of bullets. And maybe put a few into some key places. The secrets I was able to get after that, the influence I was able to build... off the charts. That's why NID keeps me here. The networks I've built." He shook his head.

"Did you give them the ship?" Mike said.

"No," Elliot said, "No! Absolutely not! I'm not a

traitor. Internal Security doesn't even know that I know about her. When they picked me up, I thought that's what they were going to ask me about, but they were just trying to turn me..." He trailed off, shook his head again. "I'm always so careful. But... I think somehow I blew it. Somehow *I* turned them on to her. That maybe they picked up a connection I created, maybe saw the signal bounce out, I don't know. I have no idea how they managed it, how they took her over. But I'm sure they did... and I'm sure it's my fault."

"They've been running you since before we came in," Wright said.

"I know Gregor's part of it for sure," Elliot continued, ignoring the comment.

"And how do you know that?" she asked.

"Because I..." He stopped himself, considered his words. "... I was trying to figure out what they knew. So I dropped him a hint, a piece of information that would only be useful if he could put it together with another piece that I knew SUNGRAZER had. And he did. He put them together and then he... acted on them."

It took a moment for Wright to make the connection between his words and his mannerisms, to figure out both what he was saying *and* what he was telling them. Then it clicked. That explained what had happened during the Guo hit. Thumper said it before Wright could.

"Ready Vector Solutions..." Thumper said. "That's why you suggested it. You set us up."

"I had to give them *some*thing," Elliot said. His flat delivery of the confession made it all the more shocking, as if he'd just admitted to something as mundane and arguably understandable as lying about his age to get into a bar.

Wright didn't even think; her body did it all on its

own. The punch caught Elliot full in the face, left side near the jaw, tipped him back in his chair and sent him sprawling into the corner of the table, then down to the floor.

The next moment, strong arms wrapped hers in a bear hug from behind, held her fast. Firm enough to contain her, reserved enough to let her know they could get plenty stronger if she tried to break free.

Sahil. He didn't say anything, just held her there until she relaxed. Once she stopped straining against him, he released her, slowly, and then patted her back firmly. He stepped up alongside her, wordlessly showing his support while making it clear that he wasn't going to let anything like that happen again.

Elliot rolled up to his hands and knees, but stayed there, head down, maybe braced for another assault.

"I didn't think they'd really be able to catch you," Elliot said. "And I figured even if you got into trouble, I could get you out. I was half-right about that, at least."

"And what was your plan after that?" Thumper asked.

"My plan... was to figure it out," Elliot answered. "That's always the plan. It's the only plan anyone can have in this line of work. The only one that actually holds up. Keep your options open, figure it out as you go."

"That's not how it works!" Thumper said.

"Oh, it's not? You know so much, why don't you tell me how it works, then?" Elliot said, his voice steady, and tone calm despite the acid in his words. He rocked back to his knees, looked up at her then. "I've been here for fifteen years, kid. *Fifteen*. My assignment was supposed to be for *five*. Any guesses on how I'm still standing? Or why NID keeps refusing to pull me? But sure, you've been here a couple of days, you've got it figured out, why don't you tell me how it works."

"How long did you last once they took SUNGRAZER away?" Wright said; she couldn't stop herself from twisting the knife.

Elliot moved from his knees to sitting on the floor, now looking truly defeated, and helpless. Her words crumpled him more than the blow she'd delivered.

"When I gave NID the *Ava Leyla*," Elliot said, "I had to make up a story for it, because I wasn't even supposed to know about SUNGRAZER then. I knew something had gone wrong, I just didn't know what to do or… or how to fix it. And then Gregor… having to figure out what he thought I knew, and what he knew I knew… this whole thing has been a nightmare, just trying to remember what I was supposed to know when, who told me what, and what I found out on my own."

He looked at his hands in front of him, spread his fingers, flipped them over to look at his palms.

"I'm not asking for your sympathy," he said. "I don't expect it, I don't deserve it, I don't want it. But I'm not a traitor. It's just… they ask me to do the impossible. And I guess I'm too stupid and stubborn not to try."

The room went still after that. Elliot, spent by his confession, had nothing more to say. And everyone else was waiting for Wright to take the lead. Her mind swirled with the dump of new information, of all the possible implications. Of what it meant for Lincoln, out there somewhere, waiting for them to come rescue him. He was counting on her, too, to lead.

"You said we can get both at the same time," Wright said. "I'd like to hear how that's supposed to work. But before we get to that," here, she crouched down in front of him, locked eyes with him. "You're going to have to convince me that I shouldn't put you down right here in this room."

"I'm a dead man no matter what, master sergeant," he said, and he meant it. "If I go home, they'll kill me for treason. If I stay here, they'll execute me as a spy. At least give me the chance to clean this mess up before I go. It's on me, I made it. Let me fix it."

He held her gaze with the steadiness that only someone with truly nothing left to lose could manage.

It was probably suicide to trust him. It was a dead end not to. But just about anything they chose to do was better than the grey hell of wait and hope they were facing now.

"This guy you know," Wright said. "Tell me everything."

TWENTY-THREE

The series of events leading from the car ride to wherever he was now were so confused that Lincoln had no idea how long it'd been since they'd grabbed him. At the moment he'd realized he was caught, that there was absolutely nothing he could do to escape that car, he had embraced his cover identity fully, in the hopes that he could buy enough time for his teammates to bail him out.

Apparently that had been a miscalculation of epic proportions. He'd been bound, gagged, and drugged in the vehicle. His memories since that time were a jagged blur of jumbled voices, rough hands, and humid darkness. It took him until this most recent span of wakefulness to realize that they'd put a thick hood over his head. He took inventory as best as he could in his current condition. Seated, hands bound behind him. Lincoln swiveled his head around slowly, testing his neck while simultaneously trying to see if he could catch any light through the hood. No luck on that front. The muscles in his neck and upper shoulders were tight, but he didn't detect any signs of damage. Next he inhaled deeply, held the breath in his lungs. Same deal; sore muscles, no pain. At least they hadn't beaten him while he was out.

Lincoln turned his attention then to listening, to see what he could discern about his environment. There wasn't much for him to go on. It was quiet, which was something. A heavy sort of stillness, like a library. More than that. An enforced silence.

"Hello?" he said, loudly. "Is anyone there?"

There was no answer, but Lincoln hadn't expected one. The sound of his voice died off quickly. Not just an empty room then, but one designed to absorb echoes and sound reflection. Possibly to make recording of conversations easier. Possibly to muffle the cries of the interrogated. Neither boded well.

"My name is Simon Kim," Lincoln said. "I'm a Senior Operations Officer for Ready Vector Solutions. Can somebody help me?" His throat was a little dry and rough, but no more than if he'd slept with his mouth open for a couple of hours. They'd kept him hydrated, then.

"Hello?" he said, giving it one last try.

"Hello Mr Kim," a voice answered, warm, feminine, surprisingly close.

The hood lifted from his head; cool air refreshed him even as the sudden brightness stabbed his eyes. Lincoln blinked through the blur as his eyes adjusted. It didn't take them long; the lights in the room were pleasantly dim, like a quiet restaurant or a firelit study. A woman sat opposite him, her chair turned off-angle from his. More therapist than interrogator.

She wasn't wearing a uniform, but still looked as squared away as any soldier or police officer Lincoln had ever seen. A crisp, dark suit, her hair pulled tight in a bun.

The room wasn't anything like Lincoln had anticipated.

He'd imagined the cold, sterile, institutional decor of a police station or military base, function only, designed to create feelings of exposure and isolation. Instead, the atmosphere was warm and relaxed. Soothing colors, rich woods, comfortable chairs beside a round table. If his hands hadn't been bound, he could have believed they'd realized their mistake and were about to apologize and let him go free.

"Sorry about the ride," the woman said. There was the apology. Dare he hope for freedom to follow? "I'd like to remove your bindings, if you'll allow me."

"Uh," Lincoln said. "Sure? Please?"

The woman nodded and walked around behind him, touched his wrist, and leaned to speak in his ear.

"I'm sure a strong man like you could harm me if you so chose," she said. "I'm going to trust you not to do so."

Lincoln nodded, thrown off guard by her manner. But even while his natural instincts flailed, his training detached and ran down the list of what she'd just done; an apology, a favor with request for permission, a compliment and implied submission, an offer of trust. A shotgun blast of social techniques designed to loosen his defenses. Even with his awareness of what she'd done, Lincoln had to shake off the powerful urge to respond in kind. There was an added layer of complexity too, in needing to appear to respond as any normal male would, without actually doing so. A chess game, against an obvious master. And Lincoln had never been great at chess.

The woman released his bindings and dropped them on top of the hood on the table as she returned to her chair. She sat legs crossed, arms folded, with an expression of mild disappointment on her face.

"Look," Lincoln said, taking the initiative, and slipping

a little desperation into his voice. "I'm not a wealthy man. I'm not important. If you're looking to ransom me, there's not going to be any money there."

"You aren't in any danger, Mr Kim," the woman answered. "My name is Mei Dimasalang. I'm an officer with the Martian People's Collective Republic Internal Security Services." She produced her credentials and showed them to him, then smiled and said. "I know that's a mouthful. You can just call me Mei."

Lincoln still hadn't decided how to play it yet; scared traveler, outraged executive? He didn't have enough information to go on to decide. Some of each, perhaps.

"OK, Mei," Lincoln said. "Can you tell me what's going on?"

"Of course," Mei answered. "We're just going to have a conversation. I'm going to ask you a few questions, and if you answer them honestly, then we'll get you on your way."

"I find that hard to believe," Lincoln said, "given what you put me through. You could have just stopped by and knocked." He put a little heat on the words.

"I understand," she said. "I know this is upsetting. I assure you that we all want to get this matter cleared up as quickly as possible."

"What matter?" Lincoln said. "I'm here on business. I'm out for a walk last night, and next thing I know your thugs are kidnapping me and treating me like a common criminal. Worse. Am I under arrest? Do you even have the legal authority to detain me?"

"Some unusual methods were used in your case, Mr Kim," she said, her tone neutral, unmoved. "But I'm afraid your circumstances are equally unusual."

"Then why don't you tell me what my circumstances are, exactly."

"We were made aware of the presence of a number of foreign agents operating within the Republic. Given the current political situation, I'm certain you can appreciate the level of concern this has raised for us."

"That does sound bad, yes," Lincoln said. "I don't know what it has to do with me."

"You work for...?"

"Ready Vector Solutions," Lincoln answered. "We're in navigation. Collision detection and avoidance, really."

"You are employed by the Earth-based corporation Ready Vector Solutions?" Mei asked.

"Yes," Lincoln said. "As a Senior Operations Officer."

"For Ready Vector Solutions," she repeated.

Lincoln nodded, and waited for the next question. It didn't come. Mei sat there, looking at him expectantly. She hadn't moved, hadn't changed her position or posture since she'd sat down, a sure sign that she was an experienced interrogator.

"I'm sorry, but I really don't see..." Lincoln said. "I just... I really don't understand what's happening right now. I was sent here by my employer to evaluate whether or not the Republic was a good candidate for setting up new operations. I'm an operations guy, that's what I do. They told me all the travel arrangements were made properly, that everything was cleared. If there's a problem with my paperwork, I'm sure we could get it sorted out with a call to our corporate HQ."

"And you say your employer is Ready Vector Solutions?"

"Yes," Lincoln said, not having to feign annoyance at the repeated question.

Mei nodded. "You're aware that Ready Vector Solutions is a front company for the United States National Intelligence Directorate?"

Lincoln hoped the surprise didn't show on his face. He chuckled, as if she'd made a joke. She smiled warmly.

"I'll take that as a yes," she said.

"Well," Lincoln said. "You can take it however you want to, but this is… this is all so ridiculous. I don't know what your game is here–"

"This isn't *my* game, Mr Kim," she interrupted. "These are games of state. But it is my *job* to identify and neutralize threats to the security of the Collective Republic. You're only being detained for as long as it takes me to determine that you are not, in fact, a threat. I'm afraid so far, you haven't given me a lot of help."

"I can't help you prove a negative," Lincoln said. "Whatever information you have, I don't know how any of it connects to me. It's obviously wrong."

"Some kind of mistake?" Mei said.

"Must be," Lincoln said.

Mei nodded, and stood up. "Perhaps you need some time to consider your situation."

"You keep acting like I have some say in any of this," Lincoln said, and he started to stand. From the way she looked at him, he understood very clearly that he shouldn't get out of his seat. He perched on the front of the chair. "I don't know what you want from me!"

"I know you have friends in the area," Mei said as she walked to the door. "And I'm sure they're looking for you. But you shouldn't expect them to be able to find you. Not until we're ready for you to be found. I apologized for the rough ride, and I meant it, even though it was absolutely necessary. We couldn't safely leave you inside the Republic."

She watched him carefully to see how he took the news; Lincoln let the genuine feeling of shock register, knowing no pretense was necessary now. He didn't necessarily believe her. It could be an easy psychological trick, to lie about his location, to undermine his hope of rescue and thus hasten the inevitable break. Everyone had their limits, Lincoln knew. Everyone broke, eventually.

Mei knocked on the door three times, and looked back at him over her shoulder.

"I may be *your* enemy, Mr Kim," she said, as the door was unlocked from the outside. "But you are not mine. I hope the next time we talk, you'll remember that." She paused there for a moment, and smiled at him again, though a little sadly.

Once she'd exited, two men entered and took him by the arms and Lincoln wondered just how long he would last before they broke him.

TWENTY-FOUR

Wright checked the time, then glanced out the side window of the car. Two minutes. Thumper was running another pass over the target site, using three skeeters to provide overlapping coverage over a wide perimeter. Elliot had selected the meeting point with ample input from the team, all of them knowing full well that every advantage it gave them, it also presented to their opposition. By the same token, every vulnerability they accepted was one they also forced on their adversary. This was the Game at its highest possible level. Spooks and ghosts; mist fighting shadow.

And they were down a man. Wright had given up on trying to prevent her concern for Lincoln from creeping in. Now she was embracing it, inviting it in, letting it focus her. They wouldn't be getting him back tonight. But this was the first step in the chain of events that would bring him home. They would get it done. She would make it happen, no matter the odds.

"Go time," Sahil said from the front of the car. He'd let the AI handle the trip in, but he'd jacked his console in to override it, just in case.

Wright nodded, opened the team channel over comms. "Thumper, we good?"

"Good to go," Thumper responded.

"Mikey," Wright said. "You set?"

"Set," Mike replied. "And I've got the place all to myself." During planning, he had identified every viable position for a sniper nest, as well as each point he would use for counter-sniper work. He'd made a joke before they'd left the safehouse, about just hoping he wasn't going to have to share his spot with the enemy. "At least for now."

"Sahil?"

"Good," Sahil said from the driver's seat.

"Roger that," Wright answered. "We're stepping out now."

She opened the vehicle door and got out first, checking up and down the sidewalk before motioning for Elliot to follow. At her signal, he clambered out and stood by her side. Alert, but relaxed. His demeanor surprised her, for some reason. For the first time since they'd met, he seemed solid, capable. Almost trustworthy. In his element, maybe. It occurred to her that she'd never actually seen him in action.

"Thumper, you got us?" she asked.

"I got you."

"Mike," Wright said, "if any of this starts to go sideways…" She turned to look at Elliot, waited until he met her gaze.

"Yeah?" Mike said.

"Kill him first," she answered.

"No sweat."

Wright gave it a moment, staring hard into Elliot's eyes for any sign of betrayal. But there was none. His eyes held hers, calm, steady. Resolute.

And then, while she was still staring him down, a smile broke across his face like a slow sunrise; he bowed slightly, and offered his arm.

"Shall we?" he said. Definitely in his element.

"We're moving," Wright reported. She didn't take his arm.

In another life, Wright may have enjoyed such a walk, on such a night, in such a place. They walked alongside one another for about a kilometer through the quiet streets, in a residential area, removed from the bustling night life on the other side of town. It was a place of families; of dinners around a table, and bedtime stories, and evening routines. The windows were mostly dark, reasonable people in bed at a reasonable hour. Dreaming children, probably, all safe in their beds, with parents sleeping close at hand. And not a one of them aware of the deadly dance playing out on their streets.

They reached a low apartment building and stopped, their break-off point. He escorted her up the steps to the entryway, and as she was reaching to open the door, he took her by the elbow and gently halted. Wright turned halfway back to look at him.

"You're a good woman, Ms Wright," Elliot said. "Wish I could have gotten to know you under other circumstances."

Whatever response he was hoping to get, she didn't have one for him. After giving her plenty of time to reply if she'd wanted and receiving none, he nodded.

"Well," he said. "Here I go."

"Yep," she said.

"You won't have to shoot me, I promise," he said.

He looked at her for a moment, held her gaze long enough that it might have become uncomfortable, if Wright hadn't been used to staring people down. There was something more he wanted to say, but for once, he didn't seem to know how. To her surprise, he leaned forward and kissed her cheek. She didn't react. Just held still as he drew away.

"So... bye," he said, flashing his easy smile. And without another word, he turned and trotted down the stairs, turned right, and started his route to the meeting point at a brisk pace.

Wright stood there and watched him go. She wanted to be angry with him, wanted to hold him solely responsible for the situation they were in. But no matter how hard she tried, her heart wouldn't let her. He was just a man, after all. Everything she'd ever done, she'd had a team to do it with. He was out here alone, finding his own way. *Making* his own way. He'd made a mistake, that was certain. An enormous one. One that was finally too big for him to handle on his own. But it was still just a mistake. Wright had lost count of the number of times she'd screwed up, only to have a teammate pick up her slack. Who did Elliot have, she wondered.

Her mind answered its own musing. Them. He had them. And that was it.

They'd find a way. That's what they did.

Wright entered the apartment building, gave it a couple of minutes in the dim, silent entry hall, and then exited out the opposite side. Elliot's route would loop out and around. Hers would intersect his not long after he passed and, if her timing wasn't too far off, she'd be able to shadow him the rest of the way to the rendezvous. He had talked them through his planned surveillance detection route; a shallow, ineffective one more for show than to actually pick up any tails. The target was supposed to come alone, but of course he wouldn't. And according to Elliot, they would make sure he saw at least one of them, just to reinforce the point. It was the ones they didn't want him to see they all had to worry about.

And it was those that his route was meant to expose to the Outriders.

It didn't take them long. Wright was just reaching her point of intersection and starting to scan for Elliot when Thumper came in over the team communications.

"Mark one," she said. "Grey coat, glasses, off your left shoulder, about a block behind Elliot... half-block ahead of you, Mir."

Wright kept her hands in her pockets, her head down, but directed her attention in the general direction. Sure enough, across the wide street, a man in a grey coat was walking at a brisk pace. And further down the street, Elliot. Timing had been pretty good after all.

"Got a possible shooter here," Mike said a minute or two later. "Building nine, third story, second room over from the easternmost corner."

During their far-too-brief planning session, they'd numbered all the buildings around the courtyard Elliot had arranged for his meeting site. "Not a bad spot," he added. "But not a great one, either."

"That makes two," Thumper said.

"Watcher on the wall," Sahil chimed in a moment later. An elevated position adjacent to the courtyard, with good lines of sight on the western approach, but too exposed for a shooter, according to Mike. "Woman, brown coat and hat. You got her, Mike?"

"Negative," Mike answered. "Don't have a line on her from here. Should I reposition?"

"Negative, hold there," Wright said. "Sahil, Watcher's yours unless you hear otherwise."

"Watcher's mine, roger," Sahil said. "Movin' to."

"Three," Thumper said.

Wright continued to shadow the man in the grey coat, as he trailed Elliot. At one point, Elliot took a right, requiring the man to cross the street to follow him. Grey Coat wasn't there to track Elliot to his destination; both parties already knew that final location. His job was to watch for any extra hands Elliot might have brought along with him.

The man in the grey coat undoubtedly noticed her when he checked the road before crossing it, but if he'd had any suspicion that Wright was following him, he didn't reveal any signs of it. Not that he would, if he was a pro. To be safe, Wright kept her eyes in front of her, blissfully ignorant of her surroundings, and continued on her way another two blocks before she cut over on a parallel track. She fully expected at some point that Grey Coat would drop off the trail, and his replacement would take over. She hoped she could catch the hand-off herself. If she missed the moment, Thumper would catch it on one of the skeeters, but Wright preferred getting to see them firsthand, with her own eyes. Easier to size them up that way.

As she completed her parallel circuit, and was rejoining the caravan of spies, Thumper came in over comms again.

"They just handed off, Mir," she said. "Grey Coat's going perpendicular. Replacement is a woman, dark hair, long coat with some sort of dark pattern on it... huh."

"What's the 'huh' for?" Wright asked.

"She kinda looks like you," Thumper answered.

"Great," Wright said.

"Hope I don't shoot the wrong one," Mike said.

"That's four," Thumper said. "Elliot said three to five, in addition to the primary. Anyone got eyes on any other suspicious persons?"

No one responded with new targets. Wright wasn't able to get a look at her twin before Elliot made the

turn for the final approach to the courtyard. She didn't
want to risk it this close to the site, in case Grey Coat
had warned the doppelganger to be on the lookout.
Wright continued past the route, and finished her circuit
around the perimeter, looking for any stragglers they
may have missed. She couldn't pick any out. If only that
guaranteed they weren't there.

With the four extra bad guys identified, Wright loosely
assigned the targets.

"Sahil's got the Watcher on the Wall. Mike you've
got the shooter, obviously. I'll take the man in the Grey
Coat. And Thumper. Going to need you to do a little
work on my twin."

"On it," Thumper said.

"Lucky," Mike replied.

"Get set," Wright said. "And hold for my call."

Wright crossed over to her final position, and readied
for action. Once it went down, they were all going to
have to move fast. The order was going to be the trickiest
part. Assuming they hadn't overlooked anyone.

It was another bad meet. Elliot knew that. He'd known
it when he set it up. There was no way around it. And as
usual, he was walking in, deaf, blind, practically naked.
Sahil had tried to convince him to carry a pistol, or at
least wear a vest, but Elliot had refused both. He'd never
had either before, and he knew anything he changed
about himself was likely to be taken by Gregor as a
warning sign. He'd even declined to wear any comm
device to connect him to the team, fearing that keeping
them informed on their progress might interfere with his
ability to read the situation. And he was most definitely
going to need all his focus to play this one right.

The space where they were supposed to meet was

an open, brick courtyard. Elliot stepped out into it first, even though there was no sign of Gregor yet. If they wanted to kill him, he was giving them the perfect opportunity. There were a dozen good angles. He knew them all, because Mike had painstakingly evaluated and categorized each of them. Elliot couldn't help but glance up at the one in the four-story building a few blocks over. That was the one Mike had said he'd use for sure if he was going to take Elliot out there in the courtyard. Clean sightlines, easy access in and out, not an obvious location from the courtyard, but an easy shot from elevation. The windows in the building were all dark. Not that Elliot would have seen his would-be murderer even if there was a sniper stationed there. In fact, he never would have even noticed that particular building if Mike hadn't pointed it out to him. And just then, he wasn't especially grateful that Mike had.

But Elliot knew if they wanted to get him, they would get him. He'd known that for a long time. Ever since he had volunteered to serve as an undeclared officer for the Directorate. Somehow coming to terms with his own death many years ago had made it easier to take all the ridiculous risks over his career that had kept him alive for so long. At least, up to this point.

Elliot moved under one of the lights in the courtyard, presenting himself as conspicuously as he could manage. He could almost feel the crosshairs on him. But he figured this too was a show of courtesy to Gregor; giving Gregor's people a chance to take the first shot, before Gregor himself had to commit. Maybe Elliot's willingness to step out first would ease the other party's concerns of compromise.

Gregor was out there, Elliot knew. He was watching, evaluating. Moving his people around, undoubtedly.

Elliot stood there in the open, in the light, waiting as the game pieces moved all around him. He would wait, however long it took.

It was nearly twenty minutes later that a figure appeared in the wide arch at the opposite end of the courtyard, a shadowy silhouette back-lit by the ambient light from the street behind him.

Elliot didn't move or acknowledge the figure, once more giving Gregor the opportunity to initiate. Assuming it was indeed Gregor, and not a decoy.

Another five minutes passed before the individual moved. Instead of stepping forward into the courtyard, it receded, and a second figure came out from under the arch. So the first had been a decoy after all.

Gregor.

"Well," he said. "Let's get on with it."

Elliot stepped forward out of the light, raising both hands in front of him as he did so, in a show of being unarmed. And as he brought his hands back down to his sides, he hoped he hadn't done it too quickly for the Outriders to catch the cue.

"Target's confirmed," Wright said. There had been a fifth man after all, and that man was now providing close security for the primary. His proximity to the courtyard made him Wright's responsibility, but there was no way she could take out the man in the Grey Coat and cover the distance to the fifth man in time. "First was a decoy, say again, first individual was a decoy. Decoy is mine. Mike, I need you to take Grey Coat. Do you have a shot?"

"Hold one," Mike said. Wright held her place, resisting the urge to change positions now in hopes that Mike could get the shot, knowing every second they delayed increased Elliot's danger. But if she moved too early and had to double back, the man in the grey coat would certainly notice. Ten seconds later, Mike answered, "Roger that, I can get him. First or second?"

"Shooter first," Wright said. "Moving to Decoy, hold for my call."

She left her position then, restraining her pace, circling around, losing time. She hoped Elliot could keep the man talking.

It took her over two minutes to reach her new position. The Decoy was watching whatever was going down in the courtyard, his back exposed.

"Wright's in place," she reported. "Execute, execute, execute."

As soon as the words were out of her mouth, she left her position and crossed the street. And with them, the team went into action, working their targets from outside in, each layer of security peeled away to expose the next.

"Shooter's down," Mike said.

And seconds later, Sahil responded, "Watcher on the wall, down."

"Twin, down," Thumper reported. As the reports from her teammates came in, Wright closed the distance to Gregor's nearest guardian. Ten meters.

"Grey coat, neutralized," Mike said. "That makes four, last one's yours, Mir."

Seven meters. Wright couldn't tell if she was going too fast or too slow.

She was still five meters away when her target started to turn.

"Don't worry," Elliot said, "I won't take too much of your time."

"I know you won't," Gregor answered. And in a

motion as casual as brushing lint from his sleeve, Gregor drew something from under his coat and pointed it at Elliot. If the movement had been faster, Elliot might have understood his danger. As it was, he simply stood there, trying to figure out what Gregor was doing when the something in his hand emitted two muffled pops, and currents of raw pain lanced through Elliot's belly.

It was only when he found himself sitting on the ground, struggling to breathe through his spasming diaphragm, that he realized he'd been shot.

"There," Gregor said, standing over him. "Now. Whatever you had to say, you should probably say it quickly."

"I was wrong," Elliot gasped out through gritted teeth. He pressed his palms into his abdomen, trying to staunch the bleeding.

"I'm sorry?" Gregor said. "Speak up, Elliot. You're mumbling."

"I was wrong," Elliot repeated. "About... the guy you grabbed."

Gregor holstered his weapon with a sigh, and settled into a crouch in front of Elliot.

"No, you weren't," he said. "I confirmed it through other sources, you see. Suffering from a little guilt, are we?"

Elliot shook his head. Where was his back up? He hoped they had seen his signal.

"Oh? Huh. I had heard that was common amongst traitors," Gregor said. "Particularly here, at the end."

"I'm... not... a traitor," Elliot said.

"A man of opportunities, if you prefer," Gregor said, and he smiled his corpse grin. "*Formerly*, a man of opportunities. Pretty sure you're all out of those now. Goodbye, Elliot. You've been... useful."

Gregor patted Elliot on the side of the face, and then stood and started to walk towards the exit. Elliot had to stop him somehow. But there wasn't much he could do from the ground, with two rounds in his belly. Unless...

"The ship," Elliot said.

Gregor stopped, stood in place for a few seconds. Was he waiting to see if Elliot would say more? Or was he trying to decide what to do? He hadn't known that Elliot knew about SUNGRAZER; neither that it existed, nor that Gregor was aware of her.

Still no sign of the others. Maybe they'd decided it was too dangerous and they'd bailed out. Or maybe they'd left him out to dry. The thought made him sad, but he couldn't really blame them if that's what they'd done. Maybe they were off raiding Gregor's office, while Elliot sat here and bled to death.

If that was the case, then he'd still buy them as much time as he could.

"You..." Elliot continued, forcing the words out despite his protesting lungs, "shouldn't have messed... with the ship..."

"What ship, Elliot?"

"You know... her name."

Gregor turned at that, strode back in front of Elliot and crouched again, so close his nose almost touched Elliot's. Angry now.

"What about her?" he growled.

"You should have... left it. They're going to find you, because of it."

"Not unless they hurry," Gregor said with a chuckle. "I really hope you didn't bring me all the way out here just to try to feed me more of your stories."

Elliot's mouth moved, but the words he'd meant to say didn't come. He squeezed shut his eyes against the wave of pain rolling through his gut.

"Stop gaping," Gregor said. "It makes you look like a fish."

"I... didn't," Elliot said.

"Didn't what?"

"Bring you... out... for stories," Elliot managed to say.

"Are you sure?" said Gregor.

Elliot nodded.

"Then what, exactly, did you bring me out here for, Elliot?"

Elliot forced his eyes open, just so he could see the look on Gregor's face.

"I brought you out..." Elliot said, "for them."

Gregor's eyes narrowed at the words. And then they widened, and he started to turn.

But Wright was already there.

The blow had been aimed at the base of his neck, but it caught him instead on the cheek just under his eye socket, and flashed electric blue as the stunner in her hand fired off on contact. Gregor sprawled limp, like Wright had punched the life right out of him. She hovered over the man for a moment like a storm cloud ready to deliver a second dose of lightning if necessary.

It wasn't. She seemed disappointed.

Once it was clear Gregor wasn't getting up any time soon, she turned and looked at Elliot.

"You get him?" Elliot asked. His eyes didn't want to focus.

"We got him," she answered.

"I thought you... had a stunner," Elliot said. He was pretty sure he'd seen a flash of light, but maybe he'd imagined it. "Did you have to hit him?"

"Didn't *have* to," she answered. She knelt down beside him. "How bad is it?"

"Eh… nothing a couple of pints of blood and… a couple of fewer holes can't fix…" he replied. The pain wasn't so bad now, for some reason. That probably wasn't a good sign. Her face became clearer all of a sudden, and he realized his eyes had teared up, and just now spilled over. He hoped she didn't think he was crying. That would be so embarrassing.

"Lie back," she said. "Lie down, let me see."

Elliot tried to comply, but once he started back, his abdominal muscles refused to cooperate. He would have smacked his head on the brick if Wright hadn't caught him and eased him to the ground. She moved his hands out of the way; he hadn't realized they'd still been pressed over the wounds.

"Told you," he said.

"Told me what?"

"That you wouldn't have to shoot me."

"Sahil," Wright said, "Sahil I need you here, now."

Elliot didn't hear a response. But based on the sudden appearance, either Sahil had been mere steps away, or Elliot had blacked out briefly. The man's face materialized above him, close, looking down at him.

"You're OK, Elliot," Sahil was saying, though his voice sounded strangely thin. "We're takin' care of ya, don't worry."

"Did you get him?" Elliot asked. He'd meant to ask before. Or had he already?

"Yeah, we got him. Be still now. I'm gonna get you patched up, you're gonna be all right."

Elliot smiled, warm and drowsy.

"You have a nice face, Sahil," Elliot said. "But you're a terrible liar."

TWENTY-FIVE

Lincoln was slipping. He knew it. He could feel it.

He'd been through the training before, on multiple occasions, had learned a number of techniques to minimize the effectiveness of every known interrogation tactic. He could name them while they were being used on him, and in naming them, he could master them. Counter them. In some of the darkest corners of his training, instructors had tortured him to help him understand it, to take away the fear of it, and to educate him on how to combat its effects. But here, now, everything he'd ever learned was failing him.

Not because his captors were harming him. Apart from the drugging he'd suffered in his initial capture, they had done nothing to cause him injury. Though the meals were always cold and the water tepid, he had plenty to eat and drink.

It was the room. He'd never been in anything like it before.

It was stealing his mind.

His cell was large by usual prison standards, perhaps as much as twelve feet square. But there was no furniture. No bed, no chair. A toilet was in one corner, but it was sculpted into the floor and wall in such a way that he hadn't identified it as such at first. A small recession in the wall served as a sink. Other than those two things, the room was empty.

And when they'd first brought him in, he'd found its shape bizarre; the walls and ceiling were strangely contoured, the material unpleasant to touch. The floor was flat, and vaguely spongy. It wasn't until they sealed the door that he understood.

As total darkness was to the eyes, so was this room for the ears. In pitch blackness, you could touch your palm to your nose and still not see your fingers; it was this same uncanny sensation, but for sound. Lincoln had never experienced anything like it before. At first, it had seemed merely ridiculous. A novelty, even. He had yelled, clapped his hands so hard they ached, even thrown himself against the walls and floor, experimenting and marveling at the deadness of the room. And no matter what he did, the sound dissipated immediately, no louder than a soft exhale. Even screaming as loud as he could, the wordless cries died as soon as they left his mouth. For a while he'd tried raving about the illegality of his imprisonment or pleading for release, but there had been no response and the lack of sound quickly became too unsettling for him to continue.

It wasn't deafness. He could still hear. The noises he could detect were simply all internal; his breathing, his own heartbeat, the rushing of his blood.

Or was he just imagining that constant rushing sound? Surely it would be impossible to hear your own blood moving through your body. But what else could be making that endless noise?

The temperature was too cool, by a degree or two. Not enough to cause hypothermia, by his estimation, but uncomfortable. The thin shirt and pants they'd given him to wear held little heat. No matter what he did, he couldn't seem to get warm. Couldn't sleep. Couldn't think.

And how long they had given him before they introduced the next phase? An hour? Two? Ten? He'd lost his ability to track time.

When they made the switch, Lincoln felt himself cry out reflexively, even though the scream was virtually silent. Had they known about the anxiety open space caused him? The walls, the ceiling, the floor, had all ceased to exist. Every direction he looked was the vastness of space. Except for down. Below him, far, far below him sat Mars, spinning on its axis.

He had fallen to the floor then, thrown himself upon it on hands and knees, to remind himself that the room still existed, that he hadn't really, truly been ejected into space. But even with his palms pressing hard into that strange, springy material, the image was so convincing Lincoln nearly started to hyperventilate.

He shut his eyes against the vision, drawing up the image of the room as it had been, reminding himself of its many surfaces, of its solidity, of its *realness*.

And it was then that he understood the insidiousness of the room's design. Shutting his eyes magnified the isolating effects of the silence; opening them made his mind swim and reel at the all-encompassing emptiness, and his utter insignificance in its midst.

Lincoln's only refuge, his only coping mechanism, was sitting tucked in a ball, hugging his knees, his back pressed into the corner with his feet flat on the floor. Sometimes he would run his palms back and forth across the floor or the irregular walls to increase the sensory input. When he was brought food, he forced himself to eat it slowly, a small bite at a time, regardless of whether he was famished or wasn't hungry at all. Anything that could help him stay grounded, to stay present in his body.

His captors were, most likely, providing food for him at irregular intervals. Forcing him to go hungry for eighteen hours, and then giving him two meals less than an hour apart, to further deteriorate his sense of time.

It all worked. When the room reappeared and the door opened, Lincoln had lost all concept of time. They could have told him he'd been held for a day or a year and he would have believed either of them equally.

The return to reality was shocking to Lincoln's senses. Lights dazzled, and the sounds... they were a nearly unbearable confusion assaulting his mind. The two guards that escorted him to the interrogation room practically carried him, and not roughly. A man and a woman, they didn't speak or make eye contact, but even so, their hold on him felt more protective than controlling.

They left him sitting in his chair in the interrogation room he'd been in previously. Or, one so like it as to be indistinguishable. The questions were coming. Lincoln knew it. He used the time he had alone to try to prepare his shattered mind.

The door opened some unknowable span of time later, and the woman who had questioned him before came in, a pleasant look on her face. Lincoln struggled to remember her name. He had always been so good with names before.

"Mr Kim," she said. "So good to see you. Can I get you some coffee?"

Mei. Her name was Mei. He should refuse. You always refused. It was their way of putting you in their debt, of making you feel the need to reciprocate, to return a favor.

"That would be great, thank you," Lincoln heard himself say.

Mei nodded, opened the door and stepped out into the hall. She left the door propped open while she spoke to someone outside. When she returned, she was holding two steaming cups of coffee. It wasn't until Lincoln heard the sharp clicks of the door locking that he realized he hadn't even considered getting out of his chair while the door was open.

"Black is OK, I hope?" Mei said, as she handed him the cup. "I'm afraid we don't have a lot of extra luxuries here."

Lincoln accepted the cup with both hands, savored the warmth that ran through his palms up through his forearms.

"Black is perfect," he said. "Thank you."

He took a sip and scalded his lips and tongue. He didn't care.

"How are you finding your accommodations?" she asked.

Lincoln blew on his coffee, watched the steam swirl across the surface. Fighting to come back to himself. He inhaled deeply, let the aroma draw him into the present.

"Quiet," he said. "Nice view."

Mei sipped her coffee, her sharp eyes monitoring him over the rim. She looked a little different than the last time he'd seen her; still a dark suit, still squared away. Dark hair in a loose pony-tail.

"Mr Kim," she said, and then stopped herself. "... Do you mind if I call you Simon?"

"Simon is fine," he answered.

"Simon, then," she said. "Are you feeling up to answering a few questions?"

"I would love to answer some questions," Lincoln

JAY POSEY   379

said. "As long as you ask me ones I *can* answer."

"Good. Excellent. Let's start with Elliot Goodkind."

Lincoln took another sip of coffee, trying to keep his reaction neutral. He shouldn't have been surprised that they would know about Elliot. But that was a connection he didn't have to worry about trying to hide, either.

"OK," he said.

"How did you come to be connected with Mr Goodkind?"

"Through work," Lincoln said. "First time I met him was when we arrived. I don't know him personally." It was nice to be able to answer that one with complete honesty.

"And what role does he play in your work?"

"Liaison, mostly. Part tour guide, I guess. He was supposed to show us around, set up a few meetings... I don't remember seeing you guys on the itinerary though, so I'm pretty sure he wasn't supposed to let me get caught up in your crazy spy story."

"If that were true, then perhaps an undeclared covert intelligence agent was a poor choice of guide," Mei said.

Lincoln shook his head.

"So now Elliot's a spy too?" he said. "Are you guys just trying to stir up trouble? Pick a fight with Earth? Is that what this is?"

"The Collective Republic is neutral in such matters, and will remain that way for as long as it is within our power to do so."

"Is there anything I can say to help you understand that I'm not a spy?"

"No."

Lincoln let his exasperation show.

"Why not?"

"Because, Simon," she said with a smile, "if you were

simply a man on a business trip, you would have gone insane by now. Your training is showing."

Lincoln tried to prevent his face from revealing his realization, and knew he had blown it. How had he been so stupid? He had become so focused on enduring, he had forgotten what such circumstances would do to his cover identity.

"It's been a long time since I've had a moment to myself," he said, trying to deflect. "Nice to get a breather."

Mei chuckled.

"I still don't know what you want from me," he continued. "I wish you would just tell me what you want me to say, so I could say it."

"I think you do know what I want you to say," she said.

"I really don't."

"I want to know why the United American Federation wants to go to war with my nation. The United States in particular."

"We don't want war," Lincoln said, before he could stop himself.

Her eyes narrowed just enough for him to pick up on it.

"Then why are *you* here, Mr Kim?"

He'd given himself away completely now. She'd gotten him. He looked down at his coffee, took a sip to buy himself some time and to help keep his mouth occupied. Mei watched him intently for a long moment. And then suddenly got to her feet.

"OK," she said, as she walked over to the door. "Well, maybe next time you'll have more to say on the matter."

Even knowing what they were doing, it was hard to resist. This room. This comfortable room, with light, and warmth, and a human voice. They would let him stay here as long as he liked. As long as he talked. As long as he told them everything.

"No... wait," Lincoln said, reflexively. He took a breath to say more, but then regained control. It had been close. His body had nearly betrayed him again. He didn't know what words had been about to come out of his mouth, but he'd only caught them in the barest nick of time. They were going to stick him back in that room again. He closed his eyes, held that breath for a moment to settle himself, then exhaled. Opened his eyes, looked down into his half-finished cup of coffee.

"Yes?" Mei prompted.

He looked up at her. "Can I finish my coffee first?"

She didn't answer, but her expression showed clear disappointment and, Lincoln thought, perhaps a flash of frustration. Maybe he wasn't losing as badly as he thought. She knocked on the door three times, and while the guards came to get him, Lincoln drank in as much of the warmth as he could before they took it away.

TWENTY-SIX

When Gregor came to, his first sensation was the feeling that someone had filled his mouth with scalding water while he was out cold. His half-numbed tongue felt too big for his mouth, and his teeth ached with a dull throb. He couldn't remember ever having felt his heartbeat in his teeth before. It was decidedly unpleasant.

Seeing that he was awake, the right side of his face joined the pain party with the gift of a blowtorch impression, along his upper cheekbone below the eye socket. He went to touch it, but his arms didn't work. It took him a moment to realize he was strapped down.

"Mornin'," a man's voice said.

The sound drew Gregor's attention to the larger surroundings, outside the borders of his personal world of hurt. He opened his eyes to find himself quick-cuffed, hands and feet, to a chair, in the middle of a small, otherwise empty room. It was damp, with a sharp odor of fuel. A man leaned against the wall in one corner; tall, long limbed. He was smiling, but he didn't look happy, or friendly.

"Let me put it to you like this, buddy," the man said. "The only reason you woke up with eyes is because I wouldn't let her carve 'em out while you were out cold."

He pointed to a woman seated on the floor.

Dark skinned, her face vaguely familiar. Gregor knew her, from somewhere. Cooper. Allison Cooper, though he knew now that most likely wasn't her real name. The other NID agent. Gregor looked back at the man, tried to bring up anything he might know, but came up blank. Apparently Elliot hadn't given him *all* the information. Gregor regretted not having shot him more.

"And why is that?" Gregor managed to ask.

"Figured it'd be better if she waited till you were awake," the man said.

"You seem angry," Gregor said. He sat up as straight as he could in his chair and made a show of stretching his back and neck, to draw attention away from the fact that he was testing the strength of his bonds.

"They're strong enough," said the man. "Don't you worry about that."

"I work for Internal Security. I hope you realize you've assaulted and imprisoned an officer of the law."

"You'll have to pardon me if I don't think you're much of a lawman."

"Well, I'm sorry, I'm at a bit of a loss," Gregor said. "You'll have to remind me what it is in particular I've done to upset you."

"You killed a friend of ours," the woman said. "And kidnapped another."

"Oh," Gregor said. "Ah yes, I could see how that might be upsetting. But if you're referring to Elliot Goodkind, let me assure you that he was no friend of yours. I probably did you a favor." Good to know the man was dead. Gregor still wished he had shot him more.

"Then maybe you'd be kind enough to do us one more," said the man. "What are you doing with SUNGRAZER?"

Gregor kept his face neutral. For what was supposedly an above-top-secret asset, an awful lot of people seemed to know about that ship.

"I'm afraid I don't know the reference," Gregor said. "But I do understand that you're hostile spies operating in the colony I'm sworn to protect. I'm sorry about your friends, but I'm not sure what else you would expect me to do, exactly."

"Think harder," the woman said. "Do your best to remember. It's important."

"Hmm," Gregor said. "SUNGRAZER you say. OK, let me think about it. Nope, no idea."

Cooper, or whatever her name was, got up off the floor then and walked slowly towards him, with a predatory look. She stopped in front of him, her legs touching the front of his knees, and started to unbutton her shirt. Underneath she was wearing an athletic compression top, sleeveless. Her arms were well-muscled, covered from shoulders to wrists in intricate tattoos. She tossed her shirt to her companion in the corner.

"Don't get excited," she said. "I just don't feel like trying to get the blood out of my shirt." Her hand disappeared behind her back for a moment, and when it returned it brought with it a claw-shaped blade. She straddled him and sat on his lap; Gregor reflexively leaned back in the chair. When he did, the woman grabbed the top of his head with one hand and forced it back further, to the point of pain. The next instant, he felt cold steel press into his cheekbone, the blade flat against his skin, but the point of that claw-tip uncomfortably touching the lower eyelid, just under the eyeball.

"I hope it doesn't pop like a grape," the man said.

"You sure you don't have anything you want to say to me?" the woman asked.

"I have many things I'd like to say to you," Gregor answered. "But I fear they would only anger you further."

The woman pressed her body into him, her weight and strength constricting his abdomen; with his head tilted so far back, he found it difficult to breathe. Even without the knife blade threatening to pluck his eye out, Gregor had to fight against the natural panic rising. It was almost like drowning on dry land. But Gregor held on. He was strong. He could beat her. He held still, silent, did his best not to give them the pleasure of seeing his discomfort.

"Don't break that neck," the man said. "Gonna be hard for him to talk if he chokes on his own tongue."

In response, the woman lightly dragged the curved inner blade of her knife along the hard edge of Gregor's eye socket, not enough to cut, but uncomfortable, like she'd dragged the back of her fingernail roughly across the soft flesh.

"Torture me all you want," Gregor said. "I assure you I have nothing to tell you."

"That's OK," the woman said, suddenly casual. She stood and backed away from him, and held up a small device for him to see. His badge. His credentials. Access to Internal Security Systems. "I only needed a little bit of your DNA and a couple of minutes of voice sample anyway. I was just hoping you'd save us the trouble."

She tucked his badge into her pocket, and held the blade of her knife up to the light, looking undoubtedly at the skin cells she'd scraped off. The man moved closer to her and returned her shirt.

"You want to say SUNGRAZER for me again, nice and clear?" she asked.

"I don't know what you think you'll do with that,"

Gregor said. He couldn't stand the smug look on her face, as if she'd beaten him somehow. She had no idea what she was up against.

"I do," she said.

"It's too late," Gregor said. "You can't stop it now. Not even I can." He wouldn't make the mistake of revealing anything they didn't already know, but he couldn't let them leave that room with any sense of hope. Maybe they'd kill him. But not without knowing it was for nothing.

The woman hesitated by the door. "Things starting to come back to you a little clearer now?"

She gave Gregor a few seconds to answer. When he didn't, she left the room.

"'It takes the knowledge of but one shark to fear the entire ocean'," Gregor said, as the man was about to leave.

"Say what now?" the man asked.

"A wise woman once told me that."

"Sounds fancy," the man said. "What's it supposed to mean?" He didn't strike Gregor as being particularly bright.

"You'll see," Gregor said, smiling.

"Maybe," said the man. "Too bad you won't."

Gregor stopped smiling. The man flicked the light off and left Gregor sitting in total darkness, the scent of combustible fuel suddenly heavy in his nostrils, and on his mind.

"You're not really going to burn him alive down there," Elliot said, lying on the sagging couch. His voice was rough-edged and thin, but it'd lost the concerning wet wheeze from an hour or so before.

"Nah," Wright said, shaking her head. "*Probably* not.

But he doesn't need to know that. We'll give him a little while to think about it, see if maybe he decides he's got something to tell us after all."

"I wouldn't count on it," Elliot said.

"I'm not," Thumper answered. She sat down at the makeshift workstation they'd set up for her in the dingy space, and ran what looked like a needle along the blade of her knife. This she inserted into a receptacle attached to Veronica. "He thinks you're dead."

"He might be right," Elliot replied.

"Don't be a baby," Wright said.

"What's with the knife?" Elliot asked.

"Took a little bit of Gregor's DNA," Thumper said. "We'll sequence it real quick, and then with that and a vocal imprint, I can spoof his credentials to give us access to Internal Security's systems. See what he knows, and what they know."

"Stay on target, Thump," Wright said.

"Yeah, yeah," Thumper said. "I won't waste time. It's just… while we're in there, we might as well grab what we can, right?"

Thumper held her hands up in front of her like she was climbing the face of an imaginary cliff, looked up at the ceiling, and then started moving her hands around like she was manipulating oversized pieces on an invisible chess board.

"OK, so, Veronica's still crunching C&C encryption data," she said. "We have the device from the *Ava Leyla* – that's busted but has some pieces we might be able to use – and a bunch of design schematics from Guo Components. With our friend Gregor's creds, we can get into the Republic's Internal Security Service and see where the ridealong I injected back at the research facility ended up. There's got to be something in there, with all those pieces... We've got everything we need except a way to connect with..."

She trailed off, her hands still hovering in the air in front of her. Then her gaze dropped from the ceiling and fell like a hawk on Elliot.

"Wait a minute..." Thumper said. "Elliot."

"Yeah?"

"How were you getting intel off SUNGRAZER?"

"Through a bounce, with my rig," he said. "Secure comm set up. But it doesn't work anymore. My creds aren't valid."

"But you can still submit requests for access?"

"Yes..." Elliot said.

Wright could see Thumper's mind working; she was putting pieces together faster than anyone else and, Wright guessed, had pieces the rest of them were missing.

"How does that help us, Thump?" she asked.

"Because with his credentials," Thumper said, pointing vaguely towards the downstairs room where they were storing Gregor, "and his rig," she said, pointing now to Elliot, "we just might be able to locate SUNGRAZER."

"How?"

"Ehh neh neh neh," Thumper said, waving her hands and leaning forward so far that her face was almost touching Veronica's interface. That wasn't the first time Wright had seen that reaction; it meant Thumper had an idea and no time to explain. Thumper not having time to explain was a rare thing indeed.

"I don't know what's going on right now but–" Elliot said.

"Shut up," Wright interrupted. "She's thinking. And she's probably about to crack this whole thing wide open."

For nearly half an hour, they all waited around trying

not to break Thumper's concentration while she worked furiously with Veronica. Wright wasn't actually sure she *could* have broken Thumper's concentration; Thumper seemed to have lost all contact with the physical world. But there was no reason to risk it.

Finally, without warning, Thumper let out a little cry and said, "We gotta go! Guys, we gotta go, we gotta go!"

Everyone immediately went into action prepping to bug out, except Elliot, who just laid there on the couch, looking confused.

"What does that mean?" Elliot asked.

"It means," Wright answered, "we better get a call into Papa Charlie Bravo and see about getting ourselves off this planet."

TWENTY-SEVEN

Two days. It'd been almost two days that they'd left him in the room since his last conversation. This most recent stretch seemed longer than the first session, though Lincoln couldn't know that with any certainty, since he genuinely had no idea how long he'd endured before. He was pretty sure about the two days, though, because of Mars down there. Mars, spinning on its axis. He didn't know why it hadn't occurred to him before, but they'd given him a clock of sorts. All it took was an eye for detail, and the patience to stare at a planet long enough to recognize features when they reappeared. Of course, maybe none of them had thought about that either.

That little game of focus was his lifeline, and it was single-thread thin. Exhaustion had finally enabled him to doze off briefly, but the effect had not been welcome. The first time it had happened, he awoke in a cold panic, screaming and flailing, convinced he had fallen out of a ship. When his brain caught up with the reality, it did little to calm him. Somehow, in his deteriorating mental condition, the idea that he had lost track of the Martian revolutions was more than he could handle. It hadn't been until he had managed to find a recognizable landmark below that he had been able to regain some measure of control. And when he did the rough math, he realized he'd only been out for maybe half an hour at most.

After that, realizing how critical timekeeping apparently was to his sanity, he found that, if he set his mind to it, he could sleep and then force himself awake after a short interval. Twenty minutes seemed to be the magic number. In that manner, Lincoln had been able to combat the fatigue without losing his now critical watch on Mars. He wondered for a time if that was the actual view from his cell, or just a projection they found useful for their psychological torment. He had been assuming it was the latter, but once the thought occurred to him, he couldn't shake it. Mei had made reference to having moved him outside of the MPCR. Would they have gone so far as to have taken him off-planet? It seemed like that would be overkill. But Lincoln knew all too well that the National Intelligence Directorate had black sites on a number of space stations between Venus and the Belt. He had in fact broken a captive out of one not all that long ago, in order to keep a promise.

The recognition that his cell might in fact be ten thousand kilometers from Mars sent Lincoln spiraling down a dark path. He'd been fighting to keep it together, holding on as long as he could, knowing that his team would be doing everything in their power to find him. But if he was in an off-world black site, what hope did he have? And how much of their short time would they be wasting, looking for him? Or, the thought sprang suddenly to mind, would they be focused on the mission first, focused on recovering SUNGRAZER?

Wright would be making the call. If they *were* trying to find him, the time lost could have catastrophic consequences. If they weren't... well, the idea that his teammates weren't coming for him was almost more than he could bear. But he knew Wright. He knew what she would do. And he knew it was the right call. Mission first. He was on his own.

It was then that a thought he had never before had in his life first presented itself to him. Lincoln had known others who had entertained such thoughts, and when he had heard them speak of it in their hushed confessions, he had imagined it as a demonic voice dripping sickness. But when he heard it for himself, it came cool, calm, rational.

Would not the easiest escape be simply to take his own life?

It would deprive the enemy of a valuable source of intelligence. There was no doubt; they would break him eventually. Possibly soon. And what harm might come to his team then? His family? His nation?

And the Process. Wouldn't that make it OK? There was a risk that it wouldn't work, of course. It wasn't a guarantee. But if he died here, and woke up back on Earth, at least then he could contact his team, and support them from there. At least he could guarantee they weren't trying to find him. And if it didn't work... well, they'd have to find a new team leader, obviously. But the Outriders had gotten along fine without him before. Surely the colonel could find a replacement.

There weren't many options, but Lincoln started working the problem. The shirt they'd given him to wear. It was thin, but had long sleeves. If he twisted it up sufficiently, he thought, he might be able to tie it around his neck tightly enough to choke off the blood supply to his brain. A blackout would soon follow and, if he was lucky, death not long after. It might work. In his shattered state, he actually went so far as to remove his shirt and start the process of twisting it into an improvised rope.

But when he put it around his neck, that was as far as he could get. Even while the coldly rational voice in his head told him it was the best choice, the noble sacrifice, a heroic death, Lincoln knew it was contrary to everything he'd been taught and everything he'd been trained to do. Through all his evolutions, every test, every trial they'd ever put him through in the military, his instructors had forged in him a spirit that was supposed to find a way to fight on as long as he drew breath. Blind, crippled, deaf, as long as his heart continued to beat, he was to carry the fight to the enemy.

What would they say if they could see him now? What would his teammates say? Or Colonel Almeida? The rational voice wasn't his ally. It was his enemy. He'd never surrendered before. This seemed like the worst of all times to start.

Lincoln removed the shirt from around his neck, unrolled it, and put it back on, feeling suddenly foolish as the clouds cleared from his mind. What would Wright say, if she ever found out what he'd been about to do? Nothing probably. But he knew the look she would have given him, and he knew he would never have borne it.

Thinking about his senior enlisted teammate, he realized he was wrong. She would have had something to say; she would have told him, right there, in that moment, sitting in that cell that he was thinking about this all wrong. Trying to endure. Counting on others to rescue him. Buying time until someone else did something. *Wasting* time.

He was sitting in the middle of a secret facility operated by a foreign intelligence service who may or may not have been responsible for an assault on his nation's interests. And here he was, focused only on himself, on his own discomfort. The mission. Wright would have told him to focus on the mission. And she would have been right.

Whatever fire he had just passed through, Lincoln emerged from it changed. Another evolution. Whoever Mei was, she had no special power over him. And Lincoln hadn't just been trained to resist interrogations; he'd been on the other side of that table as well. Enough planet watching, he decided. He needed a new perspective. A new approach.

A new plan of attack.

Lincoln accepted the coffee again, but not from a place of weakness. He'd already established the precedent; refusing it now might signal renewed resistance, and he needed his interrogator to believe he was continuing to deteriorate. He blew the steam from the top, and took a tentative sip, but didn't allow himself the same instinctive pleasure of the heat that he had so greedily consumed before. This time, he thought of it in purely tactical terms and noted with some small satisfaction that the coffee wasn't as good as his anyway.

"So," Mei said, sitting across from him. She was shifted sideways in the chair, angled towards him, relaxed and casual. "You think you're finally up for talking with me today?"

Lincoln nodded.

"Ready to stop pretending you're not an agent for the NID?"

"I'm not an agent for NID," Lincoln said, and he saw the shadow of disappointment fall across Mei's face. "But... if I *were*... there might be a few questions I would be trying to answer."

"Oh?" Mei said. "I don't suppose you'd like to

elaborate on them?"

Lincoln let his gaze fall to his coffee, as if finally coming to terms with his resignation to betraying his country. In reality, it was because he needed to catch her unguarded reaction to his words, and he knew his chances to do so were best if she didn't already have her mask intact.

"If I were," he said. "*If* I were… I think the first thing I'd be interested in finding out is why the Collective Republic would be openly pursuing a return to normalized, peaceful relations with Earth," and now he sprung his tiny trap, flicking his eyes up to hers as he finished the sentence, "while simultaneously engaging in a shadow war with the UAF."

And there it was. The microexpression, the fleeting narrowing of the eyes, the slight pursing of her lips. She hadn't expected that. Either she hadn't known, or she hadn't known that he knew. If the MPCR were, as a matter of state, actively trying to push Mars and Earth towards war, then Internal Security was undoubtedly Lincoln's enemy. And from what he knew of the Service, its agents would be perfectly equipped and positioned to pull off an operation like the SUNGRAZER takeover. But if actions were being taken by a group within the Republic, but not sanctioned by it, then that would make Internal Security a natural ally. The trick now was to determine which side Mei was on.

"Interesting," she said, her tone neutral. "And why would you believe that was the case? *If* you were an agent for the NID."

"If I had to guess, and obviously I do… I would start with the usual things. Loss of an asset, maybe."

"Spying is inherently dangerous, Simon. People lose things all the time. That doesn't mean a war is on."

He shrugged. "I wouldn't know about that."

Mei dropped her eyes briefly and suppressed a smile, then after a moment reached up and tucked a tendril of hair behind her ear. For a brief second, the gesture inspired an instinctual reaction in Lincoln; he realized he found her attractive, and the almost-girlish motion charming. And that reaction set off alarms that woke him, as if scales had fallen from his eyes. He'd missed it during the second meeting. But it seemed so obvious now.

Lincoln closed his eyes and recalled his first meeting with Mei, pictured her clearly, firmly in his mind. The sharp attire, the severity of her appearance. With that image fixed, he reopened his eyes and looked at her again, took the image in all at once; the unbuttoned collar, her hair down. Her posture was more open, more inviting. Even the color of her clothing was softer.

Such a simple, social trick. Now that he thought back, he remembered the loose ponytail from their second session. Midway between a bun and hair down. She'd been gradually adjusting her appearance, presenting herself on warmer, more familiar terms, as though they were growing closer. But now that he saw it, now that he recognized it, Lincoln saw also the opportunity it presented. He knew how much the body affected the mind; it was the reason the military drilled such strict rules into recruits in boot camp about things like polished boots, made beds, and grooming standards. Disciplined bodies led to disciplined minds.

"You seem like a good woman, Mei," he said. "Honest. Trustworthy."

It was true.

"Thank you," she replied.

Over his career, Lincoln had seen all kinds. And though it was obvious that Mei was a skilled interrogator, Lincoln could tell that under the carefully controlled veneer she was the genuine article. She truly believed she was doing the right thing. And she had a distinctly different demeanor than the man who had captured and drugged him. He hadn't contrasted one with the other in his mind before now, not as separate individuals. But once the comparison was made, he couldn't believe they were part of the same agency.

And that thought triggered another; if this whole operation *was* the work of an independent group within the MPCR, that didn't necessarily mean the Internal Security Service as a whole was clean.

"I thought Internal Security was about protecting your people," he said.

"It is," she answered, her brows furrowed slightly at the incongruity of the statements.

"Are you sure?"

"I should certainly hope so," she answered. "I've devoted my life to it."

"May I ask you a question?"

"Of course."

"You mentioned Elliot Goodkind earlier. That you believed he was a... what did you call it? Unapproved agent?"

"Undeclared," Mei said, and she smiled again. "But I appreciate the effort you're making."

"What brought your attention to him?"

"I wish I could take the credit," she said, sipping her coffee. "But that was my partner's work."

"Your partner? The man that brought me here, by chance?"

"You have met him, yes."

"And this was a case you had been following together, for some time? Watching him, gathering evidence, that sort of thing?"

She didn't answer.

"Or perhaps your partner just got a lucky break?" Lincoln asked.

Mei cocked her head; he'd touched on something there. A doubt she'd harbored, perhaps. Or she was starting to process the hints he was dropping on what NID's interests might be within the MPCR, and realizing that maybe Lincoln wasn't an enemy after all.

"I want to trust you, Mei," he said.

"You can," she answered.

He leaned forward, lowered his voice. She mirrored his movement.

"Sometimes... the people you want most to trust," Lincoln said, watching her closely. "The ones you want to believe are on the same mission... they're the ones you have to most closely guard against." He said it like a confession, as if he was about to break, and flip on Elliot. But there was something else wrapped in the words, a hunch he was delicately exploring, a leading question he would hope she would answer without realizing. "Trying to serve your country..."

"... or protect your people," Mei added, almost to herself. She broke eye contact immediately after she said it, looked down, her eyes widening for a fraction of a second. Betraying her. She hadn't meant to say it. She'd slipped. The familiarity she'd been so careful to cultivate had caught her in her own trap.

He couldn't prove it logically, not even to himself. But after that, Lincoln was convinced that Mei was clean, that she didn't know about SUNGRAZER, that she wasn't a part of the shadow war. And maybe, if he hadn't misread her, just maybe she had already been concerned that her agency might have been compromised. She had just never considered her partner as a potential threat.

But maybe she was now.

"I want to help you," he said. And then leaned back and added, "But I'm not an NID agent."

Mei coughed a single laugh, and fixed him with a sharp-eyed stare. Whatever exchange they had just had, he'd given her more to consider than she'd expected. As she searched his eyes, he could see the wheels turning in hers. Finally, she sat back, and then got to her feet.

"I think we're done for the day, Mr Kim," she said. "But we'll talk again. Soon."

"I look forward to it," he said.

She didn't reply, but gave him a little look over her shoulder as she knocked on the door. He didn't know what conclusions she'd reach, whether she'd think he was genuinely trying to help her or that this was all a disinformation play. But no matter what, he felt like he'd gained some insight for himself. At least he had something useful for his mind to chew on while he sat in his cell.

Lincoln stared up at the stars on the ceiling that wasn't there, wishing he had paid a little more attention when a navy girl he'd known had tried to teach him the Martian constellations. Watching Mars spin had lost its appeal, and his mind had enough to keep it occupied for a while longer. Now that he had a mission, the loss of the sense of time didn't bother him as much.

He'd won a small victory today. If it was indeed still today. Not that he knew what he'd do with the information. Use it during his next interrogation, if he could. Maybe he'd get a chance to share it while it still mattered. If not, at least he'd made it one more day without breaking. He was just beginning to wonder how many more he'd last, when something strange happened to one of the stars above him. It winked out. And then so did its neighbor.

As Lincoln watched, the dead splotch in space grew wider, consuming more stars as it expanded. He could only assume this was some new stage of torment, one his captors reserved for the toughest cases. As disturbing as it was, he couldn't stop watching the void progress; it even looked like it was bulging into the room now, as if space itself had somehow taken on substance and invaded.

And then Lincoln heard a crackling sound, like a footstep on broken glass. It took a moment for him to realize he had *heard a sound*.

Whatever was happening to the ceiling, it was definitely growing or getting worse; a dark, thick, rope-like substance oozed towards the floor, slow like tar. If Lincoln hadn't already been pressed into the corner of the room, he would have backed away.

But then it plunked to floor, dragging something bulky behind it. Lincoln's first thought was that something had damaged the roof above his cell, and that some sort of structural component had broken through. But then the thing on the floor writhed around like a serpent made of swarming insects, and formed into a more familiar shape.

Poke.

It was the team's little foldable. Lincoln knew he must have fallen asleep. Surely this was some sort of dream, or hallucination. Even so, he crawled on hands and knees over to Poke and whatever package it had brought along. When he approached, Poke flexed its back and sort of sat up, like a pup greeting him. That meant Thumper was on the other end. He indulged her and patted the uppermost part of the bot before he turned his attention to whatever it had dragged in.

The bundle had been tightly compressed and sealed in a thinskinned material; when Lincoln picked it up, Poke helpfully reassembled itself and made an incision in the packaging. As soon as it did so, the contents blossomed, and Lincoln was able to tear away the rest of the outer container without any trouble. It wasn't until he'd gotten the packet completely open that he realized what Poke had brought him. It was an emergency environmental suit, the flexible kind a ship's crew might employ in case of a hull breach. This one was missing most of the larger components, though. They'd obviously stripped it down to the bare minimum to be able to get it inside. There were no instructions with it, but he didn't need much prompting. He put the suit on as quickly as he could, all the while knowing he wouldn't last more than a few minutes in open space.

Once he'd sealed himself in, the suit automatically pressurized. The built-in comms activated at the same time.

"Check check check," Lincoln said.

"We read you, Lincoln," Wright answered. "Good to hear from you."

Tears welled at the sound of her voice.

"Not as good as it is to hear from you, Amira," Lincoln said. The joy, the relief, the surprise of it all threatened to burst his chest, but he knew there wasn't time to let emotion overcome him. "What's the plan?"

"Thumper's got the cameras rerouted," Wright said. "But we don't want to hang around. You sealed up?"

"Roger that," Lincoln said. All the indicators inside the suit were green. "Suit's sealed and green."

"Then get against the wall, the one closest to the door," Wright said. "Tuck yourself up as tight as you can. We'll have you out in a second. Let me know when you're set."

Lincoln didn't love the sound of that, but he did as she instructed. He curled himself fetal at the base of the wall by the door.

"I'm set," he said.

"Copy," she answered. "Five seconds… might want to cover your ears."

"Don't think that's going to be necessary," he said, but she was already counting down.

When she got to zero, the wall opposite Lincoln imploded with a *whump* that he felt more than he heard. The image of space vanished and the room returned to its original appearance, but Lincoln barely had time to register it as he rocketed across the room and out into open space with the sudden depressurization of his cell. He tumbled helplessly, and quickly lost all sense of direction.

A few moments later, he collided roughly with what he assumed was debris from the explosion; it folded around him, clung to him. Lincoln windmilled his arms to try to get free, but he was caught fast. Then, his wild tumble started to stabilize.

"I gotcha," Sahil said. "Quit your flailin'."

Lincoln looked down to find arms wrapped around his chest. Sahil, in his suit. Once Sahil got their spin under control, he started hooking a harness around Lincoln's torso, strapping him in. As soon as Lincoln's senses settled he could feel the acceleration, dragging them along a vector that was up, from their perspective. It was a steadily increasing pull, and it wasn't long before they were moving much faster than Lincoln knew the suits could move on their own microthrusters.

"Might get bumpy," Sahil said. "We're gonna hook it."

Lincoln looked up and saw the source of their acceleration. Spooled out on a tether a good twenty meters was a canister; they were essentially being towed through space by a rocket engine, with no ship attached. He couldn't remember the official name for it, but mostly it was just called star-hooking. He'd never actually done it before, though he'd heard about it. It was partially because he had heard about it that he had never done it.

"There's our ride," Sahil said. "Comin' in, about nine o' clock."

Lincoln didn't recognize the ship; it was small, sleek, and looked like it was built for speed. It was coming on at a good clip and at an angle. Or rather, he and Sahil were on line to intercept the ship; the vessel's forward thrusters were firing, slowing its approach. Knowing what they were about to do, it didn't seem to be slowing nearly enough.

"All right, we see you, we've got you," Wright said, "Hold on to your teeth."

Lincoln figured it was better not to watch what came next. He felt the shudder of the impact as the grapples on their freestanding engine found purchase on the passing ship, and in the next instant he and Sahil lurched forward, dragged along. The difference in velocity apparently hadn't been quite enough to rip him in two, but Lincoln was pretty sure it hadn't been too far off.

As they were being reeled in, he finally had time to look around; a station was receding in the distance, small and unimpressive, looking like some half-forgotten outpost rather than the black interrogation site he knew it was. Glancing around he realized that the view they'd been projecting on his walls and ceiling and floor had actually been the same view he would have had if there had been no walls at all. He might have found it beautiful, if he hadn't been tortured by it for some unknown amount of time.

One of the indicator lights in Lincoln's suit went amber, an early warning that the e-suit was running out of life support. Lincoln glanced up at the ship, gradually growing closer as the line they were attached to retracted. He'd make it with plenty of time to spare. He would make it. He *had* made it.

And with the realization that his freedom had been made sure, that his imprisonment was over before they'd broken him, the emotions did overwhelm him, and Lincoln allowed the tears to fall without shame or restraint.

TWENTY-EIGHT

Lincoln's welcome home was intense, but brief. After all the hugs, shoulder punches, and "I love you"s disguised in insults and cutting jokes, Sahil gave him the shortest medical once-over he'd ever experienced, while Wright gave him a shotgun blast of a briefing. When both were completed, they led him back towards the main compartment of the vessel. Before they got too far, Lincoln stopped and turned the opposite direction. The cockpit of the ship was at the top of a short, steep staircase; Lincoln jogged to it and called up.

"Hey Will," Lincoln said. "You ever pick anyone up without yanking them out of something else?"

This was now the second time the Barton boys had towed Lincoln out of harm's way.

"Not if I can help it, Lincoln," he answered with a laugh. "I can refer you to a good chiropractor when we get home."

"I think you did that work already, buddy," Lincoln said.

"We live to serve," Will replied.

"Heya up there, Noah," Lincoln said.

Noah leaned over and stretched his fist as far down

as he could; Lincoln hopped up on the second step and bumped knuckles.

"Good to have you back, Link," Noah said. "Now quit walking around the boat and go get strapped in. We've got a hard burn coming up, and we're all waiting on you."

"Roger that," Lincoln said. "Thanks boys."

Lincoln hustled back down the length of the vessel to the main cabin, and rejoined his teammates. They were already strapping into crash couches. Sahil was still suited up, but he'd removed his helmet. The rest of them were wearing street clothes. None of them looked like they belonged in this ship.

But it wasn't until Lincoln plopped down and got himself hooked in that he really took notice of the surroundings. The compartment was luxurious to the point of bordering on extravagant.

"Is that a wet bar?" Lincoln asked.

"Yup," Mike said with a chuckle. "Planning to break that open on the trip home."

"Where'd you guys get this ship?" Lincoln said.

"Papa Charlie Bravo," Wright answered.

"Where'd *they* get it?"

"Told us not to ask."

"Man," Lincoln said. "I must have missed all kinds of fun."

"Nah," Wright said. "Mostly just the bad stuff."

"You folks locked in?" Will said over the intercom.

No one replied for a moment; Lincoln realized his teammates were all looking at him expectantly. He couldn't help but smile.

"Roger that," Lincoln answered. "We're good to go."

"Then settle back, and relax," Will said. "We're going to crush you for about half an hour."

The ship's grav field automatically compensated for acceleration up to a certain point, but it could only do so much. From the g-forces Lincoln felt stacking on top of him over the next few minutes, he got a pretty good idea of just how little time they had left to get the job done.

After Will's promised half-hour crush began to subside, he cleared them to unstrap and get to business. The team moved out of the compartment to another one that Thumper had taken over. Whatever it had originally been designed for, it now looked like someone had set off a small bomb in a hardware store. Veronica was set up on a table at one end of the room, but that was the only easily identifiable thing around. Every other available flat surface had some jumble of parts on it, or devices Lincoln had never seen before, or things crammed together that seemed to be doing something, even though they looked like they shouldn't be doing anything at all, except maybe smoking or spitting sparks.

"All right," Lincoln said. "So where are we at?"

He and Wright followed Thumper in, but Mike and Sahil both hovered out in the passageway.

"Veronica's got the command-and-control encryption scheme cracked," Thumper answered. "Enough that I should be able to abort the fire mission. And that's the only good news we've got."

"Aw, that's not true, Thump," Mike said. "You found a way to track her, too."

"Sorta," Thumper replied, sounding disappointed. "It's still intermittent. We're going to have to do some best guessing, and probably get a little lucky."

"If you got C&C cracked, does that mean you were able to decipher her target?" Lincoln asked.

"Yeah, and her post-strike instructions," Thumper said. "Looks like they're trying to hit the MPCR."

"Makes a pretty strong case for them to forgo neutrality," Wright said.

"And the kicker," Thumper said, "is what comes after. They want her to crash land. Put her down hard somewhere up north, but not so hard as to render her unidentifiable."

A deadly strike on a neutral colony, incontrovertible proof of US involvement, with an asset so secret not even the United American Federation knew of its existence. Lincoln couldn't think of a much better way to guarantee immediate retaliation against the United States. And he was plenty aware of the Collective Republic's outsized production capabilities. He could only guess what would happen if that entire populace mobilized for war.

Lincoln looked over at one of Veronica's many displays, and saw a pattern he thought he could almost decipher.

"That's her current trajectory?" he asked.

Thumper nodded. "As far as we've been able to track her. White dots for when we were able to establish her actual position, orange for our calculated positions when we lost her."

"And the red?"

"Those are the calculated positions that we got wrong," Thumper said. There were more oranges than reds, but not by much. "See what I mean about getting lucky?"

"I do," Lincoln said. "She's not moving in a straight line?"

Thumper shook her head. "I wish. But no. What she's doing... you gotta understand, Lincoln, the math involved, the variables she's working with, adjusting to on the fly. It's not just about getting into range; she's got to take into account planet rotation, position of the planet in its orbit, weather factors all the way down at the target site. She's doing all of that in real-time. She's really impressive."

"Keep in mind we're trying to *stop* her, Thump."

"Yeah, of course," Thumper said. "Doesn't mean I can't appreciate what she's doing. But look... the adjustments she's making, they might only be half a degree here or there, or a light tapping of the brakes... at the velocities and distances we're talking, we could end up missing her by a few kilometers and never even see her. If she gets by us, it's pretty much game over."

"I assume we're trying to intercept," Lincoln said.

"Sort of," Thumper said. She gestured at Veronica, and a second line appeared on the trajectory display. "We've got to come in line with her, try to match velocities. If we go straight out to meet her, we'll lose her in the turn and never catch up. We're swinging out wide, and cutting inside, then once we're running in the same track, hopefully she'll catch up with us, and we can match from there."

"Sounds complicated."

"It is," she said. "I don't envy the work Noah's having to do up there to figure it all out."

"Pretty sure she's got a crush on him," Sahil said.

"I don't," Thumper said, a little too quickly. And then a few moments later, "Just a little one, maybe."

"And the loss of contact?" Lincoln said. "We know what's causing that yet?"

"Sure do," Thumper said. She waved her hand at all the gear around the room.

"Basically," Mike said, still standing in the doorframe, "... don't touch anything."

"OK," Lincoln said. "So we get in line, and then what?"

"Well, I never could get this device put back together exactly, but a couple of the techs at NID really came through for us. We've got a way to rig ourselves up. We just have to get close enough to the ship to make it work."

"Apparently," Wright chimed in, "the magic words were 'hey we found your missing secret ship and need you to tell us how to stop it'."

"And we can shut her down?"

"Theoretically," Thumper said. "No one's ever done this before. But the NID folks seemed optimistic."

"Sounds like you guys got this all under control," Lincoln said. "Not sure why you bothered to come get me."

"Sahil's idea," Wright said. "Wouldn't leave me alone about it."

"What'd you find out about potential bad actors?"

"Positive ID on one, at least. Gregor Petrescu, of the Republic's Internal Security Service. He was definitely using Internal Security's infrastructure... secure comms, surveillance, all kinds of stuff. That's actually how we were able to locate SUNGRAZER, using his setup, paired with Elliot's rig. But based on *how* he was using it, I'm going to guess it wasn't sanctioned. Seems like he went to a lot of trouble to hide it."

"I agree with that assessment," Lincoln said. "I don't think his own partner even knew what he was up to."

The others looked at him. "I get stuck in a cell for a few days, you think I'm just going to sit around feeling sorry for myself?" He shrugged. "Speaking of Elliot, we need to make sure we get him out of the Republic. Internal Security knows he's NID."

Wright and Thumper exchanged a look.

"I missed something," Lincoln said.

Wright nodded. "Couple of things. We'll get you debriefed later, when we have more time."

"And beer," Mike added.

"So what do you need from me?" Lincoln asked. "Anything I can do?"

"Not much we can do until we reach SUNGRAZER," Wright said.

"And even then, well," Thumper said. "Probably most of it's going to be on me. Figured you'd want to be here for the big moment, at least."

"That I do. Until then, though…" he said.

"Need to go have a good cry in the shower?" Wright asked.

"Dunno about the cry," Lincoln said.

"Definitely need the shower, though," she said. "Come on, I'll show you to the head."

She escorted him out of the compartment and down the passageway. When they were out of earshot of the others, she stopped and turned to him.

"How you doing, Lincoln?" she asked.

"Wrecked," Lincoln said. "Glad to have something to do, though. Got bored with all that sitting around back there."

"Serious question, sir," she replied. "I don't know what they put you through, so I don't know whether I should consider you operational or not. I need to know, just in case."

He knew he was pushing it. He'd seen it plenty of times before; prisoners, hostages, anyone coming out of captivity had to deal with the emotional whiplash at some point. Some of them felt it immediately, others weeks later. And he knew he wasn't as sharp as usual. The lack of sleep, the psychological stress, he couldn't ignore it completely. But he was functional. Being back with the team was already burning away the effects of his utter isolation; knowing they still had a mission gave him something to focus on. He'd deal with the baggage when it came, as inevitably it would. But until then, there was work to do, and for now, at least, he could detach himself enough from what he'd been through.

"I'm good, Mir," he said. "I know it'll all crash down at some point. But not right now. I think I'm still trying to figure out how you pulled that off. Seems like everything happened all at once... guess I know how it feels from the other side now."

She watched him for a moment, evaluating. The intensity of her eyes reminded him of the first time he'd met the master sergeant, when he'd walked into the team facility unannounced. He'd thought she was going to throw him right back out.

"All right," she said.

"Not that I'm upset at the call," Lincoln said. "But I have to admit, Mir... with time so short, I'm surprised you came to get me."

"That's what I tried to tell them," Wright replied. "But I got overruled." She said it deadpan, but after a moment the corner of her mouth pulled back in a smile. "Turned out we needed time to track SUNGRAZER down, and the hop they were holding you on wasn't too far out of the way. Figured there was no reason to sit around twiddling. Plus... well, I wasn't sure what they'd do to you once we got her back. None of us were. Figured we better get you out while we knew where you were."

"Well, I appreciate it," he said. "You did a good job holding it all together. A great job."

"Thank you, sir."

He felt like there was more he should say, but the words just didn't come.

"You really ought to get that shower," Wright said.

Lincoln chuckled. It was good to be back. Wright turned and led him the rest of the way, then left him on his own. Lincoln took a long, hot shower, and let the water wash away the last vestiges of his captivity.

Lincoln had enough time to get cleaned up and even got a couple of hours sleep before the big moment. Between Thumper's technical prowess, Noah's insane gift for complicated navigation, and Will's piloting skills, they got lucky enough to match trajectories with SUNGRAZER.

But that, apparently, was as far as luck and skill could take them.

The team was all gathered once more in Thumper's makeshift mad-scientist laboratory.

"So according to NID," she said, working with both Veronica and whatever device the techs had helped her cobble together, "we send this packet to her, wait for her reply, and once that comes back, we issue the abort command."

"No need to wait for fanfare, Thumper," Lincoln said. "Get it done."

"Roger that," she said. A few gestures, and the initial request for connection went on its way. Several tense seconds ticked by before Lincoln realized he didn't know what kind of response he should be expecting, or how quickly it should come.

"How long until we know if it worked?" he asked.

Thumper sat forward. Gestured again.

"Thumper? How long do we wait?"

"We don't have to wait," she said, grim. "I can tell you right now, it didn't work."

"What didn't work?" Wright asked.

"The connection request," she said. "Rejected."

"So NID's trick didn't work?" Lincoln said, clarifying.

"It did," Thumper said. "Connection request went through. It just came back rejected. Invalid."

She turned and looked at him. "They changed the command-and-control encryption again. They must have done it after…" She trailed off, and then pounded her fist on the table. "That's what he meant. That's what Gregor meant when he said we couldn't stop it. That not even he could stop it."

The team stood in shocked silence. If they could have stuck their heads out of the ship, they could have seen SUNGRAZER from there. Their objective was that close, and there was nothing they could do about it.

"We should have burned him alive after all," Mike said, but even he didn't seem to be able to find any humor in the moment.

"Can you crack the new scheme?" Wright asked.

Thumper shook her head. "It took Veronica days to get the last one, and that was only because she had samples of both the old and new to compare. This would be starting over from scratch… worse than that."

She swept her eyes around the room, looking at all of the gear she'd set up, all of the effort they'd put in to get this far. And then slammed both fists down hard on the table. So hard, some unidentified bit of gear bounced off and rolled away.

"Let's look at our options," Lincoln said. "We're this close. We've got to have a few."

"We shoot her down?" Mike said.

"Not with this ship," Wright answered. "It's a civilian vessel. Got some defensive capabilities, but nothing that could do much more than scratch her paint."

"What if we ram her?" Mike said.

Everyone thought that over for a moment. It might

be possible, but it would almost certainly spell death for them all. Thumper was the first to respond.

"If we just try to nudge her, I don't think our engines are enough to redirect her. And if we come in hot enough to pose a threat, she'll obliterate us before we reach her. That's if we could even hit her which, at the velocities we're talking isn't a sure thing at all."

"I got a bunch of charges in my kit," Sahil said. "If I freespace over, you think I could blow her up from the inside?"

There seemed to be something to that. SUNGRAZER had self-destruction capabilities; charges at key points might not destroy *all* of the critical components, but there was a good chance it would be enough to stop her from carrying out the strike at least.

"Depends on how much heat you're packing," Thumper said. "But even that might not help. The munitions she's carrying, they're designed to penetrate atmosphere." She brought up the trajectory display and pointed at it. "She's already on vector to impact Mars. We blow the ship, we would end up scattering those munitions, and at least some of them are going to continue on to target. We'd just be taking a city-killing sniper rifle and turning it into a nation-killing shotgun."

The team fell silent again, each silently taking inventory of what they had at their disposal, working the problem in their own way.

"Unless," Thumper said. "Unless… if we stage it right. If we could adjust her angle enough, and then detonate her, we might be able to make her miss. Send it all skipping off the atmosphere."

"So what…" Mike said. "Ram her, *then* detonate her?"

"Something like that I guess…" Thumper said.

"You got a schematic of SUNGRAZER?" Sahil asked,

walking over to Thumper.

"Sure," she said. She gestured and Veronica produced the requested images.

"Can I?" Sahil said.

"Of course," Thumper replied, and she scooted over so Sahil could manipulate the imagery. He was the team's demolitions and explosives expert. As he spun the three-dimensional image around, zoomed in and out, he talked them through the points of vulnerability he saw, and asked for Thumper's input on what they'd have to do to make it all work. After about twenty minutes of discussion, they had the rough sketch of an idea.

"Gonna have to time the detonation sequence pretty tight," Sahil said. "You can run those numbers?"

Thumper shook her head. "It's not going to be predictable enough for timers. We'll have to hook up some kind of remote detonators, monitor the ship's reaction, adjust on the fly. I can set Veronica up to run it, but you're going to have to help me with the detonator part."

"How much time do we have until she launches?" Lincoln asked.

"She could have already," Thumper said. "She's in the window. Could be three minutes, could be three hours."

"Any way for us to know?" Wright said.

"Well, I have a monitor set up. We'll be able to tell when she arms and starts going through her launch protocol."

"How much warning will that give us?"

"About five minutes," Thumper answered. "She's an AI. She doesn't take long."

"So whatever we're going to do," Lincoln said, "we better do it now. That star-hook we rode in on, how much does it have left in the tank?"

"Should be enough to get over and back, with some to spare," Sahil replied. "If that's what you're thinking."

"It is. I'll suit up, and handle planting the charges," Lincoln said. "While you work it from this end."

"That's a negative, sir," Sahil said. "My job, I'll handle it."

But Lincoln shook his head. "None of us can handle the detonator side, Sahil. If we plant the charges and they don't go off, the whole thing's a waste. You can direct me on placement, but I want you here working with Thumper to make sure we get that part right."

It was obvious Sahil didn't like it, but he couldn't argue. There was no point in sending him over, and having to wait until he got back to verify the detonation protocols were all proper. Not when timing was of such essence. And not when there was no guarantee he'd have time to make it over and back.

"It's a lot of ground to cover, Lincoln," Thumper said. "And you got to remember, SUNGRAZER isn't made for people. It's going to be zero-g, working in maintenance tunnels. Just getting around is going to be a chore."

Thumper was right. Looking at that schematic and the points that they'd identified as vulnerabilities, the work wasn't going to be quick. Several points were within the central portion, deepest into the vessel.

"It's fine, I'll go with," Mike said.

None of them had mentioned it explicitly, but Lincoln knew they were all thinking it. There was a chance that whoever went over might not have time to make it back.

"And I'll go instead," Wright said. "Mike and I will handle it, Lincoln. Ranking officer, you need to stay here and coordinate."

"No," Lincoln said. "I'm not going to sit here and watch, not when I can do the work. I'm going over."

"Captain," Wright said.

"Not a discussion, master sergeant," Lincoln said, loudly. "But I will take some help."

Wright and Mike both looked at him expectantly. It was risky, going himself, to take Wright along with him. If it went wrong, that was the ranking officer *and* senior-most enlisted wiped out. But Mike. Mike was suffering some unknown effects from his last brush with the Process. Lincoln couldn't put him through that again. Not knowing what he knew.

"Wright," Lincoln said. "Suit up."

"Roger that," she said.

"Thumper," said Lincoln, "keep working C&C. Maybe there's something else there we missed."

"Yes sir," she replied.

"Sahil, come help get us loaded up. I'll need you on the line in case we have questions about placement."

"'Course," he said.

"Let's get to it," Lincoln said.

"Sir," Mike said. "What do you want me to do?"

"Well," Lincoln said. "If you're the praying sort, now's a good time."

Mike held his gaze for a moment, then gave a little nod. Lincoln couldn't help but feel Mike knew why he'd made the decision he had, and resented him for it.

"Be back in a few," Lincoln said, nodding back. He exited, and went to the rear of the vessel to get armored up.

Getting on board hadn't been difficult, but it had been nerve-racking. Without a grav field, moving around on the surface of SUNGRAZER required Lincoln and Wright to use the magnetic capabilities of their suits, which made movement stiff and unnatural. And there was the constant fear of falling off. At the velocity they were traveling, and with SUNGRAZER continuing to make her microadjustments, Lincoln knew if he became detached from the vessel, there was a very real chance that he wouldn't be able to get back on board.

Once they made it inside the first access, movement wasn't much easier, and the fear of falling was replaced with the fear of getting hopelessly lost. When Thumper had said SUNGRAZER hadn't been made for people, she hadn't been kidding. There were indeed service and maintenance tunnels running all through her, but none of them afforded much room to work. It was, of course, pitch black, but his sensor suite absorbed electromagnetic radiation and heat and converted it all into useful imaging. He and Wright split up, each laden with demo charges. Lincoln headed forward to his targets; guidance, navigation, fire control, and forward and port steering thrusters. Wright would handle aft and starboard steering, the main engines, and the reactor core. If everything went according to plan, they'd meet in the middle, work their way back up to the surface, and star-hook their way back to the rest of the team before they detonated the charges.

Unfortunately, their targets weren't neatly aligned. Instead of being able to plant charges in a nice row and get out, they both had to weave their way in and out through the ship's infrastructure. Lincoln kept a wireframe schematic up on his display to help guide him to his targets. Sahil had marked the locations for the charges precisely on the schematic, and his positioning was reflected in the display such that when Lincoln had one set, it appeared highlighted by Sahil's markings.

Lincoln moved through the ship by pulling himself along, with the occasional boost or stabilization from the microthrusters on his suit.

"Starboard one in place," Wright reported over comms, while Lincoln was placing his first portside charge.

"Copy that," he said. "Port one, in place."

He double-checked the settings on the first charge, then set a second right below it. Once the backup was in place, he checked the first charge again, just to be sure. Time was of the essence, but so was getting it right the first time.

Those charges in place, Lincoln moved on to his subsequent targets; three additional port thruster placements, then fire control, then navigation. He was actually moving a little slower than Wright, though her work at the main reactor would be more complicated than anything he had to deal with. If they both held pace, they'd finish up at practically the same moment.

But as Lincoln was placing the back-up charge on the guidance system, he felt a strange sensation that he could immediately place. A dragging sort of feeling, as if he were slowly sliding towards the rear of the ship. His first thought was that he was suffering vertigo from the zero-g. Then he realized he wasn't in zero-g anymore. That sensation was fractional gravity.

They were accelerating.

"Lincoln," Thumper said over comms. "SUNGRAZER's picking up speed."

"Yeah, I can feel it," he responded. He activated his microthrusters to counteract the force and finished setting the back-up charge. "What's it mean?"

"Crossing the approach threshold," Thumper said. "I think it means she's less concerned about detectability now, and is moving up to strike velocity."

"Understood," he said. "You guys set?"

"We're ready to go," she answered. "If you can move

any faster, it'd be good."

"I know. I've got three more points on forward steering, and I'll be wrapped. Wright, how're you doing?"

"Second aft right now," Wright answered. "Then just reactor left. Ten minutes, max."

"Roger that," Lincoln said. "I expect about the same for me, Thumper."

"Understood. Let us know as soon as you're clear."

"Don't you worry about that," Lincoln said. "Guidance is set, moving to forward thrusters now."

Lincoln continued his way forward, stopping and turning to follow a branching tunnel with a long ladder. Looking at that thing made him glad for the first time to be operating in zero-g, or close enough to it. As he followed the yellow ladder's trail, he kept having to boost his microthrusters to maintain his movement. Soon enough, he found himself pulling himself along as much as flying, and not long after, his arms were doing more of the work. Within another minute, he shut the thrusters off completely and was forced to actually climb the ladder.

"Thumper," Lincoln said, "what's going on? I need an update."

"Still accelerating, Lincoln. You're up over a full g now."

Lincoln looked up at how much more ladder he had to climb, and as foolish as it was, hoped SUNGRAZER would reach her strike velocity soon. He activated the suit's motion-assist systems, lending his limbs some extra muscle against the increasing g-forces, and started climbing as fast as he could manage. By the time he reached his destination, acceleration forces had climbed to twice Earth's pull, and it was beginning to fatigue his whole body, even with the support of the suit.

It took considerable effort for him to get the charges in place at the forward steering thrusters, but he managed it. As he was placing the last of them, it seemed like the acceleration had stabilized. Still a little over two-g, but at least it wasn't getting any higher. It was exhausting, but manageable.

"Forward three in place," he reported. "I'm wrapped and headed back to the exit. Wright, what's your status?"

"Aft's complete," Wright answered. "That's everything but the main reactor. I haven't gotten there yet."

"How far are you?"

"I can get to it," she said. He could hear the effort in her voice, and her breathing. "You get on out."

It was down for him. Up for her.

"I'm on the way."

"Lincoln," she said.

"I'm on the way, Amira," he answered. "I'll take topside, you get the base. We'll go out together."

He rerouted the map on his display, and started following the tunnel back down towards the reactor. The hardest portions were the cross-tunnels that forced him to hop from his ladder to a different surface, or from a surface to a new ladder. Nothing that would have been particularly difficult or worrisome under normal circumstances, but the elevated gravitational pull made it hard to judge the jumps.

There, finally, below him, he could see the top of the reactor.

"Lincoln," Thumper said, her voice measured. "SUNGRAZER just kicked off her preparation for firing. You've got five, maybe seven minutes to finish up and get out."

"Understood," Lincoln said. "Sahil, what's the absolute minimum number of charges we need on this reactor to get good effect."

"Four," Sahil answered after a moment. "Two up top, two down low. Forget the backups. If you get the two centermost, that should be good enough."

"Be sure, Sahil," Lincoln said. "We still need to get the job done."

"It's good, Link, get 'em down, and get out."

"Wright," Lincoln said. "You got that?"

"I got it, I'm almost there."

Lincoln worked as quickly as he could, sweating profusely despite his suit's attempts to keep him cool. As he was placing the second charge, he started to feel lighter. A sure sign that SUNGRAZER was nearing her strike velocity. It was a mixed blessing. Time was short, but their escape would be much faster.

"Second upper charge is set," Lincoln reported. "Sahil, you're sure that's good?"

"It's good, cap'n, get out!"

"Roger that," Lincoln said. "Wright?"

"Placing now. Right behind you."

"Understood. I'm on my way out."

G-forces continued to drop as he clambered his way back out towards the access hatch they'd used.

"I'm going to light my beacon," Lincoln said. "I don't think we're going to have time to rig up the star-hook."

"That's fine," Thumper answered. "We'll pick you up, just make sure you go off aft of the ship, thrust away from the ship, to aft."

"Bail to aft, understood," Lincoln said. He was bounding now, using his microthrusters to help him make superhuman leaps. "Wright, status?"

"Finishing the second charge now," she replied. Her voice was steady, calm. But there was intensity behind it. She knew how close they were cutting it.

"Move it, Amira!" Lincoln called.

"Done," she said a few moments later. "Coming up."

Below one-g now, and steadily falling. Lincoln had to force himself to slow down, to adjust and not pull himself along too hard and risk losing control. The exit was painfully close, but there was no straight route to it. He still had a couple hundred meters of service tunnel to navigate.

"Munitions bay just opened," Thumper called, her voice loud with urgency. "Are you clear yet?"

"Almost," Lincoln said.

"SUNGRAZER's hot! She's prepping to fire!"

"Almost," Lincoln said. "Come on, Amira, come on!"

He risked a glance back down the tunnel, fearing it would be empty.

It was. She wasn't going to make it. And he couldn't leave her. He couldn't leave Amira to die alone.

And the moment before he turned back around, she came hurtling into the tunnel, used her momentum to bound off the wall and rocket herself his direction.

The exit was there. He could see it, twenty meters ahead, towards the front of the ship. Fifteen.

Ten.

And then, without warning, the side of the tunnel spiraled up and crashed into him hard enough to disorient him. When he got his bearings, he realized he was pinned to the tunnel, an invisible hand crushing him into it, grinding him down the side. He glanced up and saw the access hatch. Getting farther away.

"No, no, no!" Thumper cried over comms, her words matching Lincoln's thoughts.

SUNGRAZER was accelerating again, harder this time, adjusting her trajectory. Achieving her strike vector.

The pressure was too much; three and half, maybe

even four gs. They weren't going to make it.

"Sahil," Lincoln said. "Blow the charges!"

"You clear?" Sahil said.

"Sahil," Lincoln said, as calmly as he could manage. "Blow the charges."

The response didn't come immediately.

"Fire, fire, fire," Sahil said. And Lincoln heard in his teammate's voice that he understood what was unfolding.

Lincoln felt SUNGRAZER shudder, felt the vibration from somewhere deep in her belly roll up and through him. Another, stronger shockwave followed, and from above him, Lincoln saw an orange star blossom into existence.

TWENTY-NINE

Lincoln woke to warm feet, a pleasant hum, and the unmistakable antiseptic scent of a medical facility. When he opened his eyes he didn't recognize his surroundings exactly, but they were familiar enough. The dim lighting, the various machines, the rough white sheets. A military hospital.

He couldn't remember how he'd ended up there. The last thing he could recall was calling in that he'd finished placing the third of three charges on the forward steering thruster controls aboard SUNGRAZER. Wright had responded that she'd completed charges to aft, and was moving towards the reactor. And then, warm feet, a pleasant hum, and an antiseptic scent.

Lincoln tried to imagine that they'd found him somehow, that the blast had thrown him clear of the ship, and his teammates had picked him up and brought him home. But the gap in his memories was too clean. Too surgical.

He picked his hands up, looked at them, ran his thumbs across his fingertips feeling the sensation. He sure felt like himself. There was a knock at the door.

"Come in," he said.

A woman poked her head in the room.

"Good afternoon, captain," she said. "How are you feeling?"

Lincoln took stock. A little thirsty. But other than that, he was surprised to find he actually felt pretty good. Really good, in fact. As if he'd just had the best night's sleep of his life.

"Not bad," he answered. "Could use a swig of water, maybe."

The woman entered and extended her hand.

"Dr Marcos," she said.

Lincoln sat up and shook the woman's hand.

"Lincoln Suh," he said. She smiled, and he realized the introduction had been obviously unnecessary.

"You understand why you're here," she said.

"I believe so," Lincoln said. "It's safe to talk about?"

"Yes, captain," Marcos replied. "We're in a secure facility. You're back on base."

"Then yeah," he answered. "You had to put me through the Process."

"That's correct. How do you feel about that?"

"Fine," Lincoln said, with a little shrug. "Is that weird?"

"No," the doctor answered with a chuckle. "That's what we always hope for. But it is, unfortunately, not always the reaction we get. Obviously, you may experience some emotional impact, particularly over the next week or two. We have a number of specialists you can talk with at any time, if you feel that any sort of counseling might benefit you. We have a packet of information prepared, which we'll give you on discharge. If you don't mind, I'd like to take a quick look at you."

She pulled out a pen light and gave him a check over. Between her soft tones and gentle way of directing him to turn his head this way or that, Lincoln felt like he was being treated by a pediatrician.

"All your vitals look good," she said. "Look very strong. Have you noticed any metallic taste in your mouth, or ringing in your ears?"

"No ma'am," he said.

"Good, good. Well if you do have either those, or a sudden loss of balance, let us know immediately, OK?"

"Sure." Lincoln remembered that bit from his inaugural run through the Process, during one of the last stages of selection for that other unit he'd been hoping to make. If he recalled correctly, any of those symptoms could indicate an incomplete sync with his nervous system. He'd never actually followed up on what the long term effects of an incomplete sync would be.

"Good, good. Any questions for me?"

"That's it?"

Dr Marcos smiled and nodded. She was probably the most relaxed and cheerful doctor he'd ever met.

"Were you expecting something more?" she asked.

"I don't know," he answered. "I don't guess so. Just seems like it ought to be a bigger deal, I guess."

"We hear that a lot. But, of course, our ultimate goal is to make these transitions as seamless as possible. So if it seems a little underwhelming, we're OK with that. Anything else?"

"No ma'am."

"Great. A nurse should be around shortly to handle your discharge papers. You can go ahead and get dressed, it shouldn't be long."

"OK, thanks, doc."

She nodded, smiled once more, and started to leave.

"Oh, Dr Marcos," Lincoln said before she could close the door.

"Yes?"

"What about memory loss?" Lincoln asked.

"Oh, a good question, captain. A certain amount is to be expected," she said with a kindly smile. "We do excise a certain portion deliberately, which I believe you've been briefed about?" Lincoln nodded. "Good. And things may be a little fuzzy for a couple of days, that's perfectly normal. But if you notice anything you're especially concerned about, just give us a call. OK?"

"All right," he said. "Thanks again."

"Mm-hmm."

After she was gone, Lincoln noticed a cup of water with a straw in it on a table by the bed. He sat there, sipping water for a couple of minutes, waiting for the truth to dawn on him. For the emotional wavefront to crash. But it didn't. When his water was gone, he set the cup back on the table and got out of bed. His uniform was hanging on a hook on the back of the door. He was tying his boots when another knock sounded.

"Yeah?"

The door opened and Colonel Almeida strode in. When he saw Lincoln sitting there he let out a big breath and shook his head.

"Hey kiddo," he said.

"Colonel," Lincoln said, standing and saluting. The colonel flapped a return salute like he was annoyed at the formality. "How'd we do?"

Almeida nodded, furrowed his brow, and then nodded again. If Lincoln hadn't known better, he could have believed the old warrior was trying to contain his emotions.

"That good, huh?"

"You got the job done, son," Almeida answered. "You got it done. And I'm glad you're all right."

It was subtle; Lincoln almost missed it. But the

Colonel had put the slightest emphasis on *you're*. And now that he looked at Almeida, really looked at him, he realized he'd never seen the old man look so beaten down. Lincoln's thoughts immediately went to Wright.

"Where's Amira?" he asked.

Technically neither of them was supposed to be in the room, but no one was going to argue with the Colonel, not if they valued their lives or their careers. Almeida escorted Lincoln a few rooms down and scattered people out of the way. She was there, lying in a bed just like Lincoln's. But she was hooked up to so many machines it was hard to tell it was her under all of it.

"What's going on?" Lincoln said.

"Bad sync," Almeida answered. "Been trying to get it under control all afternoon."

They stood in silence for a few moments, the soft, rhythmic chirp of some monitor the only sound in the room.

"She already burned one replica, Lincoln," the colonel said.

"What does that mean?"

"It means if they can't get her here," he said, "that she's only got one more shot. And I gotta tell you, I've never seen it go like this. If it doesn't work in two, chances aren't good the third's going to make any difference."

Lincoln's hand went over his mouth.

"Please don't tell me..." he said, though he didn't know who he was talking to. "Please don't tell me I just killed our senior-most team member."

"She's not gone yet, son," Almeida said, putting a hand on Lincoln's shoulder. "And it wasn't you. It wasn't you. It was the mission. It was the job. You did what you had to do."

The words had no meaning to Lincoln, not there, not in that room. Not with Master Sergeant Amira Wright lying there plugged into all those machines. Lincoln had made that call. He'd sent her to that fate. And not necessarily because she'd been the best one for the job. He'd done it because he was trying to protect Mike.

"What happened," he asked.

"I think you can guess," Almeida answered. "You and Mir went in, got the job done. Didn't quite have time to make it back out. It was noble thing, Lincoln. They'd give you both the highest honors of the land for what you did, if anyone could ever know about it."

"Probably gonna need a new suit."

"Afraid so."

"What happened to SUNGRAZER?"

"You mean the transport ship that had a catastrophic entry on approach to Mars," Almeida said, "and ended up spilling most of its cargo across the upper atmosphere and out into space? I believe some portion of that vessel burned up on entry, and the other bits went on to parts unknown, captain. Terrible loss of the company. Pretty impressive show for people in the right areas."

"Anybody buying that?" Lincoln asked.

"The general public," Almeida said. "Which is good enough, for now."

"What about the security compromise? All that intel?"

"NID black ops managed to contain it," he said. "Thanks to the work you did with Manes-King and the Internal Security systems, they were able to cover some tracks. Not all of them, of course. It wasn't a perfect solution, bad guys got away with a lot of intelligence. We couldn't hide the fact that they'd found *some*thing. But the cleanup effort made it look like they'd been targeting a less sensitive asset. It's going to ruffle some diplomatic feathers of course, but given the posture of both planets right now we've all got to expect a little reconnaissance going on. Everybody seems to think we got off light on this one."

Lincoln didn't feel that way. Not looking at Wright in that bed. Two KIA, from a team of seven. In the grand scheme of things, he knew the numbers were right. A couple of deaths in the face of what might have been were hardly worth mentioning. But it was hard to take that perspective when one death had been his own and the other, the one that mattered most to him, was his dear friend. His sister-in-arms.

"Turns out the easiest way to keep a big secret," Almeida said, "is to confess to a smaller, less damaging one."

"Can I get a few minutes with her, sir?" Lincoln asked.

"Sure, of course," the colonel said. He turned to leave, but paused at the door. "Lincoln…"

"Sir?"

Almeida stood there for a moment, looking for the words. But whatever he'd been about to say, he couldn't articulate. "I'll uh… I'll be right out here."

"Yes sir."

After the colonel stepped out, Lincoln walked over and stood next to Wright's bed. He could see her better from here, in the dim light. They had her on an oxygen mask and a number of IVs snaking into both arms. It seemed strange, because apart from all the medical paraphernalia, she looked in perfect health.

He knelt down by her bed then, reached up and took her hand in his.

"Come on, master sergeant," he said. "Come on, Mir. Don't do this to us. We need you here. *I* need you here."

He sat there for a time, trying to will her back.

Wondering what their final moments had been like. Had he said anything to her, anything meaningful? Had he done everything he could to save her? Or had he, in those last desperate moments, abandoned her to her fate to try to save himself? He'd mocked the eggheads before, forever believing that remembering your own final seconds of life could be anything but traumatic. But now, on this side of the Process, he saw the value in it for the first time. Every warrior wondered about how they would face death; for Lincoln, that question had been answered, but it had been hidden from him. And that was, in its own way, maddening.

A mentor of his had once told him that to really understand a thing, you had to watch it die. Lincoln had had his chance to understand himself in a way that practically no one else ever could, and he'd missed the moment.

He just hoped now that he wouldn't have the opportunity to gain that understanding from his trusted teammate.

Lincoln had no idea how long he stayed there, knelt by her bedside. Long enough for his knees to ache, at least. She hadn't moved since he'd taken her hand.

"Amira," he said. "If you can hear me, I need you to come back. I need you to find your way back here. I'm trusting you to do it."

He waited a few more minutes, just in case some miracle was underway, but nothing changed. Finally, he pressed her hand to his cheek, then to his lips. And he rose to rejoin the colonel in the hall.

When he touched the door handle, he heard a noise behind him.

"Cap'n."

Lincoln snapped around, hoping he'd heard what he

thought he heard, almost certain he'd imagined it. He held there by the door, trapped between hope and fear.

Then again, clearer this time.

"Captain," Wright said. Her voice was raspy, barely more than an exhale. But it was her voice, for sure.

He practically leapt back to her side.

"Yeah, Amira, I'm here."

She didn't open her eyes.

"Sir," she whispered. "Did you…" She paused, drew a deep breath. "Did you just… kiss my hand?"

Lincoln couldn't help it; he laughed.

"Negative, master sergeant," he replied. "It would be inappropriate for an officer to take such liberty with someone under his command."

She cleared her throat. "I concur with that assessment."

She opened her eyes and looked up at him. "Did we get it?"

"We got it."

"Good," she said. Then she closed her eyes again. Lincoln couldn't tell if she'd gone back to sleep, or if she was slipping away again. Turned out to be neither.

"After all you put me through," she said, "seems like you could at least give me a day off to relax." She opened one eye again, and gave him a thin smile beneath her mask. Lincoln couldn't think of a single smile he'd ever seen more beautiful.

"*One* day, master sergeant," he said. "Don't waste it lying around in a hospital bed."

"Roger that," Wright replied.

Lincoln left her to rest, and sent the colonel and a couple of doctors in to check on her. But he didn't wait around for the report. He knew she was going to be just fine.

•••

Lincoln touched base with the rest of the team as soon as he was allowed, to let them know the situation, but it was a few days before they all made it back on planet. Once they reunited on base there were reports to file, debriefings to give, general housekeeping to take care of. Lincoln got the full story on Elliot, at least as much as he could follow. In the end, he was happy to learn that certain details had been forgotten in the official report, and that Elliot had received a promotion that took him out of the MPCR. Lincoln wondered if the man was finally going to open his pub.

After all the formalities were handled, Lincoln arranged for them to have the traditional celebratory cookout, with ample steaks and plenty of beer to go around. He was a little discouraged by how it began; the whole team was more somber than usual. After some needling, he discovered that Thumper and Sahil were both wrestling with how everything had gone down with SUNGRAZER; Sahil, for having initiated the detonation sequence while two of his teammates were still on board, and Thumper, for not having found another way to solve the problem. Each saw the loss of life as their fault, and held the other blameless. And even after both Lincoln and Wright had talked with them about it, about how it had been the right call, and the only real choice, they still wanted to hang on to it. It was almost like a competition between them. So after they'd all had a couple of beers, Lincoln went to the team gym and dragged one of the wrestling mats outside, not far from the grill, and told them to fight it out. Winner got to keep the blame.

They both seemed to get the point after that. But they went at it anyway, in their mixed martial arts version of horseplay. Sahil had to get his eyebrow stitched up after it. He claimed victory anyway.

Mike on the other hand was more reserved than usual, a little less quick with the quips, a little more lost in thought. When Lincoln was able to catch a moment with him, the conversation was short and to the point.

"I know why you did what you did," Mike said. "I don't want it to happen again."

"I understand," Lincoln said. He still couldn't decide whether he'd made the wrong choice or not. Mike was taller and stronger than Wright, there was no doubt. Maybe he could have covered the ground faster, and gotten those charges in place. But Wright was hard to the bone, and nimble. It was a close call, either way. But he knew he'd made the decision based on the wrong parameters, and he vowed to do better next time. "Won't happen again, Mikey," he said. "Promise."

Mike warmed up after that, and at any rate his emotional state didn't interfere with his appetite; Lincoln was pretty sure the man ate more steak than was healthy for any living being. Will and Noah got inducted into the ways of the Outriders with a couple of rituals that were special to the team; at least one of which involved getting dunked in a cooler full of ice water.

The cookout went on until well into dark, but as it was winding down Lincoln found himself sitting next to Wright, watching Mike regale the others with one of his legendary stories. He had half a steak in his hand, and he took the occasional bite from it whenever his storytelling allowed.

"I think Mikey's probably half beef by now," Lincoln said.

"Gross," Wright said.

"Hey," Lincoln said, turning to look at the master sergeant. He leaned towards her on the arm of his chair, and tipped a little farther forward than he intended to, sloshing his beer.

"Easy, tiger," she said, with a chuckle.

"Mir," he said, having an earnest moment. "I'm sorry I put you through that."

"You didn't, sir. Comes with the territory."

"I guess," he said. "Doesn't mean I like it. Or that it's right."

"No, it doesn't," she said. "Don't see how either of those matter much."

Lincoln sat back in his chair, looked at the rest of their team. *Their* team. His and Wright's.

"I don't know... with all that went down... I'm not sure what it means, as a team leader."

"Doesn't change a thing, sir," Wright said, clinking her beer against his. "Except now you're really part of the club."

EPILOGUE

"Lincoln," a voice said in the darkness, waking him instantly. When Lincoln opened his eyes he saw Thumper's silhouette in the doorframe, dim light from the hall spilling in behind her.

"Yeah, Thump," Lincoln said. He really hoped she wasn't waking him up to apologize again. She was still beating herself up for what had happened, and nothing he had said had done anything to assuage her guilt. He cleared his throat, "What is it?"

"I need you to come look at this."

Lincoln checked the time. 0319. His body demanded that he roll over immediately, but the tone of Thumper's voice had his mind arrested.

"OK," he said. He stuck his bare feet in his boots and didn't bother to tie them. Thumper led him down the hall to her workspace, and took a seat at Veronica.

"I had Veronica running through everything we pulled from Internal Security's systems," she said. "They had Elliot under surveillance for a couple of days before they picked him up." On Veronica's display, a blurred image sat frozen, video captured by a skeeter, paused mid-motion. Thumper gestured, and the feed played.

The footage showed Elliot meeting with someone

in a low-traffic area, behind a building or in an alley, perhaps; the angle clearly indicated that Elliot was the subject. But at one point, the person he was with turned, and Thumper paused the feed again. It was a woman in profile. Though the fact that she had frozen the image there suggested the woman was important, nothing stood out to him immediately about her.

Until he saw her eyes. He knew those eyes.

"That can't be…" he said, though his instincts told him of course it was.

"It is," Thumper said. She gestured at Veronica again. Another image appeared, this one identified as Amanda Flood. Veronica helpfully highlighted the matches in the facial features. "Amanda Flood. Or whatever identity she's taken now."

The woman they'd hunted down on his first mission as an Outrider. The woman he had confronted in her compound in the Martian People's Collective Republic. The woman who had killed herself right in front of him.

In quiet hours, the memory of her had nagged at him, like a riddle only partially solved. The obvious answer he had rejected outright; the capability for the Process was a closely-guarded secret, the cost to run the program obscene. But now that he saw her again, he knew the truth.

"She's like us," Lincoln said. "She's deathproofed."

He didn't know how that was possible, but of course she was. It gave meaning to her last moments. Her great escape. He hadn't believed it before because he hadn't wanted to, not because it was impossible. If the US had the capability, there was no reason to believe they were the only ones. But if Amanda Flood had access to that technology, then that put her into an entirely different category of adversary.

"No," Thumper said. "It's something else. Something worse."

She gestured, and Veronica produced another image. The hair was different, the clothing more expensive; facial features had been modified somewhat, but genetic markers were identical.

"This is from SUNGRAZER, footage from the Meridiani Administrative Region," Thumper said. "NID was keeping tabs on the Minister of Finance. And here," she pulled up another surveillance clip, "is something else from the Internal Service archive."

"So she's operating in multiple areas around Mars, not just the Collective Republic," Lincoln said.

"Look at the time stamps, Lincoln."

He compared the date and the time from each frozen image. He looked again. And a third time.

They were identical.

Amanda Flood was literally in two places at once.

"How…" he said, but trailed off. Shook his head. It was impossible.

But even as his conscious mind refused to answer the question, a memory bubbled up unbidden. An image he had wrestled with not long ago, when he'd gone to visit his replicas, seeing the three of them there together, each waiting to be imbued with his self.

Not replica. *Replicas.*

"Thumper," he said. "Is it… With the Process, would it be possible… What would happen if you tried to put the same mind into multiple bodies?"

She turned and looked at him then, her eyes ablaze. It was the conclusion she had reached, and that he now had confirmed.

"I've never heard anything like that before," she said, "but… theoretically, a branch…"

Thumper shook her head, and looked back at the images on Veronica's display.

"Dear God."

There was no obvious connection between the loss of SUNGRAZER and Amanda Flood. Nothing to indicate any of this was her doing. But ever since the *Ava Leyla*, the thought that this whole matter had been a continuation of a plan from before, one he'd thought they'd stopped, had been nagging at him. And now, here, at last, with the possibility raised, it seemed inescapable that her hand had been in it, somehow, some way.

There was no way to know for sure. But one thing Lincoln didn't doubt: their paths were intertwined. And just as they had crossed before, so they were certain to cross again.

ACKNOWLEDGMENTS

Every book has proven to be its own challenge, and it's always taken a team of people to rally around and help see me through to the end. My heartfelt thanks to:

… Jesus, for second chances, and third, and fourth, and for all the grace I've required.

… My wife and children, for your everlasting patience and support, and for making every day the best day.

… Marc Gascoigne, Phil Jourdan, Mike Underwood, Penny Reeve, Nick Tyler, and all the various Robots for your continued trust and support.

… Sam Morgan, for your guidance and encouragement.

… Joshua Bilmes and everyone at JABberwocky for all your work and kindness.

… David Mooring, for your faithful friendship and steady support.

… Judge Braswell, for giving your precious time to pass on your wisdom and memories.

… Jocko Willink, Echo Charles, and Leif Babin for your instruction, encouragement, and for sharing your lives and wisdom.

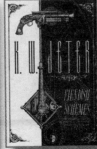

THE LEGEND OF THE DUSKWALKER

31192021280522